TOUCHING NOW FAMILIAR THINGS

BOOK 1: THE MEN OF JEWEL STREET

ROGER V. FREEBY

Touching Now Familiar Things
Book 1: The Men of Jewel Street

Copyright © 2019 by Roger V. Freeby

Editor: Wayne Smith
Cover art: David Wayne Fox
             www.davidwaynefoxart.weebly.com
Author photo: Lorikay Stone
             www.lorikayphotography.com

ISBN: 978-1-7333233-0-7

Published by Blue Dogwood Press

To Mark,
my Sweet Man since 7/8/96

1

A pale, slender young man dashes out of the math building ignored by passersby as just one more nerd regularly spit from the department. Leo rushes, running late, always late these days.

His meeting with his advisor ran long, making him later getting to where he hopes to live. He had promised one of his new roommates, Benji, he would be there by ten. It is almost eleven. The place is supposedly near, but he does not know which way.

Benji had explained, "The city is on the Front Range. The mountains are always west. Head east to the edge of campus."

Without his current disorientations, simply noting the angle of the sun relative to the time of day would be enough. Instead, standing in place, he turns a full circle. Buildings surround him. The minimal gaps between them offer little information: no mountains in sight. Hot, sweaty, and irritable, he steps around the corner of the math building and sees the massive Rockies in the background, giving him a modicum of relief.

He turns his back and heads across his new scholastic home, smaller than the very familiar University of Arizona where he spent roughly half of his life. The campus seems crowded. Arriving new students unload their belongings while anxious parents hover.

Leo pauses briefly to rub his temples with two fingers of each hand.

When am I going to feel normal again? Hell, when was I ever normal, whatever that is?

He makes his way rapidly across the unfamiliar campus.

Bus delays caused him to arrive late yesterday. He had trouble finding the building, causing him to be late meeting with his advisor. They went over details of his program and information on a project the department runs as a contest every year where the winners receive a small stipend. After his advisor, he met his project partner, George, who seemed impatient and a bit odd.

Of course, most find me pretty odd.

He has been foundering since his parents' sudden death last spring. A cold pair, they didn't know how to deal with any child. The insurance paid the funeral expenses and little more. Scant savings were left.

His only known relative, his mother's sister, helped him though the legal issues but could not offer much more. How could she? Leo's parents had never even told him he had an aunt. His first knowledge of her was when he received her call regarding his parents' crash. How was it she knew before he did? One of many lingering questions irritatingly beyond comprehension.

An adult now, he could not be expected to move in with a woman who, although a relative, was otherwise a stranger. She had been more than generous taking him in these past few months while his mind drifted through dense fog. So much paperwork. He paid bills from money he earned from a tutorial job that lasted through summer.

The decision to pursue a doctorate in math was made before the wreck. Once his mind started to clear from the shock, it seemed the only realistic option. He has a full scholarship for the program. There was no money, however, for living expenses. With nothing else to do, he decided he may as well go. Details of how the move came about remain hazy.

Once the estate settled, he sold everything. There was no one to say goodbye to other than Aunt Jean. He boarded a bus three days ago and headed northeast to this place he hoped would lead him to the future.

Of primary concern was how he was to live and where. Given his limited finances, living alone would not work. A dorm was not an option. He would never put himself in that position again. Even the scrawny roach-infested studio apartment Leo could afford in Tucson was better. Here in Colorado, the ad that caught his eye simply read, "affordable housing to share with two gay men in large home with lots of character. Close to University." Jay was the contact name, and his information was given. The price was certainly right. Living with gay men intrigued him. He'd accepted his attraction to men years ago but had never known really what to do about it. He experienced some encounters but none of significance.

After a surprisingly easy conversation, for some unknown reason, Jay offered Leo the room. When Leo told him his arrival date, Jay explained he would be out of town and gave him his roommate Benji's number.

Pulling out his phone, he punches that number. "Benji? It's Leo. Sorry I'm running so late, but I'm on my way now. I'm pretty turned around. I'm on the edge of the campus… Yes, I see the post office. Good I'm headed the right way. See you soon."

The short conversation inches his mood up. Benji's friendly laugh and "no problema" comment helps. Quite the contrast from his impression of Jay who came across with more authority while still welcoming.

He crosses the street and heads away from campus.

The late summer day becomes hotter than expected. Leo wishes he hadn't worn his jacket. Removing it, he loops it though the strap of his backpack. A river of sweat runs down his back. Very thankfully, he finds Jewel Street lined with shade trees offering some relief. The house lies somewhere down this street. For the first time today, he consciously notices his surroundings. Unfamiliar trees run along the appealing street, so different from the omnipresent palms of Tucson. Older homes line each side. Nothing like the carbon copy homes of the neighborhood where he grew up. Down the street, a man unloads boxes from a van into a house.

Looking to the house on the other side of the van he realizes he is almost there. Certainly, the largest on the block like Benji had said. Leo likes the look of it: solid with its own charm, an older Pueblo style home painted pale blue. The trim, done in white and darker blue, brings out unique features. So very different from the ugly cinder block box of his childhood. He finds his hopes raising that he could live in such a welcoming place.

As he approaches the door, he finger-combs his pale blond hair, generally as precise as his grooming gets. He knocks, hoping for the best.

A shorter, powerfully-built man wearing shorts and a cropped t-shirt opens the door. His dark, round face suggests affability, soon confirmed by the brilliant smile that crosses his features, lighting up nearly black eyes. A hand, small compared to the massiveness of the body, reaches out.

"Are you Leo? Benji Martinez."

Leo takes it. "Yes. I hope I didn't keep you from anything."

He's much more appropriately dressed for this weather than I am.

Leo steps into a spacious foyer. In front of him, a door he assumes is a closet stands next to the landing that begins the stairway. Stairs head right to another landing before crossing back and rising steeply to the second floor.

To the left, a wide archway offers a glimpse of the bright main floor. On the other side of the opening, a small alcove with a table and two chairs offers a view of the street.

Benji leads them through the arch and turns right to the spacious living room. The furniture is slightly old, clearly bought for comfort, not show. One long sofa backs against the outer wall. It is flanked by a smaller sofa on one side and an easy chair on the other. A sturdy coffee table rests in the center of the arrangement. Above the sofa, a painting of a mountainous landscape adorns the cream-colored wall. Toward the top of the wall, a row of five windows, barely a foot tall, hover near the ceiling, allowing diffused light to brighten the space. Leo likes it.

The dining room tucks behind the stairs. A doorway from the dining room opens into the kitchen. It fills the back of that side of the house.

Leo has a vague unease as he relates to the depth of the living room. No windows or doors on the back wall explain its sense of shallowness.

Benji looks Leo over. The light blond hair tops a pair of pale blue eyes. His beard is close cropped and just a few shades darker. Benji imagines what it would be like to kiss those lips that are a bit redder than most. And that fine crop of hair peeking out of the top of Leo's t-shirt promises a nicely furred chest. Benji is infatuated, a fairly common state for him.

He starts the house tour trying to concentrate on showing the place. The living room and dining room are first. "You're welcome to anything in here. Dinner is pretty informal, so you can use the dining table for school work when needed."

Benji's mind runs an entirely different program as Leo removes his back pack.

Those crystal blue eyes gaze into mine. We get naked. I bet he's a good kisser.

Leo sizes up the dining table, judging it more than adequate for his needs. For the most part, he won't need that much space, usually just a spot to sit where he can have his laptop running. A large, comfortable looking chair in the living room may suit his needs. Several outlets are noted where he could plug in his printer.

They head into the kitchen, fully equipped with modern appliances. A table with three chairs sits in front of a window. Leo comments on how nice it looks but admits his worthlessness as a cook.

"I play around in here," Benji says. "You'll get good at heating up leftovers 'cause when I cook I tend to make a ton of extra unless I am making something special, then I don't want it again too soon. There's also a pretty decent grocery store within walking distance where you can get almost anything you'd need."

Leo turns and focuses out the kitchen window to the house next door. The man he saw earlier is setting a box down in the kitchen for that house. Glancing up, he gives Leo a slight wave. As Leo automatically returns the wave, he wonders if the neighbor is also a student but he appears older, probably mid-to-late-forties.

When Leo turns, Benji notes his sweat-drenched shirt. "Babe, you must be thirsty. Where are my manners? Sit and let me get you something. Juice? Water? Coffee? Tea?"

"Water's fine." He selects one of the kitchen chairs and stretches out his legs.

"Here you go. You look tired."

Leo focuses back in this kitchen and shrugs his shoulders.

"Jay mentioned you're from Arizona."

"Yeah." That one word seems to require so much energy. He gulps down most of the water and sets the glass down, resting his hand on the table.

"I think Jay said you're from Tucson." He waits for a response, then since none seems coming, "Probably not used to the altitude. It took me a couple days to get used to it. I'm originally from El Paso." Benji pats Leo's outstretched hand then explains how to get to the garage from the kitchen. "There's plenty of room if you have a car. Jay has one, but I don't."

"I don't drive. Pretty much walk everywhere." Walking fits his solitary personality. It also has kept him in better shape than he would have been.

That's why the living room is shallow. The garage is on the other side of the back wall.

Benji notices Leo's not quite snug jeans hint at promising musculature.

I crouch between his legs. His cock begs to be sucked. I want to drive him crazy.

"Let's head upstairs," Benji suggests as he lightly pulls Leo to his feet.

Leo grabs the glass and downs the rest of the water in a second gulp. It bothers him to set the used glass on the table. "Where can I put this?"

"Dishwasher is next to the sink," Benji motions.

The glass properly settled, Benji leads the way back. Passing into the dining room, Leo notices the large built-in cabinets on the wall opposite the kitchen. Next to these stands a small room with a closed door.

Benji, noting Leo's focus, explains the door is to a small powder room that was built during an early renovation of the house to provide a bathroom downstairs.

As they pass through the living room, Leo understands its proportions, giving him a better sense of the hospitable nature of the house. He likes this place. It's full welcome blossoms beyond what he is able to process in the moment. Plus, the man leading him up the stairs is unlike men he has known. The frequent touches Benji bestows are not quite comfortable but seem harmless.

Is this the way friends act with each other?

Continuing on the tour, Benji glances back making sure Leo follows to the second floor. He realizes with a tinge of embarrassment if Leo looks up, he'd be staring right into his ass.

I lean down and offer myself up. It would feel so good to have him eat me out right here.

At the top of the stairs, Benji stands at the head of a hallway dividing the floor. He explains the layout. "There are four bedrooms. Yours will be one of the ones on the left. Mine is the one on the right toward the back. Jay has the master suite at the end of the hall. He has his own bathroom."

Benji opens the first door on the right. "We would share this." They go into a bathroom. It is good sized with a double sink on the left side. The toilet is at the far end, partially concealed by a half wall. The other side holds a generously-sized tub with a showerhead. "It's pretty easy for us to share. We can always work something out if our schedules are too similar."

Leo takes thorough scrutiny of the bathroom, judging it to be as wonderful as everything else he has seen in this house.

Benji takes a seat on the counter between the two sinks. He is fascinated how Leo seems to take in every detail of the room before facing him to signal he is ready to see more.

He steps between my legs and surprises me with his forwardness. I know he wants me now.

They move into the first bedroom directly across from the bathroom.

"You can have this one if you like. It's bright, but a little smaller." He waves an arm around the room. "As you can see, it is fully furnished."

Leo steps into the room. "Jay mentioned that."

"Of course," Benji continues, "if you need more, I'm sure we could find a way to oblige."

I'm ready to crawl on the bed so he can take me from behind with his arms reaching around me.

Benji calls it small, but it's larger than any bedroom Leo has ever had. "There's more here than I'll need." He feels he should add more. "It's nice."

"Let me show you the other bedroom, and then you can choose." He heads down the hall and ushers Leo into the second bedroom. "As you can see this one is a bit larger. Lot more shade too. You can decide which you'd prefer. We're only renting one. The other will be for company."

Both are presidential suites to Leo. He eyes the bed with envy, wanting to simply fall onto it and pass out for a week.

Benji notices how Leo's gaze lingers on the bed. He moves to it and flattens the covers. "Both beds are very comfy."

I want him to flip me over and reenter me while on my back. I want his whole body as sweaty as his back.

Leo doesn't really know which to choose. He does like the house. Benji is very different from anyone he has met, but one of the things he promised himself before signing up for this program was that he would try new things. Maybe having this energetic man as a roommate would be good. "I don't know which room I like, but I like the house. I'd like to move in if that works for you guys," he says, trying hard to mask his fear of everything.

"That's great!" Benji leads Leo back into the hallway and closes the door to both the room and his fantasy.

They head back down the stairs. "Jay will be back late tonight, and you can meet him tomorrow morning." Jay already told Benji he was pulling the ad as Leo was the one. "He already likes you, I can tell. Now, I believe you and Jay already worked out the rent and deposit and all that on the phone."

"Yeah," he hesitates. "Crap. I still have to find a bank."

Leo's panic is starting to work its way to the surface, and Benji's heart opens up to this shy, clearly frightened man. He takes Leo's hand and pulls him down so they can sit on the bottom stair.

"This is all quite a change for you, isn't it?"

Unaccustomed to touch, Leo is briefly wary. When he gives Benji a quick glance, he is somehow reassured.

"It's all pretty intense."

"I think you'll be happy here. It took me a while to get used to living here, and I had a pretty rough start."

Leo waits. This is usually when people start telling him what they think he should do. Realizing Benji plans to do no more than acknowledge the situation, he relaxes. "Where's the nearest bank?"

Benji laughs. "The nearest is a couple blocks away back towards campus. But they're terminally rude. Do you have to be anywhere soon?"

"Classes don't start until Monday. I guess that's not too soon." It is the closest he can get to a joke.

Benji's phone rings and he pulls it out of his pocket. "It's Jay. He'll want a report." He makes a raspberry sound as he shakes his head and laughs. "Control freak... Hey babe. Yes, he did come by and is sitting right next to me." There is a pause as he listens. "Well, all I can say is can I keep him? Please?" He playfully shakes Leo's knee with his free hand.

Leo withdraws slightly.

Benji, not noticing, hands the phone over. "It's for you."

"Leo?" a deeper voice on the phone addresses him.

"Yeah."

"Sounds like everything's fine. I can't wait to meet you in person. I'll be in late tonight, so if you want to come by around 9:00 tomorrow morning, that would be great. I'd say earlier, but I will be exhausted when I get home."

"That sounds fine. It will be good to meet you too. I, um, mean see you in person finally." He hopes that is the correct response.

Laughing, Jay says, "Put Benji back on. Bye."

Leo hands the phone back. They chat a bit then Benji returns the phone to his pocket.

"Where were we? Oh, yeah, bank. Okay, there is a sweet bank down where I work. I have to start getting ready to go in, so if you want to hold on I can walk you over and give you a little neighborhood tour."

"Um, yeah, sure. Why not?"

"Wander around while I get ready. It's your home, so feel free to snoop anywhere."

He heads up the stairs leaving Leo to his crazy spinning thoughts.

What is this marvelous place?

He doesn't know if he can do it. Fear entrenches. Wanting to look around, but even with Benji's assuring words, he doesn't know how to start. Slowly standing and moving into the living room, part of him wants to break down and cry, but even he knows that's not the best thing to do in front of someone he just met. A hand reaches to keep in contact with anything as he wanders: the warm, richly-toned wall...the front drapes currently open to the bright day...

Crossing to the living room, he sits on the larger of the two couches like it may bite. There are barely noticed interesting things around the room.

How can this work?

The stipend offered by the project is his logical source of income.

I have to do it. I must stay here.

Unsteadily he moves to the large reclining chair, finding it as comfortable as he had hoped...

Leo jumps when Benji touches his shoulder.

"Wake up, sleepy head."

He sits quickly forward and rubs his face with open hands. His eyes dart around the room noting the two sofas set at a right angle, the sturdy coffee table a smaller rectangle in the center of them and the landscape painting. It is all so welcoming, not matching the unease of evaporating images.

"You've had a hard day, haven't you, babe?" He extends a hand to help Leo up.

If only it had been just today.

"Yeah, I guess so." Leo accepts the hand, rising to a wobbly stance.

"You all right? Looks like you've had a fright."

He turns to Benji and sees the look of concern.

"I think I had a bad dream."

He looks out the window to the bright day. A woman across the street checks her mailbox as a dog plays for her attention.

Must have been a dream.

"Well, I have plenty of time, so we can take time and walk it off. I manage a coffee shop you can see from the bank, so after you open your account, come by for a cup on me."

Leo, truly tired, lets Benji lead the way. Somewhere in the back of his mind it has registered that Benji keeps calling him "babe." Too new.

As Benji starts to lock the door, he looks at Leo, "Didn't you have a backpack?"

Leo laughs for the first time in days and turns beet red. "Yeah, I did. I'm sorry. It's just so overwhelming."

"You do that a lot? Blush, I mean?"

"I guess. Never noticed."

"There's just no end to how cute you are, is there?"

As Benji goes back in and retrieves the pack, Leo tries to identify the warmth he feels. Despite his embarrassment of forgetting his pack, a rare joy races through him.

Heading down the street, Benji briefly puts his arm around his new friend's waist. Wondering how accurate he was in imagining Leo's body, the only remnant of his fantasy.

Leo starts to think maybe this whole idea will be okay. Even the arm around his waist does not bother him like it would have an hour ago. But he is completely in over his head in trying to figure out this short powerhouse leading him down the street.

Babe? Cute? Me? Sweet bank?

As soon as Leo returned to his motel, he fell asleep before removing his shoes. He awakens now to a new day, his body sore from being in a chair overnight. Pulling out his cell shows he slept almost fifteen hours.

He needs to calm himself before panic overtakes him.

"Okay, Leo. You are in a new place. You have committed to this PhD program and met a project partner who will depend on you. You have a bank account. You will be moving into a house today."

Standing and stretching his stiff body, he kicks off his shoes, strips off his shirt and jeans. He wishes he had another cup of that wonderful coffee Benji treated him to after the bank. How good it would taste now and would probably help the dull ache in his head.

What is Benji about? Is this what a friend is? Did he really call me cute?

Growing up, there were no friends. Now there is this energetic, diminutive muscle man who asked questions and kept touching him. What will it be like to be around that energy?

And Jay, so direct over the phone with something soothing in his voice, a confidence Leo wishes he felt.

Sitting on the unused bed he takes up and examines his checkbook.

There it is, every cent I have in the world.

In his head, Leo calculates the total rent for the year, including deposit. Remembering phone charges, his calculations for all other living expenses shrinks to only $253.72 a month.

What the hell was I thinking committing to this program?

Looking around the sterile room, he takes survey. All clothes and toiletries are packed in a good-sized suitcase. His one splurge, a powerful laptop and printer sit next to the suitcase. Another smaller bag holds his extra two pairs of shoes and his day pack that is large enough for his laptop and supplies he may need during the day at school. At 25 years old, his entire estate.

He runs his hands through his hair and realizes at some point it will need to be cut, another expense.

I could let it grow out, not a bad idea, probably have to figure another option, though.

He adds his shorts to the pile of clothes on the floor and realizes he did not ask if there was a nearby laundromat.

One more expense. At least another $15 per month.

He asked his advisor about any positions for T.A.s or tutoring, but none have opened. Naked, he sits fighting the urge to give in to the depression he has lived with for the past several months. He heads to shower, running the water as hot as he can stand.

While washing, he pays rare attention to his body. Believing himself that gawky kid of his youth, he wonders if anyone will ever truly caress him.

Will having two gay roommates help him or make him feel even more out of it? He had met a few men in college but was always too busy studying to know any of them more than casually.

After the shower, he examines his face in the mirror while brushing his teeth, seeing nothing appealing in his angular features. Growing up a skinny unkempt kid kept separate from other kids provided no peers to give feedback. Teachers confined themselves mainly to his academic skills. College professors understood him better, barely. He could so easily spiral into a vortex of self-pity but remembers his new home.

He rushes to the bedroom, throws yesterday's shirt and underwear in the suitcase and pulls on the jeans, figuring they'll be good for at least one more day if nothing gets spilled on them. New ones will be needed eventually.

Another expense.

He slips on a clean t-shirt, steps into his shoes, then naturally straightens the already neat room. Picking up his phone, he sees the time. "Late again." Gathering his belongings, he checks out and heads toward his new home.

Home?

―――――――――

"He seems nice but so quiet," Benji says to Jay as they sit on the smaller living room couch. "I don't know if he's terribly shy or was very tired. I thought about bringing him back here after work, but he disappeared before I could offer. Even with that, though, there is something in him I really liked. Kind of a lost puppy I just wanted to bring home."

Jay listens. On the phone, he sensed that Leo has been a loner. His responses were certainly terse, not so much rude as lacking social grace, but there was a sweet tone in the quiet voice that somehow told him to take a chance. None of the others who had responded to the ad came near what he wants.

His glance meanders across the dining room to the man moving in next door. Carrying an obviously heavy box with no problem, Jay likes the way the arms of the man's t-shirt stretch tightly over his muscles and doesn't mind the burgeoning gut.

Benji notices and gives Jay an impish whack on the arm. "Play later. Leo should be on his way now."

"Bet he's late," Jay says.

Benji refuses the bet. Given what he has seen, he figures schedules are probably not Leo's strong suit. They chat a bit more, comfortable in periodic silences, having little need to fill every gap. Several minutes after Leo was to arrive, Benji moves to the alcove, glances out the front window, and spots him. "There he is."

Jay moves to the window and watches the slender man make his way down the street. They lean against each other watching Leo struggle to get everything down the block. "We should help him," Benji says.

"No, I want to study him." He watches as Leo stops to readjust. "That guy is the most awkward and sexy man I have ever seen. You're crushing on him."

"Hush, I know better. Think he'll work out?"

"Completely. There's something about him, Benji. I don't know what, but after talking to him on the phone and now seeing him, he is the right man for this house."

Benji trusts Jay's instincts.

"Let's meet him," Jay says as he heads for the door.

Leo, still not adjusted to this higher altitude or walking with so much in tow, pauses to catch his breath. He looks up to see Benji and another man exit the house and head toward him. It must be Jay. Taller than either Benji or Leo, Jay moves with confidence matching what he heard in Jay's voice on the phone.

Jay waves and extends his hand as he approaches, "Leo. Welcome home."

Leo takes the warm hand that is offered.

He said I'm home. Am I?

Jay and Benji relieve Leo of his load. He is not comfortable with them taking over, though not sure what else to do. Jay drapes an arm on Leo's shoulders as they head to the house, talking easily about working out details and who knows what. All Leo can think is that someone is touching him...and he doesn't want to run away.

Halfway back to the house, the new neighbor steps out to get another box. Jay stops the little group to introduce them. "Hello, new guy. I'm Jay Freed. This is Benji Martinez, and this is even newer guy, Leo Graham. We live next door."

The man smiles and takes Jay's hand. "Tommy Jelinek. Thanks for the greeting."

Jay tilts his head toward Leo. "Gorgeous here needs to get moved in..."

Gorgeous? What is this?

Leo doesn't know Jay is simply paying a compliment.

Jay grins at Tommy. "...but I'll drop by later to welcome you more properly."

"Sounds good, just walk on in, the door will be open," Tommy says.

Inside they deposit Leo's things at the foot of the stairs before heading into the kitchen where Benji offers Leo coffee and pours more for himself. Jay refuses another. Benji opens the cabinet to select a mug for Leo. Examining the rather large collection, a good-sized sky blue one is selected. This will be his new roommate's mug. Finding out how Leo likes his coffee, he prepares it.

"You look like you could sleep for a week," Jay says to Leo. "Classes start Monday?"

He answers with complete disorientation. "Yeah to both, I guess."

Benji sets the mug in front of Leo, tells him he can keep this one on the mug tree next to the sink, and asks, "Which room have you picked?"

"I don't know."

"The front one. You need light more than space," Jay states, settling it as easily as that.

Leo pulls out his checkbook. "I need to give you rent. Do I make it out to you?"

"Yeah." Jay spells his last name. "We can work out a rental agreement later. You look like you are going to hardly make it up the stairs."

Realizing Leo is not up for conversation, Jay and Benji allow him to finish his coffee. Then the three head to get Leo's things.

Jay asks Leo, "Do you need help getting anything else?"

"This is everything."

Benji and Jay exchange glances.

"Oh, I forgot to ask yesterday, where is a laundromat?"

Jay softly laughs, "I'm not sure where one is, but the washer and dryer in the basement are available to you. There is also quite a bit of gym equipment down there you're very welcome to use, though you may prefer to use the gym at school. You get a lot more visual vitamins there."

Leo mentally sighs a bit of relief, one less expense to worry about. He barely knows what a gym is, much less how to use equipment.

Visual vitamins?

"I guess you can handle this yourself. I think Benji is planning to cook dinner for all of us tonight to celebrate your addition to our home."

"I will if I can figure out the recipe," he scampers to the kitchen returning with a cookbook. "It's written for eight people, but I need to cut it down for three." He reads out the ingredients with measurements.

Leo, without missing a beat, glances at the recipe and starts, "Twelve ounces sliced chicken breasts, a third of a cup chopped onions..." and continues to call back all the ingredients with the corrected measurements. Benji stares in amazement.

Jay goes up to Leo, "We have a genuine genius in our midst. Fucking cool! This house has needed you desperately." He takes Leo by the shoulders and gives him a kiss on the cheek. "Welcome to your home, Leo. Now, I need to go fuck the other new addition to the neighborhood." He hurries out the door.

Leo sinks to sit on the stairs, very confused and so tired. "What just happened?" he wonders aloud. Benji comes to sit next to him and leans into his new friend.

"You have been welcomed into your new home, silly. Jay likes you. So do I." He turns Leo's head to face him. "You are so tired and overwhelmed. Your eyes are so bloodshot red, the blue is clashing. Let's get your things upstairs. I'll run you a bath, and then I think you'll probably take a nap."

"Did he just say what I think he said? I mean about the neighbor?"

"He did. You'll get used to it. There's a lot you'll learn about Jay... and me. There's a lot we'll learn about you, but believe me when Jay said you are home, you are indeed home. Now come on." He grabs Leo's suitcase and heads up the stairs. Leo gathers his computer gear and follows.

Home. What does that mean?

Jay bounds up Tommy's steps. He enters and calls out, "Your personal welcome wagon is here."

Tommy straightens. "Jay, welcome to my home. Want something to drink?"

Jay shuts the door and leans back on it. "Nope."

Tommy looks at Jay. He smiles. "Tour?"

"Nope."

"What do you want?" Tommy asks, though he has no doubt.

Jay pulls his shirt off to reveal a broad chest and tight torso. Tommy follows suit, revealing a considerably heavier, far less developed body.

Jay crosses the room. He takes Tommy's face between his hands and begins to kiss. Tommy reaches his arms around Jay and readily returns the kiss.

"Where's your bedroom?"

"This way. I knew there was a reason I set it up first."

Jay induces Tommy to sit on the edge of the bed. He steps up, hard cock brushing Tommy's lips. Tommy takes Jay's cock, sucking eagerly.

He guides Tommy back onto the bed then climbs on so they can provide mutual pleasure. On their sides, both men explore with their hands as they continue, Tommy paying attention to Jay's torso, Jay to Tommy's ample ass.

The new neighbor knows he will be getting fucked and is fine with the idea. He'd be fine the other way around, but that seems very unlikely.

Jay fingers Tommy's ass as he sucks, getting Tommy even hotter. Jay wants inside. He breaks off to ask for a condom.

Tommy reaches into the drawer in his nightstand and pulls one out. Jay takes it and slips it onto his erection.

Jay rolls onto his back. Tommy mounts him, easing himself down. He leans in for a kiss as Jay begins.

"Damn, man, best welcome ever."

Their sex is that of friends establishing a bond.

They casually laugh as they continue. Both laughter and sex grow until Tommy lets go onto Jay's stomach, accompanied by a grunted roar of hilarity. Very soon, Jay cums inside Tommy.

Tommy pulls off, and they kiss.

"Welcome, neighbor," Jay says. "By the way, what do you do?"

Tommy laughs. "Most guys ask that first. But clearly you are not most guys."

"No, I am not."

"My passion is creating things from wood. I have been working on a series of sculptures, but I also love fashioning boxes. I like to play with inlay."

"That sounds cool. Have any I could see?"

"Sure." He runs a finger through some of the cum that is covering Jay's torso. "Maybe we should clean you up a bit first. Come on, there's a bathroom on the way to my workshop."

Tommy leads Jay to the backyard where he has been setting up a workshop and studio. The space has not been fully enclosed yet, so a slight breeze glides over their naked bodies.

"I'll finish this before starting any heavy work, so you won't have to worry about too much noise."

Tommy sets out several boxes. One, made from a honey-colored wood with two deep blue lapis circles, catches Jay's eye. Thin bands of silver separate each lapis, creating a simple, stunning effect.

Jay reaches for it. "Do you sell them?"

"If I didn't, I'd have to work some shit job full time. You want that one?"

"Yeah, it's the perfect gift for someone. How much?"

"$200."

"Done. I'll bring a check right back."

"Must be for someone special."

"Someone who doesn't know he's special. I need to grab my clothes so I can make a call." They head back in, and Jay gets his phone. "Benji, have you gone to the store yet?"

"I was about to leave." He laughs when Jay says what he wants. "Don't you have enough of those already?"

"Not for me. Leo. How is our wounded bird?"

"I made him take a hot bath and put him to bed. I hope we can wake him for dinner. I swear I don't know how he'll be ready by Monday."

"He will be. He's stronger than he looks and a hell of a long stronger than he knows." He ends the call and smiles at Tommy. "We are still naked."

"We are."

"Why don't we break in your workshop?"

———————

Midafternoon, Leo awakens feeling tired but much better, and he realizes this was the first time since boarding the train he has not slept sitting up. He takes time gazing around the room, his room. Somewhere along the line, Jay told him the room was furnished but not how nicely. The bed, covered in a soft cream-colored spread, is bigger than his normal single. Two firm pillows in cases of a slightly darker color and softer fabric span its head.

He gets up to explore.

A shoulder-height six drawer chest, much larger than he needs, stands on the wall between the two front windows. Head cocked to the left, he studies it before moving to one side to push it very slightly, centering it more perfectly. His hand runs across the top. The beautiful dark wood feels so solid. Opening the top drawer reveals a contrasting interior of a lighter wood, closer in color to the wooden floor beneath him. Turning, the rest of the room gets scrutinized.

Jay was right about the light. In addition to the two front windows, another graces the wall to his left, overlooking the house on the other side from Tommy's. Under it, a nice-sized desk and chair sit, perfect for his computer and printer. On either side of the bed at its head, nightstands match the chest. Each bears a small lamp. The door to his room is on his right almost in the front corner. At the far end of that wall, he sees what must be a closet. Very pale yellow walls add to the overall sense of airiness.

He goes to the closet. It is deep, far larger than his needs. A full-length mirror hangs on the inside of the door.

Unpacking begins with setting up the computer. He checks e-mail for anything from school. Nothing, but there is one message bearing an unfamiliar name. He'll deal with it later.

Next, all clothes are arranged neatly on the bed. The suitcase and computer carrier go into the closet. Leo hangs his day pack on the back of the chair then lines his shoes up on the floor next to the bed and takes survey: walking shoes, a pair of sneakers, and brown loafers for dressier occasions. "Damn," he realizes, "I need something heavier for winter." Six pair of pants, four jeans, two dress; a stack of a dozen variously colored t-shirts; six button-up shirts, half short-sleeve and half long; stacks of briefs and socks; three sweaters; and his jacket from yesterday and a slightly heavier coat.

The final item, a folder containing personal papers and the reports from the wreck, arouses painful stomach knots. He'll have to deal with it sometime but not yet.

He starts putting everything away. There are plenty of hangers in the closet for his shirts, coats, and pants. He puts his shoes in there also. T-shirts, socks, and underwear would fit in one of the drawers of the chest, but are spread out meticulously using two. He doubts he will ever fill the chest. The folder remains on the bed. He frowns at it. Snatching it up testily, he shoves it in the back of the bottom drawer.

Finally, he gathers his toiletries kit and heads to the bathroom. As soon as he steps out of his bedroom, he runs into Benji who has just finished a shower.

"Babe, it's good to see you up."

Leo realizes his nakedness and mumbles an apology.

"Don't worry. We're family." Benji is pleased to see how close he was in his fantasy to Leo's actual body. "If it makes you feel better," he drops his towel, "there. Now we're even."

Leo can't help but laugh and suddenly feels what may be hope enter.

"I need put this stuff somewhere."

"Sure. I've kind of gotten into the habit of using the back sink and all my stuff is in the cabinet above that. You can use the front one." Benji can't help but notice how little this man owns as Leo puts his things away. "Okay, I'm going to finish getting dinner ready. We're pretty informal, but spills may clash with your current outfit." He grins and heads to his room. Over his shoulder he calls, "About thirty minutes."

Back in his room as Leo dresses, he remembers the e-mail. Curious, he fires up the computer and logs on. It is from his Aunt.

> Leo,
>
> I am very glad to have had a chance to get to know you these last few months. I clearly regret the circumstances that brought it about. This has had to be very difficult for you. I hope I have given you at least some help through it. I suspect you are not completely through it yet.
>
> We have been complete strangers all your life. That was not my choice. I would like to have a conversation about this. Or at least try.
>
> I hope this new city brings you much joy. And best of luck at school, though from what I know of you, you won't need a lot of luck there.
>
> With love,
> Jean

He is very pleasantly surprised. He notices that she also put her phone number at the end. There are so many questions, but he doesn't know yet what they are.

> Aunt Jean,
>
> Thanks for your message. You are right about it being difficult. It's been such a fog, I don't even remember giving you my e-mail. I'm glad I did.

Arrived safe and very tired yesterday after a long bus ride and feel like I have not stopped. School starts on Monday.

I have found a place to live with two guys, Jay and Benji. They seem very nice. It's a beautiful old house a few blocks from campus. My room is huge.

Hope I won't be too busy.

Thank you for getting in touch,
Leo

Benji has made a wonderful chicken dish for them accompanied by asparagus and a tossed salad. Jay has been praising dinner with each bite.

Leo starts wolfing it down out of sheer hunger, but after a few bites, the flavor of the chicken strikes him, and he starts savoring it unlike any meal ever. His mother was a functional cook at best. Once on his own, school cafeteria or cheap takeout provided all sustenance.

"This chicken is really good." He blushes deep red after that admission as Benji beams.

At one point, he picks up an asparagus spear and asks, "What is this?"

It takes a moment for the others to realize his sincerity. Both Jay and Benji are incredulous that he has never had it before. They tell him.

"It's always been mushy stuff out of a can. This tastes good."

"Real food generally does. I guess I should warn you about something then," Benji says leaning dramatically forward.

Leo knits his brows.

"If you truly have never had real asparagus before, there's a curious side effect."

Leo's face darkens slightly, and he hesitates taking another bite.

Benji giggles. "Oh, babe, it's not that serious. It just makes your pee smell funny."

"That can't be true." Both assure him that it is true, and it is harmless before they all break down laughing. Soon, while taking another bite, Leo murmurs, speculatively, "of course the distinctive flavor probably comes from an innate chemical unneeded by the body and therefore filtered through the kidney and subsequently sloughed off through urine. An odd smell would be logical."

"I thought you were into math," Benji states.

Leo, realizing he spoke aloud says, "I have a degree in organic chemistry too."

Jay and Benji exchange looks before resuming the meal.

After the first bite of dessert, a rich chocolate cake, Leo just sits back staring. Finally, he looks at Benji and says simply, "Wow," then continues with new relish.

Still exhausted, "I'm sorry guys. I need to go to bed again." He gets up and turns, "Thanks for the great dinner. I'll be sure to smell my pee."

As he leaves, the other guys burst out laughing. Halfway up the stairs, Leo understands they got his joke and were not laughing at him. It feels good to strip down and be naked in his room, despite an unshakeable tiredness. About to lie down, he sees a box on his nightstand with a note on top.

This is to welcome you into your home.
It is yours also. Please make full use of what's inside.

The box is beautiful. He runs his finger around the blue stone and silver circles several times before opening it. Filled with more condoms than he has ever seen and a generous bottle of lube, he can't imagine ever needing so many and closes the box.

These guys are being so nice. I can't give them things like this back.

His fear of simple survival battles the glint of happiness Jay and Benji have offered. That battle takes him into a fitful sleep.

2

Benji walks to work Friday mulling the week. He hoped to get to know his new roommate better, but Leo leaves the house long before he wakes. He can't even rely on Jay for updates as he has been gone all week for work.

The first week of school normally means a hectic time at the coffee shop. New students seek a place to hang out. Returning students want to reconnect. A steady stream of local regulars also assert themselves, resulting in a usually raucous, joyous week that slowly folds into each semester's normal. Already the crowd is noticeably smaller than at the beginning of the week.

One thing differs. Steve, Benji's favorite coworker, leaves today after graduating the end of the summer term to devote his time finding a teaching position. Benji will truly miss him. Steve, not a handsome man, has full shoulder-length dark hair and large bright blue eyes, but his real charm for customers and staff lies in his flirty personality. Everyone's day brightens around him. Benji teased with him for months, but seeing Steve do that with everyone, he never figured it seriously. He had wished he wasn't scheduled today and had thought about trading with one of the other managers, but that would not be fair to Steve.

The head manager assigned Steve to straighten out the basement storeroom today, and Steve asked Benji to help. It needs a full clearing out every few months. Not a hard task, but it can take time. It is also normal to ask for help. Usually it would be another coworker, but Benji was glad when Steve asked him.

As he rounds the last corner, he sees people waiting to get in. At first, he thinks something has happened, but as he nears, several carry small presents or cards.

Of course. The regulars want to say goodbye to Steve.

Several in the jolly crowd gently tease him about cutting in line as he passes them.

A subdued staff makes for a lower mood inside. No one wants Steve to go.

Surrounded by well-wishers, Steve exhibits his normal effervescence, giving Benji a chance to examine him. Steve's too-broad face features a somewhat off-center, bulbous nose. True, his hair and sparkling eyes add to his appeal. Somehow when he flashes his smile, Benji dismisses the crooked teeth and slight lips.

The smile glows when Steve's eyes meet Benji's. As soon as Benji gets behind the counter, Steve gives him a big, smacking kiss on the cheek with a "Welcome, Boss," something he has done from day one, always making Benji feel special.

"Good morning, Steve. It is good to have you this one last day."

Steve flashes his bright smile and retorts, "It's always a pleasure to be had by you, Boss."

Benji wishes that could be true but has no time to ruminate. The rush begins. Customers coming to bid farewell to Steve linger far longer than usual, causing a raucous congestion.

Steve accepts cards and little gifts, thanking each person by name. Every now and then he finds a way to cozy up to Benji as he has always done, mentioning frequently how he looks forward to the storeroom.

Benji forces himself to keep busy, making sure things run as smoothly as possible.

The closing manager arrives, and the shift change begins. The onslaught dwindles as fewer evening customers know Steve.

Benji goes into the office and removes his cap. As he steps out to look for Steve, he finds him waiting outside the door.

"I'm ready, Boss." He smiles at Benji in an odd way. They head down the stairs together, Steve becoming unusually quiet.

He actually seems nervous.

Benji tells Steve to get the supplies they need, enters the room, and turns on the light. He looks around at the completely clean room. Confused, he turns and finds Steve at the door wearing an uncharacteristically shy smile.

"I came in early and took care of it. I wanted time with you alone, Boss." He steps up to Benji, hugs him and kisses him on the mouth. "You don't know how much I've wanted to do that."

Benji, completely taken off guard, stands in Steve's arms. Stammering a protest, "We're at work..."

"Don't care, Boss." He kisses Benji's neck, working to his ear, whispering, "I've wanted you for so long." He pulls back to look at the man he holds.

They gaze at each other a few long moments. Benji finally nods. They kiss in earnest. Hands reach for shirt buttons until Benji pulls back and looks at Steve. "What are we doing?"

Steve faces Benji with clear confusion. He manages to stammer out, "I wanted you to know what I really think about you."

Slyly, "So you think I'm the kind of guy who'd risk his job for a few minutes of fun?"

"Oh, no. No. I didn't mean that. God, I'm so sorry." Mortified, he tries to pull away, but Benji won't let him.

"Babe, trust me. I'm not angry. A few years ago, I'd have had you down here naked the first day you showed up. I actually like you. A lot."

This was not what Steve wanted at all. Still it feels good to look down and see Benji has not let him go, those strong hands fire on his hips.

Benji looks around the room and spots a step ladder. He takes Steve by the hand and leads him to it. "Sit." Once Steve is settled, he then perches on one of his knees. "Only place to sit. You probably don't mind."

"Guess not," he admits as he starts to recover. "I'm sorry, Boss. I wasn't thinking."

He pokes him gently in the temple. "Not up here anyway. Couple of feet lower."

"You're not mad?"

"Not really. Sort of flattered. But why like this?"

He looks to the side, still feeling ashamed. "I guess I wanted to let you know how I feel." He does look up at Benji and lets out a sigh. "Boss, I really do like you." He risks a hand on Benji's thigh. "A lot too."

"I can see that." He tweaks at Steve's chest where a nipple is clearly pushing at the cloth of the red polo shirt. "Quite spirited."

The first relaxed smile since they came downstairs breaks on Steve's face. "They always give me away."

"Clearly." He leans his head onto Steve's. "Babe, whatever possessed you?"

He thinks, wanting to give an honest answer. "I wasn't sure I'd get another chance. I'll be gone soon."

Benji faces Steve. "How soon?"

"Could be a coupla weeks. Probably not more than a month."

"Good. We're going to find time to make this happen." He looks at this man who seems so much younger. "What's your schedule like?"

Steve is frozen to his seat. He planned only this option, not realizing there could be more. "Parents this weekend, then back by Tuesday to follow up on leads."

"I'm not sure this week is great, but next weekend we'll find some way for us to be together, but not rushed like this." Seeing Steve differently. "You've always called me Boss." Benji gets on his feet.

Steve shrugs his shoulders. "It's how I've always seen you." He starts to stand wanting to leave.

"Sit back down. We're not done here."

With curiosity, Steve sits back down.

"Babe, you made a misstep, nothing more. I am glad you finally showed your hand." He closes the storeroom door and goes back to Steve. "Spread your legs out and hold onto the seat." He moves between Steve's legs and crouches down. One hand is placed on each of Steve's knees. "Do you want more than a quick fuck in the storeroom? I want honesty, not what you think I want to hear. If nothing more than this, I can do that. Which is it?"

"Boss, I won't be here. There's no chance of a job here."

"I know. I want to know what you really want. Here only or more?"

He gazes into Benji's eyes, studies his features. He knows only one honest answer which emerges in a ragged whisper. "More, Boss. I want much more."

Benji smiles. "Of course, you do. We both do." He leans in and starts to kiss Steve.

Pulling back in surprise, "I thought we weren't going to do anything."

"We're not going to fuck, but no one expects us upstairs for a few more minutes. Besides, you're perky again."

"Damn, Boss. You do get me going."

Benji rubs Steve's shirt where the nipples show so prominently. "I've always liked you in this shirt. Red works on you."

Between kisses, Steve says, "It's my favorite."

Benji knows how to take care of me.

Steve's hands rove Benji's body, needing no more. Another time. Unfortunately, this time can only last a few minutes. Benji helps Steve to his feet.

A little off balance, he finds his footing. "Boss, that was amazing."

Benji takes all of Steve in and begins to softly laugh, "Looks like more than nipples are giving you away."

Steve looks down and notices a rather large dark spot in his pants. "Oh, fuck, I never do that."

"Apparently, you do." Benji fights breaking into full laughter and has to turn away trying not to burst out, but it is a losing battle. "There's an apron in here somewhere. Oh, babe, I'm sorry," he mutters through giggles.

Soon Steve is infected with a giggle fit himself.

Benji spots an apron and tosses it over his shoulder, unable to face Steve.

Once properly attired, and somewhat more composed, Steve lets Benji know he's ready.

Benji turns. Affection replaces laughter as he gazes at the man standing in front of him.

They step in for one final embrace filled with tenderness and wonder. Steve resolves to find a better way to be with his Boss before ascending the stairs. Once upstairs, they discover Steve still has a little time left before his final shift ends.

Benji declares, in Steve's honor, everyone, staff included, gets a free piece of cake. He lets Steve select his favorite two from the dessert case, and they serve the crowd until the cakes are gone.

Steve clocks out and comes up to Benji, taking him in a warm bear hug. "Boss, I want to see you before leaving." He chastely kisses him on the lips, but that elicits hoots of affection from all present.

Benji tries to hide a tear. He busies himself as Steve leaves, unable to watch him walk out.

When he gets home, he finds Leo at the dining table with a small red-haired man.

"Hey, babe, it's good to see you." He gives him a peck on the cheek.

Leo feels the affectionate kiss linger several seconds longer and has no idea how to react.

"I didn't know school would eat you alive like this." Benji glances across the table at the other man who seems distracted. He's not sure, but he thinks he is trying not to see him.

Leo introduces them. "This is George, my project partner."

George lifts only his eyes in Benji's direction and mutters a hello, but then he quickly focuses back on his computer.

Benji looks at Leo's computer screen. "I have no idea what you are looking at."

Leo explains, "There's a contest. Ten problems. Some need to be solved, some need to have corrections made. We don't know which are which. It's not part of our grade, but the team who solves it will earn a stipend lasting the duration of the program. Like this first one. It's a simple solve. You see…"

Benji stops him. "Babe, I was an English Lit major. If you want to discuss the symbolism in D. H. Lawrence or whether Virginia Woolf or James Joyce better personified the spirit of early 20th Century British thought, I am there. But this? I leave to you."

Leo chuckles, surprising Benji. "And I don't know who any of those people are, so I guess we'll have to find something else to talk about."

"Oh, I think we will find lots of topics," he teases. "I'm starving and think I'll throw something together. Want some? I'd say what I'm offering, but until I get in the kitchen I have no idea what will come out." He pauses and laughs at himself. "For an English major, that was a really awkward sentence. Anyway, whatever I make, you guys want some?"

Leo starts to feel defensive. Benji keeps giving and giving to him, and he never has any way to give back. But he has been so afraid to break his budget that he has not eaten anywhere near what he should. Hunger agrees for him.

Benji looks at George expectantly, "And you, sir?"

George finally looks at Benji, his eyes partially hidden behind smudged glasses, "Um, no. I have to go soon."

"Okay, babe, just you and me. Oh, and I plan to leave a mess, so you get to clean up." He again pecks Leo on the cheek and disappears into the kitchen.

A weight lifts. Without knowing, Benji offers him a way to give back. He will gladly clean the kitchen from top to bottom. Creases on his forehead smooth out and his shoulders drop a little. He smiles briefly to himself before returning to the screen in front of him. His smile vanishes.

3

As an academic recruiter for the university, Jay traveled last week from Tuesday through Saturday on a three-city tour. None of the students he met truly impressed him. Shining in their respective communities, they were cases of big fish in small ponds. He eventually signed one without enthusiasm. Because of where he went, there was little a decent meal after work or opportunities for play. Thankfully Benji produced another wonderful dinner Saturday night, and this time with tons of leftovers.

Leo still keeps to himself. He cleans up after meals. Jay notes he also seems to have taken on a few chores around the house that usually get neglected. But come this Monday morning, he was out like a shot before anyone could say a word to him. Jay hasn't a clue how to approach this man.

Carrying a bag ready for play, Jay turns the corner, approaches the student union, and spots the object of his concern, typically buried in his computer. A quick scan of the area shows most people looking at some type of electronic device, but Jay has no doubt Leo is not on social media. Seeing his mysterious friend who, of course, sits alone at a shaded table with two empty chairs, brings a little spark. Bounding over, he lands in the one closer to Leo who jumps at the sudden dramatic appearance.

"God, hi. Where'd you come from?"

He inclines in, saying conspiratorially. "Heading for a hookup, and I spotted you."

Leo, embarrassed by his naiveté, assumes that holds some sort of sexual meaning.

Jay leans on him to get a better look at his computer screen, "What's that?"

"Preliminary work for a paper in my calculus class."

Jay is getting used to Leo focusing on things like this. Not needing to be center of attention, he simply sits contentedly and scans the scene around him, a potpourri of this year's edition of students. Most, gathered in twos and threes, spend more attention to their phone than the people within touching distance. Jay pulls out his own phone to check for messages, noting one from the guy waiting for him. He ignores it, putting his phone back in his pocket. Latest fashions drape themselves on bodies all about him. Like any college campus there are plenty of guys worth looking at, so he busies himself until he spots a very dark-haired fellow with impossibly green eyes facing them. Dark Hair frequently glances their way, and Jay soon realizes his focus is Leo.

Damn, Leo has an admirer and a fucking hot one to boot.

"Leo, not to pry, but I know you really like the box we gave you, however, you haven't commented on the contents."

Without looking up from his computer, Leo says, "I appreciate your gesture, but I don't see me using them in the near future."

It saddens Jay to hear this. "Leo, guys want you. You have to know that."

Leo looks at Jay. "Not many."

The total conviction of the statement shocks Jay. He glances back to the man, who looks over again. "Do you not want to have sex, or is it you don't think you will have any time? You don't really believe no one would be after you, do you?"

"Something like that," Leo says.

Jay keeps watching Dark Hair. An idea formulates. Jay moves to the chair opposite Leo and checks behind him for Dark Hair. He pulls out his phone to call Benji. "Hey you. How about we have a little party this weekend? ...Friday better than Saturday? ...That works. Let's keep it a little small 'cause we don't want to intimidate our shy roommate." Jay slips a foot out of his sandal and kicks Leo gently to make sure he has caught that. "Yeah, that would be great. Love you."

He puts the phone away and looks at Leo who eyes him with burgeoning wariness. "What's going on?"

"We are going to have a party. Call it your housewarming. But you are going to ask someone to it with full intention of using at least one of your presents."

"What are you talking about? The only person I know in town other than you guys is George. Don't think that will be happening."

"No, you are going to ask a strikingly gorgeous dark-haired man with impossibly green eyes." Jay is smiling, on the verge of breaking into laughter.

"You are crazy." Curiosity edges an advantage in the battle with anger. "I don't know anyone like that."

"If you did, would you want to go out with him?"

"Maybe. Who wouldn't?"

"Well, my dear friend who needs to pull his head out of his computer and ass simultaneously, I do believe there is just such a man who is ready to give his left nut to meet you."

"What the fuck are you talking about?" Leo never said anything like that to someone and somehow it seems good rather than bad. Jay is so unlike anyone he has known.

"Look over my shoulder."

Leo does so. Jay shakes his head and lets out a soft laugh. He takes Leo's chin and guides his head. "The other shoulder."

At first, Leo has no idea what's happening, and then their eyes meet. They are green and bright.

He's looking at me.

Jay's still grips Leo's chin. "Smile."

Leo does.

"Now, nod."

He obeys that command too.

"Is he strikingly handsome?"

Leo nods.

"With dark hair?"

Another nod, his mouth opening.

"Does he not have incredible green eyes?"

Leo again nods then returns his gaze to Jay.

"And, unless I am wrong or the guy is a complete loser, he is smiling at you right now. Right?"

Leo glances up. "Yes."

"Close your mouth and return the smile."

Mechanically, Leo does.

His vision triangulates from this new man to Jay to his work.

Each time he meets the dark-haired man's gaze, Jay notices a softening in Leo's features. The chin slackens, lips slightly part allowing a glimpse of pink tongue. The crystal blue eyes sharpen in focus. Slight furrows of curiosity develop on the forehead. He meets Jay's eyes with a questioning element. Leo's lips move slightly as if trying to form words.

Leo focuses on his computer. For a rare moment, he's uninterested in coursework.

Who is this man staring at me with such remarkable eyes?

"Wow, you do like what you see. Okay, I see this needs a little help." Jay jumps out of the chair and heads right for Dark Hair. "Watch my bag," he calls back to Leo, realizing now Leo won't be able to run.

He lands on a chair and reaches a hand out. "I'm Jay. I am assuming a strikingly good looking, dark-haired guy with impossibly green eyes must have some kind of wildly exotic name."

"Extremely exotic, one of the rarest," Dark Hair bursts out. "Dave."

"One of the best comebacks I've ever had," Jay laughs. "Okay, here's the thing. You have been staring at that equally devastatingly handsome guy with fair hair and shimmering blues eyes, am I right?"

"Indeed, I have been, though I must ask why you care." The eyes, focusing on Jay, brim with amusement.

Jay knows he has made the right decision. "I care because even though he doesn't know it yet, I am one of his two best friends in the whole world."

"That is quite interesting. And who is the other? Please don't tell me about a six-foot, invisible rabbit."

Jay likes this guy more and more. "No, his other best friend in the whole wide world even though he doesn't realize it is named Benji. Only 5'6" and very visible, a veritable melding of muscles and mirth. You'll meet him next time."

Dave leans back and looks Jay over. He also looks over to Leo who quickly lowers his head to his computer. "Okay, I have had many bizarre conversations in my life, and this one is rapidly rising up the charts, possibly into the top five already, but you know something? I believe ever word of it."

"Replaying it, I see your point, but I am curious as how you arrived at the truth part."

"First, I know your name. I know the name of his other new best friend. But tell me his name, you know, the equally devastatingly handsome guy with fair hair and shimmering blue eyes." He leans forward, arms on the table, anticipating.

"Leo."

"Leo, yeah, that's good." He looks back and catches Leo looking again and jerking away. This brings a contented look to Dave's face. "Here's the thing. I saw Leo the very first day of class. He was sitting in that same chair at that same table. Evidently, a creature of habit. Anyway, I have been trying to get his attention every day since. I even said hi once with no response. I was about to give up, thinking maybe he was just straight."

"What? It's not possible he is simply not interested?" Jay teases.

"Hey, I'm a strikingly good looking, dark-haired guy with impossibly green eyes, so of course it had to be he was straight."

They both release guffaws.

Jay says, "You have officially become my second most favorite person I have met in the last year."

"Be nice if you could be my second too."

"And number one?"

They simultaneously say, "Leo."

"I just haven't been able to get his attention. Now you show up, and every time I glance over there, he is pretending not to see me. Remarkable progress. And your timing's great. Next week I go into a new rotation which means I have to hone my stalking tendencies in order to see him at all."

"So, you are not just a handsome face, but you are also smart."

"PhD candidate in creative writing. Far too pretentious sounding to admit to someone who is not potentially my second most favorite person I have met in the past year."

"Dreams of writing the next 'Great American Novel'?"

"I'll have to if I want to live. Can't do that with my real passion, poetry." He gives a self-deprecating shrug.

"Oh, you are fucked. But it is good in a way, because the equally devastatingly handsome guy with fair hair and shimmering blues eyes just started his PhD. And given your field, it should perfectly blend with his, math."

"Ouch."

"Here is the thing, in addition to his agreed upon physical attributes, he is, alas, very timid. So as one of his two best friends in the whole wide world, although he doesn't realize it yet, I have taken matters into my own hands. We are giving a party this Friday. He needs to invite you, but without help, well, you know."

"By 'we,' I assume that includes Benji."

"That is correct."

"Is this where you take me over to meet the equally devastatingly handsome guy with fair hair and shimmering blue eyes named Leo?"

"Yes."

"Good, because in addition to previously mentioned looks/hair/eyes description, I think he is utterly beguiling."

"We are in agreement. Someday he will be too. Shall we?"

Dave stands and slips his computer into its case. He wears a loose off-white shirt over dark shorts that reveal rather hairy and sleekly muscled legs. Standing, his height clearly matches Leo's more than Jay's.

As they move toward him, Leo can no longer look away. He notes the gentle glide of Dave's gait and his slender frame. But it is the eyes that hold his attention. They are indeed uniquely green, and he cannot help but hold his gaze out of fascination. They draw him to his feet as the two reach his table.

"Leo, this is the strikingly good looking, dark-haired guy with impossibly green eyes, Dave. We have agreed that you are an equally devastatingly handsome guy with fair hair and shimmering blue eyes. He understands you are going to invite him to our party as your date. He also knows he will have his work cut out in getting you to talk."

Leo's mouth has dropped open, and he is bright red. Jay starts to leave, but hears Dave say, "I think you have something to ask me."

"Would you like to come to a party as my date?"

Out of earshot, Jay turns before taking off for his rendezvous to see Leo has not bolted and Dave smiles easily with him. He also notes that Dave has moved one of the chairs closer and both lean forward.

Given the setup, Jay's lateness enhances the situation.

A couple of blocks on the other side of campus, he finds the address, the right side of a tiny duplex. The guy, Justin, was looking for someone to take complete charge.

He told Justin to leave his door unlocked and wait for him naked in the bedroom. He enters knowing the bedroom is off the living room to the left. He goes in and sets his bag down.

Justin sits on the bed, fully clothed. He looks at Jay. "I am sorry, sir, I thought you weren't coming."

"And you got dressed? I said naked."

"Please sir, forgive me." He starts to take his clothes off.

"What makes you think I want a strip show?" Jay asks in a clear tone. "I have to pee. When I get back, I better not see any trace of clothes."

"Yes, sir."

Jay has not moved. He exhales with a note of exasperation. "Do I have to search your whole place, or are you going to tell me where the bathroom is?"

"Turn right just past the kitchen." A glower from Jay forces Justin to add, "Sir."

"Ass up when I return," he tosses over his shoulder.

Scavenged furniture fills the bleak apartment, nothing on the walls, no sign of a book anywhere. He finds the equally boring bathroom and pees. Back in the bedroom. Justin waits naked, ass up. He has spread his legs and his arms are out to the side.

"Much better." Jay walks over to the bed. He runs a hand up Justin's leg. *Skinny, but not bad.*

Jay thumps his bag loudly on the nightstand next to the bed causing Justin to turn his head.

Four bindings, a dildo, and a butt plug are pulled out and laid on the bed. Briefly Jay digs through his bag as if looking for other equipment, "These should be enough." A glance at the scars on the slatted headboard confirms Justin's experience with bindings. Briefly meeting eyes, he adds, "Never mind what I'm doing. Not your business."

Justin turns his head.

"Scoot down on the bed, put your arms over your head, and spread your legs," Jay commands.

Several minutes later, Jay unbinds Justin.

"Thank you, sir." He rubs his newly unbound wrists noting the lack of chafing. "That was everything I wanted."

"You were adequate." He withholds any sign of affection or eye contact as he gathers his equipment.

"Please, sir, may I ask a favor?"

"You may ask, but I reserve the right to refuse."

"Yes, sir, you know best. May I cum, sir?"

"When do you want to do that?"

"Now, sir."

"No."

"No, sir?"

"That is right. No, not now."

"When may I cum, sir?"

"I don't care," he says with a determined note of disinterest. "I need to pee again. Do it then."

"Yes, sir."

"Use my cum for lube."

"I will, sir."

When Jay returns to gather his things. Justin is wiping the last traces of cum off his belly.

Jay packs his things up. He knows Justin's eyes follow him but does not look back, simply checks around for any missed gear and takes off.

Returning the same route, he passes the table where he ran into Leo. Part of him hoped to see the two men still engaged, but neither is in sight. The look on Leo's face the moment he first saw Dave is something Jay doubts he'll ever experience...for himself.

4

Finding themselves home in the evening during the week for the first time since Leo arrived, all three sit on the large sofa, Leo in the middle, munching leftovers from this past weekend's dinners. Benji has rolled the TV out and absently flips through channels, but nothing holds anyone's interest.

Jay asks Leo, "So how did it go?"

"How'd what go?"

"What do you think, numb nut? I leave you with the gorgeous Dave so you could ask him out, what else?"

"Leo has a date?" Benji turns off the TV.

Why do these guys always want to know so much?

"He said he'd be here."

"And..."

"And what?"

Jay and Benji exchange glances. Benji whines, "Babe, details." He gets up on his knees facing Leo with a clear note of excited hilarity. "Who is this Dave? What's he look like? Are his intentions honorable? Are your intentions dishonorable?"

"I don't know what to tell you," Leo states honestly.

"Okay, gorgeous." Jay tousles Leo's hair. "I'll start. Dave is a sweet, smart, and handsome man who thinks Leo is the hottest thing this side of hell. He's been trying to get Shy Boy's attention for days, and thanks to yours truly, they finally met. Our party Friday was so he..." Jay pokes Leo in the ribs who flinches in return. "Aha, you're ticklish...would have an excuse to ask him out."

"Yay! Leo has a date!" Benji squirms in delight. "So did you see him this morning? Come on! Details!"

Leo places his empty bowl on the coffee table and thinks. He is taking too long, so Jay slowly starts to walk his fingers up Leo's side. Leo starts to move away, but Jay doesn't stop until Leo is laughing so hard he can hardly breathe. He takes a deep breath unfamiliar with what just happened.

"Okay, okay. I did see him this morning but only for a minute. He stopped by the student union and said he had something come up in his job and would be busy all week."

Jay poises his fingers at Leo's ribs. "And?"

Leo looks at Jay's finger. "Um, he said he'd see me at the party."

Jay touches Leo with one finger. "And?"

"He is looking forward to it and meeting you," he says to Benji.

Jay waits a second before he starts to wiggle his finger into Leo's ribs. "And?"

Leo grabs Jay's hand and embarrassedly admits, "Then he took my hand and kissed it before taking off."

"That's better."

Leo is still holding Jay's hand. "Now, will you stop?" He is smiling, trying to identify his feelings.

Jay gets a devilish look. "No." He and Benji both start lightly tickling Leo, one on each side, eventually working him down on the couch with Jay straddling his belly but not pinning him down. Benji, now sitting on the arm of the couch, has his hands lightly on Leo's shoulders.

First ever tears of laughter fall from Leo's eyes.

"Babe," Benji says, "you really need to learn how to tell a story."

"That is the truth," Jay agrees. "I think it is time for him to learn to contribute."

Benji wipes one of Leo's tears with a thumb. "I would have to agree, my dear man."

Leo, still beneath Jay, asks, "What are you talking about?" Immediately he worries they want him to do more around the house, unable to let go of his financial problems. His parents left him so ill prepared financially after the wreck, not that they prepared him in any other way.

Jay leans down and holds Leo's face between his hands. So much worry clouds the sharp features. Jay attempts to smooth the rutted forehead with a finger as he continues softly, with a touch of humor. "We are going to play a game. It's quite harmless, but I absolutely refuse to let you up until you agree to join." He moves around until he is stretched out as much as he can along Leo's body, his raised head above Leo's. "Can you do that?"

"I don't know." Clearly in uncharted territory, games meant solving brain teasers in various courses. Naturally, he always won.

"What do you think, Benji? Can we trust him?"

Benji leans over as close as he can and gets eye to eye with Leo. "Definitely worth the chance." He kisses Leo's forehead.

Jay gets off Leo and helps him to a seated position in the center of the sofa. He sits on one side and drapes his leg over Leo's leg. Benji takes his place on Leo's other side and drapes his leg over Leo's other leg. Both men are laughing lightly as each takes one of Leo's hands and holds it in theirs. Unable to process all this affection, somewhere inside a tiny voice tells him it is good.

"Okay, here's the deal," Jay starts. "One of us will ask one of the others a question about his past. That man then has to tell a story to answer the question with as much detail as possible. Look at me," he says to Leo who does so. "If we are not satisfied with your details, we tickle them out of you."

"I guess I'll have to at least try." He gives Jay a goofy grin.

Am I actually enjoying this?

Benji chirps in, "And naturally, the story has to be of a sexual nature."

Leo's features freeze. His breathing loses depth. He does not like this feeling that grabs onto him so often. He thinks a bit and finally confesses. "I don't have a lot of stories to tell, guys."

"We're kind of aware of that," Jay says, "and we'll go gentle with you, given it's your first time. Benji, tell us the first time you learned to love bottoming."

Benji gets ready to tell a story, but before he begins, Leo breaks in. "What did you just ask?"

Jay suddenly realizes the depth of Leo's naiveté. "Bottom, a man who enjoys being on the receiving end of anal sex. Top, a man who enjoys being on the giving end. Versatile, one who enjoys both. It is not required that you be one or the other. Some guys don't like anal sex at all. And you do not have to get locked into one. Benji is a bottom. I am a top. You, I suspect are somewhere in between with a preference toward topping."

Leo nods more from an urge to go on although he wonders how true Jay's assessment is.

Benji starts, "Jay's heard this, but it's new for you. I was 19. Unlike you," he says playfully to Leo, "I had had *a lot* of experiences. I was always used to doing whatever my partner of the moment wanted. If they wanted me to fuck them, I would. If they wanted to fuck me, I'd let them. If they wanted to dress me as a nurse and call me Elizabeth…well, I did have some limits." After a beat, he adds, "Okay, maybe one time."

Leo actually laughs.

"Anyway, I met this guy, Gary. He was my age and cute as a fluffy kitten. He was a student here. Smart, not like you, Leo, but smart. I would see him at the gym almost every day. He would smile and say hi. I was absolutely besotted… Shut up, Jay."

Jay holds his hands up to indicate he has said nothing with an expression that speaks volumes.

Benji briefly explains to Leo, "I fall for guys too easily. There, my 236th darkest secret is out. Now to continue, I pursued him like crazy. Followed him into the showers. Tried to get my locker as close to his as possible. Real crap."

Leo begins to wonder where this is going. His arms cross his chest.

Noting Leo's tension, Benji rubs his knee and says, "It changed real soon, babe. One day, when I followed him into the shower and started to come on to him, he simply put a hand on my shoulder. 'If you truly want me, you have to go out with me. Not here.'

"That made no sense. We were there and already naked, why not?" He shrugs. "Curiosity got the better of me so I agreed. That Friday we met for a movie. I tried to get him to sit in the back row so we could make out, but he insisted we sit in prim middle-of-the-theater seats. Every time my hand started inching toward his crotch, he'd grab it lightly and only hold on. When the movie finally ended, he asked what I'd like to do next. 'Go to your place,' was all I could say.

"He laughed gently and said, 'I guess we'd better.' As soon as we got there, I was all over him. He didn't push me completely away, but he did do everything he could to slow me down. Eventually, he stopped and let me know it was time to stop playing. We either fuck this once, or we take our time and see what we might have between us.

"Completely stumped me. 'Benji, relax. Let me find out who you are.' I gave up. Let him take charge. It became real slow and sensuous. We made out. He explored my body. I thought he was going to have me fuck him when I was on top of him with his legs wrapping my waist. Boy, was I wrong.

"He slid out from under me. I stayed on my stomach. He started to massage my ass. He was so sweet and took so much time. It felt like it was hours before he even started to rim me. I was more turned on than ever. Finally, he asked if I wanted to get fucked. I can't believe he asked. After an agonizing three milliseconds, I said yes."

Leo turns from Benji to look at Jay. "Rim?"

Jay leans in and whispers into Leo's ear, "Oh, slang for analingus." He turns back to Benji, indicating he is ready to go on.

Benji stares at Leo. "Analingus, yes? Rim, no?" He shakes his head in amusement. "You are amazing, babe."

Benji thinks for a second to remember where he left off. "I remember how he reached for a condom. He asked me to turn over. I raised my legs expecting him to start fucking, but he just started to ease inside me. He just looked at me and told me how handsome I was.

"I recall how gently he kissed me. It built as we went, but something changed in me. I never felt like such a man before. From then on when I have someone inside of me, I feel strong. Like I know what life is and stuff like that."

He leans back and looks at Leo who softly says, "Wow."

"I was really upset when he had to leave."

"What happened?" Leo asks.

"Family emergency. We kept in touch a bit, but when it became clear he was not going to be able to return, we drifted apart."

Leo just looks at him. He has an urge to...do what?

Benji perks up. "But I love what life has brought me since, so that's that. Jay's turn. I told about becoming a bottom. Now you tell us about becoming a top."

Jay smiles. "It wasn't a great discovery. I found almost any time I went home with someone, he wanted me to fuck him. One or two guys wanted to fuck me, but I wouldn't let them. It really started to dawn on me that I enjoyed the control." He looks at Leo and adds, "That doesn't mean the top is in charge, but we'll save power bottoming for another time."

Leo raises his eyebrows at Jay who waves his hand dismissively.

"I need to find a book of gay slang for you." Jay continues, "For me, though, there is an element of power. You've probably noticed that I have no problem taking matters into my own hands."

Leo smiles and softly says, "Dave." This brings a new blush.

Both roommates note this with light chuckles.

Jay moves his leg off Leo's and leans against him. "After graduation I started interviewing for all kinds of jobs, wanting to stay connected to the university. I finished a very successful interview and had time to spare." He cocks his head and sits up slightly. "Wow, I just realized, that's been almost eight years now...

"I wandered over to get a cup of coffee at the union. It was a little different then. The patio was much smaller and not enclosed. Anyway, there were these two guys sitting at the table next to me. They were talking basic frat rat shit about how they were going to nail this babe or that one. Real stupid shit. One of them, the other called him Vince, was adorable. Hair blond as yours, but no beard. I knew in an instant that he was faking it to fit in. He stumbled too readily over sexual terms for women. The other one was completely full of shit too, but he was faking his experience, not his desires.

"Shithead friend got up to get more coffee or something, and I just decided to act. I called over, 'Hey Vince.' He looked at me and asked 'Do I know you?' I told him no, but he needed to stop being a shit and come with me.

"He gave me some sort of line about I didn't know what the hell I was talking about. Then he blushed brighter than you do," he says, running a finger down Leo's chin.

"I called him on his bullshit and told him to ditch his worthless friend. He sat defiantly a moment or two, and announced 'Okay, but just to show you how wrong you are.' We took off before frat rat could return and headed here. I led him upstairs into what is now the spare bedroom. 'What are we doing here?' he asked. 'This,' I replied and gave him a kiss. He put up two seconds of struggle before his arms slipped around me and started kissing me back.

"I told him to take his clothes off. He hesitated, but as I began to strip, he did so too. Man, did he have a nice body. Lean and well-toned. He was 19, so he still had a lot of boyishness. His cock was hard from our kiss. So was mine. I took him back in my arms, and we kissed more. Slowly I backed him onto the bed. I got him to lie flat and then started to make love to him. I kissed him everywhere. Neck, nipples, between his thighs. I even sucked on his toes a bit. I got him to turn around and started eating out his ass."

"Rim," Leo peeps out.

Jay gives Leo a peck before continuing. "I never heard anyone moan so longingly. We had to fuck. I hurried to my room and came back with condoms." He smiles at Leo. "I wasn't as prepared then. He sat up and was looking at me. I could tell he didn't know what to say. Part of him wanted to grab his things and run naked out of the house, but he was frozen in place. His eyes scanned me from head to toe, making me feel like no one had ever seen me before. I put the condoms on the night stand. He looked at them, then looked at me. Slowly he began to nod and slid nearer. I took out a condom and handed it to him. He could have put it on himself, but he rolled it down my cock then laid back, legs parted.

I climbed onto the bed and started to enter him. It was hard at first for him. It hurt. He wanted to pull away. 'Vince,' he looked at me. 'Breathe.' It was the first time I said that to another man. He was fine from then on. And boy did he start loving it. I kept kissing him in this position. He held on tighter and tighter. I reached down and stroked him to orgasm. I came inside him right after. He started to cry, and when I asked him what was wrong, he replied, 'Nothing.'"

Jay raises Leo's hand to his lips and kisses it. "It was that day I knew how good I could feel and could make another man feel. I did let Vince fuck me once later. It didn't work. It was the last time anyone has been inside of me."

"What happened to him?" Leo asks.

Jay and Benji both laugh. Benji takes over the story, "He went back to the frat house, told his shithead friend to fuck off, gathered all his things, and moved in here. He was living here when I moved in. He had your room."

Jay continues, "He finished school a couple years back and then got a job in Germany where he met this guy named Markus from a small town in Bavaria. Sounds like they are going to make a go of it. When I talked to him last week, I told him all about how his room has been taken over by a wonderful new man. He can't wait until his next visit to meet you."

"How many guys have lived here?" Leo wants to know.

"A few failed attempts that never lasted more than a day or two, but they don't really count. My brother, Vince, then Benji, and now you. That's all. Only very special people."

Leo looks at him.

What is special about me?

Benji, not realizing what he asks feeds right into Leo's mood, says, "Now, we get to find out a little about what makes Leo so special."

"I don't have stories like that," he says quietly.

"We'll give you an easy one." Jay starts. "I remember when we first invented this game, Vince had kind of the same problem because he was so young. I guess most of your stories are still to be created."

Leo interrupts, "You just said he was nineteen. If you had just graduated, he wasn't that much younger than you."

Jay's features harden, "I was never truly young." He shakes off his feelings and returns to the present. "For now, how about just tell us about your first adult sexual encounter."

Leo shrinks. He knows about that first time. He wants to run, not talk. "I can't," he whispers, fighting emotions.

Jay and Benji glance over Leo's head, both confused.

"I can't. Too hard."

Jay kisses him softly on the cheek. "I think you know you have to." He and Benji hold him very gently. "You're safe now. You're with us."

"Sometimes," Benji adds, "it is best to start when it's still easy, and by the time the real story starts, you can't stop."

Leo looks at him. "Thank you."

He breathes in. He feels the hands that are holding his and squeezes them back. He closes his eyes and thinks back.

When was it still not bad?

Leo leans back and takes a deep breath. "When I started college, I hadn't turned 13. People thought it was too far for me to walk from home but also too young for a roommate. So I was in private dorm rooms. It was okay, I guess. All I ever did was study and go to class anyway. I'd get out for long walks around the campus. I thought it was so pretty at times. It was covered in trees and grass. And there were so many people to look at."

He stops as it dawns on him and grins. "I guess now, though I really was only looking at the guys." He manages a little laugh at that.

"I didn't know how to meet any of them, but I remember several I would think about often at night when I was finally through studying and was about to fall asleep. I remember thinking what would it be like to touch one of them? This went on until the year I turned 17."

Benji interrupts, "Wait, you finished high school at 12, but was still in college at 17?"

He simply shrugs. "Have a few degrees," as if it was perfectly natural.

Benji looks at Jay who nods agreement and silently mouths, "Many."

Leo continues, "My advisor thought I was old enough then to have a roommate. I thought about all the guys I used to look at. I guess you could say I had a few favorites. I remember hoping I would get one of them. Funny, I never knew any of their names."

After a moment, he resumes, quietly. "But it was none of them. Instead I got..." He pauses, struggling to keep tears at bay.

"Fucking Asshole?" Jay suggests.

Leo looks at him. This time louder, "Thank you. Instead I got Fucking Asshole, a jock on some team.

"He was loud. He got drunk a lot and would bring his other jock friends into the room. They'd all join in and try to get me to drink too, but they scared me. There was one or two who would try to get..." He pauses. "...to get Fucking Asshole to lay off." He rests his head back and takes a gulp of air to steady himself before continuing. "This one really tall one especially would block him. Weekends were the worst. I started basically living in the library. It was safe. I'd walk around after it closed until I thought he'd be passed out and I could sleep.

"Sometimes it wouldn't be late enough, and he would still be awake. He'd be too drunk to do anything but kept saying how horny he was and how he wanted some pussy. I didn't even know what horny or pussy meant. I was so bad I remember thinking what does he want with a cat?"

Leo can't help but laugh and that gives him the pause he needs. He is also being helped by the two kind men at his sides who continue to gently hold him with a tenderness that eases him forward.

"I tried staying out later, but I couldn't all night. At some point, he started to say how a nice genius ass would be as good as a pussy. He would say how he wanted me to come over and suck him. I pretended to sleep. He was always too drunk to do anything but talk.

"That changed about two or three months into the semester. He started to get up and come over. He'd pull my covers down and start to touch me. 'Come on,' Fucking Asshole would say. 'Let me at your skinny ass.'"

Leo leans back again letting his head rest on someone's arm. "God, it feels good to call him that. I wouldn't turn over. I would hold on tight to the bed. He was strong, but I guess too drunk. I didn't know what to do. I should have moved out, but I didn't know it was an option. It got to where I felt safer when he had those other jocks over. He started getting really quiet around me when others were around.

"One night," Leo says as tears start to slip from his eyes, "he crawled over and started asking again to give him my ass. He pulled the covers down. He kept asking over and over."

Words force their way between gulps. "He pulled my shorts down. I fought with all my strength to not let him turn me over. He wouldn't go away." Leo's angry hand swipes his nose. "Then he changed. He stopped trying to get me to turn. He said, 'If I can't have your ass, I'll take your cock.' And he started sucking me, and I got hard."

Leo is crying now. Getting the words out is grueling, but Benji was right: once started, he can't stop.

"I was so angry with myself. I hated Fucking Asshole. Why was I hard? I found out later by reading about it how at that age it was just my body reacting to stimulation, but at the time it made me hate myself as much as I hated him.

"Sucking wasn't enough. Fucking Asshole got up on the bed and tried to jam my penis inside him." Leo squeezes his eyes shut, needing all his strength to finish. "His cum felt like poison when it landed on me. He stumbled off and passed out. I jumped up and ran to the shower. I stripped all those clothes off and scrubbed myself. It felt like I had been exposed to nuclear waste and had to get every bit of Fucking Asshole off me. I threw on some clothes and grabbed what I had been wearing. I left and started to run. Somewhere I tossed those contaminated clothes.

"I didn't come back until the next morning. I grabbed my books and hid out in my refuge, the library. I stayed out, wandering for the next few nights.

"When I came back, he was gone. His stuff was not there. Never saw him again. Some of my things had been ripped up, but he was gone."

Leo's hands cover his face as full sobs erupt. He has done it.

No one was supposed to know.

They know.

His friends hold him and let him cry it out.

Finally, Jay kisses his cheek, "You're home now. We will keep you safe. That is a promise, dear one."

Benji catches a surprising note of anger in Jay's voice, but Leo does not quite understand.

"I think someone needs to be put to bed and tucked in."

They gently guide him to his feet.

"Wait a sec." Benji runs to the kitchen and returns with a dish towel to wipe Leo's face before they lead him out of the room.

They help him up the stairs. When he tries to break free and go into his room, they continue to hold him. He gives himself over, and they go to Jay's room. Although his first time in this room, he only sees how big and inviting the bed is.

"We're going to take care of you, Leo," Jay speaks. They guide him to the foot of the bed and turn him around so he can sit. One of them, he is not sure which because he has closed his eyes, gets behind him and starts massaging his neck and shoulders. The touch is firm, not at all painful.

A hand caresses his face and again Jay speaks. "Benji will stay with you while I get a few things. I won't be gone long. Keep remembering you are safe now."

It is difficult for Leo to process that statement, not sure what 'safe' means. Oh, but Benji's fingers feel so good.

Jay returns. Leo can tell he is carrying a basin of water from the slight, sloshing sound. "I'm back. I want you to try and relax. I have a feeling this is all very odd for you."

Leo confirms with a nod. He feels Jay raising one of his feet and removing his sock. It is repeated with the other sock. The strangeness of the situation causes him to open his eyes.

Jay sees the pleading, worry, and mistrust in the sweet blue eyes meeting his gaze. He lightly holds Leo's face between his hands and leans in to kiss his cheeks. "We are here to take care of you only. We are going to undress you, then bathe you. What Benji's doing feels good, doesn't it?"

"Yes," he manages to get out.

"Stand up," Jay says with quiet authority.

He obeys but feels uncomfortable when Jay reaches to undo his pants. He takes Jay's wrists and again meets his eyes, finding a soft, unfamiliar, yet comforting gaze. With a jerk of a nod, he let's go, arms fall to his side, deciding to trust. His eyes close.

Jay continues to undo the waist and tenderly slip the pants, underwear inside, down Leo's legs.

Leo raises each leg as Jay indicates in order to remove his pants. He then raises his arms allowing Benji to doff his shirt. Once discarded, Benji resumes softly kneading tense back muscles.

They begin to bathe him by first guiding him to sit again. Jay hands Benji a warm, damp cloth to start on Leo's back. Jay begins with Leo's feet with soft, invitingly warm cloths. Each washed spot receives a gentle kiss not more than a sweet brushing of lips on clean flesh. Once Jay finishes his feet, Leo is guided back to standing.

Both men start at the bottom of Leo's legs and move steadily upward. As one cloth becomes too cool it is replaced with a warm one.

The sound of water being wrung from the washcloths provides a particularly soothing sound.

They move up his body continuing the sweet kisses.

Leo, with some embarrassment, finds he is aroused, but Jay does no more than bathe him and bestow a gentle kiss as with every other place he has touched, his erection simply one more part given love and acceptance. The relaxation deepens more than any previously known. No harm will befall. Whatever all of this means, it is good. He melts into the rest of this bathing ritual.

They re-dress him in the softest clothes he has ever felt. Wonderfully warm pants caress his fine legs. Arms are raised so an equally luxuriant top can be pulled on. Finally, they gently guide him down on the bed to encase his feet in thick socks.

They ease him onto the bed on his side. One spoons into him drawing his arm. The other cuddles from behind and places an arm around him.

Exhaustion envelopes him. Someone says I love you.

Leo sits up, noticing the morning sun casts a dimmer light in Jay's room. He looks over these two men on either side of him.

I have friends.

He looks at the clothes he is wearing: a pair of snow white sweatpants and a pale blue sweatshirt. He didn't know clothes could feel so good.

Jay stirs and opens one eye. "Good morning, gorgeous."

"Hi."

Jay gets up on one elbow and pulls Leo in for a kiss. "Thank you."

Puzzled Leo finally says, "You're welcome." He starts to get up, but Jay grasps his hand. "I have to get ready for school."

"I know, but I want to look at you." He strokes Leo's arm for a bit. He pinches a bit of the sweatshirt's fabric and looks at Leo. "This is the exact color of your eyes."

Benji stirs, sits up briefly and sees Leo. "Good morning, babe." And he flops back down fully asleep.

"Get up and walk around a little," Jay says, and Leo obeys. "Turn too. I want to see you from the back."

Leo does that also with growing amusement. His movement is awkward, unused to being examined so openly.

"Damn," Jay mutters.

"What?"

"That sweatshirt is the perfect color for you and those pants show off your ass better than anything you've ever worn. Keep them." He falls back on the bed.

Leo gets back up between them. He turns to give the sleeping Benji a peck on his cheek then turns to Jay. "Thank you." He gives him a kiss also. For one more moment, he stays.

"And now I really do have to get going." He dashes out the door. The new clothes embrace him the entirety of the walk to his room.

Jay watches Leo head down the hall until he disappears into his room.

Too much cruelty. Does anyone ever overcome it?

He reaches for Benji's hand and looks at him affectionately.

Of course, they do.

He cuddles closer to his old friend and happily falls back asleep.

5

Benji is excited. Steve is coming.

He shifts finger food on three trays he has laid out on the kitchen table and counter. Several backup trays fill the refrigerator. There's enough for twice the number of invitees.

Leo tries his best not to hyperventilate as he sits on the edge of his bed gripping the bedspread. A date. At 25, Leo Graham has his very first date. If he wasn't so excited, he'd think it pathetic, particularly since it seems there is nothing to wear. He loves the blue sweatshirt Jay gave him, but it will be too hot.

Jay, heading to his room, sees Leo sitting amongst his few clothes, looking frantic.

"What's the matter, sexy? Nothing to wear?"

Leo shrugs. He can't admit nearly his entire wardrobe arrays around him in very neat stacks.

"Come with me."

Leo takes the outreached hand, drawing assurance from the contact. It feels so nice having his hand in Jay's.

Jay takes him back to his room. "Pants. I'm sure there's something you can borrow. Let's see. You're thinner and shorter than me, so nothing recent. I may have a pair of pants I originally bought for my little brother that would do." He disappears deep into his walk-in closet, emerging with two pairs, one a dark blue and the other a pale tan. "I'm broader in the shoulders, but otherwise most of my shirts should do. Take off your clothes."

Before he moved in, Leo could not have imagined himself standing in front of another man with only underwear so casually, but this doesn't faze him tonight.

"Those too," Jay indicates the underwear. "These will look better if you go commando."

"Go what?" he says as he gets naked.

"Commando, without underwear. Both of these would show a VPL."

Leo interrupts, "VPL?"

Jay looks with fondness at his friend. "Visible panty line. The only line you want to show tonight is the vague hint of cock."

Leo reddens.

"I love to make you blush... Too easy."

"You're so kind." It is the first sarcastic comment he has ever said. He giggles. That's new too. He laughs harder.

"What?"

"I giggled."

Jay bursts out laughing. He runs at Leo and tackles him onto the bed, pinning him down. He smiles into the bright blue eyes.

"Stop!" Leo says with more confusion than conviction.

"You're naked and have a man on top of you, you realize."

"Yes."

"Good, wanted to make sure you're paying attention." He gets off disregarding Leo's semi-arousal. "Try these." He grabs the tan slacks and tosses them to Leo who puts them on quickly.

"Stand up straight." Jay notes how well they hug Leo's thigh muscles and indeed offer a tantalizing bulge. "Turn around. Yeah, those will do very nicely. Now let's see about a shirt."

Leo runs his hands down his legs. This pair of castaway, slightly long slacks feels better than anything he owns.

Jay rummages through shirts, unsatisfied. Looking back at Leo in those slacks he decides on a pullover instead. The top drawer to a chest, larger than the one in Leo's bedroom, holds a wide variety. Several are pushed aside until a deep blue V-neck appears. "Try this."

Leo pulls on the loosely fitting shirt.

Jay tugs at the base of the V. "You look damn hot. This shows just enough of your chest hair to give any red-blooded gay man ideas." He steps back. "And now you're red again."

This time Leo laughs looking at himself in the mirror, liking the improvement this outfit produces.

Jay comes to stand behind Leo and looks over his shoulder. "You're on your own for shoes, though. I wear a couple sizes larger. Barefoot would be good, but we don't want your pretty toes to get stepped on." He brushes his lips on Leo's shoulder.

Leo reflexively curls his toes under his feet feeling a rush of warmth from Jay's comment. "I have a pair of brown dress shoes."

"Slip-on or laces."

"Slip-on."

"Good. Wear them without socks." Jay steps back from Leo and finds his shoes. "Let's get downstairs and pretend to help Benji so he won't pout. And by the way, in case you don't know, he has a date too." He winks at Leo. "Guy from work. Steve."

"Oh, wow, that's great."

Jay heads down as Leo stops by to put on his shoes, glad at least one thing is his, but admits really liking Jay's clothes. He has never developed his own taste, but could easily adopt Jay's.

Guests start arriving. Leo hangs back on the stairs watching a few enter, the only recognized one, Tommy. An especially vivacious guy comes in and makes a beeline for Benji who stands in the doorway between the foyer and living room. They hug and share an enthusiastic kiss. Leo assumes this is Steve.

"Oh," Steve says as he pulls a guy over, "this is my cousin, Carl." He leans into Benji. "Please don't be upset. He came back with me this morning after visiting my folks."

Leo watches, unsure, but thinks Benji is not happy about the other guy. His attention vacillates as he watches the door for Dave. He goes down into the room and sees what he can do to keep busy.

Benji plays the charming host and welcomes Carl, hiding his disappointment.

Jay wanders past them and recognizes Steve. "Hey, good to see you. I hear you'll be taking off from here pretty soon."

"Yeah, I have quite a few interviews coming up. With luck, one will work out."

Jay squeezes Benji's hand in understanding as he addresses Steve. "Who's your friend?"

Steve introduces Carl. Jay takes his hand and welcomes him to their home. "I'll show you around."

Carl happily follows this tall, handsome man.

Jay notices Leo holding back against a wall and takes Carl to introduce him. He then leads both men into the heart of the party, introducing both to other guests.

Leo tries to remember names, but his mind stays too much on the absent Dave to fully register any. He soon slips away from the group that starts to surround Jay.

Steve turns to Benji. "I am so glad to see you, Boss."

"Me too." They sit on a couch talking, finding excuses to touch.

Leo watches from across the room. How he wishes Dave would get here. He wonders if they will be touching like those two.

Where is Dave?

The party drags on. No matter how hard Leo tries, he cannot think of any names of the men he just met except there were no Daves. He wants to just go upstairs and close the door, but Jay would be all over him if he did that. Instead he brings out another tray of food from the kitchen for something to do and fusses over where to place it on the table.

Jay, in his element, flirts with Carl, chats with Tommy, and moves around the room with ease.

Benji and Steve get up to get something to drink. Seeing Leo, Benji diverts them. "Hey, babe, how's it going?"

"Okay, I guess."

"I don't know if you remember Steve. You met him that first day when you stopped in at the shop. This is Leo."

"I remember you. You almost fell asleep in your coffee. Damn, Boss, he cleans up nice." Steve reaches out and touches Leo's arm. "If I wasn't so crazy about this guy," he places his hand on Benji's chest and circles it seductively, "I'd be all over you."

Steve's flirtation improves Leo's mood. He still keeps one eye on the door, though it feels good talking to someone. The three chat until Steve reminds Benji about getting that drink.

"Boss, I almost didn't recognize him."

"He is a real sweetheart, but kind of socially out of it. I don't think his date has shown up either."

"Yours did." Steve gives Benji a kiss.

"What about your cousin?"

Steve turns and sees Carl talking with Jay and Tommy. "He's fine. Let's get that drink."

"Not thirsty."

"No?"

"I'm hungry."

"Well, there's all kinds of things to..." Benji reads Steve's eyes. "Want a tour?"

"Tour?"

"You haven't seen upstairs."

They scoot up the stairs trying not to be too obvious. Out of sight, they grab each other and start making out.

"This way," Benji rasps out as they head down the hall.

Halfway out of their shirts when the get to the bedroom, complete nakedness arrives barely in time for the door to close.

They kiss their way onto the bed. Steve's full weight settles on top of Benji, tongue deep inside his mouth. He holds his Boss, hips pushing into him.

Steve raises his head so they look at each other.

Benji touches Steve's cheek.

"Boss, you have the cutest nose..." He kisses it. "The warmest eyes..." He kisses each. "And damn, the most muscles I've ever seen." He pushes himself up.

Benji sees him gaze down. He feels Steve's eyes caress his skin. When Steve lowers himself, how good those lips feel on his skin as he receives the benefit of lingering kisses down his torso. He watches that full mop of hair receding down his body. He feels hot breath moments before engulfment into the warm silkiness of Steve's mouth.

"God." His hips arch up. "That feels so good."

Steve's sweet ministrations of hand and mouth bring about delightful squirms. His hand runs through the generous shock of hair as tempo increases. Lips embrace Benji's cock more securely. Eyes shut, Benji gives in. Flying. Soaring.

A hand gently caresses his balls as the sensation deepens. Gentle tugging, pulling sac tight, intensifying the awareness of his cock until Benji gasps, "Babe, stop, stop."

Steve looks up with a big smile. "Anything you want, Boss."

"I want you up here."

Steve slides up his body and begins another deep kiss while they roll onto their sides.

Benji holds him in his arms, his leg draping over Steve's. They stop kissing long enough to look at each other. Words feel so intrusive.

With Benji on top, kissing resumes with a keen sense this could be their only night together. He wants to memorize this body with all his senses, causing an unhurried journey. Each erect nipple receives full, exquisite attention. The few hairs on Steve's chest obtain enough consideration that Benji almost knows exactly how many there are.

The intense stimulation causes fleeting images of pleasure unable to coalesce into coherent thoughts. Steve pushes into it, body writhing forward greedily for all he can get. Suddenly aware of being engulfed with such deliberation, he can barely handle it. Deep inside Benji's mouth, a roar begins to build. With no warning, the yell escapes his lips, accompanied by rhythmic pulses inside Benji's warmth.

Benji struggles with the volume Steve pours into his mouth but gulps voraciously, refusing to let any escape. His hand begins lightly massaging Steve's thighs, calming, bringing him back. Finally releasing the softening appendage, eyes trace up the body until he looks at the still-awestruck face. He slides his body next to Steve's and rests his head on the heaving chest.

Steve lets his arm fall across Benji's shoulders, drawing him closer. "Boss."

Both are silent for several minutes. Benji feels Steve's fingers trace along the skin of his upper arm. "Steve, I want to ask you something."

"Anything, Boss," he says huskily.

He turns to face Steve. "All your flirting. I kind of get the idea it's all bravado."

Steve's return gaze softens. "Yeah."

Benji waits.

Steve looks at Benji and knows he can trust. "Most guys don't mind the flirting, but I never know how to bring it to the next step." He takes a deep breath. "Boss, not a lot of guys find me attractive." Before Benji can issue any kind of protest, he rushes to continue, "I know what I look like, Boss. I'll never win a beauty pageant."

Benji, having heard this from many men who handed him money for favors, cannot deny Steve's self-perception. "I prefer Miss Congeniality, babe." He runs a hand across Steve's very furrowed brow. "Besides, believe me, I have more than enough experience for the both of us."

This brings a wary smile.

"How about we get some sleep. I think I wore you out."

He moves to face Benji then gives him a kiss. "Thanks, Boss."

Once he settles back down, a realization hits. "I abandoned my cousin, Carl. I should get him."

Benji places a hand on Steve's shoulder as he starts to rise. "He's fine. Jay'll take care of him. If I know my roommate there's nothing to worry about." As Steve resettles, he adds, "It's what the guest room's for."

Jay and Tommy stand together sharing a plate of Benji's incredible food. Each keeps an eye on the room. Tommy, accepting nothing much more will happen with Jay, finds him easy to talk to, and besides, they're neighbors. Like Leo, he knows almost no one here but is far more willing to meet these strangers.

Jay sees Leo fussing away with food and arrangements.

God, that poor guy is so out of his element.

He tells Tommy he'll be back and heads over. "You know there is more than just food here, Leo."

"I know. Just, well, I know what to do with this."

"Dave's not here yet?"

He keeps focus on the hors d'oeuvres, now arranged into an elaborate geometric design. "No."

Jay is surprised.

Where the hell could he be?

He takes Leo's hand to lead him back to Tommy. "You know Tommy made that box we gave you? He's quite the artist. Maybe you'd like to thank him."

"Really? It is so beautiful," he says, relieved by the distraction while pushing away the thought of what the box holds. "I like having it."

"I'm so glad you got it, more special when my little creations go to people I know. I hope it gives you much pleasure." Leo's flash of redness puzzles Tommy. "I don't think we've talked since the day you moved in. Hope you are settling nicely."

"I really like it here."

They converse for a few minutes, but soon Leo feels he is running out of things to say and makes up an excuse to make sure there's enough food and drinks for everyone while unconsciously avoiding making eye contact with other guests.

Tommy finds Jay in a small group of men. "Hey there." Eventually the others drift away.

"Hey. So, anyone caught your eye?"

"A few. What's with Leo?" He indicates with a nod toward the dining room. "I kind of get that he's shy, but is something else going on?"

"His date hasn't shown yet. I've met the guy, seems real solid, so I am thinking something came up."

"That can be shitty." He points out Carl. "What's his story?"

"Carl? Just visiting. I've kind of been watching him too."

"I wouldn't want to interfere, but he is cute."

"I have no claims." A grin creeps across Jay's face. "We could share."

"You aren't kidding, are you?"

"Nope."

"Think it's possible?" He steps slightly away from Jay and moves his gaze from him to Carl. "It is intriguing."

"He's what 20? 21? From what I've gathered, not a ton of experience, but hungry for more. Visiting from a small town that offers few opportunities. Think he'd jump at the chance to bed not one, but two guys."

"You make a good argument." His head tilted, Tommy studies Carl. "Approach together or separately?"

"Chat him up a little, I'll come and see if we can guide it to a bit of fun." He winks at Tommy and leaves to make a circuit around the room, eventually coming back to Leo who looks in near panic. He lifts his chin so their eyes can meet. "No Dave yet?"

He shakes his head.

"Don't give up. Whatever happens it will be what needs to happen. I don't know, but the Dave I met doesn't seem like a jerk who would leave you high and dry. And if he is, better to find out now. Have you been able to talk to any of the other guys here?"

Leo looks around the room. Those that aren't in knots of people are focused on their phones.

How would I talk to any of them? None of them are Dave either.

"It's hard to be here right now."

"It sucks. I wish Patrick was here. He'd be good company for you."

"Who's Patrick?"

"Dear friend and coworker. Had to be out of town tonight."

Leo likes the thought of another friend, but there is something more pressing. "I really thought he'd be here." He lowers his eyes despising his feelings.

"So did I, but I haven't given up. Meanwhile, I know it's hard. Try to talk to someone. And don't hate me."

"What?"

"I'm about to abandon you for a hot three-way. Pretty sure Benji disappeared with Steve, so that leaves you in charge."

"Well, maybe I can talk to Tommy about his boxes."

"Crap. He's part of the three-way."

Leo just looks at him. After a moment, he just laughs. There's absolutely nothing else to do.

"Leo, the party can't go on much longer. We'll talk in the morning. Keep that in mind. If you want, I can wait with you 'til people leave."

"No, I'll get through. Like you said, it can't last too much longer."

Jay hugs him before returning to Tommy and Carl.

Draping one arm around each man's shoulders he asks how things are going.

"Good, good," says Carl trying to keep his cool, but Jay's arm across his shoulder pleasantly flusters him. That intensifies as Jay begins to massage his shoulder.

"You're Steve's friend, aren't you?" He turns to quickly wink at Tommy and then back to Carl.

"Cousin, but I haven't seen him for some time."

"Pretty sure he disappeared upstairs with Benji quite a while ago."

"Yeah, he's really into that guy."

"Tommy and I were going to disappear upstairs ourselves. Be a lot more fun if you joined us."

"Really?"

"Oh, yeah, really." Jay draws Carl in and gives him a quick French kiss, turns to Tommy and does the same, then pulls Tommy and Carl together so they can also kiss. "That should answer your question. Come on."

As they head up the stairs, Tommy leans into Jay, "Damn, you're smooth."

"Years of practice."

Jay leads them to his room. Inside, he looks at them. "Fuck the preliminaries. Let's get naked." He strips and the others follow. They stand close. Tommy takes a cock in each hand. Jay pulls Carl in for a kiss. "First threesome?"

"Yes," he says, his voice cracking. Jay turns Carl's head to face Tommy so he can kiss him too. As the others kiss, Jay gets behind Carl and presses into him, signaling his intentions.

Carl subtly pushes back.

Jay reaches between the two men to play with Carl's nipples. As Jay continues Tommy crouches to start sucking Carl.

Jay sucks Carl's ear, evoking little groans of delight. He starts to kiss his way down Carl's spine. Holding him firmly at the waist with his hands, he gets to Carl's ass and licks at the crack. "Spread your cheeks."

Carl obeys, ready to accept anything that may happen.

Jay gives Carl a playful whack. "Turn around." Carl obeys and now Jay sucks cock while Tommy eats ass. Feeling how Carl is shaky on his feet, Jay asks, "Ready to test your limits?"

Limits? Carl knows nothing of them anymore. Just this morning, the idea of being with more than one man never occurred to him. Now, two men are paying attention to his body, sharing him, turning him as he stands between them.

He knows he is being led across the room, probably by Jay. That would make more sense. Soon they are stretched out on a bed, room enough for all.

Hands seem to be everywhere on his body. A mouth engulfs his erection as he readily accepts another into his own mouth. Is it the same man or the different one? Opening his eyes to confirm seems absurd, the sensations too wonderful to care.

On hands and knees, he hears the tear of a condom wrapper and Jay say, "I'm going to enter you now." Eagerly, Carl pushes back on first contact. New limit: accepting so naturally as one and then the other take turns. Letting himself be manipulated into new positions, finding new limits. The only identifiable one, for now, is he cannot bear to touch himself. Too much stimulation.

Finally Carl opens his eyes to see Jay above him, bearing into him as he lies on his back. Reaching up for that handsome face with both hands, the sensations build beyond his control. His warm semen lands on his chest and belly. Loud sighs escape his mouth. He feels Jay orgasm inside him.

Voicing unwillingness as Jay withdraws, he is assured.

The exhaustion of physical stimulation carries him too soon into sleep.

No Dave, but a few guests linger. With Benji and Jay upstairs, Leo feels he should stay up at least until these guys, whoever they are, leave.

Can this night please end?

He just wants to go up to his room and cry himself to sleep, but he is so wound up.

Finally, the last guest leaves. He starts to head upstairs, but decides to relieve tension by cleaning. If not busy, he will spiral into a grim canyon. Maybe he can tire himself out enough to just collapse. Starting with the food table, leftovers are consolidated onto fewer trays and brought to the kitchen, wrapped, and precisely tucked in the refrigerator. This takes two trips. Wiped down trays find room in the dishwasher. The buffet is cleared of drinks.

Once done, he starts with the dining table, leaving it cleaner than it's been in years. The living room is scanned for stray dishes and glasses to clear and load into the dishwasher.

The downstairs bathroom gets attention next. He cleans the commode and wipes down the sink, cleaning any spots he sees.

He gets the garbage can from the kitchen and starts throwing things scattered around the living room into it. Fighting an almost losing battle with tears, his anger and frustration is accompanied by the thump, thump of refuse tossed into the can.

Not sure, but he thinks he hears a different knock, stops and waits. Yes, there it is again at the door.

Great. One of those total strangers is back because he forgot something.

A quick scan of the living and dining rooms does not identify a lost jacket or phone.

He stomps to the door and jerks it open.

A very sheepish Dave stands there.

"Am I too late?" It's a lame attempt at humor, and he knows it. He looks at Leo taking in the scowl and the hurt.

I caused that pain. I didn't want that.

"You look really pissed. I hate that this happened this way. Please can I come in? You deserve an explanation."

Leo finally steps aside.

He enters. "I want to reassure you so badly right now. Please let's sit down." As badly as Dave wants to hold Leo, he feels he likely broke a trust.

Leo, stunned to inaction, can't look at Dave even though he dreamed of looking into his eyes all week. Eventually, he motions to the living room.

Dave goes to it and waits. "Leo, please come sit here. I don't want to yell across the room. I want you close." He sits on one end of the large sofa, patting a cushion.

Leo starts to move. He lowers himself onto the far end, faces towards Dave, draws his legs up and wraps his arms around them defensively. His eyes remain merely open, not focusing on anything, especially Dave.

Dave scoots down as low as he can to meet Leo's eyes with no luck. "Okay. This is better," he states nervously. "When I met you the other day, I felt so incredible. I'd seen you since the first day and just couldn't figure out how to reach you. You never looked up. Then Jay came along, and he started talking to me about you. God, what am I doing? You know all that." He breathes deeply. "I was disappointed when they changed my schedule with no warning. I hoped we could talk more during... I'm rambling. Get to the point, Dave, get to the point."

He has to stop looking at Leo finding it hard to deal with all that sadness and anger.

"Sorry. This morning I woke up in such a good mood. I knew I'd get to see you. I had trouble focusing. All I could think about was seeing you. I kept thinking how much I wanted to talk to you, look at you, and maybe hold you. I didn't care what. It was all so good. That feeling built all day. I would get excited then nervous, changing my clothes a thousand times in my mind. At one point, I passed a store and thought I'd buy... Rambling again." He shakes his head trying to collect himself.

Leo takes a peek at Dave. That is exactly how he felt all day too.

"But then around 4:30, my advisor called. There was some sort of mess that had to be dealt with, and for some reason I had to be at a department meeting. I only had one hour before it started. I tried to get out of it, but Dr. Lopez made it clear all T.A.s had to be there if they expected to hold their positions. I'm so new and..." Dave shakes his head to interrupt himself. "Dave, how are you going to ever be a writer if you can't tell a story right?

"I ran over to the student union and hoped to see you, but you weren't there. I found the math building to see if I could find you. I didn't know where to look. I tried to get some information out of the department secretary, but she looked at me like I was offering her a warm dish of plague."

"Dot. She's notorious." Leo picks at an imaginary speck on his knee. "Why didn't you call?"

"Leo, I couldn't call you. Here..." He pulls out his wallet and takes a small piece of paper then carefully unfolds it. He passes it to Leo who doesn't take it. "I didn't have your number." He looks at Leo who finally looks at him quizzically.

Softly, "Leo, please look at it."

He takes it. It is the written information for the party he had given to Dave. "So?"

"Read it." He does and just looks at it for a few moments until it strikes him.

"There's no phone, only the address," he says very sheepishly. "That was stupid."

Dave takes the note back and returns it as carefully as he had extracted it. "Not stupid. We were both nervous. I got here as soon as I could. I'm just glad you're still up. God, I've been running so crazy I must look horrible."

He thinks Dave looks amazing but says, "I was cleaning up."

"Can I at least help with that?"

"I don't want to clean anymore."

"This was very rough on you, Leo. I am sorry you went through that." *Leo looks so tired.*

"Guess it wasn't really your fault." Leo now picks at imaginary dust on the sofa.

Dave reaches for Leo's hand. "Is it okay if we talk a little?"

"About what?"

"About Leo, about Dave, life. I don't care. No, that's not true. I do care."

It feels good to have Dave's hand on his. Leo turns his hand up. They sit quietly. Each wanting to say something. Neither knows what.

At last, Leo manages to break the silence. "I woke up the same way this morning." He takes a peek at Dave. They finally fully look at each other.

"Are you sure I can't help you clean up?"

Shaking his head, "I guess I should put that back, though," he indicates the trash can. "I'll be right back." He takes it back to the kitchen. *He's here. Dave made it!*

Back in the living room. Dave has stood and looks around. He focuses on the painting above the sofa. "That looks like where I grew up. This place is wonderful."

"Yeah, it is."

"Should I go?"

"I don't know."

"I want to know you, Leo. I want to know all about you."

"What do you want to know?"

"God, I don't know, anything, everything." His mind spins. He indeed wants to know all. "Um, what's your favorite color?"

"I don't have..." The box flashes in his mind. "Blue. I like blue."

"Me too. We have something in common."

Leo reddens.

"Maybe I should go. You look tired."

"I'm not really. Just had a long day."

"Yeah, I guess you have. Wish it had been better."

"It's better now." A slight smile.

Encouraged, Dave asks, "Can I at least give you a hug?"

Leo nods. He steps into Dave's arms. They hold each other. They continue to just hold on. Leo's arms take Dave in tighter to him. Dave's hands move slightly down Leo's back. Their body weight shifts. Dave turns his head. His lips rest on Leo's neck. Leo's hand moves up to Dave's hair. Dave's lips soften against Leo's neck as he leans his head. Dave starts to kiss Leo's neck. Leo turns. Their lips meet. Mouths part, Dave's tongue tentatively explores. Finding no resistance, he starts to really kiss. Leo responds and starts to explore Dave's mouth also. The kissing develops as sweet as both men are at heart, as yearning as both in the moment.

As they briefly break, Leo rasps out, "Don't go."

They return to this kiss with more passion, more resolve. They step into each other as much as they can without falling over. Somehow Dave's jacket falls to the floor.

They barely pull apart again. "I won't," Dave finally answers. Slowly, Dave works Leo's shirt out of his pants enough to slip his hand underneath, seeking the comfort that touching flesh brings.

They look into each other's eyes, virtually the same height. Curious gazes become relaxed smiles. Lips yearn for contact again.

Another break. Hand takes hand. Dave raises Leo's to his lips. Leo follows suit. They move.

"Come with me," Leo invites.

"Yes" is the simple reply.

Leo stumbles slightly as he backs toward the stairs. Dave readily catches him, keeping both hands on him. They smile at each other.

Backing his way slowly up the stairs, Leo is unable to stop looking at this man. His mind wandered to Dave often this past week.

He is here. His hand is in mine. He's following me.

At the top stair, he pulls Dave in for another kiss as he fumbles back to open the door. They kiss their way across the threshold.

Once across, Dave pushes the door shut. It is very dark. "Leo, I want to see you better."

Leo turns on a small lamp by the bed and returns to Dave's embrace.

Dave's hands slip under Leo's shirt again taking the lead, unconsciously compensating for Leo's lack of experience. Inching Leo's shirt up his slender torso, Dave kneels to kiss Leo's bare flesh on his belly. He nuzzles into the smooth flesh on the sides then runs his tongue lightly down the distinct treasure trail that will obtain more attention later. Now a hand runs over the front of Leo's pants.

As he stands, his hands slide up, raising the shirt further, exposing a nice hairy chest and nipples he wants to devour but now only gently kisses. He continues pushing the shirt up.

Leo raises his arms so Dave can remove it completely. Leo's arms drop onto those broader shoulders.

Dave smiles as he massages Leo's chest. "This is nice." He dreamt of this since he first spotted him. Now this quiet man stands here accepting his touch. He allows his eyes to travel up from Leo's chest to his face. Dave reaches to pull Leo in for another kiss as he feels arms slipping off his shoulders. Leo is unbuttoning his shirt. Dave moves back enough to give him the room he needs to work his way down his body. His shirt is slowly pushed off his shoulders, and he lets it drop to the floor.

"Wow," Leo softly says as slender fingers dig into the dark fur covering Dave's chest.

Dave looks at the fascinated Leo. "And you thought you were hairy."

"Amazing."

They look at each other and again kiss. This time their bare chests crush together. Shoes are kicked off. Hands find belt buckles, buttons, zippers. They are getting each other naked for the first time. Internally, both hope it will not be the last. It takes no time for discarded pants to be forgotten.

Dave guides them to the bed. They ease themselves down as they embrace, finding their way to the middle, facing each other side by side. Dave moves his hands between them to find Leo's cock, very aware every move he makes is a first: the first time he touches Leo's cock; the first time to stroke it; the first time he feels Leo's hand on his. He loves the way Leo feels in his hand and raises up on one arm so he can watch as they stroke each other. He slowly looks over all of Leo's very slender body.

He stops stroking to run his hand over this perfect-to-him body. A finger travels up that delightful trail leading all the way from Leo's pubic hairs to his chest. Each nipple is traced. He gently pushes Leo's shoulder until he is flat on his back next to him. He continues to run his hand over Leo's chest and belly.

"You are so gorgeous," he tells Leo as he looks at him, causing a cloud of doubt to darken the fair features. Leaning down, kisses resume.

Dave rolls on top, body sinking onto this man. Hands hold the face he kisses. He feels Leo's arms take him into an embrace. Lightly he sucks a bit of Leo's lower lip into his mouth, the reddest lips he has ever seen on a man. He feels more than hears Leo's moan. He turns Leo's head to one side and brushes his hair away from his ear to know how that makes this man feel, again keenly aware this is his first taste of this part of Leo. Dave, happy to find anything giving pleasure, rejoices how Leo's body squirms under him.

He kisses Leo's neck. The beard is lighter here than on his face, the hair surprisingly soft. He is aware of hands on his body. He raises Leo's arm so he can explore the pit. He inhales and licks lightly at the thick patch. Leo reacts with a laugh and an involuntary jerk. Dave meets his eyes. "Ticklish?" he asks. Even in this dim light, he can see Leo blush as he nods yes. "I won't."

Leo visibly relaxes.

A different kind of pleasure is intended.

Dave slides down Leo's body. He rubs his head over Leo's chest, enjoying the roughness of it on his face and finally understands men who have nuzzled into him like he does now. Kisses are bestowed anywhere lips land, now a nipple. Kisses develop to licks, causing a deep sigh. He feels a hand on his head, fingers running though his hair. He moves slightly off Leo so he can reach down to stoke his cock while he continues to give Leo's nipple more attention.

Leo's fingers run along Dave's face. He is in awe. This man is here. With him.

Dave returns to exploring Leo's body, nibbling at his belly. Kissing closer and closer to his erection. His tongue touches just the tip causing a wave of sensation for Leo. Dave circles the head with his tongue then kisses it. Parting his lips, he takes in just the tip. Another first. The hand he left on Leo's chest is held. He takes more into his mouth. It would be so easy to take it all down at once, but he wants to give Leo as much pleasure as possible after this disastrous evening. He sucks just the head, transporting Leo into new territory.

Leo writhes under Dave's attention, wanting more.

Dave starts to take Leo deeper until he takes Leo's cock to its base. A sweet mass of pubic hair brushes his compact nose. Leo's hips involuntarily, then consciously, thrust forward as Dave sucks. Hips and mouth find common counter-tempo.

Dave pauses. He leans up to catch Leo in a deep kiss before adjusting his body so that Leo can get to his cock as he returns to Leo's. And Leo does so with a novel relish. It is all new tonight.

He takes Dave into his mouth. Dave hardly notices Leo's lack of experience, only thinking of how they are together, pleasuring each other. How much he enjoys this quiet man. The two are again on their sides. They mutually pleasure. Dave reaches around Leo to hold his ass, to know its sexiness.

Leo now on top, they return to kissing. Dave wraps his legs around him. He wants one more first with Leo tonight.

Dave breaks from this kiss. "Leo? I want you inside me."

Leo traces Dave's face. He wants this too. Unable to think of the word "yes," a simple nod suffices. Suddenly it hits him. He is prepared. He is going to use what's inside his beloved box. He starts to laugh softly which breaks the impasse in his brain.

Dave looks at him a bit puzzled.

Leo rediscovers words, "I would love to be inside you. I want that more than anything in the world right now." He gives the first full smile Dave sees from Leo, the first full smile he has given in his life.

He watches Leo reach for the box and open it. When returning, Dave stops him, "Get up a bit." Leo obeys. Dave sits up and takes the packet out of Leo's hand. "I want to put it on you." His smile is met with a delighted grin. Dave has a sly grin on his face as he opens the packet. He reaches for Leo's hardness, strokes it a little, and starts to roll the condom on. He takes the bottle of lube and applies some to Leo's cock and rubs some into his anus. Looking into Leo's eyes, he says, "I want you so much, sweetie." He lies back down and scoots closer, raising his legs. One hand guides Leo inside.

His ass opens, invites. "Go slow." He wants to savor every inch of Leo as he is entered. At that moment when cockhead enters, he bites his lower lip as he watches Leo's face. He breathes deeply, relaxing, taking more and more as Leo slowly eases further and further. Cupping Leo's cheek, encouragement is nodded.

Leo is inside me.

He pulls him down for a kiss.

Leo begins to slide out a bit then back into him.

Dave lets his eyes close, his head rolls back, taking deep chest-raising breaths. He finds his own hard cock and just holds it. His legs embrace the lean torso. Leo is gentle. He can take more and will, but this is so right for their first time: cock and ass getting acquainted. He feels Leo's breath on his neck, then his lips. His whole body is awake.

And Leo, how in awe he is of this man beneath him. Who he is penetrating. Who wants him inside. He has never been this aware of his cock inside another man. He is conscious of giving Dave pleasure. He pulls up to look at this marvel, unable to doubt what he sees.

He likes this. I am giving him what he wants. We both are.

We. A simple word. One Leo never used quite this way before.

Dave's hands gently knead Leo's chest, the hair rough and soft at once. He lightly digs his fingers into the flesh. And oh, god, how that cock feels. His gaze returns to Leo's eyes, and he sees this man is taking in his body, scanning him too.

His pale hair is so thick it doesn't fall forward.

A silly, yet profound observation, another Leo detail.

The pace progresses naturally. Dave finds his cock again. This time stroking. More intensity.

"Yes," one of them says, or was it both?

Leo's hips move even more insistently, more powerfully. He wants to look at Dave, but for a moment, has to close his eyes and go inside himself. His body has taken over.

His eyes open to see Dave's sweet face change, become unfocused.

He's ready.

Leo automatically increases his thrusting. Dave starts to cry out. A stream of pearl white shoots out, landing on that beautiful dark matting of his belly. Then another that goes a little farther. More comes.

Dave writhes and moans beneath Leo.

Inside Dave, a quieter but as powerful orgasm.

Both men lie still a long blissful moment until Dave reaches up to pull Leo down for yet another kiss, this time with a new urgency and breathlessness. They have made love. Their first time.

Leo eventually slips out of Dave. Dave's legs at last drop from around Leo. Bodies align. They turn to each other, soft kisses accompany gentle strokes on faces and bodies. They wait for voices to function.

"You're here."

"With you."

They sleep until somewhere in the middle of the night when Dave gently wakes Leo, needing the bathroom. Groggily, Leo leads them. They pee together and return, falling immediately back to sleep. They hold hands the whole time.

6

Saturday opens with a rare haze on the first cool day of the fall. Jay notices the first color change in trees as he stands naked at a bedroom window. He loves this time of day. It is all still promise. Wonderful or dreadful things may happen. He looks at the two naked men sprawled sleeping, softly breathing, not quite a snore escapes from one. One was taken somewhere new last night. Jay hopes it was good.

He moves to the toilet to pee and ponders if he should shower. No, he'll run later, maybe work out, plus he likes the lingering scent of last night's sex. He hears a stirring in the bedroom. In a moment, Tommy comes in to relieve himself also. Carl would have been a surprise. They mutter sleepy greetings.

In the doorway staring at Carl, last night plays out. This young man will need help getting through today. The day's scenarios run through his mind. Benji will be both happy and sad about Steve. And Leo, his sweet new friend, was in such pain last night. They take precedence over Carl.

The toilet flushes and Tommy stands next to him. They both stare at Carl as Tommy speaks. "That was intense."

"More for him."

"No doubt. Never saw that happen before." He sits with Carl while Jay stands firm in the doorway. Tommy can deal with Carl today. He won't be as raw with him.

"Take him out for breakfast."

"He probably could use food. Let's get him going." Tommy gently shakes Carl's shoulder. "Hey guy, it's morning." Jay does not hear Carl but sees his arm go around Tommy. Jay goes to the bed to urge them on, suddenly wanting Benji or Leo.

Carl, clearly not fully awake, needs help getting dressed and down the stairs. Before they leave, Tommy thanks Jay and adds, "Unreal." They will be very good neighbors.

On his way to the kitchen, Jay sees a jacket on the floor. He figures someone must have forgotten it but puzzles how it ended up there. He hangs it on the back of a dining room chair noting how clean the table is. The entire place has been cleaned.

Leo.

Whatever needs to be dealt with will be easier with very strong coffee. Once started, he goes upstairs to change into running clothes then returns to wait for coffee and those he loves to appear.

———

Leo and Dave have been awake several minutes. Leo, never spending the full night with a man, woke before Dave and studied his face: he has a day's beard now, surprisingly light given his body hair. The nose is straight, very short. There is a very slight scar under his right eye. That dark coffee-colored hair on his head, very straight, longish. He hovers his fingers over Dave's lips: thin, slightly chapped from all the kissing. They are somewhat parted and Leo imagines his tongue widening that opening. When Dave opens his eyes, there are those green sparkles.

Dave's first sight of the morning is Leo's face. He smiles. "Good morning, sweetie."

"Good morning." Leo would like to add an easy name like "sweetie" or "babe" like Benji calls him, but nothing comes.

Yet without realizing, Leo experiences none of his normal unease as they cover a variety of "this is who I am" subjects. Dave asks about school, what brought him to math.

"Numbers always made sense. I was good in everything. I could remember what I was told, reading was easy. But numbers? I don't know, I could see the connections. There was so much logic. I couldn't understand why no one else saw it, why they had to be 'taught' how to add or subtract."

Dave laughs. "I know that feeling. Why was I in a reading class? It didn't make sense it had to be taught. I honestly don't remember learning."

"Yeah, it was that way for me too. I don't remember how I figured out how to make sense of it."

"I loved books forever. My favorite was Dr. Seuss. I read everything of his."

Leo blurts out, "Who's Dr. Seuss?"

Dave looks at him. "You're not kidding, are you?"

Leo shakes his head.

"Sweetie, you led a sheltered life." That comment draws a deep blush and slight withdrawal. Dave moves back to numbers, bringing Leo back to the conversation.

They cannot spend the rest of their lives in bed, not even the rest of the day. "I could do with a shower," Leo admits after a surreptitious sniff.

"Wouldn't mind one myself. May I join you?"

This causes Leo's cock to stir. He almost says no, but agrees. "I'll get a towel for you."

Dave swings his legs over the side of the bed. He notices the box that Leo had reached into for the condoms. "This is beautiful. I love lapis."

"It is. It was my housewarming gift from Jay and Benji. Our neighbor made it."

Dave opens the box. "My, that's a lot."

"It was part of the gift. I can't imagine using all those."

Dave looks at him and grins. "I'll see you in the bathroom. We did go there last night, didn't we?"

"Yeah. Right across the hall."

Dave watches Leo head out of the room. He takes a condom out of the box and looks at it gleefully.

Sweetie, I hope we'll need to buy more very soon.

Leo showers, intriguingly visible though the opaque curtain. Dave closes the door. He leans against it and savors this sight a moment, the obscured vision of Leo's body an impressionist painting come to life. Dave pokes his head between the break in the shower curtain. He steps in, calling Leo's name softly.

Leo turns. His hands are up to his chest holding soap. He notices Dave's erection and feels himself stirring.

Dave steps closer. He looks at Leo with a mischievous grin as he places the condom on the ledge. "You never know."

Downstairs, Benji joins Jay. He brushes a kiss on the top of his head before commenting on how good the coffee smells.

"You had fun last night, I assume," Jay teases.

Benji sighs. "Damn it, it was wonderful." He plops into a chair.

"You're hooked again."

"Yeah, but this time so is he." He grins at that. "Progress, I suppose. He doesn't know how much longer he'll be here. As soon as he gets a job offer, he'll be off. Damn, he doesn't even know where, but it won't be here." His smile has become a frown.

Jay rises to get coffee for Benji. "Here."

Benji is consoled by the rich brown color knowing it is prepared how he likes it. "I suppose you had fun too."

"Yes, but all was not well last night."

"What?"

"Dave didn't show."

"That's shitty, but I think Leo's feeling better."

"Why's that?"

"He's not alone in the bathroom."

Leo and Dave head back to the bedroom leaning into each other. Dave stands in front of the closet mirror and shuffles his hair around with his fingers, then finds his underwear and slips them on.

For the first time in his life, Leo has spent a full night with a man, taken a shower with a man, fucked a man in said shower, and in doing so, had sex while standing. All in less than 12 hours. Getting used to this could be fun, but right at this minute sitting takes precedence.

Dave studies the room. Other than the mess they made, it is very neat, organized, and clean.

He sits next to Leo. "I could go for some coffee. Interested?"

"There's probably some already made downstairs if that would be okay. Someone's usually made a pot by now."

"That sounds good." He was hoping to spend a little more time together. Where they share coffee is irrelevant. "Is it okay to just wear my shorts downstairs?"

Leo laughs, "Yeah, no one here will mind." He has seen Jay and Benji naked in every room of the house but hasn't worked up the nerve to do that himself. "Go on ahead. I'll be down in a bit."

Sitting across the kitchen table from each other, the friends discuss who could possibly be with Leo. Neither imagines any of the guys who were here last night with Leo. Jay has his back to the entrance, so it is Benji who first sees Dave. He stops mid-sentence, spoon raised, staring at the hirsute man who has just entered.

"What the fuck?" Jay turns. In a second, he screams in delight, pointing. "Oh my god, it's a strikingly good looking dark-haired guy with impossibly green eyes."

"And it's one of Leo's two best friends in the whole world even though he doesn't realize it yet."

Jay jumps up and embraces him.

Dave glances past Jay. "Okay, now," he indicates Benji, "he is clearly visible, not a rabbit, much less one that is six feet tall. Can this be Leo's other best friend in the world although he doesn't know it yet?"

"My name is Benji, not Harvey. And I need an update."

Jay, his hand on Dave's chest, "This is...ready? Dave."

Benji gapes widely. "Yay!" He grabs the other kitchen chair and pulls it close. "Sit! Spill!"

"First, Leo's doing much better this morning, I believe. The rest is a long, thankfully done story." Dave and Jay are laughing. Dave sits in the proffered chair as Jay returns to his. Head spinning, Dave repeats yesterday's horrible misadventure. Unable to tell it lightly just yet, it's still painful. He hates how Leo suffered, but the story could become part of their anecdotal history.

Leo comes in during the telling in his usual jeans and t-shirt.

He's here.

The pain from yesterday disappears as he cherishes hearing Dave tell it again.

Dave sees him. "There you are. Come sit."

"No more chairs." He feels an odd fearless shyness.

Dave reaches to him. Leo takes the outstretched hand and sits on Dave's lap. Head rests on head. Hand in hand. As he focuses on Dave's hand, he remembers last night watching Steve and Benji as they held hands.

It feels better than I thought it could.

Benji breaks the silence. "You guys need coffee." He gets up, asks Dave how he takes it, and returns with two very welcomed mugs, Dave's very similar to Leo's.

There is little to say. Clearly Leo is exhausted, but Jay has never seen him so relaxed. He watches as Dave simply holds his hand.

He's good for Leo.

Benji asks if Dave will come to dinner.

"I would love to, but I have too much to do today. My advisor gave her first tests last week. I have about 200 papers I need to grade by Monday."

Leo actually pouts.

"And I think I need to take this fine young man back upstairs." Dave runs a finger under Leo's eyes and asks very softly, "You need to get to bed?"

Leo shrugs. He is not physically tired but experiences a new kind of exhaustion. They rise, but before leaving Leo thanks Jay for letting him borrow the clothes.

"No problem. Keep the pants. They don't fit me. In fact, you may as well take both pair."

Benji comments, "I thought those looked a little long on you. Bring them to me later and I can hem them up a bit."

"The shirt you can bring back later," Jay adds teasingly, "even though it looks better on you than me."

Leo shyly thanks both for their unexpected generosity.

Jay rises, addressing Dave. "And I need to get out there and run. It is very good to see you." He leans in to give Leo a kiss on his cheek and tells him softly, "I knew he'd make it." He heads out the front door.

Leo and Dave go up the stairs.

Benji prepares a tray. He pours the remaining coffee into an insulated carafe, fills a creamer and sugar bowl, followed by spoons and napkins. He puts his mug on the tray and opens the cabinet to select a fresh mug.

Will Dave's become permanent?

He wishes the one he places on the tray is.

He lugs it all to his room, larger than the two across the hall but smaller than Jay's. Along one wall, three crammed bookcases stand. His computer sits on a table with two chairs under a window opposite his door. He places the tray on that table and crawls back into bed, cuddling up to the still sleeping Steve.

─────────

"I wish you could come for dinner," Leo says.

"Me too. I want to see you again."

"Me too." He sits on the edge of his bed.

"How about dinner next Saturday. I'd love to cook for you."

Leo smiles and agrees.

"And finally," Dave finds his pants and takes out his phone, "May I have your number?"

Leo laughs and recites it as Dave punches it in, then calls it. When it rings, he holds Leo back from answering so it can go to voice mail. "Hi Leo, it's Dave. I had the most wonderful time getting to know you a little. I want to know you a lot. I live at 515 N. Mesa #513. Dinner will be served at 7:00 p.m. but come over early, say around 5:30?" He looks at Leo who nods. "Now, you have my number too."

Leo reaches for his phone on the night stand. He saves the message and adds Dave to his contacts. He gazes down his short list of numbers in his phone. "Just remembered, I have to meet my project partner this afternoon."

Dave gets dressed and then gets on the bed to kiss Leo one last time for now.

No one is downstairs. He finds his jacket and takes off.

─────────

Jay starts an easy warm-up jog, deciding to head to the university track rather than the nearby trails.

The early Saturday morning is yet still. Very few people are out. A woman walking a dog, a man watering his lawn, a few joggers. He moves from the owner-occupied houses through the houses filled with an ever-rotating band of students finding their second taste of freedom after dorm living, a fun, adventurous group mostly unconcerned about upkeep of the domiciles.

Crossing the campus, he thinks of his next trip starting Wednesday. He won't return until Saturday. Too much to think about: the trip, his powerful experience last night, life in general, and now Leo. He has rarely felt this strongly about someone so soon after meeting them: Patrick, Vince, and Benji. Leo promises a complexity far more intriguing than any.

Few populate the track, allowing a hard run. Smooth, long legs carry him well. Halfway around the track, his mind clears, and he is only running.

Steve wakes and stares dully at the ceiling. He feels Benji's arm beneath his neck. Sitting up he turns to face him. He wants to be here, next to this man, not moving who-knows-where hundreds of miles away. Gazing around the room, he focuses on the bookcases, wishing for time to read them all, maybe discover which they've both enjoyed. How? No jobs in this highly competitive market means not enough time to know and love this incredible man.

He touches Benji's face lightly. "Good morning, Boss." This elicits a smile before eyes open. Steve leans down for a kiss.

Still a bit groggy, Benji turns his back to Steve. He reaches around and draws an arm around him, nuzzling his butt against Steve's rapidly developing hardness. He reaches to open his box for a condom and passes it to Steve. Very soon he can feel his ass being opened and pushes back. His hand finds Steve's mass of hair. "God, just fuck me."

Steve obliges, holding this precious man in his arms while driving into him. No building this morning, only desperation. Steve rolls on top of Benji greedily. Benji bites into the pillow to muffle his exasperated screaming and pounds the bed with one fist.

Both want more than this one long night. Frustration builds in both men over their situation. Steve's arms force their way under Benji's body, holding him tight.

Benji reaches around and has both hands in Steve's hair. "Yes, do it! I want you." He has never been so demanding, never so furious. "More!" Benji presses his hips up. Steve has to get on his knees. Benji, on his elbows, his hands locked together, buries his head into that wedge.

Steve grabs those strong hips. He digs his fingers in and drives with all his might. A tear forms and slides out of his right eye. The intensity of his orgasm is a raw, new sensation.

He pulls out and falls onto the bed sobbing, hand over his eyes. Benji rolls over, taking him into his arms.

"I'm sorry," Steve finally says, "I didn't know. Damn, I didn't know."

Benji guides Steve's arm away from his face. "It's okay. I know. It sucks."

"Why do I have to leave?"

"You have no reason to stay."

"I have one."

Benji sighs. "You stay here and do what? Serve coffee for the next 20 years? We both know you have to do this. I wish you could stay as much as I wish I could go."

"Benji, how did this happen? I just wanted to have a little fun, you were so sexy. When did I fall for you?"

"You have it hard." He laughs ruefully. "I fell too, you know."

He smiles. "So what can we do?"

"Right now, I want to cuddle and try not to think."

"You got it," and with a sad smile, "Boss."

7

As the only academic recruiter for the university, Jay flies out early Wednesday after the party. While he enjoys meeting the kids, most shine in their communities but are not special enough. All were like that this week. One girl had promise, but in the end the best option was simply giving her more financial options than he offered the others.

All week he turned down over-fried dinners well-meaning mothers offered in hopes of improving their chances. By the end of these trips, Benji's meals cooking welcome him home most delightfully.

Workout opportunities are also rare. Not knowing neighborhoods, he mostly settles for runs around whatever lodging has been provided.

Finally, in a decent city, St. Louis, the hotel offers decent meal choices and a house gym with a sauna off the changing room. He doesn't hope for more than a few machines but is pleasantly surprised to find some free weights and benches.

Alone, he starts with a light jog on a treadmill. Most hotel gyms attract few visitors. Midway through his warm-up, another man enters: early 50's, thick in the waist with dark, thinning hair.

Jay nods a greeting.

"Morning," he receives, accompanied by a furtive look of appreciation.

He pauses his run. "Usually I have these hotel gyms to myself. Nice change." He gives the guy a welcoming smile. "Jay," he says, extending his hand.

"Bill. It is a nice change. What brings you here?"

Jay tells him about his job. "And you?"

"I'm here with a convention."

A puzzled Jay asks, "Okay, the International Introverts Incorporated? This place is empty."

Bill laughs, "Very thankfully, most are at hotels downtown. I avoid the people you meet at these things. Usually a bunch of drunk men trying to get laid. And the women are just as bad, except more of them see me as fair game. Doesn't matter that I'd rather have somebody's drunken husband. I'd rather men be more out."

"Makes total sense. Easy to have your way with a guy claiming drunkenness. Personally, I prefer men who are a bit more evolved. The drunk bit is strictly sophomore frat boy."

"Exactly."

"Want to work out together? Be a nice change from normal hotel routine."

"Sounds great."

They do a solid workout, mostly weights, concentrating on chest and arms, becoming more physical as they go. Clothing clings with perspiration. Bill clearly enjoys the attention. He is starting to get used to being bypassed for younger men.

Both work up a nice sweat. "You got time to hit the sauna?" Jay asks.

"Sure, flight's not 'til this evening."

"Great. Love getting sweaty with a sexy man."

Bill lets out a hearty laugh. "Me too."

They head into the changing room and strip off sweat-drenched clothing. Jay subtly slips a condom into the waist band he creates with a towel. Each sizes up the other's body as they head in. The squeaking door leading to the sauna lets them know they will have ample warning of anyone's approach. It is basic. Wood plank walls with one bench across from the entrance. Four men would be cramped, five impossible. Plenty of room for two.

Jay raises the heat as they enter. They sit on the bench leaning against side walls to face each other in near-mirror images: one leg on the floor, the other on the bench with knee bent. Towels, strategically draped, barely hide cock and balls. Any little movement gives the other a tantalizing glimpse. They begin a dance played out in saunas around the world. The outcome assured, the journey is part of the fun.

They speak nonchalantly. With each sentence, another suggestive gesture is added: a hand rubbing across sweaty chest, a nipple given slight attention, the foot of the leg on the bench inches noticeably forward, towel is shifted giving an enticing glance. At some point, their feet have inched forward enough to connect.

Conversation draws to a close. A brief impasse is broken when the air conditioner is heard kicking on. Jay looks down Bill's body to see his cock tenting the towel and adjusts to advertise his own erection. Each towel is withdrawn step by step, an inviting strip tease. Eventually both are exposed. They nod approval. Now the dance moves to the negotiation phase.

They start to touch their cocks. Stroking would declare only mutual masturbation, but the slow teasing tells the other: you may touch too.

Jay's foot inches over Bill's: I will take charge.

Bill does not withdraw or try to reposition: yes.

They lick or bite their lips: oral is wanted.

Bill's foot stretches out to massage Jay's cock: I am ready for more.

Jay's foot slips under Bill's balls: I want access.

Bill leans back, moving his hips slightly forward: granted.

They move closer, hands stroke as they kiss.

Bill leans forward to suck. Both know what they are doing.

Eventually Jay kneels between Bill's legs.

As Bill begins to suck, Jay keeps an ear open for the squeaky door.

Jay guides Bill so that the older man can lie back. Bill raises his legs, signaling his readiness. Condom is retrieved from the folds of Jay's discarded towel. He enters Bill. Jay wants to fuck; Bill wants to get fucked. Bill wants to cum with a dick in his ass. Jay wants to cum inside an ass. That simple. That good.

As Jay removes the condom, Bill jokes about being prepared. They laugh as they share a cramped shower area. They even decide to have lunch together. No exchange of phone numbers or promises.

For the first time, Leo decides to wear the navy pants he got from Jay and pairs them with his blue dress shirt, hoping it matches better than the white one. Looking himself over in the full-length mirror, he notes how well these pants fit. Twisting to see the reflection of his ass reminds him of the last time he met Dave for coffee. The soft fabric of Dave's shorts clung to his butt as he walked away.

Remembering the day he first arrived at this house dripping from being overdressed, there will be no jacket. He doesn't want to be sweaty when he gets to Dave's. Later? Fine.

Downstairs he looks for Benji to say goodbye. The door to his room was open but he wasn't there nor anywhere downstairs. After a fruitless glance to the backyard, he goes to the basement and finds him on one of the benches taking a pause from working out, still looking sad. He calls his name softly.

Benji turns. Seeing Leo dressed up he remembers, "You're off for your date. Babe, I am so happy for you." Looking his roommate over he is reminded, "I need to hem those up for you."

"I wanted to say bye." He is again, maddeningly, feeling shy.

"You better have a good time." Shaking a finger at Leo, he adds, "I want all the details tomorrow. Lurid details."

Leo stands unsure. He should say something to acknowledge his friend's mood, but what? At last he strides over and hugs Benji, muttering, "Thank you," and then is off.

Was that the right thing to do? It felt good.

Leo walks fast.

Slow down. Don't get all sweaty.

He deliberately makes himself look at his surroundings to slow down. There are many older houses in this neighborhood, all painted in so many different colors. Some have additions. One's porch sags, needing repair. Another has flower beds along a stone walkway leading to the front door. He starts to catch details from every house along the way until reaching campus.

Dave's apartment is on the far side in housing set aside for graduate students. He described his place as efficiently tiny, the second of four identical red brick buildings sitting close to the sidewalk. The minimal landscaping, a swath of lawn, grows between sidewalk and building. Flowers reaching their season's end languish in oversized, pretend terra-cotta planters flanking the entries. Leo finds Dave's name on the resident list, pushes a button, and is buzzed in. Dave warned him the intercom doesn't work.

He gets into the elevator, pushes "5," and exits on an identical floor. He peers down the hallway and sees Dave heading to him wearing an oversized grey t-shirt over dark blue shorts that show off his hairy, toned legs.

Dave beams as he reaches Leo and takes him into his arms for a hug and kiss. "Sweetie, welcome to my, and I can't stress the word enough, *humble* abode." He takes Leo by the hand and leads him to the back end. "I am so happy to see you again."

"Me too," Leo manages.

They enter a room smaller than Leo's bedroom. To the right is the bathroom. A kitchenette lines the far wall. On one side there is a desk with Dave's laptop and a small table set for dinner. Two chairs flank it. A sofa that folds out to a bed sits under the sole window on the final wall. A few filled bookcases cram into available nooks. One painting hangs on barely available wall space.

"Let me give you the tour." He takes Leo by the shoulders and spins him once slowly. "If you missed anything, I can take you the other direction." His hands slide off Leo's shoulders, down his arms to take his hands. "I wish I had room for more of my own things, but as you can see, not much." He gives him another kiss. "I opened a bottle of wine, if you'd like."

Leo, captivated, answers, "That would be good."

They release each other, and Dave goes to the counter. He pours the garnet-colored liquid into two glasses. Handing one to Leo, he toasts, "To finding happiness." He touches glasses and takes a sip.

Leo follows suit. The wine is slightly tart but very delicious. "It's good."

"Thanks, picked it out just for tonight. I have just a few things left to get ready before putting dinner in the oven, then I have something I'd like to share with you." Leo takes the few steps needed to stand by Dave's side as he works on the dish he is preparing. He has already smoothed a layer of cooked rice on the bottom of a casserole dish. On top, he places a couple of marinated chicken breasts. Over that he grates some cheese. "Per someone's request, not a mushroom in sight."

Leo leans forward to take in the scent. "It already smells good."

"Thank you. I love cooking. I was always in the kitchen with my mother or my grandmothers." He grins at Leo. "It may be illegal to have Italian grandmothers and not cook. I hope I can be half as good. Do you cook?"

"No. Don't really know much about it."

"Well, I enjoy it enough for the both of us." He covers the baking dish and slides it into the small oven and turns to Leo. "Come on. We should be right in time. Grab your wine."

He takes Leo's free hand and leads out of the apartment to the stairway opposite his unit.

"I want to take you up to the roof. I love sunsets. And from the clouds today, this should be a really pretty one."

On the roof alone, Dave leads them to two chairs facing west. "Sit, my lovely."

The sky has started to darken already. Sunset begins.

"Quiet up here," notes Leo. "Nice."

Dave holds Leo's hand as he gazes at the sky. "I come up here to write. The light is great at so many times during the day, but I love sunsets best."

Leo has never thought about doing something like this. He knows what causes each color. He can say what angle is needed for one shade over another. If asked, he could tell why the sky is blue. All of that, but he has never actually just sat and watched.

"What do you like about it?" Leo risks a question, finding it easier to ask than he thought.

"Apart from the sheer beauty of the sky, I love to try and describe it. Part of why I want to write. Like, look at that band over there between the two strands of cloud." He points off to their left. "What color is that?"

"Orange."

"That's the easy answer, but which orange? Is it like the fruit orange? Is it more tangerine or maybe peach? Just take a moment and think if you wanted to tell someone about that exact orange, what would it be?"

There is something different than just orange. Darker than an orange, less red than a peach, but it does make him think food. He ventures, "Pumpkin." It makes him smile.

"Wow, that is so correct. You get what I mean." He takes Leo's hand to his lips. He keeps hold and lowers their joined hands to his lap affectionately.

Leo is truly enjoying this. "What color would you call the clouds above and below the pumpkin orange?"

"They are a deep slate blue. Each has patches that approach purple."

"You're not going to tell me which purple?"

"Smartass." Dave purses his lips playfully. "Eggplant."

They scoot their chairs closer together so they can lean on each other.

"Okay, sweetie, try the dark patch of blue sky that is below that cloud and further to the left. No more food."

"What food is blue? Well, blueberries, but other than that. Oh! Lapis."

How could saying a word bring so much joy?

"Yes, that's really it." They settle into simply watching the sunset develop then fade. Taking occasional sips of wine, Dave's arm is around Leo's shoulder. Leo's head lies on Dave's chest, feeling the mat of Dave's chest hair beneath the cloth of his t-shirt.

Dave kisses the top of Leo's head. "I love the color of your hair."

Leo smiles. He turns to face Dave. "What color is it?" he asks with a coy grin.

"Oh, it's a newly discovered color. No food, gem, or flower dares lend its name. It's unique in the annals of colordom. Salons across the world are trying to duplicate it as we speak. We need to be very careful and protective of your head. Mad colorists skulk, scissors in hand, trying to get a sample. It is called simply 'Leo.'" He kisses Leo's nose. "It will go down in the Color Hall of Fame once that is created, the first inductee."

They laugh and meld into each other and reach to hold hands. "Sweetie, dinner may be ready." He finds his wine glass. "But first, to sunsets and new colors."

The aroma from Dave's dinner seductively draws them down the stairs. Leo can't wait. They kick their shoes off as they enter. Dave has him sit at the dining chair facing the kitchen. He removes the chicken dish from the oven and places it on the counter.

He brings two salads, dressed with a homemade herb vinaigrette to the table, then pours more wine. Seating is invitingly cramped. One of Dave's feet settles on one of Leo's.

"This is all so good. I've never tasted wine like this." Leo laughs at himself. "I seem to be saying a lot of that. Nothing has been the same since I got to town."

"I hope it's been mostly good."

"Yeah. I mean living in that beautiful house with Jay and Benji is unlike anything I could have imagined. They're so nice and, I don't know, just good to be around." A look of worry crosses his face. "Can I say something?"

"Sure, anything."

"Well, it's that Benji has been kind of quiet lately. I feel like I should be doing something but don't know what."

"Quiet in what way? Sad or angry?"

He ponders, salad-filled fork halfway to his mouth. "I think sad. Definitely not angry. And Jay's been gone, so it's kind of strange."

"Have you asked him?"

Chewing, Leo shakes his head. "I kind of gave him a hug on my way out, but I don't know what to say."

"Hugs are good. When did it all start?"

"Not sure," he looks down, feeling good suddenly. "I've been distracted."

Dave grins, "How so?"

He looks up briefly into those amazing eyes. He lightly pokes Dave's chest with a finger. "You."

Dave raises Leo's face with his forefinger under Leo's chin and leans in for a kiss. "I like being your distraction. Kinda been happening to me too." He is a pubescent teenager around Leo. "I'm glad you like living there. Haven't had a chance to talk to Benji. He seems naturally amiable. It would be upsetting to see him sad. I really like Jay. I think he could be a great friend, for me and for you. And I'm ecstatic to be a distraction. At least with my field I can write sappy, purple verses. Don't imagine you get that kind of inspiration in yours. How's that project going?"

Leo, very pleased that Dave has remembered, doesn't like his answer. "The best I can say is no one seems closer to an answer than us."

Dave removes the salad dishes and serves the chicken and rice. The aroma that promised delights delivers beyond what Leo imagined.

The conversation flows in ways Leo never knew he was capable. His full present life makes it easy to avoid his troublesome past, keeping a smoldering dread at bay. He sits here flirting with this fascinating man, a skill Leo did not know he possessed. And that electric shock of Dave's touch…

Dinner over, Dave clears the dishes.

Leo watches Dave, not fully aware he focuses on Dave's ass move to the kitchenette. He wants to make love to Dave. How does that happen? He believes Dave would like to also, but insecurities kick in.

Dave finishes while Leo is pondering. "I am stuffed," he declares. "How about a little walk?"

Disappointed, Leo agrees. That improves once they put their shoes on and Dave takes him by the hand as they leave. In the elevator, still hand in hand, Dave leans over, "You're cute."

"Am not."

Dave is not sure if Leo's playing or being serious.

Outside Dave leads. He enjoys having Leo's hand in his, a simple gesture announcing we are a couple. The walk is short. Dave, suddenly in a hurry to get back, almost pulls Leo along the hall as they get off the elevator. Once inside, he takes Leo in his arms and begins to kiss him, not the friendly flirty kisses they have shared so far this evening, but full, desirous. "God, how I've wanted to kiss you like this again." Dave almost rips his t-shirt as he pulls it over his head.

Leo shoves his pants down. They need their naked bodies pressed together, hands exploring. They want deep kisses.

Dave zeroes in on Leo's neck. He loves the slight roughness of the beard and gives Leo gentle nips that in all likelihood will leave a mark. Hungry for this man, he dives into an armpit, inhaling a spicy musk, teeth tugging at the hair.

Leo shudders.

Dave returns to those lips, his hands in that glorious mane. He feels Leo's hands around his waist, their cocks aligned side by side between them. He pulls back to look into the most beautiful blue eyes he has ever seen. Can he feel this deeply so soon? He knows everything and nothing about Leo.

Dave wants Leo. Now. He squats down to take him in, shoving one of the dining chairs aside for room. Confident in this moment there will be other times for toying or teasing, now he wants exactly this. With steadying hands on Leo's thighs, fingers press into flesh, taking the cock to its root and holding it there to breathe in the finer scent of that full bronze pubic bush. Though tempting to have Leo cum like this, he wants more. Lightly stroking, he looks up to Leo. "I want you so much."

Leo, overcome, nods.

He pulls Leo to the sofa on top of him. Hips grind into each other. Hands on Leo's ass, Dave holds him close. Sweat from their exertions allows their bodies to glide. They roll, now side by side. Dave, on the outside slips off the sofa to reposition himself so they can provide mutual pleasure. A foot knocks something off the side table, but neither notices.

They move around with Leo on his back, Dave kneeling above. Dave cups Leo's balls as he sucks. Leo's hands cover Dave's ass.

Dave reaches back for Leo's hand, guiding it to his crack for Leo to play more. Dave releases Leo's cock from his mouth enough to groan, "Yes." Encouraged, Leo starts to stroke between Dave's cheeks, noting the hair here is longer, more velvety, than the hair on Dave's ass cheeks. He touches the anus and Dave gasps.

He wants this.

He starts to circle the smooth softness. He presses, eliciting more groans of pleasure. His finger starts to work inside Dave.

So warm and silken. It feels different than with my cock.

Dave raises up and takes Leo's hand, steering it to his mouth where he sucks on the finger that had been inside him, then adds a second. Crouching over Leo's chest, he then guides Leo's hand back. He feels the now moistened finger enter him, then the second one.

Leo had no idea this could feel so good. He remoistens his fingers to continue this unique pleasure. His eyes are riveted by the sight of his fingers moving in and out, loving the contrast of smooth inside and hairy outside.

Dave has his own, plainer box by the sofa bed. Reaching for Leo's hand, stopping him, he turns to watch Leo's face as he takes him inside, the pleasure so intense Dave's head rolls back reflexively. Mouth agape, taking in air, breathing out, "Oh, fu, oh." He slowly brings Leo's face into focus as he steers Leo in.

Leo's face is a wonderment of pleasure.

Both utter sounds, a primitive language spoken in the dance of sexually engaged men. They try smiling, but mouths won't quite stretch that way now, needing to be open for the deep gulps of air and released sighs.

Dave rolls his hips back and forth. Leo is tensing.

Dave increases his movement, his hands gripping Leo's shoulder. His body rises as Leo thrusts his orgasm into him. Dave's ass muscles involuntarily grasp more tightly. His own milkiness sprays Leo's belly.

Leo's hips relax back to the couch. Dave releases himself. Smiles emerge. Leo looks at the pool on his belly, still warm when touched. Dave takes Leo's finger and raises it to his lips, sucking his own juices. Leo takes another finger full and brings it to his own mouth, noting the slight difference in taste from his own. That makes him happy.

Eventually Dave raises up enough for Leo to fall out, then sits back on Leo's hips. He touches Leo's face.

"We should pull the bed out," Dave says.

"We should."

"I don't want to move."

"I don't want you to move."

Dave chuckles softly, "Legs are falling asleep."

"Guess we better move."

They open the sofa up to a bed and get on. In the warm room, they lie on top of the covers, Leo's head on Dave's chest. He can stroke Dave's body, breathe his scent, and hear his heartbeat. He likes this.

"This isn't what I'd planned, you know," Dave says with soft affection.

"Oh?"

"No, I wanted to go on a long romantic walk after dinner. We were supposed to stroll around campus, find places that would come to have special meaning. Then I was going to bring you back here where I planned to light some candles and slowly seduce you."

"What changed?"

"With every step, all I could think about was getting you naked. Walking was difficult," he admits laughingly.

Leo raises to look at him. "I guess I should admit something too."

"What?"

"I've been kind of turned on the whole time I've been here." They kiss. "You've shown me something that I never saw before even though I've seen hundreds of them. I mean I think whenever I see a sunset, part of me will think of you."

Dave holds him closer. That is the most romantic thing anyone has ever said to him. Sleep sneaks up on them, leaving them sweetly entwined. Dave drifts contentedly.

Leo's demons show their heads a little. He successfully brushes them aside when his fingers lightly grasp Dave's chest hair.

9

Benji considers his shy, admittedly odd friend. The hug felt very good. Maybe Leo will be okay. He picks up a 40-pound weight and resumes arm curls.

Usually here every spare moment, this is his first workout in a week. Thankfully that awkward hug refocused him. Sweat develops, soon soaking both shirt and shorts. A welcomed soreness will visit tomorrow. Nearly two hours later, he emerges and heads for the refrigerator, pulls out a pitcher of water, and guzzles it halfway down in big gulps. He looks down at his sweat-soaked clothes. On his way upstairs to shower, a rapid knock sounds on the door.

Steve sheepishly stands on the porch. "Hi, Boss. Can I come in?"

Benji steps aside. "Of course."

Even as Benji protests his sweaty condition, Steve takes him into his arms. Gazing into Benji's dark eyes, a confession falls out. "I have news that is not great."

"You got an offer, didn't you?"

Steve nods.

"It's great news, but yeah." Sweaty clothing becomes irrelevant. "Let's sit. Tell me about it."

"They called a few minutes ago. It's at a small private girls' school in San Diego. I'll be teaching math to third and fourth graders."

"Girls' school?" Benji leans back and tilts his head.

"Yeah, probably a bunch of princesses, but the pay is great and San Diego is gorgeous. They'll cover moving expenses and help me find a place to live."

"Wow, so it's happened. When do you start?"

He looks down. "Benj," he says softly, "right away. I have to get everything ready to be there in three days." Facing away, he tries not to tear up. "That part really sucks."

"Fuck," plops out before Benji can check himself, then he leans in to kiss him lightly. "Way, way down, I really am happy for you, just kind of hard to feel that right now."

"Yeah."

They sit silently.

"We should celebrate," offers Benji, sullenly. "I could take you out."

"I don't want to be around people. Not other people. This is my last free evening. I don't want to be around anyone but you. Can we do that? Just you and me?"

So many emotions churn inside a speechless Benji.

"Look, Boss, I know we're going to promise to stay in touch. I know I'd love to have the chance to see what we could genuinely have. We'll even try. But damn, I'll be a thousand miles away. I want to be selfish. I want..." He pauses for a breath. "I want you, goddamn it. Please say yes." He takes hold of Benji's hands.

"Of course, yes. Yes!"

They head up the stairs.

In his room, Benji stands looking at his bed.

Steve comes up behind him and takes him into an embrace. He holds him close and nuzzles into his neck.

"I love holding you."

Steve begins to kiss his neck. Benji reaches back and grabs his wrists behind Steve. Steve's hand slips down to get under the sweat-laden shirt to find smooth warm flesh of a flat belly. He pulls up the shirt to get access to the finest chest he has ever known.

"Undress me," Benji says, releasing his hold.

Steve eases the shirt over Benji's head. He again holds him from behind. He reaches lower to undo the drawstring of the shorts. Fingers sliding into the waistband, he eases the shorts down enough so they drop to the floor.

Benji steps out of the shorts.

Steve starts to tug the jockstrap down but is stopped.

"Leave it for now." Benji steadies his hands back on Steve's hips. "Get naked. Put on a condom. I want you holding me like this, your arms around me, inside of me."

Steve complies, concentrating on entering that beautiful ass instead of thinking how this could be their last time together.

"I remember the day you applied," Benji starts after a slow exhale. "I had just been made full manager. You strode up to the counter. I just watched you. How assured and full of energy you were. I was scared when I heard you ask about applying. I thought, 'How can I work around this guy?' But oh, how I was thrilled I might see you every time I came in. I avoided you that day. I didn't want you to see me." He moves his ass just slightly.

God, he feels so good in me.

Lips brushing against skin, "I did see you. As soon as I walked in. You were looking down. You were...are...so attractive." His hands slowly roam on that chest he dreamt of so often. "I tried to catch your eye, but you disappeared into the office."

"It was scary interviewing you. Did you know you were the first person I hired? I wanted to offer you the job on the spot. I had that horrid porn movie fantasy about clearing the desk and letting you take me right then and there." He flexes his ass.

"Ah. Oh god, that's good." He counters with a gentle thrust. "I never wanted a job so much." He needs to take in a breath. "I had the same fantasy."

"You had on that red polo shirt. It fits you so well. I had to force myself to think about the questions. Your nipples were erect. I wanted to rip that shirt off you. Every time you wore that shirt, I wanted to slip my hands under it and get your nipples hard again. No shirt shows your body as well. You wore it the last day." His hips sway side to side.

"Damn, my nipples always do that when I'm turned on. Like right now. Yours too." He rubs them.

"Ah, ah." Leaning his head back, hands reach back to hips. "I wanted to treat you special. Give you more than anyone else. I couldn't. I was your boss," he says, slightly starting to rock his hips back and forward.

"It was special. Every time you looked at me, or our eyes met, or I touched you, you were always kind and patient. I came in thinking you were so fucking hot and then found out how sweet and caring you are." His hand stays on Benji's jock strap.

"The most difficult were nights we closed together. After I turned on the alarm and we'd walk out, you would hug me goodnight. I wanted to say, 'Let's go somewhere.' I hated those hugs to end and us heading off in opposite directions." He takes a step closer to the bed.

Steve steps forward also. "I'd watch you walk away. I would have gone anywhere with you."

"I thought you were flirting with me like you do, but now I see it was different. You were more deliberate. It lasted a little longer." Another step.

"Sometimes I wish I'd never learned to flirt. The wrong people take it seriously, the right one didn't." Another step.

"I hated the day you said you were leaving. I wanted to say, 'No, you can't!' Of course, I knew you'd have to go." Close enough to the bed, he leans forward and braces himself with his arms causing his hips to rise invitingly.

"I hated that day too."

"I don't want to talk more. I love your gentle pace. Keep doing that."

Steve's hands loosely take Benji's hips as he eases in and out. He watches his shaft penetrate rhythmically. Slowly he guides his erection into this man and just as slowly, withdraws it. The sweet ass squeezes down, giving as much pleasure as he hopes he provides. He leans over to wrap his arms around this body, kissing smooth flesh.

Benji slides forward, bringing their bodies down as their feet remain on the floor. He can turn his head so they can kiss. "A little more."

Steve increases pace. Keeping his strokes steady, he knows he can't last. "I'm so close, Boss."

"Yes. I want it," Benji says quietly.

Steve does not need to increase his pace. Permission is all he needs. His hips thrust deep, his body shudders. His weight drops onto the man beneath him as his breath starts to return.

He pulls out and gets Benji to turn over. He starts to remove the jockstrap, but is stopped.

"Not yet."

He sits up to meet Steve in a kiss. "We need a break. I want to fix something light to eat. Then we are coming back up here. I'll want you back inside me."

Steve starts to put some clothes on as they get up.

"Babe, we're all alone today."

Downstairs, Steve sits at the kitchen table, eyes on ass still framed by the jockstrap.

A simple salad on a single plate with only one fork is brought over but not placed on the table. Benji, sitting close, feeds them. Once the food is gone, the plate is set on the table.

Steve feels the fork lightly graze across his chest, toying with his nipples. He starts to look down at it, but his gaze is guided back up so that he stares into those dark brown eyes. Fork tines explore his body: stomach, flanks, and hips. Arms are raised, and the fork drags along the sensitive underside and into his pit.

Steve continues his gaze even during a break in the stimulation. Two powerful knees between his press them apart. Then the fork is on his thighs, the tops, the sensitive inner flesh. It combs through his pubic hair and starts to graze his balls. It is dragged up the length of his erection. And he cannot look away from those eyes, even when they do not look back. The gaze will return, and he cannot miss it.

He hears the fork being put down. "I wanna go back to my bedroom."

Up the stairs, Steve is led to the bed. A condom is rolled on.

"The first was yours. The second, when you bring me to orgasm, will be mine. The next, ours."

He smiles broadly. "You're in charge, Boss."

When waking in the morning, Steve will know for at least this night, they loved each other.

10

The sun creeps over the building next door, its light falls directly onto Leo's face, discourteously waking him. He squirms away from it and sees Dave in the kitchenette working away naked. Leo knows that body better than any other man's.

I need to get busy. I don't have time. How can it all work?

He meets George this morning. They must succeed if he has any chance of staying in this place he is coming to love. And if he has any chance of staying with this man... He can't go there, too frightening. He rolls onto his back with an arm over his eyes blocking the glare.

This has to work.

He sits up, "Good morning."

Dave turns. His smile melts Leo's worry momentarily.

"Good morning, sweetie. Sleep well?"

"Yeah."

"Coffee?"

He gets a nodded reply and pours a cup, knowing already Leo takes it with sugar and extra milk. He brings it over, gives Leo a kiss, and hands him the cup.

"I am so glad you're here," he says as he gets back into bed. "I wish we could stay and cuddle all day."

All Leo can say is, "Me too."

Dave wants so badly to take this melancholy man into his arms and tell him everything will be all right, but until Leo can say what is going on inside that brilliant mind, there is not much to do. He wonders how much the accident that took Leo's parents has affected him.

"You have things to do today, don't you?"

"Yeah, meeting George to make a dent in that project then I have other work to do for my classes." But, he wants to add, I want to stay here.

"Me too. More work than I thought." Their legs press together tempting them to get lost in each other again. "When you meeting George?"

"He's coming over at 10:00."

"We need to get you going." Dave says with a sigh as he scoots off the bed. "I shouldn't have let you sleep in so late. It's nearly 9:00. I'm sorry, Leo, you looked so peaceful."

Leo just shakes his head. He wants to be here so badly but desperately needs money. He slips to the edge of the bed and starts pulling on clothes as he finds them. His normally smooth movements are unconsciously slowed, delaying his unwanted but inevitable departure. He sits back on the bed to pull on his socks and shoes.

Dave sees the emotions roil in Leo and sits back on the bed. He reaches out to touch Leo's shoulder. "I'm so sorry. I don't want you to be angry."

Leo's hand covers Dave's. He turns to look at him. "I'm not mad at you. I couldn't be. There's just, well, so much." He wants to tell him all of it, but where can he possibly begin? Leo looks so lost.

"I was all set to make a nice breakfast."

"That would have been nice. Dinner was wonderful." He starts to get up.

Dave gets up too and throws on some shorts. He grabs two pieces of toast he has made and wraps them in a paper towel. "Here, you'll need something, and you can eat this as you go."

"Thanks." He looks at Dave.

So much I should tell him, I don't understand it myself.

"Look, you have to get going. I have a lot to do too. I would rather be with you, but we'll find time later. Let's talk tomorrow and see if we can figure out a time during the week to at least grab a cup of coffee. Would that be okay?"

A smile conquers Leo's funk. "That would be a lot more than okay."

Benji and Steve woke and made love for the both of them through the long night. It left both more exhausted yet happier than either could remember, yet culminated with profound sadness with the unwelcome sunrise.

Benji aches from the physical workout downstairs and the passionate one upstairs.

Steve dresses in harsh silence, looking at his Boss too difficult. He swallows hard and squeezes his eyes shut in a losing battle with his emotions.

Benji watches, then gets up to walk him out but can only make it to the stair landing where he sits heavily, incapable of another step.

Steve takes two more before knowing he needs to turn and look through tears into those eyes he will miss. He reaches to hold him one more time. They kiss hoping there will be more.

"I love you, Benji," he barely verbalizes.

Benji can only nod.

Steve turns and hurries to the door but pauses to turn for one more glance, seeing his beloved struggling against breaking down. He rips the door open and begins to run. Halfway down the walk he crashes blindly into Leo. His tear-stained face looks into a shocked one. "Take care of him!"

Steve escapes, racing down the street leaving a very confused Leo.

Take care of him? Is something wrong with Benji?

He takes the entry stairs two at a time and calls for Benji, seeing him as soon as he enters, looking very small on the stairs.

"Benji," he moves to him. A shaky hand reaches up, and he takes it.

Benji pulls him down to sit next to him and, with no other warning, curls into Leo and begins to bawl harsh, shuddering sobs.

Never having seen anyone so broken, he can only hold his friend, letting him cry it out, not knowing if this is the exact right thing to do, emotional support as new to him as watching a sunset was yesterday.

It takes several minutes for the crying to subside. Once Benji quiets, Leo continues to hold him.

Eventually Benji sits up. He touches Leo's tear-stained shirt and looks up at him, "I've made a mess on you, babe."

"It's okay."

Benji cuddles into Leo. "Thank you. I needed that."

There is a knock on the door. Benji momentarily hopes for Steve until Leo says flatly, "That'll be George. We're supposed to meet."

"Oh, lord, that odd little man is the last one I want to see right now."

Leo starts to get up.

"Babe, I will not allow you to greet anyone in our home covered in my tears and snot." Not totally himself, but Benji is back. "You go change. I'll get him settled."

Leo looks down at the mess on his shirt. He then surveys Benji, "You're kind of messy too."

"I have lower standards to maintain. Go get presentable."

As Leo gets up, Benji takes his hand. "Thank you." Leo smiles back and gives Benji an extra, brief hug.

More knocking ensues. "Oh, hold on, I'm coming." Benji swipes his open hands across his face to remove as much tearing as possible then wipes them on his shorts.

He jerks open the door and is greeted by a very frightened look.

George was not expecting to be greeted by a nearly naked man with tear-red eyes.

"Come on in. Leo's upstairs getting changed after his hot date." He can't resist teasing. "May take him a while to get respectable."

George moves warily inside, and Benji directs him to the dining table.

"There will be coffee soon. You want some?"

George gives a quick nod.

Benji slightly shakes his head.

God, I scare the pants on this guy.

As he starts the coffee, he remembers teaching Steve how to make the various drinks at the coffee shop. He forces himself to focus on the rest of this day. It doesn't last. A replacement needs to be found at the coffee shop, not what he wants to think about now. Dinner. An elaborate feast is required.

Coffee done, he prepares a tray for Leo and George, adding sliced fruit and a bowl of walnuts.

"Here you go, guys."

George forcibly focuses on his screen as Benji leaves the two of them to put himself back together.

When he returns, Benji squats by Leo. "Sorry to interrupt. I'm going to the store if you want anything." He takes Leo's hand adding softly, "And thanks,"

Leo smiles back. "You're welcome. No, can't think of anything."

Thinking out loud, Benji adds, "Better get laundry soap. Have to do some today."

"I'll do that for you. I have to do mine anyway," Leo volunteers.

"Thank you, babe. I'll put a stack outside my room. Sure you don't mind?"

"I am going to be at this stuff all day. Going up and down the steps is probably all the movement I'm going to have."

Benji steps out. A breeze kicks up, cooling the day. Benji buttons his jacket as he heads for the store. Refocusing on dinner lasts only a few steps before noticing the color of the leaves on a tree to the left are turning to the color of Steve's shirt, that girl getting ready to run has a similar haircut. The nibbling wind makes his eyes water. People can assume that. He bows his head, refusing to see anyone. This will be a long walk to the store.

"I think we've made pretty good progress," George yawns out.

Leo looks at him disbelievingly. To him they should have been done with all the problems, not just making progress.

Both push away from the table, and George gathers his work. Neither being a talker, the walk to see George out processes silently with a simple goodbye shared at the door.

Leo watches George stumble on a crack as he heads away, thinking even this quirky little man is a better friend than he has ever had prior to moving to this new city, though the relationship pales compared to what he has found with his roommates, and certainly unmatched to what he may have beginning with Dave.

Looking down, he notices the slightly off-kilter welcome mat and crouches to straighten it, unable to remember ever having one in any previous residence. He moves back into the house looking at all the marvels in this world. A book, one Benji always seems to have open, lies on the table next to the sofa. Turning it to read the unfamiliar title, like so much here, new, all pieces of a life unlived until now. A hand on the sofa confirms its firm, caressing support, so unlike the utilitarian furnishings of his previous life. Even the one time he tried living off campus in that roach-infested one-room converted storage shed he called home for a year held flea market furnishings.

Leo must return to his work but cannot stop his brief caresses on anything within his reach as he heads back to the dining room table.

With George gone, Leo shifts to course work. He moves to the easy chair and squirms into its comfort, realizing how stiff the dining chair was. Now breezing along, fingers float easily over the keyboard. The frustration of the project dims. He can think about other things.

What is keeping Benji?

The front door opens, and he thinks "Benji," but hears Jay's voice, "Honeys, I'm home."

He puts the computer down and stands, calling out, "Hello."

Jay comes around the wall separating the foyer from the living room and goes to hug Leo. "I am so glad to see you." He happily notes Leo not pulling away. "Did you have a good week?"

"For the most part, yes. Had a wonderful time with Dave."

Jay manages to urge details out of Leo regarding the date before eventually asking, "Where's Benji?"

Leo steps back to tell Jay about how Steve ran out crying and how he had found Benji. He also says he is worried that he is not back from the store yet.

"He said he was going to fix dinner. Probably walking out some of whatever is going on. If Benji promised a meal, it will take a hurricane in Colorado to interfere. Help me with my bags." In his room, Jay strips out of his travel clothes, tossing them into two piles, one for washing, the other to be taken to the dry cleaners. "Glad to get back to normal." They continue chatting as Jay unpacks, tossing most of his clothes into the laundry pile. "Ugh, laundry."

"I told Benji when he comes back I'd do his with mine. If you want, I can throw yours in too."

"You are volunteering to take that glorious task of washing clothes away from me?"

"Unless you want to do them. Is it weird for me to offer?"

Jay motions for Leo to join him on the bed. "This all very new to you, isn't it? Do you just wish it would go back?"

"No," he says with more decisiveness than Jay expected. "This is all very new and scary. I have no idea what I'm doing day in and day out, but go back? No."

Jay waits.

"You, Benji, this house...yes, this home I have never known anyone or anything like it and...?" He hesitates.

"And Dave?"

"Yeah, Dave." A shy smile plays on his features.

"I like him. I suspect you may be on the verge of a lot more than that."

Almost inaudibly, "Maybe." His head dips, hiding his smile.

Jay laughs, pulling him in for a hug and a kiss. "There's a lot we don't know about each other. Someday…you'll know when…you'll let us know. What I do know is I'm very happy this is your home. Very happy you have all this scary world to deal with and very happy and honored you're a part of my life. Now, I suspect you have more work to do. Oh, wait. I bought something for each of you." He opens the side of his suitcase and pulls out two sweatshirts, one blue and one red. Each has the simple design of the Arch on the front. "Can't go to St. Louis and not get something with the Arch. Benji loves red, and I figured blue for you." He tosses Leo the blue one and then heads for his bathroom.

"Thanks. Don't you get one?"

"They rarely have purple, which is my color," he calls back. Turning, he adds, "Remember that."

Leo gathers up the laundry and takes it to his room to add to his meager pile. He lays the sweatshirt aside but looks at it.

Well, I'm that much better prepared for cold.

Benji returns through the back laden with ingredients for an enormous turkey meat loaf to be accompanied by an assortment of roasted root vegetables, just coming into season. There are apples for pie.

He spots an absorbed Leo in the living room and remembers about his promise to do laundry.

Leo has earbuds attached to the computer and doesn't hear Benji, who touches him to get his attention. "You're back. Are you okay?"

"Much better, thanks to you and a long walk in the cold wind. If your offer stands, I'll put my laundry outside my door."

"Yeah, it does. Jay's home."

"Great! Where is he?"

"Not sure if he's in his room or downstairs working out."

"When did he get here?"

Leo checks the time on his laptop. "Twenty minutes ago."

"Downstairs by now and will be there for some time. I'll get dinner started and join him. Maybe someday you'll join us. You've got a nice body naturally, but it doesn't hurt to do some maintenance."

"Maybe, but I don't know the difference between a free bell and a dumb weight," he declares with a slight smile.

Benji is dumbstruck a moment. "Oh my god, you have a sense of humor." He laughs. "I better get started."

Leo shuts down his computer. "Guess I can get the laundry started too."

Morning drifts into afternoon. On Leo's final trip to the basement while neatly separating and systematically folding clothes, he watches the others who have worked out together for years.

Jay raises a bar with large weights on either end as he lies back. Benji stands at the head of the bench, hands not touching the bar, but poised just under them. Leo thinks it may be nice to someday join them. He has never done anything more physical than walking.

Jay's phone rings. "It's Tim. Hi, little brother." Facing away from Leo, he is silent for some time, but from Benji's reaction, something is going on.

Jay closes his phone. "Tim's coming next weekend. He has some papers that need to be taken care of. Seems the bastard has died." He looks at the weights. "I think I'm going to take a nap 'til dinner." He leaves hurriedly.

Leo watches him and turns to Benji who motions Leo over. They sit side by side on the bench.

"You don't know any of Jay's background, do you?"

Leo shakes his head.

"You don't know ours anymore than we know yours. Tim is Jay's brother, the only member of his family he talks to. The bastard is, or I guess now was, Jay's father. Very hateful man. Long ugly story. Jay's told me the full nastiness of it bit by bit."

"But Jay seems so confident and happy." Leo shakes his head in dissatisfaction, "I'm not sure what I mean."

"I know. Jay is everything you see. He was by the time I met him too. Anyway, there was a lot of fighting and a lot of legal shit. Part of the deal that was worked out involved Jay getting this house and some kind of settlement. He's never returned to his family and changed his name. Jay was his nickname, short for James. He took it legally. I don't know his original last name. When Tim became an adult he also changed his name."

"Wow. Is he okay?"

"Probably. He isn't sleeping. Think that was his way to say he wanted to be alone. Look, babe, that all happened a long time ago. Jay is happy now."

"This has been an intense weekend."

"No shit. Damn, I never asked how your date went."

"Wow...that was only last night." He sits for a minute gathering his thoughts. Carefully he covers the events of the date, ending shyly with, "It was wonderful."

"At least someone has good news. When you seeing him again?"

"Not sure. We're going to try and find time to meet for coffee this week. His program is as busy as mine." He pauses. "Can I ask something?"

"Anything."

"What was this morning about?"

Benji's takes his turn to divulge details.

———

Laundry done, Leo takes it back to everyone, pleased to give back any little bit. He puts a meager stack on his bed then, since the door is open, leaves Benji's stack on his bed. He hesitates at Jay's door but finally knocks lightly.

Jay opens his door showing no reaction until he notices the laundry in Leo's arms. "Forgot all about this. Come in."

Leo starts to say something about the laundry, but Jay interrupts. "Leo, that was upsetting. My past rearing its ugly head. Partly because I thought it was just that, the past. But I guess there is more to still deal with. Come in." Papers are neatly covering Jay's bed and part of the floor.

"Benji told me a little."

"Then you know that my father was a fucked-up bastard. I got scared when Tim told me there are papers that need to be signed. I don't trust the bastard not to reach out from the grave to fuck me. I've been up here pouring over the paperwork from back when it all went down, trying to make sure this house is safe for us. I can't find anything that suggests otherwise, but I can't be sure. I'd like you to look through all this and see if you see anything I don't."

"I don't know about this kind of stuff, Jay."

"No, but you are the smartest guy I've ever known, so it would reassure me. I have a call in to my lawyer to meet this week."

"Fine then, let me see if anything doesn't make sense. That's all I can promise."

"Leo, you flinch anytime someone tries to tell you about your looks, but just now you accepted my judgment of your intellect in a heartbeat."

Leo doesn't let him finish. "Jay, I graduated high school at 12, could have at 10 if I'd been allowed."

Jay, who researched Leo before the move, acknowledges this. "I know about your degrees and honors. You have a pretty impressive cyber trail." He tilts his head, wondering something, "Why are none of those degrees or honors on display?"

Leo ponders for a moment, "I left those all at my aunt's. Haven't even thought about them 'til now."

"All that evidence is overwhelming."

"As for good looking, how do I tell? It was rarely mentioned 'til I moved here. I know what I think is good looking in men. You and Benji are attractive in entirely different ways. Dave certainly. I don't know why I know that about you guys, so how could I know anything in that regard about me?"

Jay is nodding, "Fair enough. But you have made it extremely clear why I would want you to look at all this."

"What should I be looking for?"

"I want to make sure my ownership of this house is safe for me and for anyone, including you, that may choose to live here. I want to make sure I can leave it to whomever I choose in case something happens, and I want to make sure that no one in my family other than Tim can ever threaten to interfere."

"How are they arranged?" Leo sweeps his hand across the room.

Jay indicates the bottom left corner of his bed, "Chronologically starting in this corner, going up the bed and then back to the bottom for each row."

He digs in, picking each in order and placing it back in the same spot before moving to the next. At one point, he halts. "Jay, do you have anything to flag a couple spots I want to come back to? Nothing that would make a mark."

"How about these?" Jay hands him a few coins.

It takes him the better part of an hour to read all the documents. Jay notes Leo only looks up to glance back at a previous document.

"Jay? I know very little about these. The language is uniquely legal, so I can't guarantee anything. But everything looks good. There's no debt on the house and the title looks clear, I think. I didn't see anything to interfere with how things stand now just because your dad..." There is obvious distaste using that term.

"You can now and forever refer to him as 'the bastard.'"

Leo nods. "I don't see anything that would change anything. There are a couple spots," and he points them out, "here and here that concerned me, but I think that was all taken care of by this document." He touches another paper a row down. "Of course, that's mainly conjecture."

Jay amazes how quickly Leo came to this conclusion. "Thank you. I feel a hell of a lot better."

"Um, Benji told me not even he knows your full birth name. I do now, but it will never leave this room."

"Appreciate the reassurance. I trusted you from the second I agreed to have you move in."

―――――――――

The roommates enjoy Benji's dinner, supplementing it with lavish, sincere compliments. Leo listens to Jay and Benji nonchalantly ask questions about the other's weekend and ventures a few himself once comfortable to try a few. He is starting to believe this is home and has a little bit better idea what that means. He hopes more than ever he and George can succeed. Losing all of this would devastate him.

Leo takes his laptop back to his room to do some more work. Before closing down for the night, he checks e-mail and sees one from his Aunt.

Dear Leo,

Your reply was so encouraging to me in so many ways. I am glad you seem to be off to a good start. I assure you it was not a mistake to leave this place. Your life should not be lived in this shadow.

I like what you say about your roommates. It is good for you to meet people.

I will always wish the best for you.

Love,
Jean

He didn't think this day could get better.

Dear Jean,

Thanks for the encouragement. I am feeling more and more this is the best thing I could have done. Jay and Benji are remarkable guys. We are all getting to know each other and that makes me feel great. I have met one other guy. His name is Dave. I like him a lot.

It's late.

But one thing I should say. I have always been pretty much a loner, more so since the wreck. I think with all the support you gave me over these last few months, it never occurred to me to find out much about you. That wasn't nice. I don't know what to ask, but I do want to know more about your life too.

Leo

11

Tim, a smaller, younger version of Jay, hair several shades lighter and the same basic build, flies in late Friday night. He is not as driven as his older brother. They greet in a warm hug.

"I have all the paperwork in my carry-on. Do you want to go over it when we get home or wait until morning?"

"The sooner the better. I won't sign anything until my lawyer looks at it. Of course, maybe I'll just have Leo look at it." He relates the story with a touch of warmth.

"So this guy who has never looked at a legal document in his life spots two mistakes that it took a lawyer a full day to find and then recognized the document that fixed the issue and all in less than an hour?"

"Total complete genius. Awkward socially, unfortunately. Reluctant to share."

"Not fitting in?"

"No. There's something bothering him he hasn't been able to voice, but both Benji and I love him to death."

"How is my favorite jockette?"

Jay tells him about Steve.

"That's shitty. Sounds like they could have had a chance. Hate that for him."

At home, Leo, in what has now become his favorite chair in the living room with laptop fired up, doesn't hear them.

Jay gets his attention. "Leo, this is my brother, Tim."

He rises to greet him. "Welcome. Good to meet you."

"You too. Heard a lot of great things about you." Tim can tell from Leo's deep blush not to continue. "Benji here?"

"He's at work." Leo averts his eyes. "Um, I was told to not let you look in the refrigerator under penalty of death."

"I bet he has created some fabulous dessert. Oh, I bet I know what it is. Well, we don't want to upset him, so I promise, no looking." He turns to Jay. "Let's get my stuff to the guest room, then we can look at those papers."

On the way upstairs, Tim says to Jay, "You didn't tell me he's sexy. What's the story?"

"He somehow missed the memo on his looks. He started dating a real sweet guy named Dave."

"You'd do anything for him, wouldn't you? Leo is very special to you."

Jay acknowledges this with a nod. "Indeed, he is. Dave is too."

"That's very unusual."

"Everything has been since that beautiful man came into this house. I believe he brings a bit of magic."

Leo joins the brothers for a light dinner of leftovers before leaving them to review the two documents. The will states all business concerns are to be entrusted solely to their older brother, Bo. Tim is given a miserly cash settlement. Their mother gets all other properties and accounts. Jay is not mentioned. A second document's purpose seems to reinforce the original agreement that cut Jay out of the family. It contains a clause saying no one not listed in the will may claim any family ties to his father.

"I think he's trying to make sure you get nothing else from him. And you don't try to re-establish yourself as part of his family. I ran it by our old lawyer, Matt, and he came to that conclusion."

"Like I would ever re-establish contact?" Jay shakes his head in disbelief. "Surprised he left you something."

"I also had Matt draw up an order to anonymously transfer all of it to an organization in Chicago that takes care of homeless gay youth. I don't even want to touch it unless I have to sign a check."

"Like that idea. I'll bring this in to my lawyer, just to make sure before sending it along."

They both lean back in their chairs.

"It's finally over?" Jay ventures.

"Hope so."

"No more family?"

"You."

"I love you too, little brother."

They hear the back door open. "Timmy!" Benji pounces on him. "I am so happy." He looks back and forth between the brothers. "Everything all right?"

They both nod.

"Great! Now Leo made you promise not to look in the fridge?"

Another nod.

"Get Leo so we can celebrate."

They gather up the documents and get Leo. All three sit at the table.

"Those the documents causing all the worry?" Leo inquires.

Jay hands him the second document. "This is the one that is of concern."

He reads it over in a few minutes, "It's just saying all those other papers you showed me the other day are still valid and cannot be challenged. I don't see anything alarming."

Tim looks at Jay, "Leo, are you sure you shouldn't be studying law. You really have a knack for it."

He puts the document back with the will. "I'm a mathematician."

Benji enters with dessert service for four. "Jay, you put these out. Leo, on the wine rack get the bottle from the bottom row, very middle. Here's the corkscrew."

"What can I do?" asks Tim.

"You just sit there and let us all take care of you, Timmy." He returns to the kitchen.

"Leo, he is the only one that ever gets to call me that."

Leo struggles opening the bottle. "Maybe."

Did I just tease him?

Then he adds, "Is he bringing glasses?"

"Let me do that," offers Jay. "You get glasses."

Leo goes to the cabinet against the side wall. He pulls out four stemmed glasses. "These all right?"

"Perfect," states Jay.

Leo sets the glasses on the table. Jay fills each halfway with a pale yellow liquid.

The three wait a moment until Benji leans in and tells them to turn out the lights. That done, he backs into the dining room carrying a large dessert on a platter. Four lit sparklers glisteningly decorate it. "Ta-da!"

"Ooh, I know what that is!" Tim squeals with glee. "Blueberry cheesecake!"

"With no crust," adds Benji. "Now, everybody, grab a sparkler and have fun. Leo holds his tentatively until he sees the rest waving theirs around creating wonderful trails of light. He soon laughs along.

When the sparklers fade, Benji turns on the lights, and they dive into the cheesecake.

"Oh my god, where'd you find fresh blueberries this time of year?" Tim gushes. "You make this better than any bakery."

Conversation flows. The other three have a lot of history, so Leo mainly listens, not feeling left out as the stories are mostly funny and enjoyable. For a few moments, they keep his mind free from the worries of the project. As night deepens, fatigue intrudes. Tim retires first, followed soon by Benji.

Alone, Jay takes Leo's hand. "I hope you didn't mind us telling all those stories."

"No, it was kind of fun. Your brother's nice. I don't know what that's like." He wasn't expecting to say anything like that. It kind of fell out.

"Not all brothers are the same. You will probably never meet our oldest brother. But having one like Tim is kind of like this," and he raises Leo's hand that he is still holding. "And now it is time for me to retire." He gets up, kisses Leo on the top of his head and is gone.

Leo takes the cheesecake to the refrigerator then clears the dishes and takes them to the kitchen where he washes, dries, and puts them away. He rinses the empty wine bottle and puts it in the recycling bin. Finally, the table is wiped down before retiring.

He will think about Dave and try not to think about the project. He will think about the three men with whom he has shared a sweet evening and try not to think about how tentative his hold is.

12

Although the temperature is not quite in the mid-sixties, Jay stands naked in the backyard.

A long run, a very long run may be ideal today. Can all of that finally be over? That would be closer to perfect.

The morning light enfolds his flesh. Birds sound extra sweet this morning like they know these trees are safe for them too. The backyard needs a little work. It was planned as low maintenance, but overgrown patches flourish. Perhaps adding some flowers here or there. He squats to feel the earth.

This is my yard. It is part of my home but not really mine.

It belongs to all the marvelous men who have lived here. From Tim to Vince to Benji and now Leo. A most challenging man: his genius, his fear, his amazing potential for life, so much more.

Although cut free too, Tim won't be coming here more often. After all, he does have his own life complete with peculiar partner in Chicago.

Back in the kitchen, Tim leans against the counter while pouring coffee and just nods. A quick gulp follows. "Better."

"Thinking of going for a long run. Wanna join?" Jay prepares his own mug and joins his brother.

"Nah, think I'll use the gym. Benji cooking one of his magical dinners?"

"Couldn't stop him. But he'll be gone most of the day for work, I think."

"And Leo?"

"Probably doing school work. Maybe with his project partner. Dave's out of town, so he's not likely to go anywhere."

"He really is something. Closed off. Nothing about his past?"

"Bits and pieces. His parents died suddenly a few months back. I don't get the impression they were close. Cold and distant from what little he has said. Still there is something going on there."

"He's very sweet under it all. Whoever Dave is, he is very lucky."

"They both are."

Done with his shower, Leo wipes down the tub, shower curtain, and wall with his washcloth. Out of the tub, the sinks and counter receive attention. Extracting paper towels tucked under his sink with other cleaning supplies, Leo dries the mirrors. The floor needs no attention beyond inspection. The toilet was cleaned before showering. Glancing in the mirror, he contemplates spending time on the project but wonders if time might better be spent exploring outdoors. He rewashes his hands before drying himself with the best towels he has ever felt, his initial reluctance to use them long evaporated and replaced by an understanding of the sharing aspects of the house.

Laundry next, he wraps the towel around himself instead of hanging it and almost runs into Tim while crossing the hall. They exchange good mornings. Leo goes into his room and drops the towel and washcloth on the pile of dirty clothes. Opening the closet, a shirt is deemed ready to add. Catching himself in the mirror, he steps back.

Curiosity about his body springs up. Jay and Benji are certainly in better shape. Both have more muscles but in such different ways: Jay lean and tall, all taut and defined, Benji bulky. Dave has a nicer body too, lean like Jay's, with more sinewy legs, probably from swimming. And then all that hair. Thinking of Dave, several masturbatory images arise but are shelved for later. Leaning in to study the angular face reflected back, he doesn't get why these guys say he is handsome.

Donning jeans and t-shirt, Leo seeks coffee. Downstairs he grabs his mug, pleased Benji honored Dave by putting a mug for him on the tree. The unfamiliar one must be Tim's.

What is it really like to have a brother? Is it what Jay had told him last night? No, that was honorary. Dave talks about his sister. Is that different than brothers? Does Benji have either?

Somehow, knowing even less of his history, Benji is easier to comprehend.

———

Later, Benji showers. He wishes he wasn't working today. Spending time with Tim would be more fun.

He doesn't visit enough.

Working today also limits his time to make dinner, but at least there is more than enough cheesecake for dessert.

Benji knocks on the guest room door on his way back to his room.

"Hi, sunshine."

"Hi, Timmy. Gotta get going to work soon but wanted to see if you had any special requests for dinner. Has to be simple."

"Been on the road so much anything you make will be heaven."

"Wish you could stay longer. You need to get that husband of yours down here for a really, really long weekend."

Tim's features momentarily harden. "He doesn't leave home."

"What's up for you today?"

"Working out while Jay runs. Maybe we'll catch a movie or something. Or just catch up. I'm open."

"Okay, well whatever, have fun." He pecks him on the cheek and leaves to get ready for work.

The brothers switch to juice when they touch base in the kitchen. Jay, in running clothes, heads out, going to the trails in the nearby green space. Tim, in shorts and a muscle shirt, heads to the basement and starts with curls. He works his arms several minutes, employing high reps with low weights, then rests before moving to shoulders.

Leo, loaded with laundry, comes downstairs, and sets the pile down without noticing Tim. He cleans out the lint trap. Selecting a dirty sock, the washer and dryer get dusted. Then two piles are formed, and the darker one is loaded into the washer.

Tim lingers, fascinated by Leo's precision and purpose of movement. Once the washer starts, he calls out his name.

Leo jumps.

"Sorry. Didn't mean to startle you."

"I thought everyone had gone."

"All but me." He pats the bench. "Come sit down."

Leo goes over. The bench is not very big, so they nearly touch.

"Hope you don't mind, but I was watching you."

"Um, okay." Leo furrows his brows.

"That didn't come out the way I meant. Must have sounded a bit strange."

Leo nods.

"I like watching people when they don't know it. You have such grace to your movements. Everything seemed almost choreographed. It helps that you're very easy on the eyes too," he pauses. "That doesn't seem to have made you any more comfortable. I'm sorry."

Leo looks down at the narrow gap of bench between them. "I'm used to people telling me how smart I am. And I get that. But all of a sudden, I get all this about my looks. Jay calls me gorgeous. Benji calls me all sorts of things that come down to the same. Then I meet Dave, and it's even more. Now you. It's just, I don't know…confusing." He raises his eyes to meet Tim's.

"The genius part is loud and clear. The way you understood that legal document. It was really what I could see when I was trying to tell you about watching you at the washer. There's an exactness to your movement. But you don't think you're handsome?"

"It's not what I see." A washer signal goes off. "Need to add softener. Be right back." He takes a couple of steps before stopping and looks back. "I am going to be very conscious of your watching me. Turn around. Do something with those weights."

Tim laughs and faces away.

"Okay, I'm back."

Tim turns around. "Tell me about Dave."

"Dave. I've never... Seems like since I've moved here, each time I turn around, I'm doing something I never did before."

"Unsettling but probably good. What's new about Dave?"

"Boy, what isn't? I know I like being with him. He's cooked dinner for me. I've only known him, what? Just a few weeks. We talk on the phone. We meet for coffee."

"Are you in love?"

"I don't know what that means." His tenuous hold on all this new life and how it could be over in a flash unsettles him, but he says, "I don't know."

"I don't mean to be so pushy. Probably because I have very limited time. Going back tomorrow."

"That's too bad. How come?"

Shrugging, "Life. I have a partner too. Eddie. He doesn't travel. Plus this trip wasn't exactly planned. I was already on another trip when I got the call. Haven't been home for three weeks."

"Your dad was really that bad? I mean, reading all that paperwork, he just seemed so cruel."

"Families can be that way. Was yours any better?"

That stops Leo. He is learning how isolating his parents were. He tries to think how to explain it.

Tim breaks in with a bit of concern, "Surely they weren't that cruel?"

"Cruel? No, not cruel," he states without elaboration.

"Let's talk about something else, this is getting a bit deep." The washer signal goes off. "Good timing."

Leo starts to get up but looks at Tim sternly.

"I'm turning," Tim says as he goes back to his workout. "Promise I won't watch."

Leo takes care of the laundry, moving the first load from the washer to the dryer, then piling the second load into the washer. Before turning the dryer on, he watches Tim who faces away, straddling the bench, and raising a barbell overhead. Leo doesn't know the name for this exercise. Tim's shoulders and upper arms bulge out as the bar is raised. The top of his back spreads as the bar is lowered. When raised again, just a hint of Tim's bare torso shows at the bottom of his shirt. Leo continues to watch until the finger poised over the dryer's start button slips and the machine turns on. The sound breaks him out of his reverie.

It also causes Tim to turn and smile at Leo.

Leo crosses the room, not sure what to do.

Is it wrong to look at another man like this?

No other man has caught his attention since Dave. In many ways, no man did before.

He sits back down. Tim turns fully around. Their knees are touching.

"I was watching you this time," Leo confesses.

"I like that." He reaches to run a finger down Leo's chin line. "You have such a strong jaw." He gazes into Leo's eyes. "And your eyes are such a crystalline blue. I want to kiss you. Is that okay?"

"Maybe." They lean in closer. "Yes."

Their lips touch softly, tentatively. Tim's hand moves down to Leo's chest.

Leo's hands alight on Tim's thighs.

Tim's other hand gently pulls Leo's head closer to deepen the kiss. Tongues begin exploration.

Leo's legs stretch out, and Tim moves close enough for embracing.

They break the kiss and pull back slightly. Tim explores Leo's face both with his eyes and a hand. Hair is brushed back. Eyebrows smoothed.

Finger traces the full redness of his lips. "I don't want to do anything to hurt you."

"I know."

"We won't do this if it will cause problems between you and Dave." He lightly outlines those piercing blue eyes.

"I know."

"We can stop."

Leo clasps his hands lightly behind Tim's head and rest his forehead against Tim's. They stay still, pondering.

Leo raises his head, looks into Tim's eyes. His focus darts from eye to eye.

"Do you want to stop?" Tim asks.

A deep breath. "No."

"Do you want to continue?"

"How?"

"Promise something."

"What?"

"Whatever we do, no matter how far we take this, don't be ashamed. Don't make it a secret." He leans in and kisses Leo gently.

"I can do that, I think." He pauses. "No, I can promise that."

Tim kicks his shoes off.

"Should we go up to one of the bedrooms?" Leo wonders.

Tim gives Leo several soft pecks on his face. "Better here. More like friends. Bedroom's too intimate." He presses his lips to Leo's as the kiss becomes deep and lasting.

This touch differs. Tim, not as urgent, somehow commands more than Dave. His sure hand explores Leo's body. Fingers tug teasingly at his chest hair. Playfully.

Leo's own touch is more curious.

This is how that patch of flesh I saw at his waist feels, smooth, almost cool. And his body is smooth too as I remove his shirt. But not off yet. Let his lips stay on my chest a bit longer first. Those teeth pulling at me. Not painful but close.

Leo continually thinks how this is nice, but not like with Dave. *This doesn't feel as important. Fun only.*

Clothing is removed from upper bodies as the two mutually explore. Soon naked, Tim sucks a standing Leo.

Tim clearly wants more and has him sit back down.

They face each other more closely. Tim has his legs over Leo's so they can slowly stroke each other while they kiss.

"You're okay?" Tim ventures.

"Yes, this is nice, really nice. Different too."

They continue to gently stroke.

"I know. I'm not Dave."

Leo starts to protest, but Tim stops him.

"I'm not Dave, and you're not Eddie."

Leo understands. "Not like you have with Eddie?"

"Or how I think you hope for with Dave. But I do hope we can go a little further."

Leo is cautious. "Meaning?"

Tim gets a mischievous look; his shoulders shrug up. "I was kind of hoping to get you to fuck me."

Laughing softly, "Maybe."

"Now, if I know my brother, we should have everything we need nearby." Looking around the room his eyes spot a box on the shelf above the washer and dryer. "I'll be right back." He gives Leo a kiss and heads for the box. "Aha, I knew it. Jay would never be unprepared."

Leo watches Tim.

I was hoping for change when I moved here. Boy, did I get it. Tim is so different from Dave. Such a smooth fluid body.

He can see the resemblance to Jay, but even they are so very different. He reconfirms his commitment to making all of this work.

Fortunately, Tim is back and touching him again before he gets too lost. Tim's lips find Leo's.

Leo feels the condom now encasing his erection. Tim's hand smooths lube onto it.

Getting up and turning around, Tim guides Leo inside as he lowers himself. Leo feels those smooth powerful thighs as Tim raises and lowers his body. Leo synchronizes hip motions.

They move so both men stand, straddling the bench. Tim bends over, his hands bracing. Leo has one hand on Tim's firm smooth hip.

There's so little hair.

The other hand runs up the curved spine until he runs it into the longish hair on his head.

It's silky, finer than Dave's. It moves freely.

Tim pulls his body off and lies back on the bench raising his legs. He wraps them loosely around Leo as the slender man reenters.

With those nearly hairless legs holding his body, Leo bucks his hips reflexively, erupting inside Tim.

In a very few strokes, Tim follows. His legs tense around Leo, pulling him deeper inside. His eyes focus on Leo's chest.

They stay still for several moments, allowing breath to normalize. Both grin.

Tim speaks first. "That was very sweet."

"Yeah, it was." He is surprised by how relaxed he feels.

"I'll admit to thinking about Eddie about every ten seconds if you admit to thinking about Dave."

Leo laughs, "Every five, but not how I thought I would."

"How so?"

"I kind of expected to wonder how I would tell him. I won't forget my promise. But it wasn't that. It was more like comparing, not one was better or worse. More noticing differences. He's hairy, for example, more than me, and you're so smooth."

"Yeah, I get that. Eddie's a little older, 42. He has long red hair that falls onto my face as he fucks me."

They are back to sitting up and facing each other. Their fingers entwine.

"You are really a sweet man, Leo. I am very glad you're here. You're very good for Jay and Benji. I suspect they're very good for you."

"They have been very good for me," he realizes. "I've known that. I am not sure how I'm good for them."

"I see changes in them. Honestly, I don't know how to explain it, but trust me." He reaches for his shorts and pulls out his phone to check messages. "Speaking of Eddie, he called this morning. We should get moving. No telling when Jay will get back. And I'll bet your mind is already on some chore or homework."

A rude buzz erupts from the dryer. "Like how I need to pull those clothes out of the dryer and fold them?"

"Something like that." He leans in so they can share a friendly kiss. "I'll see you at dinner, if not before."

13

Jay stretches on the porch ready to release pent-up tensions, his long, lean legs uncharacteristically stiff. All this legal nonsense took up too much time. His eyes wander this street he chose to establish his home.

He steps onto the path leading to the sidewalk and turns, standing with a wide stance, noting the solidity of house. He liked that from the very first. It needed work. The roof was replaced. He selected the paint scheme and did a large portion of it on his own. Why choosing such a large home for himself and Tim was unclear.

He twists toward Tommy's and holds that stretch. How could he know what amazing men would come to share this home? Vince, a lovely man who needed a nest from which he could learn to fly, Benji finally finding a safe place for his gentle spirit to emerge, and now Leo. Too early to know his role in this home.

Facing forward, he notes repainting will be needed next year. The sun faded the blue just a bit. Windows probably need attention. Recognition only brings happiness instead of worry.

He turns the other direction facing the Powell's, first of the original neighbors to truly welcome him. They used to bring occasional meals for the brothers. Now very old, Benji returns that favor.

Finally, he faces away from his home. Instead of going left for the campus track, a slow warm-up jog to the right begins. It's easier for his mind to clear on the trails.

An established neighborhood, homes were built at the same time as his though most are smaller. Many have been refurbished, some ornately, some simply, a few tragically updated with unsuitable choices in an attempt to modernize. A smaller group could even benefit from this attention.

The street steepens as he nears the green space, the beginning of the mountains looming farther away. A few runners are out this morning. The nice turn in the weather gives hope winter will hold off. He picks up his pace, not a full-out run like at the track. Too difficult to run at this pace once he hits the trails, it is the last chance for a sprint until he returns. He passes the first few trails. Those draw people wanting to stroll and enjoy the scenery. Weaving through them annoys walkers and runners alike.

Methodically seeking a steeper, more challenging trail, he enters his selection. Another runner exits and raises a hand in greeting that Jay returns. No longer on pavement requires more caution. The uneven ground takes a moment's adjustment. This trail begins sharper than he remembers, resulting in a brief pause when he reaches a fork. It gives a chance to evaluate choices. The one going straight disappears around a bend after a few yards. It could be appealing to throw caution to the wind.

He looks up the slightly steeper trail that angles to the right with no bends for quite a bit. But there is something definitely of interest. About 30 yards up the trail, a young man stretches. From Jay's vantage, he appears to be twenty, maybe twenty-two. Moving from one stretch to another displays a remarkable flexibility. Turning, not quite fully facing Jay, a great profile emerges of strong, well-defined features. A full head of curly chestnut brown hair shows flashes of gold. Even from here, his lissome, slender body possesses finely developed legs. Dressed in white with slender silver piping trimming the revealing tank top, his visage pops against the dark background of russet trail and forest foliage.

My god, he's an angel.

The rough terrain requires he split concentration from the trail to his angel whose features become more defined as the gap closes. The legs prove extremely well formed with heavy thighs and fairly rounded calf muscles for someone his age, clearly someone who left boyhood behind and entered full adulthood. Standing firm, he turns toward Jay, simultaneously lifting his shirt to wipe sweat from his face, exposing a flat hairless stomach. He lets his shirt drop and sees Jay for the first time, meeting his gaze full-on, curiously. As Jay nears, full lips form a contented smile on a face more oval than round. The straight nose, leads up from the generous mouth to large, nearly gold eyes.

Jay watches the smile deepen as he nears, the lips never parting, even when the eyes join in. He doesn't stop when he reaches the angel, but nods a greeting and raises his hand that is met in kind. He looks over his shoulder. Angel has turned, the smile warmer.

He returns to his stretching, keeping his eyes on this tall man until Jay turns the bend.

Jay slows without looking back. Soon he hears the steady beat of some-one approaching. Angel catches up and raises his eyebrows. Jay winks. Angel runs ahead. Jay's focus travels down the slender body ahead of him, eventually concentrating on the firm ass muscles so clearly displayed by clingy running shorts. He allows a decent gap before increasing his pace.

Around the next bend, he finds himself not surprisingly close behind, his turn to pass. He reaches out and pats Angel's bottom as he overtakes him. That is met with mock surprise followed by a hearty laugh.

Angel comes running around the next bend at full pace again catching up, his turn to race ahead. When passing Jay, he turns and winks before disappearing around another bend.

Jay rounds the bend and spots his angel standing in the road facing him with arms open. He slows enough to run into the welcoming hug.

A kiss develops, but Jay feels himself being guided off the track to a small clearing.

Angel pulls Jay's shirt up, his hands soon on Jay's chest. They hook their shirts behind their necks. Now both men have hands on the other's chest. Jay's is developed, full pecs with large dark nipples. Angel's is starting to expand, but very defined. Jay, fascinated, lowers himself to lap, then nibble, nipples while shoving Angel's shorts down. Part of him wants to spend hours on this beautiful young man, but the location prohibits a leisurely romp. The nearby tread of other runners breaks the morning silence too frequently.

His angel takes him by the hand to lead them a little further off the path but stops short, causing Jay to bump into him. Angel starts to speak, but Jay stills his voice with a single finger on those full lips.

With an outstretched foot, Angel points out a small patch of vegetation.

"Poison ivy," He pulls the younger man close. "My angel is watching out for us." Jay surveys their surroundings and leads them to another open space to their left.

Angel looks around and nods his satisfaction to Jay.

Jay crouches to take Angel into his mouth, causing a deeper intake of breath from his immortal. A hand cups the generous balls while tongue rolls around the head's crown. He takes Angel to the root hungrily before rising to peer into flashing eyes. A finger covers the full lips, restating his Angel's mute role.

Angel takes that finger inside his mouth, bemused eyes locked onto Jay's. His hands push Jay's shorts down. Preferring something more vital than a finger in his mouth, he crouches. Hands run up and down Jay's tight body. He kisses the tip of the erection. With a slender finger, he raises the cock up so he can start licking from its base methodically. Looking up into Jay's eyes, his mouth opens as if to speak, but Angel uses Jay's cock to mimic a finger on his lips, signaling acceptance of his mute roll while knowing the environmental limitations. Specific words are indistinguishable, but occasional voices annoyingly reach into their lair from the trail.

Angel looks up, no ordinary angel, his golden eyes communicating the yearning muteness forbids. He focuses down for a moment and, from his running shorts, produces a condom. Gazing back up, he sees the approval. That intriguing smile again forms on his lips as he readies Jay.

He stands. His hands on this mortal man's face.

Jay fingers slide into Angel's curls. Hands caress the neck and chest working to the waist of this marvelous creature standing eagerly in front of him. Hands now on that willowy, taut waist, he begins to turn a compliant immortal.

Wetted fingers inserted result in a long ethereal sigh. Entering this special being deserves great care.

Once penetrated, Angel reaches back, stilling Jay's hips as he fully opens to this man. When set, the hand raises to Jay's head. His head turns to find a kiss signaling readiness.

They soar across the sky, lost in sensations.

Jay has his arms wrapping this beautiful man. "You are my beautiful Angel."

Angel, accepting the role this man has given him readily, leans his head back onto Jay's shoulder in consent.

Both Angel's hands reach up to hold Jay's head, knowing the end nears. Breath in his ear becomes husky. Throughout, his silent role is maintained. Soon he feels it. This solid man who has him in his arms fills him with final hard, deep strokes. The body pressed against his relaxes and releases tension. Then...too soon...the withdrawal.

He lets himself be turned back to accept a calmer kiss. This would be enough, but this man wants more.

Jay crouches again to pleasure his immortal. Fingers slip in where his cock had just been. Hands press his head forward as his mouth fills with surely the sweetest nectar.

In a moment, Jay stands. He pulls Angel's shirt back over his head, smoothing the fabric over Angel's chest. He leans down to pull the running shorts up those well-muscled legs.

Angel regards him as if in a trance.

Jay re-dresses himself then takes Angel into his arms, kisses his cheek and lips. "You really are an angel."

Angel's smile develops. He watches Jay return to the path to head back down. He will follow soon but needs a moment. He looks around spotting a condom wrapper. He picks it up, realizes it is an older one, but pockets it anyway and begins his descent walking.

Done with laundry, Leo studies in his room. From time to time he glances at the project. He and George will meet tomorrow to give it more serious consideration. The rest of his work, not producing frustration, takes only a couple of hours.

Hoping for something from his aunt, he checks e-mail, sends George a confirmation for their meeting, and shuts the computer down.

Remembering his thought earlier about going for a walk, he decides to do just that.

Jay and Tim sit on the front steps. They contemplated various options, but this gives them the needed time together. Leo finds them when he steps outside.

"Leo, what's up?" Jay invites him to join, patting the space between him and his brother.

He briefly assesses the brothers. They are so alike physically. He notices the similarity of their legs as both wear shorts.

"Taking a break, thought I'd go for a walk." He says, sitting and turning to Jay. "Is there a way to get up on the roof?"

Puzzled, Jay answers, "There's a ladder attached to the back wall, but nothing much is up there. Why?"

"I was just thinking it might be nice to take my computer up there sometime and do some work. Would be nice to have a place to look at the sunset or something."

"It's pretty gross up there. Only dirty roofing and the air conditioner. You could sit on the edge, I suppose, but that would be a bit dangerous."

"Oh, well, just a thought. What are you guys doing?"

Tim answers, "Catching up."

Leo puts a hand on Jay's knee and the other on Tim's. "I'm off then. See you at dinner, if not before."

The brothers watch him turn toward campus.

Tim breaks the silence. "I am very glad Leo's here..." He catches Jay's wry look. "...and not just because we had sex, but, well, just glad he's here."

"Understood. He's coming along." He watches Leo move down the sidewalk. "That was positively gregarious, for him anyway."

"He doesn't talk a lot. He said enough about you guys, living here, his program, and especially Dave. But his past? Curtain comes down fast."

"His past is an enigma. Something not right with his family, I gather." Then he laughs. "Unlike our exemplary parents."

This gets them back to what they really need to say.

A half block toward campus, Leo chastises himself for heading that way. *I've never gone the other direction.*

But he has not done much exploration this way either, only the math building, the student union, the library, and the English building to meet Dave. He visited Dave's apartment, Benji's coffee shop, the bank across the street from it, and the grocery store. The only other place he can think of in town is the motel he stayed in the first nights.

He walks, hands in pockets, still in the direction of the campus, but when he gets to the entrance, instead of crossing the street, he turns to the right toward the coffee shop hoping it's not too busy. Thankfully, few customers visit this Saturday afternoon. Almost before giving up, he spots Benji behind the counter at the far end with an employee, possibly showing him how to do something. Benji looks up and spots him.

"Leo," he calls warmly with much delight. Leo has not stopped by, except with Dave, since that first day. He waves him over.

"This is Seth Ng. Seth, this is one of my gorgeous roommates, Leo Graham." The young man and Leo exchange handshakes. "Seth is just starting. What's up, babe?"

"Not much, decided to take a break and go for a walk."

"Let me get you something."

"No, I'm really just passing by. I didn't see you this morning. Thought I'd just say hi. And that I'm looking forward to dinner." He says to Seth, "Benji is one of the two best cooks I know."

"Two best?" Benji asks, feigning shock. "Have you been cheating on me? Who's the other?"

Shyly smiling, "Dave."

"Oh, well, that's okay. Sure you don't want coffee?"

"Had enough at home. I'll see you tonight." He turns to head out.

"Bye, babe." Benji delights in that wonderfully strange interlude. He turns his attention back to Seth who watches Leo. "Yes, he is adorable, but Dave is his boyfriend, so we must live with bitter disappointment." Laughingly, they return to task.

Leo heads beyond the coffee shop, strolling along the street that marks the campus's border. Several trendy shops and relatively cheap places to eat, primarily catering to students, line the block.

His mind drifts, thinking about that sweet, enjoyable encounter with Tim. It contained a playfulness very different from any sex of his experience. Which leads him to the incredibly amazing sex with Dave, but what is it? It just seems so important. Is that the right way to describe it? Tim was nice, but Dave is like he's more than inside him. They're inside each other.

He stands in front of a clothing store with a display of winter apparel. His wardrobe, even with what he has been given since arriving, is inadequate for winter. Jay has passed on to him the finest clothes he has ever owned, given like "Naturally these are yours. They've been waiting for you."

And Benji providing those huge meals. He would have been surviving on rice and noodles without that loveable man who also simply gives, no, shares. Cleaning, his most viable option of assisting at home, yes home, feels the only thing possible for now.

A woman comes up next to him and openly admires several sweaters and scarves. Giving him a conspiratorial glance, she reaches for the entrance. "That green sweater has my name all over it."

Her nonchalance about money sets his resolve deeper to solve the project. He has seen it enough and doesn't need to have it in front of him. It is so frustrating. Parts of it were easily solved, but the remaining portions seemingly have no pattern. There must be some logic. He and George have played around with transposing this symbol for that, breaking it into smaller chunks. Nothing moves it forward. At least no one else is having success. So much rides on winning the stipend.

Stop! Not now! This was to be a break from that.

Screeching brakes followed by a loud thump cause him and others on the street to turn. The accident, a mere half block away, seems to take him several minutes to spot. A steadying hand rests on the store window as he watches. Someone seems to be consoling the driver who has emerged to inspect the damage.

He withdraws his hand, regarding it curiously.

Turning back to the accident, he studies the person consoling the driver. He could swear he saw someone wearing scrubs running toward the wreck, not this vividly dressed woman.

Wasn't she standing right next to me?

A quick head shake clears his mind.

Focus returns to the store briefly before he continues his wandering. A bookstore window has a display called books for all ages, running from early readers thought adult including a section devoted to Dr. Seuss. Again, he thinks delightfully of Dave.

He's had enough of looking at things he can't afford. Instead he starts to look for places that might be good for watching sunsets in winter. If only he could keep his mind on that.

14

"**B**enji, you remember Patrick?" Jay jokes, knowing their history. The roommates share dinner on Wednesday.

"Hmm, Patrick." He leans his elbows on the table and looks Jay head on. "Is that your coworker with the rich mane of auburn hair, smoldering dark eyes, chiseled features, body of a Greek god, and an ass you could balance a martini glass on?"

Something in Benji's tone makes Leo pause. He looks back and forth between his roommates wondering why Benji answered in such a deliberate tone.

"That would be the one," Jay says.

"Vaguely." Benji exaggeratedly tilts his head, wondering what is next.

Leo is puzzled. "Benji, you have a great body, all that time you spend in the gym shows."

"Thanks, babe. I have muscles." He flexes an arm to demonstrate. "Patrick's body is sculpted to perfection with careful attention as to which exercises need to be done and in what sequence to make this or that muscle blossom into perfection." Turning to Jay, "Anyway?"

"He's in town for an extended stay. We're all invited to a party at his lake house this weekend."

"Oh, boy."

The lack of enthusiasm in Benji's statement perplexes Leo.

"Benji," Jay resumes, "he asked specifically to make sure you could come. You haven't had a day off since Steve left. Almost two weeks now. You've earned the weekend. He offered to let us all stay over until Sunday."

"I'll think about it."

"How about you, Leo? Think you and Dave would like to join?"

"We are going to get together Saturday. I can ask if he wants to."

"I'll understand if you guys bow out."

"Hey, how come he gets off so easily, not me?" Benji demands.

Jay leans toward Benji saying in a stage whisper, "Because this is the first chance they'll have to get naked in every room of the house if we're both gone and they chose to stay." He reaches behind him seeking Leo's hand. "And, Leo, I am purposely not looking at you because I know I have made you turn beet red."

Leo playfully slaps Jay's hand.

Benji strokes his chin as he considers. He purses his lips and delivers his assessment. "Closer to tomato soup."

"But seriously, Leo, if you and Dave want to join, you'd be welcome. Patrick is my oldest friend. I also work with him. The guy is as nice as he is handsome. Very welcoming."

"I'll see. But I admit," he adds sheepishly, "I kind of like your insinuation."

"Good, thought you might." He turns back to Benji. "Benji, it would do you good to get away."

"I'll be dead tired. I have been driving myself pretty hard."

"I know." Jay glances at Leo. "We both know. It sucks. I'm sorry so much has been happening for me. I am here for you, you know that."

"Thanks, Jay. Means a lot to hear it. But listen, I know the world can't stop because Benji got a bad break. I haven't really told you guys."

He pauses and noisily sucks air in between teeth. "Steve and I have been communicating nearly every day. We've talked on the phone, and I have sent and received more e-mails or texts since he left than I have since owning a computer."

"Really?" Jay inquires.

"Yeah, and now my computer seems to be acting up, which is one more frustration."

"What's happening?" Leo asks.

"Freezing, acting real slow, that kind of shit."

"I'll look at it after dinner. Let me text Dave and see what he thinks." He gets his phone.

> Re Saturday. J & B going to an overnight party.
> We're invited. Party or home alone?

"What time does it start?" Benji asks.

"Around 7."

"I guess I could trade for Saturday morning. Be easier to take Sunday off if I do that. It will give us plenty of time, but I'll have to change on the way."

"Yay. And you?"

"Hold on." Leo opens his phone.

> Home alone!

He starts to grin.

Jay looks at the phone. "Looks like just you and me, Benji." He turns to Leo. "Other than the obvious, any plans?"

"He'll probably cook."

Benji starts to protest about leaving a mess but realizes Leo leaves the kitchen cleaner than a neurosurgical operating room. Though not discussed, everyone is aware of Leo's habits. No one minds.

Jay asks, "Is he good?"

"It was very good the one time I spent the night. He says he learned to cook from his Italian grandmothers. If that means anything."

"It means Benji will have very serious competition in the kitchen." Jay laughs.

Benji, feigning petulance, "Bet I'll be able to out-bake him." He adds, quietly. "Okay, tell him to knock himself out, but I expect leftovers."

"I'll let him know."

> YAY! B has given full kitchen privileges.
> Must promise leftovers.

Dinner finished, Leo lets Benji know he's going to look at his computer. "Thanks, babe. I'll take the dishes in and clean up in here tonight."

A few minutes later, Benji enters his room to find Leo finishing up. "You should be good now. Nothing serious, just clean up. I added a couple upgrades that should help too."

Benji sits down and is stunned how easy it is running now. "Amazing. I was afraid I'd have to take it in. I hate talking to those techie guys. I never know what they're saying."

"Most of those guys throw jargon around to intimidate you. Helps to be fluent in Geekinese."

This produces a laugh. "I'll keep that in mind next time I need to go in. Thank you very much."

Leo heads back to his room. He checks his own computer to see if it needs any work itself before checking e-mail, happily finding one from Jean.

> Dear Leo,
>
> I've been traveling so didn't see your e-mail 'til I got back. Guess that's a good place to start letting you know about my life. Sweet of you to ask.

I have a group of friends who, like me, are retired or semi-retired. We took a cruise in the Gulf of Mexico. I won't bore you with the details of how a bunch of old folks spend a week on a boat, but it's fun for me.

I retired a couple of years ago after many years as a social worker. It was both rewarding and frustrating. I was there quite some time so could retire very early. Now I go on these trips and am trying to discover or rediscover other interests, like paying attention to my garden. Something I rarely did while working.

I was married, but John died several years ago. We didn't have children, but it didn't matter. We were happy, I suppose. No, we were happy, although I miss him still.

I assume from your last message you're making good friends with your roommates. Friends are treasures.

May I also assume Dave is more than a friend or at least you would like him to be so? I find that wonderful and exciting. You will have to tell me all about him.

I have some unpacking to do and am still feeling the rigors of my jaunt, so will sign off for now.

Take care,
Jean

He smiles at his computer then glances at that bottom drawer wondering why his parents kept him from knowing this woman who has been so supportive.

Dear Jean,

You are right about Dave. He is more than a friend. New
territory for me, so I don't even know what I hope for other
than to be with him whenever I can. There isn't a lot of
time given both of us are pretty busy with school. He is
also working on a PhD, but in a very different field: poetry.
We're getting together this weekend. He has promised
to cook a big dinner. He really likes cooking. I can barely
throw a sandwich together. Oh, one more thing. He has
the most amazing green eyes I have ever seen. Emeralds.

It was nice to know a little more about you. I don't
understand why I never knew about you. So much makes
little sense to me. I am glad to be getting to know you
now, though.

Always,
Leo

He checks his phone for a message from Dave and is very pleased to see.

Envious of kitchen from day 1. Can't wait.
Don't know how to cook w/o leftovers.
Can you be dessert?

He replies before turning in.

15

Jay knocks on the doorjamb of Patrick's office.

"Hey, come in." Patrick, a fixture at the campus gym when not on the road, greets his old friend. His maroon shirt, open at the collar suggesting a promising chest, sets off dark facial features.

"Wanted to give you an update for the party."

"Great, I assume you'll be there. What about Benji and the new roommate?"

"Leo won't be coming. He and his very new boyfriend aren't quite at the stage where they want to share each other." Jay takes a seat across the desk.

"Too bad, I've been looking forward to meeting him. Kind of surprised about a boyfriend. From what you've said, I figured him for a loner."

"He's being a delightful surprise all around. Very quiet and keeps to himself more than he should, but, how do I put this? Very quietly he shows a thrilling thirst for life."

"Sounds like you could go for him yourself."

"Crossed my mind, have to admit. But ultimately, he makes a much better friend. Besides Dave is ideal for him."

"Sorry he won't be there, both actually." Patrick leans back in his chair and habitually tosses a pen from hand to hand.

"You may have seen Dave. He swims every morning in the pool next to the gym."

"What's he look like?"

"Nice. Decent body. Dark hair. Very hairy chest and legs. Incredibly bright green eyes."

Patrick swivels in his seat as he thinks. "Did he just start this year? Not a freshman, but transfer or grad student, maybe?"

"PhD."

"Has to be the same guy. There every morning early. Swims for miles. Definitely those eyes. Phenomenal. PhD makes sense too. No nonsense. Finishes swimming, showers, and is gone."

"That's him."

"Pity they won't be there. How about Benji?" he asks with a hopeful smile.

"He's trading shifts so he can be off Saturday evening and all of Sunday. We'll arrive about 5."

"Well, I at least get to see sweet Benji."

Jay sighs. He fills Patrick in about Steve and how hard it has been on Benji. "I am afraid, my friend, Benji will only be available on rebound. I know you'd like more."

"Crap, I have no luck," he answers disappointedly. "You know, Jay, it's the nature of this job. Rebound seems all I can hope for." He flips the pen onto the desk with a sigh.

"You've always had soft spots for each other. But, you're right. Timing isn't easy."

"Never was with Benji." He looks up at Jay. "You ever want to just stop? Find something else?"

"Sometimes," he answers honestly. "Probably would more if I worked your population. You get kids who've been at the top of the social ladder. I get the little nerds not used to being picked for anything much less having someone come swooping in with a promise to get them out of their lives where no one likes them."

Patrick grimaces, "Ouch, that hurt."

"Yeah, but you know what I mean. How many spoiled narcissistic kids do you meet?"

"Two out of three... Two and a half."

"Mine? Mostly misfits. Some are flat-out rude because their social skills trail way behind academics. But things are rarely handed to them, no questions asked."

"Believe me I get it. Sometimes I want to throw up on some of the ludicrous demands I hear. 'You're fucking 16, kid. The world owes you nothing,' I want to scream. But I write the demands down and present them to whatever coach is creaming for them. They usually get more than they ask for."

"I never get that. They mostly don't know they're allowed to ask, much less what for. Leo's like that. He has these incredible gifts. He is the most intelligent person I've ever met, flat-out genius. But doesn't know how to ask for anything."

"Jay," Patrick says with a laugh. "If we don't stop this, we are going to have to storm the infirmary and demand their entire supply of anti-depressants. We have good lives. Not perfect, pretty good. No, I don't have more than a week or so at a time to see anyone I meet, but that's better than none. Plus, we are going to have a great party this weekend. Who knows what can happen?"

"Easy to get caught up in shit, isn't it?" He rises. "Well, I need to see about scheduling my next round of travel."

While Jay steps out the door, Patrick offers a suggestion. "Jay, I am fully booked through this academic year. Next year, you and I need to find some place to plan a trip together. There has to be at least one city in the whole country that has both jocks and nerds who need recruiting."

"That is the single most awesome idea you have ever had."

Benji wishes he had not made this commitment. Turnaround from late shift to opening the next day is not advised. At least nice weather accompanies his walk as fall merges into winter.

He had to remember to bring his keys, not needing them mid-shift or closing. The doors lock automatically after setting the alarm. Being tired from too little sleep doesn't help his unfamiliarity with the shift's routines. Not knowing the staff, many hired for their perky morning personalities, doesn't help either.

No major crises occur, and he gets through the shift without ever completely waking up, largely due to avoiding coffee all morning. One cup would have led to ten on a day like this.

Jay arrives while Benji closes out. Benji takes the clothes Jay brought and changes in the bathroom. He now wears a pale green muscle shirt with white panels down the sides. It fits snugly across his chest and hangs loosely from there. His shorts are slightly shorter than the style of the day, but he has spent too much time building up his thighs to hide them. He climbs into Jay's car and tosses work clothes into the back seat.

"Ugh, glad to be out of those. This is not the shirt I laid out."

"Did you really want to show up wearing an oversized university t-shirt of indeterminate color? I know you're not really trying to attract anyone, but no sense making them run for the hills. That one looks good without saying 'come fuck me.'"

"Yeah, it is virginal compared to what I've worn to Patrick's." He lets out a yawn. "I hope I make it to the party, much less through it. Why am I doing this again?"

"To have fun, see Patrick, and leave Leo and Dave to their own devices."

"Patrick. Two months ago, I would be reaching over to make you go faster."

"I told him about Steve. Thought it would be easier for both of you."

"Thanks, I guess. Not sure as tired as I am I could put up much defense. 'Course if I had to give my ass up for someone, I could think of a few billion less desirable men."

"I am sure he'd like to hear you put it like that."

Benji laughs. Jay reaches over to rub his friend's thigh.

"Oh, hell. Getting it on with Patrick again would be fun. Lord knows we burn up the sheets. Steve wouldn't even mind. Half of our communication is, 'Don't wait. We can't predict the future. Don't stop living just for me.' But I don't know. This really is different." He scrunches down in his seat. "The only thing I know is I need sleep. I'm going to try and doze a bit, if you don't mind." He leans the seat back.

"I'll wake you when we arrive."

The drive takes them south on Interstate 25. Jay has loved this route from the first, especially on days like this when traffic remains light. The mountains rise to the west; the Great Plains open up to the east. The contrast remains constant the length of the route well into New Mexico, breaking most significantly when the road crosses from Trinidad in Colorado into Raton, New Mexico.

Reaching the turnoff, he leaves the plains behind and faces the Rocky Mountains' rough, stark beauty.

Sooner than expected, they pull into Patrick's driveway. The house, a 4-bedroom structure built as an homage to Frank Lloyd Wright, mostly succeeds. Only the edge of the deck facing the lake is visible from this vantage.

Benji slept fitfully, making him even more tired. Jay carries both their bags as Benji barely manages walking.

Patrick greets them at the door.

"Quick drive, traffic was non-existent." Jay places his hands on Benji's shoulders. "This puppy is dead on his feet, so might do him good to take a bit of a nap first."

Benji protests, "Not puppy." He reaches his arms out. "Want hug."

Patrick takes him in, laughing. "Okay, then we find you a place to nap."

"No nap. View." Every visit, he wants to get out on the deck and look across the lake, one of the prettiest places he knows.

"Okay. View first." Arm around him, Patrick leads the groggy Benji to the deck. Jay follows. "Here you go."

"Pretty." He spots a padded chaise in the corner. "I sit, you two look." He plops down.

Jay and Patrick look at each other and shake their heads in amusement. They turn to look at the view.

Jay asks, "How many expected?"

"Not many. Bill and Todd from work. Kev, Paul, Levi. A few others."

"Let's get Benji to bed, then I'll help with set up." They turn and find him fully asleep.

"May as well leave him here and wake him once people arrive. I can always pull one of those screens over to block this corner if he's still out of it as he seems." Patrick indicates a stack leaning against the house, used to block sun in summer.

"Good idea. I'll get a blanket just in case."

Guests start showing up about an hour later. Patrick checks on Benji, who is deeply asleep, so a screen is set up to give him privacy. He looks at him with a touch of sadness.

Patrick displays food and drinks in the same manner as Benji but with a more catered feel: arranged, rather than placed, on the serving trays in the most flattering way. Music plays softly in the background for the men in attendance. Patrick's female friends prefer meeting one on one or at more organized events like a play.

Jay engages in many conversations as the evening progresses, eventually wandering into a conversation with Todd and Diego, a recent transplant. Carlos, also present, is an old friend who asked Diego to help him set up a business, a tech endeavor that neither Jay nor Todd fully grasps.

Jay states, "I have a roommate who would better understand what you're doing. Leo's very good with technology."

"Is he here?"

"Stayed home to be alone with his boyfriend."

"Ah, we are talking real, not euphemistic roommate."

"Indeed."

Todd, getting the sense of where this may go, eases away.

"Same with Carlos." Diego points out a man talking to Patrick.

Jay looks over to see a carefully groomed dark-haired man with a close-cropped beard outlining his chin. A thin moustache dips down to connect with the beard. He wears a pale cream-colored shirt with a bright embroidered design on the left upper side over pants of a slightly darker color that hang down to almost cover sandaled feet. When hands are not cupped together at the beltline, small, precise gestures enhance statements.

"People think since we moved here together, we must be involved, but it's strictly business."

Jay shifts his gaze from Carlos back to a slouching Diego who wears a tight t-shirt over strategically torn jeans. "Business partners make sense."

"I am very available." Diego, a slight man of 5'4" and at most 110 pounds, grins. His dark face has a scattering of old acne scars.

"Available can be nice." Jay casually says as they start to drift away from the party.

"And are you available?"

"Depends on what you mean by that," Jay says as they step out onto the deck.

"Given my current status of devoting time to starting up a business, I'd have to say, only for fun."

"Fun is good."

At the rail, Diego says, "Nice view."

"This where I am supposed to look at you with obvious desire and say 'Yes, it is?'"

"That is the cliché."

"But not unwanted?"

"True enough. Does that make me cheap?"

"Inexpensive."

"Kind of exposed on the deck."

They are standing very close, touching. "Not into giving a show?"

"Not particularly."

"Have you had a house tour?"

"No, I haven't. Any places of particular interest?"

"Many. The kitchen is a marvel, terribly bright though." Jay turns and points to windows off to the right.

Diego also turns and looks where Jay indicates. "Harsh lighting. Not good. Too much reflection off my glasses."

"The bathrooms are very nice but cramped."

"One does like to spread his wings."

Jay leads him along the deck.

"The dining room is lovely, but...all that food to work around."

"True." He glances back through the sliding doors. "Kind of crowded too."

"Several bedrooms at the back of the house."

"Negotiating all those people could be distracting."

They are at the top of a stairway. "There is one other place of interest."

"Go on."

"Under the deck is a sheltered alcove. Safe from wind, semi-dark. Can be reached either by these stairs or the basement." Jay outlines Diego's lips with a finger. "Patrick never uses the basement."

"Sounds charming. Any furnishings?"

"Picnic table and benches. Kinda rustic."

"There's a bit of lumberjack about you."

They head down the stairs, Jay one step ahead. When reaching the bottom step, he turns and pulls Diego in so they can kiss. His arms around the smaller man's waist, he easily raises him off the stair.

Diego wraps his legs around Jay who carries him under the shelter of the deck above them. He sits him down on the edge of the picnic table. They race to unbutton shirts, expose chests.

"Nice," Diego says, hands rubbing Jay's considerably larger chest. He leans in for a lingering kiss.

Jay tosses Diego's shirt aside. He slips his hands down Diego's back. One hand slides under his waist band to explore his ass crack. He feels Diego's hands on his belt, hears it being undone, followed by pants being unbuttoned.

He pulls Diego up. "Get naked."

"Yes, sir," he answers and obeys. Shoes and socks come off and are tossed aside. Pants and underwear follow, leaving his arms at his side. His torso is narrow with longish, dark hair flowing across his chest. Each nipple holds a small post, one catching a reflective glint from the weak light filtering through the deck slats.

"Turn around."

Jay grabs his small ass in his hands, massaging the slight muscles thereby spreading the cheeks. "I'm going to fuck you."

"Yes, sir. I would like that."

"Not yet. Turn around."

Jay strips as Diego watches. Jay kicks off his shoes and slowly removes each sock. Jay draws his undone belt out of the loops and teasingly runs the tongue down Diego's chest, then along the length of his erection, producing a ragged breath. The belt, tossed onto the table, thumps loudly when the buckle hits. Diego flinches at the sound, then glances back, eager to see where it landed.

"Eyes on me."

"Yes, sir. Sorry, sir."

Jay removes his pants.

Diego's tongue darts around his lips.

Jay fold his pants and places them carefully on a picnic bench, reaching past Diego and letting his body brush the slight man's arm...

Diego's eyes are riveted.

"Don't move." Jay gets up on the table behind Diego and removes his underwear. He holds Diego's head between his hands and rubs his erection into Diego's very dark, somewhat thinning hair. "That feels good, Diego."

"Thank you, sir."

"Keep silent. Tilt your head back." He is obeyed. "Good. Now, arch your back, way back. Brace yourself with your hands on the table. I want you all the way back, your face turned up."

Diego acquiesces.

"Open your mouth."

Jay moves forward and stands with legs apart, his balls above Diego's mouth. Lowering his body, he commands, "Take them in, first one, then the other. Use your tongue." He raises up and down, making Diego's tongue reach.

Jay looks down at Diego and leans slightly forward. "You're very hard down there, Diego. Do you want to stroke it? You may answer."

"Yes, sir, if you want me to."

"Good. Silence again. Grab lightly, that's right, that's the way. Now, you may give five slow strokes on my count. Start at the base and go all the way until you almost let go before returning. One... Two... Three... Four... And five. Very good. Hand back to the table."

Jay moves slightly forward. "You are very good."

A long strand of pre-cum oozes from Diego's rod.

Jay raises up. "Leaking. Very sexy. You may speak."

"Thank you, sir. I am glad it pleases you."

"It does. Quiet again." Jay steps back while still standing on the table so he can look Diego in the eye. "I want you to take a finger and coat it with that lovely liquid coming out of you. Not yet. Wait for full instructions. Coat your index finger. Be careful not to touch yourself too much... That's good. Nice and wet. Now reach your hand up, finger pointed. Feed it to me."

He leans and sucks the proffered finger. "Very good. Now, stand up. Like before. Don't turn."

Diego is upright again.

"Move a half step forward." Jay sits down behind him on the edge of the table. "Okay, now slowly back up until you can feel my hardness on your back. That's right, all the way. Raise your arms." Jay closes legs so his thighs hug Diego's waist. "Rest your arms on my thighs. Shake your head yes or no. Do you like the way your skin feels next to mine?"

A nod yes.

Jay wraps Diego in his arms. "You may answer now when I ask you something. No more than three words. Do you understand?"

"Yes, sir."

"I am going to touch you with my strong hands. Tell me where you should be touched."

Diego is pondering. He is very quiet. Finally, "Your choice, sir."

"Three, very good." Jay's hands start to rove over him. "You must answer honestly. I give you full permission to say no. Do you understand?"

"Completely, sir."

Jay runs his tongue up the back of Diego's right ear. "I like that, not just yes or no. Now I want to know..." A rustle of footsteps on the deck above, causes a quietly added, "Do you like to have your nipples played with?"

Again, a slight pause. "A little, sir."

"Good. Honesty pleases more than submission. Tilt your head back and turn. That deserved a kiss."

Diego complies.

"Back forward. Tell me what you don't want me to do with your nipples."

"No pain, sir."

"It's good you know your limits. Do you like them rubbed?"

"Yes, sir."

Jay brings a middle finger to Diego's mouth. "Get it wet." He then starts to rub Diego's left nipple with the moist finger. He nuzzles into his neck, kissing it. "Do you like this, Diego?"

"A lot, sir."

"Your nipple is very erect right now. I am going to spread my legs. Let your arms drop to your side again." Easing Diego forward, Jay again stands on the table.

Another rustling intrudes. Someone is walking down the stairs. Jay wonders which one of the guests would be fun to add to this mix.

Being caught in such a compromising position appeals far less to Diego.

From above, a voice sounds. "Come back up. It's too dark to see anything now."

Footsteps retreat.

Both men remain immobilized for a moment until Jay states, "Turn around, Diego. I want you to face me." Obedience. "Look up. Beautiful mouth." His thumb traces Diego's lips. "I'm going to feed you my cock. Would you like that?"

"Very much, sir."

"Place your hands on my legs while I fuck your face. You do not need to keep them in one place, but legs only. Open your mouth." Jay holds Diego's head gently between his hands, more guide than restraint. He feels Diego's hands on his calf muscles, tentative at first, but as Jay slowly eases in and out, the touch grows stronger and begins roving.

He pulls out of Diego's mouth and sits in front of him. He takes Diego's hands, kissing the palm of one, then the other. "Time to fuck you, Diego." He pauses, knowing Diego wants to say yes, but the pocket-sized man remains obediently silent. "You are very good." He kisses him. "Remember where I put my pants?"

"I do, sir."

"I folded them very carefully. When I tell you, go to them, and in the top pocket you will find a condom. You will not need to search any other pocket and you may not unfold the pants. Go now."

He returns with condom in hand.

"Put it there on the table. Look at me. Do you trust me?"

"Completely, sir."

"Take the condom out of the wrapper and put it on me... Very good, Diego. Remember my belt?"

"Yes, sir"

Jay reaches and lightly strokes Diego's erection. "Will you let me spank you with it?"

"No, sir.

"Will you let me bind your wrists with it?" He can tell Diego is thinking. "Not too tightly."

"Diego, you are fucking hot as hell." He reaches behind him and finds the belt. "Hold your wrists up, almost together."

Diego obeys exactly.

Keeping his eyes locked on Diego's, he binds his wrists, then gets off the table and moves behind Diego. "Step up to the table and rest on your elbows on it. The belt should be on in a way that will not dig. Let me know otherwise. I only intend pleasure."

Diego gets in position. Jay's hands start to massage his small, muscled ass. "You have a beautiful ass." Jay lets a drizzle of spit fall from his mouth onto Diego's ass crack. He rubs it in and lets another lubricating drizzle fall. Jay starts to enter.

Diego's ass, small with quite narrow hips, readily accommodates Jay. Diego's head raises up, arching his back as Jay penetrates. A satisfied moan materializes.

Knowing already this guy can take it, Jay does not start gently, not rough, but no building. He merely fucks.

Jay glides his hand up Diego's back and reaches into his hair. Pulling firmly, not yanking, he guides Diego to a standing position and slows the pace. Reaching around to grab Diego's erection causes a sharp gasp. He stops. "You really want to cum, don't you, Diego?"

"God yes, sir."

Jay pulls out. "Turn around." Jay unbinds Diego's wrists. "You're very close. I want to watch. On your back." He does so. "Is that comfortable?"

"It is, sir."

"I'm going to enter you again. When I nod, start jerking. I want to see your cum fly." He raises Diego's legs, spreads them apart, reenters, and resumes. He continues until Diego starts to pant in regular deep gulps. A slight nod from Jay lets Diego know.

It takes very few strokes before several sprays of cum shoot out. Diego lets out one elongated moan, shooting the largest load Jay has ever seen.

"Damn, Diego, when was the last time you came?"

He has trouble catching his breath, but finally rasps out, "Three fucking weeks."

Jay starts to laugh. "Amazing. Still kept it to three words. I want to cum so bad, Diego. Where do you want it?"

"Your choice, sir."

Jay leans forward and kisses Diego. He takes his chin between thumb and forefinger. "My choice is for you to tell me where you want it. Understand?"

Nodding. Thinking. "Face, mouth, sir."

"On your knees." Done. "Open your mouth." Done. "Lightly pull my balls." Done.

He starts. Diego looks up, mouth open, eyes eager. The first stream lands in an angle crossing Diego's face from forehead across the bridge of his nose to the opposite cheek. The second lands on the other cheek. The third, from the tip of his nose to his chin. The rest is fed inside Diego's mouth. It takes a while before he can let Diego release him, then he helps Diego to his feet.

"You can talk freely now"

Grinning broadly, "Thank you, sir."

They both crack up.

"Uh, we both made a mess on your body. We should clean it up." He starts to look for underwear.

"Jay?" He waits for him to turn. "Can we just leave it be for a moment? I kind of like it." He studies Jay briefly. "You're not a cum and run kind of guy, are you?"

Jay thinks of Angel. "It happens. Sit." He puts his arm around Diego's shoulder.

"I don't always do that," Diego starts. "The submissive thing, but it was really amazing tonight."

"You're good at it. Sure brought out the dominant in me. But then, he comes out a bit more frequently."

"I thank you."

"You're starting to drip."

"The cum thing. That is pretty usual. Love the way it feels on my skin. In the right circumstances, I let it dry. Bit of a fetish."

"Hurts no one. Have to admit you look pretty hot that way. That why you haven't shot in three weeks?"

"Kind of. I mean I don't always wait until I can have sex, but yeah, it's cool to shoot such a huge load and get the kind of reaction you gave." He gets quiet for a bit. "This was fucking wild as hell, and you are amazing. But I kind of get the feeling you're not really that available for a steady thing."

"True, though this was fucking intense. I do want to know how to get in touch because I think at some point you should meet Leo. He's crazy busy between school and boyfriend, but if your ideas are good, he'd be someone to know."

"Sounds good. I suppose we should get back." He looks down at himself. "Damn hate to see this go."

Jay laughs and finds Diego's underwear. He very carefully wipes Diego clean. He looks at them once done, "Not sure you'll be able to wear these again."

With a sly smile, Diego, takes the underwear and slips them on. "They still fit."

"Of course."

Both finish dressing and head up the stairs.

The party lingers on. About half the guests have left or gone to bed.

Jay spots Patrick. "Did sleeping beauty ever make it?"

"Still out cold. I take it you've had a good time. You and a certain other guest have been invisible for some time."

"What are you talking about?" he says in mock astonishment. "Turned into a real fine party."

"If you want him to stay over with you, that's fine. I'll make room for Benji with me."

Jay looks at Patrick with concern. "You sure?"

"I'm aware of his limits. Besides, I can't leave him on the deck all night."

"I should check on him."

"He's okay, I've been checking every now and then. Still dead to the world. Go have fun."

Jay finds Diego talking with his friend, Carlos.

Diego introduces them. "Carlos, this is Jay. He has a friend who may be able to help us with getting set up." Carlos, skeptical, agrees to trade contact information. He then wanders off, picking up that there is more going on between his friend and Jay.

"Carlos seems pretty sharp. Think you guys have a shot?"

"I can hope. I think he's getting ready to leave and since he drove, means I'll be taking off too. Guess this is my cue to say it was nice, hope to see you again, knowing I won't. Not like this anyway." He reaches for Jay's hand.

"Here's what will happen instead. Tell Carlos you are going to stay here. I'll make sure you get home tomorrow."

"Really?"

"I'm staying anyway. You can let the cum dry this time."

"Be right back."

16

Patrick finishes in the kitchen then scans the living space.

He envies Jay's ability to sweep someone like Diego up. Tomorrow? Jay moves on. Diego gets over him. Good for them. He is tired of moving on.

A man sleeps on his deck. Maybe they could have had something, but neither found time. Still, he needs to be dealt with. A plate of food and a glass of juice is placed on a tray and carried out to the deck. Patrick sets the tray next to the lounge then puts the screen back. Finally, he sits on the edge of the lounge. Sometime during the party, he covered Benji with a blanket, now twisted around the brawny body. Benji curls on his side facing Patrick, who stares down at him. Lightly he traces his jawline with a finger. "Benji."

He stirs, rolls onto his back. Patrick repeats the gesture, lingering a bit. "Benji."

Dark eyes open and a smile forms. "Patrick."

Patrick, his hand still on Benji's cheek, says, "Hello, sleepyhead."

"Mmm... I needed that." He stretches and props himself up on his elbows. "Time to get ready for the party?"

"You slept through that. Everyone's gone home or to bed."

"You're shitting me. I slept through all that?" He sits up and finally notices the darkness. "Damn, I *was* tired."

"Tried to wake you several times." He picks up the plate. "I brought you something."

"No wonder I'm hungry. Thanks."

"Some juice too."

Benji looks at him. "Thanks. This is good." He continues ravenously, having had nothing since lunch. He reaches for the glass of juice, takes a big swig, plunks it down and returns to the food, finishing it off quickly.

"More?" Patrick offers.

"No." Benji sets the plate on the tray, gets up, and walks to the deck rail. He leans forward resting his crossed arms on the upper rail looking at what he wanted to see when he first came out here. Even in the dark, distant mountain silhouettes lazily make their presence known. Lights from other houses dot the landscape, many reflected in hazy approximations on the lake. A serenity he loves resides here.

Patrick stands next to him facing away from the lake with his elbows resting on the top rail. He looks at Benji who is refusing to look back. "Benj?"

Benji turns further away.

"Benj," he starts again. "Jay told me about Steve."

The dreaded moment. Benji feels Patrick's hand on his arm, and he covers it with his. He hears, "It's okay," and turns, saying, "Is it? Really?"

Now, Patrick cannot look. "It has to be."

Benji releases Patrick's hand and returns to the lounge, raising its back. "Sit." Following Patrick, he climbs on, leaning against Patrick's chest, drawing his arms around him.

They fall silent, trying to gather their thoughts.

Benji finally speaks. "This is the first time I feared coming here."

"We've had wonderful times here."

"You know me better than anyone except Jay. You know how easily I fall. I fell for you that first time I came here. Remember?"

He laughs, "Of course. Jay and Vince brought you. You had just moved into the house. You wore that way too tight, cropped scarlet tank and painted on shorts. But you had an overriding sweetness." Patrick runs his hands on Benji's shirt. "Can't imagine back then you would have owned anything like this."

"Damn, I was so raw. I was ready to hustle every guy here. Everyone saw me for the street trash I was."

"Not everyone."

"No, not everyone."

A chilling breeze lifts from the lake causing them to huddle together.

"Patrick, I was so frustrated with everything that whole weekend. I wanted you to ravish me to oblivion. But you wouldn't. You took me to bed. And then just held me. You wouldn't let me do anything."

"I wanted to."

"Yes, but at the time I couldn't understand why you wouldn't. I learned, I just wasn't ready for that kind of touch, that kind of sex. You taught me how to connect sex and emotion and caring. Damn all of it."

"This is where we first made love."

"That's why I always have to come out here first thing. I must look at that view. I need to look at what I saw when you came up behind me. I thought we'd end up together, but we never did. You would go away for weeks, even months. I would fall in love with one man after the other."

"Different this time?"

"Yes. And he's hundreds of miles away. I don't even know if I'll see him again."

"Benji, you and I are always going to love each other. It's not enough. We never get beyond what we find here."

Benji sits up and turns around to face Patrick. "I still want you," he leans in to kiss Patrick. "Is that wrong? I want Steve with all my heart, but I still want you."

Patrick puts his arms on Benji's shoulders and gets up. He reaches his hand to Benji who rises. Patrick brings them to the rail. "You were standing just about here that night. Facing out. I wasn't sure you knew I had come out to join you, but I had to hold you, just like this." He embraces Benji from behind. "You relaxed back into me. Desperation gone. I was Patrick at last to you. I will always want that."

Benji closes his eyes, taking himself back to that first visit, still operating on survival instincts. Then he saw that perfect body. The man who owned that body, owned this house. Patrick was a god he had to have. He flirted; nowhere. Looked for a reason to blackmail; none. He even tried to use his background for pity; zilch.

Patrick, as did Vince and Jay, let him play his games, willing to wait. On his third visit, it gelled. He was standing in the living room looking out and moved to the door. The lake and the mountains were beautiful, bringing him to silence. Patrick opened the door to the deck and urged him to go out. Look, Patrick urged. He stood at that rail for several minutes. This is beauty. Patrick's arms were around him. They made love on the deck that night.

They didn't get together every time Patrick threw a party. Sometimes Patrick was seeing someone. Once Benji brought Gary. Often enough, they found themselves in bed.

They have been down this road so often. Benji wants one more trip down that road.

Benji flexes his hips back into Patrick, acting almost as he had that very first visit.

Patrick whispers softly, "It's okay. We're fine."

Embarrassment overtakes Benji. He tries to pull away, wanting to run, but there is nowhere to go. Plus, he is held fast in two strong arms.

"It's really okay, Benji." He nuzzles against his friend's neck. "Let's just go to bed."

Fighting emotions, Benji allows himself to relax. "You're right. Funny, I feel like I could still sleep even after that long nap." Now released, he leads the way back but turns briefly. "We are going to your room. Right?"

A confirming nod accompanies Patrick's warm smile.

Patrick watches Benji as he follows. He loves how those powerful legs move, how nicely his ass flexes. When they first met, Patrick could hold both cheeks in one hand. Now, he's not sure both hands could fully contain one.

17

Jay idly watches a tennis match on TV while suppressing laughter at Leo fidgeting in one of the seats at the table in the alcove, his open laptop a poor cover.

Leo pretends, rather unsuccessfully, not to be nervous. He will see Dave the first time face to face since before Tim's visit. Schedules have only allowed electronic communication. He pulls out his phone and feels disappointment. Only one minute has passed since the last time. Both men have a view of the street, only he pays it attention.

Jay stands, moves toward the window when Leo perks up and gazes out to see a small blue car parking.

Leo rises from the chair the same time Dave exits the car. Leo opens the door as Dave hits the top step. Blue eyes meet green. Radiant smiles from both.

Leo's concerns about what he has to say are momentarily forgotten in the joy of seeing and holding Dave.

"I have missed you so much," Dave murmurs.

"Me too."

Jay, enjoying the interaction, allows it to continue for a few moments as he slowly crosses the living room. Eventually he clears his throat.

Dave looks past Leo. "Oh, hey. How've you been?"

Jay crosses the distance between them in easy loping strides. Dave reaches out a hand, the other arm still around Leo. "Good. And you?"

Nuzzling into Leo, "Too busy. So you guys are going to an overnight party?"

"Yeah, won't be back 'til tomorrow. Have errands to run before Benji's shift is over. We'll head out from there."

"Dang, sorry I won't see him. I was hoping he could show me where things are in the kitchen."

"Whatcha gonna cook?"

He and Leo are just holding hands now, "Something Italian. Depends on what ingredients we find. And I promise plenty leftovers."

"Like that. Like your car too. What is it?" he indicates with his chin.

"Yeah, my little guy. It's a Yaris. Very reliable and perfect for me. Plus, I think he's cute."

"Use the garage. Plenty room. There's a lock on the left side. Code is 245#."

They move toward the kitchen, Leo and Dave still holding hands. "We can show you around pretty well in the kitchen. It's Benji's domain, but we should be able to help you find anything you may need," starts Jay.

"Mostly where pots, pans, and mixing bowls are. See what kind of gadgets he has."

Leo, having cleaned so often, starts, "Pots on the bottom cabinet to the right of the stove. Pans in the same cabinet on the upper shelf. Bowls in the cabinet over that counter. The far cabinet on top has all sorts of gadgets. I don't know what most are. Cooking utensils are in the drawers closest to the stove on that side also. But Benji mostly uses the stuff that's in those containers across the counter."

"How about baking dishes and cake pans?" Dave asks as he explores the cabinets.

Leo opens another cabinet, "These?"

Jay comments, "You know this kitchen as good as Benji. And on that I need to get my stuff ready." He leaves the two.

Dave peers into the gadget cabinet. "My, my, what have we here?" He pulls out two items unfamiliar to Leo.

"What are they?"

"This," he indicates, "is a pasta maker. This is a food mill. Great kitchen toys. Okay, now staples and spices."

They continue to work through the kitchen, Leo pointing things out, Dave making mental notes for things he may need. Leo takes a seat at the table as Dave continues. This side of Dave is entrancing, making it clear why Dave calls it a passion. Once done, Dave turns to Leo. "I think I have enough information here. Ready to shop?"

Before Leo answers, Jay enters with his and Benji's bags. He sees the pasta maker and food mill. "Wow, haven't seen those in ages. You're really pulling out the stops."

"You don't know how much I've been wanting to go crazy in a real kitchen. My place has this dinky galley excuse. This is heaven."

"You do pretty well there," Leo injects. He and Dave look at each other warmly.

"Thank you, sweetie."

Jay interjects, "Well, dear ones, I'm off. See you tomorrow." He heads out the back to the garage.

Those two hug standing 15 feet apart.

Dave addresses Leo, "Are you ready?"

Leo is looking at Dave. He pauses, takes a breath. "Sit a minute. I want to let you know about something."

Dave studies Leo as he sits, noting Leo's sudden discomfort. "What's going on?"

Leo rehearsed this in his mind, but seeing the doubt in Dave's face worries him. He haltingly begins. "You know when Jay's brother was here?"

Dave nods. "Yeah."

Leo can't face Dave as the encounter pours out. He tells it with a little bit of fear. Without sexual details, a thorough account is presented. "I

promised I would tell you and not let you find out from someone else,"
he ends. They sit silently for a bit. "Please say something, I don't want
you to be hurt."

Dave scoots his chair closer. "Give me your hand." He holds it in both
of his. "Does Tim look like Jay?"

Leo is puzzled, "What?"

"Just processing. Does he?"

"Younger, pretty much the same features, same body, smaller all over."

"Okay, pretty hot, got that."

"I guess, yeah, he is."

"Okay, let me run this all. Make sure I have the whole scenario. This
good-looking guy comes from out of town for the weekend. He's committed to someone at home and has no desire to screw that up. He offers you
basically no strings attached sex and constantly reassures you nothing
you do with him should be allowed to interfere with what we may have
between us."

"Yeah, and I kept talking about you and he kept talking about Eddie."

"How so?"

"Well, things like how you are so different physically. Tim's smooth
and you have that great hair all over. How Eddie's hair falls onto his face,
things like that." He keeps his focus on how Dave's hands still hold his,
which confuses and pleases him.

"Anything else?"

"I don't think so unless you want actual details."

"Um, no. Can do without those." They are silent for a bit.

Leo ventures a glance up to find that Dave is calmly smiling at him.

"Sweetie, I would have done it too."

"You're not mad?"

"More surprised than anything. I'm glad you told me. Not the best
news, but far, far from worst. Look, I don't know where this is heading
between us. But it feels very special, and I want to find out what's possible."

"Really?" Leo sits up and cocks his head. "You really feel that about us?"

"Yes, Leo. I do." Dave leans in and kisses him. "I feel that about us."

Leo glows. "Me too."

Dave pulls back, "Much as I love this, we do have plans. Unless you want to blow it all off."

"I guess we should go." He pouts playfully, unable to remember doing that before.

Dave gives him a little peck, "We'll pick it up from there later." They get up, both adjusting their pants. "Are there bags we can bring?"

"Tons." He goes to a narrow closet that also houses cleaning supplies. "How many?"

"Grab the stack, better to have too many."

"Okay. The grocery store and where else?"

"Actually, not the grocery store. I found a few specialty stores. I plan to be as over the top as possible."

Leo laughs, then adds, "Dave, I know I say things like this a lot, but this is all kind of new for me, so I have to ask. Is this a date?"

Dave gently takes Leo into his arms. "You are so adorable. Yes, this is a date. Non-traditional, but definitely a date."

Hand in hand, they step outside.

"Hey, Leo," they hear and turn. Tommy leans on his lawn mower, very glad for this diversion.

"Tommy." Leo pulls Dave. "Come on, you haven't met our neighbor. Tommy, I want you to meet Dave."

Tommy wipes his hand on his shorts before offering it to Dave.

"Tommy made my box."

"Really? Awesome. It's beautiful." Dave accepts Tommy's hand with both of his. "You're quite talented."

"Thank you. Always glad when my work is appreciated. Hoping to have enough work for a show next year."

"Really?" from Leo. "A whole show of boxes?"

"No, all my work. Boxes, sculpture, jewelry. All kinds of things."

"I'd love to see your work," Dave says.

"If you have time now, I could show you."

"Have to be later," says Leo, "we've got a lot of shopping to do."

"No problem. Nice to meet you. Dave. See you around."

They turn and head for Dave's car as Tommy starts his mower. Dave opens the passenger side for Leo, who tosses the bags in the back seat and gets in.

Leo fastens his seat belt—

Instantly, his world flashes into a white void. Sound dissolves. He sees nothing but endless white. He feels nothing. Colors flash randomly and develop into quick-moving, nonsensical images. Strange, unknown people. A policeman. A woman in a lab coat speaking gibberish. A man in a suit sits on a desk speaking an unknown language. These people pass him; no, he is passing them. There's more of them, too many. An angelic woman in the background waves at him through a window. He tries to get to her but is up in the air being pulled away. Papers fly around and gather into a vortex swirling down to a rectangular opening. Then he is drawn into it, but it is empty. Frightening. He goes deeper and deeper. The papers are above him, cutting off his air. Breathing is difficult. He is lost and tries to reach but can't move. He is cold. Nothing he knows exists. He is not in the box, but floating above, maybe below, all the papers are inside, joined by all those people. The box shuts and disappears into a hole at the bottom of this now-again white world. The edges of the whiteness start to erode. Slowly colors that seem to make vague sense creep in. There is a tree to his left. He knows that tree. More trees start to appear. Then there are, what? Yes, houses. He knows these houses. There is a street becoming visible in front of him. From a distance, he hears a steady roar. To his left, he hears a voice. It is saying one thing over and over. "Leo. Leo..."

...That's my name. It is so hard to turn to that sound, but I must force my neck to move. It takes forever, but a face is coming into view. It's a man. It's a beautiful man, maybe a god. He is looking at me scared, but oh, he is the most beautiful man. I know him, I think. Yes, I do know him. My, he looks so worried. He is reaching out to me. Why can't I reach back? I know him, I know I do. He is Dave. That's it. Dave. Dave.

"Dave."

"Leo. Leo, what's going on? Leo, talk to me." Dave turns Leo's head to fully face him. He feels tears threatening to break. "Leo, say something, please."

Leo gains more control. He feels his mouth move and finds his smile. "Dave."

"Sweetie, are you all right? Talk, please."

"Where'd you go?" Leo asks, still somewhat hazy.

Dave near panic, starts to calm now that Leo speaks. He opens a glove box and pulls out some tissues to wipe Leo's forehead. "My god, sweetie, you are sweating like crazy. What's going on? Please, sweetie, talk."

"Dave, I'm okay."

"Can you get up?" He runs around to the passenger side and opens the door. "Leo, come on. Let's walk a bit."

Tommy has run over, noticing something is not right. "Can I help?"

"I don't know. Come on, Leo."

Leo's hands are still gripping the seat belt. Dave takes one. It is cold, but he warms it. He repeats with the other hand until Leo can let go. He starts to unfasten the seat belt, but Leo stops him.

"I'm okay now, Dave. I'm fine."

Tommy dashed into his house and returns, sweaty from the extra exertion, with a glass of water, not knowing what else to do. He offers it.

"Thanks." Leo takes a swallow and hands it back. Shaking his head, he reaches for Dave's hand. "I am okay now. Can we get started?" He looks at Tommy. "Thank you, Tommy, for the water. It's really okay now."

Dave goes back to the driver side. He exchanges a worried look with Tommy then gets in and starts the car.

Tommy watches them turn around and head down Jewel, continuing until they turn the corner.

They drive in silence for some time. Dave pulls Leo's hand onto his thigh to maintain contact. He places his on top every chance he gets while he drives. At a stop sign, he squeezes Leo's hand. He is scared and doesn't know what to do.

Several blocks later, Leo finally breaks the silence. "I don't know what happened. Everything just went away."

"Has that ever happened before?"

"I don't think so."

"Should we go to the hospital?"

"No, I'm really fine now."

"Can you tell me what happened?"

"I don't know. I'm not really sure." He pauses. "Dave, it was very scary. Still is. Can we talk about it later?"

"Sure, Leo. We have all day to talk about anything we want. Except, of course, when I'm busy cooking." He adds, wanting to lighten the mood. It works.

Leo squeezes Dave's leg.

Whatever happened was connected to the car. Not this car surely, but something.

He then realizes something. "You know I have not been inside a car since before moving here. I'm always on foot. Come to think of it, this is the first vehicle of any sort I've been in since I arrived. Is that weird?"

"Understandable. You live close to school. School keeps me busy enough, and your program seems even more demanding. This is only the second or third time I've used Bart since school started except to visit my family."

"Bart?"

He pats the dashboard. "This is Bart."

Leo giggles.

"Hey, hey. Don't laugh at my car."

"I'm not." He giggles again. "I'm laughing at you." He bursts out laughing. Dave joins in.

Dave pulls into a delicatessen parking lot. "First stop, cheeses." He looks at Leo. "I am so glad and amazed that you agreed to actually come shopping with me. It's fun for me, but most guys would rather wait until it's all done."

"Guess I'm not most guys."

"I am keenly aware of and deeply grateful for that."

Leo grins and reddens.

"I need to give you a bit of a warning. If you've never been into a store that specializes in cheeses, it can be rather pungent. You want that. If it smelled all clean and fresh, I wouldn't trust it." Dave leads the way and sure enough Leo is assaulted by astonishing aromas. "Kind of stinky. Just what I was hoping for. You'll adjust soon."

They wander around looking through the cases. Dave knows what he wants, but has half an ear on the older woman, clearly a regular, who is ordering from the man behind the counter.

The man behind the counter, noticing them, says he'll be right with them.

Dave answers, *"Niente di fretta. Mi place tanto il vostro negozio. Si dice che il miglior formaggio in città si trova."*

The man and woman brighten.

"Benvenuto, amico," says the proprietor. *"Sono Salvatore Lucci, questa è la signora Caputo."*

Mrs. Caputo adds, *"Mr. Lucci ha i migliori formaggi nello stato."*

Dave answers, *"Il mio nome è Dave Azzurri e questo è il mio carissimo amico, Leo Graham."* Then to Leo, "Leo, say hi."

"Hi."

Mrs. Caputo eyes them appreciatively, *"Ah, due bei ragazzi, ma il tuo amico è troppo magro."*

Leo, delightfully awestruck, had no idea Dave could speak Italian, and this little scene quickly makes this store a wonderland. The previously piquant odor assumes a sweet caressing element. Spotting a few small tables with chairs, he sits, fascinated, understanding only the jovial tone of the conversation.

Mrs. Caputo approaches Leo on her way out. He rises, and she cups his cheek. "You take good care of my friend, Mr. Azzurri. And eat his cooking, skinny boy." Laughing, she heads out.

Mr. Lucci, at one point, leans his head back and roars out a laugh. *"Ma com' è bello essere giovane e pieno di speranza!"* He calls over to Leo, "Hey, Mr. Graham, it's true, no? Great to be young?"

An astonished Leo nods.

Everything packed and paid for, Mr. Lucci adds, with a mock gesture indicating not for Leo's ears, *"Ma se ti stanchi mai di magro, ho un figlio, Roberto. Grande uomo forte. Non si sa mai."*

Dave burst out laughing and shaking his finger at Mr. Lucci, *"Capisco. Dillo Roberto ciao, ma io resterò con il ragazzo magro, credo. Ciao, signor Lucci."*

"Salvatore."

"Ciao, Salvatore."

"Ciao, Dave. Ciao, Leo."

Leo waves. "Ciao," he says tentatively.

"What was that?" he asks Dave when they are outside.

"Basically, I have a new friend, and we are welcome here for the rest of our lives. However, Salvatore let me know if I ever want to dump your skinny ass, he'll set me up with his big butch son."

"What? You're making that up."

"No, his son is named Roberto. But don't worry. I told him I preferred skinny guys." He starts laughing.

Leo soon joins in. "Is this what shopping with you is like?"

Leo hesitates briefly before getting back in the car, fearing a return episode, but nothing happens.

Dave also takes a moment watching Leo before he slides into the driver's seat.

"That took me completely off guard. Delightful! I'm pretty sure when we get all this sorted out we'll find he slipped in a little extra. We better hurry and get the rest done. That took charmingly longer than expected."

The rest of the shopping goes along without incident...in English. Produce is obtained, including several pounds of carefully selected Roma tomatoes from another store. The final stop, a wine shop, Dave selects one for dinner, one for cooking, and another as a gift to Benji for allowing him to use the kitchen. It seems to Leo, Dave has bought enough food to feed at least twenty.

Dave directs the set up for the meal's preparation. Cheeses go onto a side counter to bring to room temperature. Tomatoes are washed, stemmed, and placed in a large pot on the stove. Other vegetables and fruits are washed and set aside on the counter or in the refrigerator. Dave pours a little water into the bottom of the pot and turns it on low. Leo cleans as they go.

"We are done for now." He sets the timer on the stove. "We have twenty minutes. Wanna go for a walk or make out on the sofa?"

"Sofa!"

They race to the living room, Dave diving onto the larger sofa first so Leo ends up on top. Their kissing remains playful, not yet the time to get truly physical. Leo looks down on Dave's handsome face. He feels Dave brush his hair.

"You're so handsome," he tells Leo and watches as he winces. "I wish you'd stop doubting that."

"I don't see it."

"I know, but I happen to strongly disagree."

Leo almost understands.

"Let me approach it this way. You think I'm handsome, don't you?"

"Yeah, of course I do."

"Well, if I'm so handsome," he kisses Leo, "why would I..." Kiss. "...want to have anything to do..." Kiss. "...with you?" Kiss.

"Um, because you are a kind gentleman who does not want to treat a poor soul like me badly?" Kiss.

Dave guffaws. "Well, that too, but no, silly..." Kiss. "...because I think you..." Kiss. "...are drop dead..." Kiss. "...absolutely..." Kiss. "...gorgeous..." Kiss. "And maybe I just have different tastes."

"So, you're saying?"

"You're just not your type."

He starts to tickle Leo who howls for him to stop. Growing up with a sibling gives Dave a distinct advantage in a tickle fight.

"Not until you can admit that you are gorgeous and handsome and all around cute."

Between laughs and gasps for breaths Leo squawks out, "Okay, okay, I give up. I'll admit it. I'm handsome."

Dave's hand hovers. "And?"

"Um, gorgeous."

Hand gets closer. "And?"

"Crap, I forgot the third one."

The tickling lightly resumes. "And all around cute."

He is laughing so hard, tears form. "And all around cute." The timer bell goes off, and they sit up. Leo gets a sly look. "To you anyway." And he dashes to the kitchen before Dave can resume.

Dave races after him, grabbing him as they reach the stove. "You are just lucky the tomatoes need attention." He holds Leo, and they share a deeper kiss. "Okay, time to make sauce."

"These are going to become like that sauce that comes out of a can?"

"I hope better than that, but yeah, it's going to start looking like that real soon." He takes the lid off the pot to check. He reaches for Leo to join him. "See how the skins are split? It means they're ready." Grabbing one of the two large bowls he set out, he fastens the food mill to its lip. "Two things need to be done now. One is press all those tomatoes through the mill, the other is to chop up and sauté some vegetables to start the sauce. Would you like to do one of those?"

He touches the handle of the mill. "This thing has me intrigued. Show me what to do."

Dave moves the bowl and mill next to the stove. "Put some of the tomatoes into the basket. Then you just start turning the crank. The pulp and juice from the tomatoes will fall through the screen into the bowl. The skin and seeds will be trapped. Start with six or so, and add them as you can until all the tomatoes have been processed. Here," he moves a smaller bowl to the other side of the big bowl. "If there gets to be too much skin and seeds, scoop them into this bowl and keep going."

He selects a slotted spoon and lifts out a few tomatoes into the mill and turns the crank a few times to demonstrate. "That's kind of it. Pretty repetitive, but it gets the job done."

Leo moves in and starts cranking tentatively until he gets the feel for the mill. This simple task feels so meaningful.

Dave grabs a large cutting board and sets it on the counter on the other side of the stove. He selects an onion, several celery stalks, a head of garlic, a container of olives and a large carrot. He peels the carrot and starts chopping up all the vegetables, making separate piles on different parts of the board for each one.

Leo, now that he has the rhythm of the mill down, watches Dave.

Dave's smooth movements clearly show his confidence. Before Leo makes his way through half the tomatoes, Dave has chopped all the vegetables. The final thing tackled is garlic. Several large cloves are cracked with the side of a broad knife. After their skins are discarded, they are minced to a fine pulp.

Dave rinses and dries his hands, and then goes to hold Leo from behind. "How's it going?"

"Good, I guess." He smiles back at Dave.

Dave places a hand over Leo's to stop him momentarily. "Look. More like sauce now?"

"Amazing."

Dave checks the pot and sees there's five tomatoes left. He selects a wide skillet and pours enough olive oil into it to barely coat the bottom before placing it over a medium heat. Once heated enough, the vegetables, starting with onion and carrot, then celery are slipped into the skillet. The garlic paste follows, but olives are held aside. Turning the heat down after Leo removes the last tomato, he grabs that pot. "Hold on a sec. I'm going to pour off the liquid into the sauce." Leo steps aside.

Dave returns it to the stove then dumps the sautéed veggies in, scraping as much of the oil as he can. He turns on the heat to low, opens the bottle of wine selected for cooking, and pours a generous amount into the pot.

"Does this go back in the pot now?" Leo indicates the pureed tomatoes.

"Not quite. Give the wine a few minutes to reduce. In the meantime, we can clean up the mill and get a little bit of lunch ready."

"I'll clean. You get lunch. Cleaning, I know."

"Works for me."

Leo clears the grit out of the mill and washes it out. Skins and seeds are dumped into the compost container before washing that bowl.

Dave finds the mystery cheese that, as he suspected, Salvatore slipped in. The mild scent suggests it works with fruit. It is cut up onto a plate with grapes. He pours a finger full of the opened wine into two glasses and sets plate and glasses on the table. The meal is completed with herbed crackers and Dijon mustard. Before sitting for lunch, he checks the pot and turns the heat way down.

Leo sits, waiting for Dave's final lunch preparations.

Dave joins him and raises a glass. "To new adventures." They clink glasses and dig in, completely devouring all.

"What's next?" Leo asks.

"The tomato puree goes back into the pot, then we put together the cheese filling."

As they begin to stand, Leo asks, "Filling?"

Dave reaches for Leo's hand. "Might be more clear if I called it cheese sauce." Back at the counter, Leo lifts the bowl to pour it into the pot.

Steadying the bowl with one hand on Leo's closer hand, Dave uses a spatula to scrape the rest from the bowl which then goes into the sink. Dave runs water into it and rinses off the spatula. Another large bowl is brought to the counter bearing the cheeses.

As Dave preps what needs to be done with the cheeses, Leo washes out the first bowl, dries it, puts it away, then joins Dave at the counter and leans on him. "Okay, ready."

"You had no idea how much I was going to work you today." He pecks Leo on the cheek. "This one," he hands Leo the package of mozzarella, "goes in the refrigerator for now. The rest will be used in the filling."

"Sauce," Leo says over his shoulder as he puts that package away.

Dave grins as he opens the ricotta containers and empties them into the bowl.

He lines up the other cheeses. "From softest to hardest, we have fontina, provolone, Romano, and Parmesan. All the fontina and about half of each of the others needs to be grated and added to the ricotta."

And so, they dig into the task, hip-butting each other as they work.

"What happens to the rest?"

"The provolone can be sliced for sandwiches. The other two can be grated onto whatever you want later." He eyes Leo who stares agape at all their work. Dave picks up a piece of cheese and pops it into Leo's mouth. "Tasting is perfectly allowable."

Leo samples each cheese noting the differences. "These are really good."

"Wait until they sit and blend their flavors." He steps away to grab fresh parsley from the batch of herbs he bought. With a broad knife, the herb is chopped into small bits then added.

"This is a lot of work," Leo adds as he grates the last of the Parmesan to be used.

"This is the last of the hard work for now. You want to fold this all together while I get a couple other things?"

"I would if I knew that that meant."

"Sorry, cooking term." Dave grabs a big wooden spoon. "It's kind of stirring, but less vigorous." He demonstrates. "This is too thick for stirring."

Leo takes the spoon from Dave and tries his hand, soon getting the hang of it. Dave gets three eggs out of the refrigerator and brings them to the counter. "We'll add these in later, but for now that looks good. We just cover it up and let it sit 'til we're ready for the next step."

"Which is?"

Dave checks the time. "We let this and the sauce sit. In a couple hours, I can start dessert. Then, make the pasta and assemble the lasagna. Those both go in the oven and then another break."

"Cooking seems lot of work and a lot of wait."

"Yup, that's about it. Except for the best part." They lean against the counter, arms around waists. "Eat!"

"Yay!"

"And we have some time to fill. There are so many things I want right now. Part of me wants to rip our clothes off and have mad crazy sex right here. Another part wants to go for a long walk and enjoy the day and talk."

"Yeah, I feel the same."

"When I committed to this program, I was thinking I would pour everything into it, really go after it. I signed up for extras all over the place, I'll be a T.A. for the duration. I signed up for extra seminars. I had it all plotted out. 'Dave's Plan for the Future.' I was sure I had thought of everything. I had scheduled visits for my family." They move across the kitchen. "Everything, but you. I had no idea I'd meet the most fascinating, brilliant, frustrating, all-of-it man. There's not enough time to do everything I want to do with you."

Leo drops onto one of the kitchen chairs. He slowly starts to laugh. "Oh my, that's incredible. You didn't plan on me." He continues laughing.

Dave sits with him. "Did that come out wrong, sweetie?"

Leo continues laughing. "No, no. Sorry. No, it didn't." He pauses and takes Dave's outstretched hand. "How do I begin?" He looks around the room. "I am living in this huge, beautiful house, easily 10 times larger than any place I've lived. I have these two men who have taken me in, insist this is home, my home. They treat me like I'm important. Then I meet this outrageously magnificent man who is here cooking a meal in this kitchen that is a complete mystery to me, and he wants to cook for me, because he thinks I am significant enough to share that. And then to top it all off, you burst out into Italian on me. You didn't plan on me? Yeah, that is striking me as a bit funny." He resumes laughing.

Dave sits for a brief second then joins the laughter. He kisses Leo's hand. "I just want more time with you is what it comes down to. Come on, let's see how the sauce is coming." Hand in hand, they return to the stove. Dave stirs the sauce and takes a taste from the spoon. "Yeah, that's developing nicely." He dips the spoon back, blows on it, and offers a taste to Leo.

"Wow, that's good."

"It'll get better." He puts the spoon down. "I know what I want to do now."

"What?"

"I want us to go up to your room, get naked, lie down and cuddle and talk."

"Sounds good, but not sure we can just talk."

"If something else happens, I won't complain."

Both naked, legs entwined, they face each other on Leo's bed. Initially they have no desire to speak.

"I like this."

"Me too."

Dave, on his right elbow traces his left hand on Leo's chest. He knows what he wants to ask and the discomfort it will cause. "Leo," he finally starts, "I have to ask you something. Please trust me and answer."

Leo rolls onto his back. "I trust you."

"I want to know what happened earlier. In the car. It was very scary. Please tell me, if you can."

Leo covers his eyes with his right arm. He reaches out and finds Dave's hand with his left. His voice comes out small, barely a whisper. "I don't know." He squeezes Dave's hand but leaves his eyes covered. "I'm not trying to hide. I just don't know." Struggling to keep his voice from breaking, "It scared me too."

"You froze. Your eyes were open, but it was like you weren't seeing. You wouldn't respond. I kept trying to get your attention. I called you name over and over, but you wouldn't answer. Finally, you turned to look at me. Even then you still didn't come back right away. I was afraid you were having a seizure."

Leaving his eyes covered, he tries to process this.

Yes, I trust Dave. More than that. I have to try and tell him what I can.

He shifts his body closer and squeezes Dave's hand, knowing somewhere inside Dave will not let him go.

"No," he starts, "it wasn't a seizure. That I know. Everything went away suddenly. Like someone threw a sheet over me, but instead of it all going black, everything was light. Then it was like I was having a crazy dream, but I knew I was awake. All these strange people started showing up from nowhere. They were all talking gibberish or their lips were moving but no sound came out. A kind woman was there at one point, but some barrier was between us. There was a hole or a box or something that all this stuff kept falling into and then I was in it and then I wasn't.

Dave gently strokes Leo's chest.

Leo continues, "I did hear you, maybe not at first, I don't know. I couldn't understand you. My name was called, and I didn't know what that meant at first until I could make my head move. Then I finally could see you. I didn't know you first, but then I did and I could understand my name again. You were so scared and so kind. Was someone else there? Yes, Tommy. He brought me water. That was nice of him. Then you held my hands, and it was over."

"Sounds very scary, sweetie. You have no idea what that was all about?"

Something frustratingly stays just out of reach. "No, not really." He wants to tell him everything but simply does not understand. "Things have been really confusing since the wreck. That's all I really know."

"You mean with your parents, how they died? You weren't with them, were you?"

"No."

Dave thinks how he was when his father died, what a mess that made of him, but that was expected. He had been ill for some time. But to lose both at once with no warning is an unimaginable horror. "Leo, I think maybe you're still in shock. It had to have been devastating."

"Maybe. I just don't know." He finally removes his arm and looks at Dave.

I will tell you, Dave, I will. When I can figure this out, I will tell you, and Jay and Benji too. I want all of you to know, but mostly you, Dave. I promise.

Unable to speak aloud, eyes brimming with tears, he has no more for now. He reaches out and pulls Dave into him. Both arms are around him.

Dave, at a loss for what to say, rolls on top of Leo. He looks into those beautiful, sad blue eyes and ventures a smile. "Maybe we should check on dinner."

Relief flowers in Leo. They get up and dress.

In the kitchen, Dave checks the slowly simmering sauce. He takes the olives that had been set aside and adds them to the pot. "Ready for the next step?"

"Lead the way."

He grabs the remaining herbs and instructs Leo, "You're going to pull the leaves off the stems." He shows him how. "Good. Once you get a good pile, maybe about five or six stems of each one, just chop them up." While Leo does that, he takes several leaves of basil and rolls them together before slicing them up. They work standing close in silence.

"Great. Now mix them all up with your hands, and then throw about two thirds into the sauce."

"What about the rest?"

"They'll be used in the salad."

Leo does as instructed. Reaching for the faucet to rinse his hands, Dave stops him.

"Brush the excess off, don't wash your hands."

Once Leo does that, Dave takes both of his hands in his own.

"Cup your hands." He guides those hands up to Leo's face. "Breathe in."

"Mmm."

"Rub it into your face and neck, then you'll smell that good too." He takes Leo's hands, "Me too."

Leo brushes Dave's face tenderly with his herbed hands.

Dave spots a fleck of herb and with a moistened finger, lifts it off Leo's face, then touches it to his own tongue.

"Let's walk," Dave suggests. "I've never explored this neighborhood."

"I haven't much either actually."

Outside, Dave looks away from campus and asks, "What's that way?"

"There's some walking and running trails Jay uses. Otherwise as far as I know, more houses. Kind of like this. That's all I've seen the little I've gone that way."

"Trails might be nice but don't want to get too far." Hand in hand they head up the street letting the conversation ramble and lapse. Dave sees something that catches his eye and points it out. Leo asks about some late-blooming flower. They say hello to people who greet them. Once they hit the beginning of the trail heads, they decide to head back, invigorated and happy, vowing to return.

The final push for dinner starts with the last of the major work, leaving a few last-minute touches. Dave pulls out the largest pot in the house, fills it with water, adds a healthy portion of salt and sets it to come to a boil. In a small sauce pan, he pours most of the rest of the opened wine, enhancing it with a bit of sugar, ginger, and ground clove. This he sets on a burner and tells Leo to turn it to low as soon as it starts to boil. He pulls out the six pears he had bought, washes them, and sets them on a towel to dry. The vegetable to be served with dinner will be steamed green beans. With everything else, this one thing remaining simple as they only need a quick trim for now. He stands at the sink, surveys the room, and plots the course.

"Leo, get me three or four clothes hangers. Plastic is best, but wire would be okay. Not wood."

As Leo dashes to get those, he sets up the pasta maker and pours a large mound of flour next to it. He also checks the water. It is almost ready.

Leo bounces back in, four hangers in hand.

"Okay, you ready? This is going to get messy, but we'll start with the not-messy part, dessert." He takes the pears and finds a corer and sets a small round casserole dish next to them.

"What can I do?"

"This will be an easy one. Once I've cored each pear, put one of those cinnamon sticks in the center." They fit snuggly on end in the casserole. Dave pours the reduced wine sauce over the pears and covers them. "The pears can sit while the oven heats up, then in they go, but off to the side so we can get the lasagna pan in. Next, we get the cheese sauce ready. All you need to for that is add the eggs and fold them in."

"I know how to fold!" Leo says excitedly, hardly believing his level of enjoyment.

Dave gets more eggs and cracks them into the flour mound and with a fork, whisks them steadily in. Gently scraping the sides of his flour bowl, more and more becomes incorporated into the eggs. Eventually a dough ball, too heavy for the fork, forms, so he continues mixing by hand.

Leo calls over, "I think I'm done. it looks all mixed."

"Great. This is the messiest part. Noodles. Bring the hangers."

"I admit freely I know very little about cooking, but what do hangers have to do with it?"

"To hang the pasta."

"Naturally."

"Here we go." Dave cuts off a portion of dough and forms it into a ball which is dusted with extra flour and starts cranking it thought the pasta machine. "I have this on the widest setting. I'm going to run it through to see if it will hold or needs more flour. He starts to crank the machine. "See how it is coming apart and kind of sticky?"

Leo, leaning on Dave and looking over his shoulder, answers, "Yeah."

"That means it needs more." He rolls that back into a ball and the coats it with more flour. He works that into the ball. "You want to try?"

"Sure."

As Leo cranks that ball through, Dave adds more flour to the main dough, knowing it also needs more. "That looks good. Now you fold in three then run it through several times until it comes out very smooth and somewhat rectangular."

Once a fairly good, smooth rectangle forms, Dave moves to the next step. He dials the machine to the next setting and runs the pasta rectangle through. It becomes thinner and longer. He continues on narrower settings until he reaches the desired thickness, creating one very long noodle.

"Okay, hold up a hanger."

Dave drapes it over the hanger. Soon the kitchen is hung with long, limp noodles.

"Boy," Dave comments, "I'm really glad Benji isn't seeing this." He leans against the counter and reaches to caress Leo's cheek. "Final stage, sweetie."

He gets the largest baking pan he can find and sets it on the counter between the sink and the simmering pot of tomato sauce.

"Bring the cheese fill-, ah, sauce over and put it behind the pan."

The water boils.

"Grab a hanger. The noodles are way too long. Cut them down to about the length of the baking pan."

While Leo does that, he places a colander in the sink, then gets a ladle for the tomato sauce. Dipping the ladle in, a thin layer of sauce coats the bottom of the pan.

"Let's get started. I'm going to cook off the pasta one layer at a time then build the lasagna up, pasta, sauce, cheese. I almost forgot." He goes to the refrigerator and pulls out the mozzarella. "That's the last of each layer."

"Isn't it going to take forever?"

"Nah, fresh pasta cooks in seconds." He drops four of the cut noodles into the boiling water and grabs a large slotted spoon. "See that? As soon as they float, they're done." He scoops them out with the spoon and puts them in the colander to cool a few seconds.

"Anything else I can do?"

"After you finish cutting up the pasta and give me a kiss, I guess you could start cleaning up. There's not much else to do at this point."

Dave works methodically building the layers. "What time would you like to eat?"

"Seven?"

"Okay, that gives plenty of time." He sets the oven relatively low as they have a couple of hours to wait.

"I'm going to clean up in here. You go rest. I'll join you in a bit," Leo offers.

"That sound like a plan. See you in the living room."

"You bet."

"I'll set my phone. Need to pull the pears out in an hour or so. Oh, the pasta maker, don't wash it, water will rust it. Wipe it off as best you can. Use one of those brushes," he indicates one of the utensil containers on the counter, "to remove excess flour."

Restoring the kitchen to pristine condition, Leo starts with the pasta maker following Dave's instructions. He washes, dries, and puts the pots, bowls and utensils away, and then wipes off the counters. Every spot on the stove disappears. Finally, the floor gets quick attention. Double checking everything with satisfaction, he finds Dave fast asleep on the larger sofa.

He considers waking him, but stops. Sitting on the floor next to the sofa, he scans Dave's body starting from his now bare feet and working up his legs, torso, and face. There is such a difference in his face without the animation that normally plays so easily. A light day's growth of beard adds darkness and contour to his normally carefully groomed face. His lips are slightly parted, a bead of saliva visible in the corner. One of Dave's hands tucks between his legs, the other reaches out, its fingers loosely curled around the edge of the sofa. Leo has gotten used to holding that hand as they walk or sit at a table over coffee. He slips a finger between the sofa and the warmth of Dave's hand. He leans down and kisses those fingers. Dave stirs, moving slightly onto his back, but his hand remains connected to Leo. The motion gives room to sit next to Dave's knees, causing the striking green eyes to flutter open.

Dave's sleep-slackened features resettle into a smile. "I fell asleep."

"Um hmm."

"Come here."

Leo leans down then gets on top of Dave so they can kiss. Dave holds him. Just as their kissing starts to deepen, Dave's phone alarm goes off. "Darn," he pouts. He reaches out and turns the alarm off. He shuts his eyes briefly, then opens them and looks around, thinking. "Pears, that it. We need to take the pears out."

"I'll get them. You wake up." Leo goes off to the kitchen and pulls the pears out. He sets them on a trivet he has placed on the counter.

When he returns to the living room, he finds Dave sitting up, leaning forward, his elbows on his knees. Leo sits next to him.

"Man, that nap wiped me out. Don't usually sleep during the day." He flops back, arms fall to his sides. He turns his head in Leo's direction. One eye closed. He scans Leo with the open one, reaches out and tugs lightly at Leo's t-shirt. "You got too much clothes on."

Leo laughs shyly but removes his shirt.

Dave leans into him. "That's better."

Leo drapes his bare arm behind Dave's head.

Resting his head on Leo, Dave looks down his own body. Pushing his lip out, he whines, "Now, I got too much clothes on." He pulls his shirt off and nestles back, soon adding, "Nope, still not right."

He wriggles around to face Leo. Raising his right arm and pointing down with his hand, he starts making a spinning motion. "Turn around. Face me." He pretends to still be sleepy and keeps his voice muted.

Leo does as he's told. He is sitting cross-legged on the sofa facing Dave.

Dave pokes Leo's left leg. "I want that one..." He pokes the sofa next to his right side. "...here." Leo stretches his left leg out and Dave covers it with his right leg.

Dave stretches his left leg next to Leo's right side. He pokes Leo's right leg. "That..." pokes his left thigh, "...here." They now sit facing, legs over legs.

"Good. Now I can see you. I like seeing you." Dave smiles. "I like seeing you a lot." They automatically take hold of the other's hands.

He slowly takes in all of Leo's torso with his eyes. The pale skin has occasional moles. He reaches to touch one. "Lean back. I want to give my eyes a feast."

Dave concentrates on Leo's body, not seeing the flash of a tear that sentence produces.

Leo subtlety brushes it away as he reaches his arms back to support his body.

Dave inches forward slightly. He rubs his right hand into Leo's chest hair. "I would love to see this in full sun. I want to see how it gleams when you face into the sun. I would like to see how it looks when the sun brushes across from the side, making it all look pale and as blond as the hair on your head, and how that would cause shadows on your body." He touches a finger to his tongue and smooths the moistness into one of Leo's nipples causing a slight gasp. "You have such sweet nipples. That got perky." He steals a look up to Leo's incredible eyes. "Bet something else is too."

Leo nods slightly.

Dave smiles and returns his gaze to Leo's chest and smooths the chest hair. "Wish I had a comb." Instead he uses his fingers to rake Leo's chest hair. Not as thick as his own, but still far more generous than most men.

He moves his gaze to Leo's shoulders. He almost laughs when he starts to think Leo is too skinny, reminding him of Salvatore and Mrs. Caputo. He wonders briefly if he is following a cultural preference but realizes Leo is too thin, worrying Leo doesn't take care of himself.

His gaze drifts higher. He touches Leo's beard. "Are you in need of a trim or growing it out?"

Dave watches Leo redden as he admits he needs a trim.

Damn, I've embarrassed him.

"Yours is more balanced than mine. It'll get heavy if I let it go a week or so, but uneven. Yours is very symmetrical." He caresses the beard, runs a thumb over the moustache.

He leans forward and inhales deeply, "You still have some herb scent. It's faded but there."

He finally gazes into Leo's rich blue eyes. "I've been sitting here pawing all over you. Hope you don't mind, but your body fascinates me."

"Don't mind. S'nice." He grins.

Dave glances outside. "It's getting dark. We'll have to draw the curtains soon. I don't think Tommy would mind, but I don't know about your other neighbors."

Leo starts to get up, but Dave doesn't let him. "We can close them when we get up to finish cooking."

"There's more?"

"Just the salad and veggie. Nothing much." He continues to fully look at Leo. That thick shock of pale blond hair that tops his face is probably longer that Leo would normally have it, but Dave likes it. He touches the edge of it, just to move it off the forehead so often lined with worry or concern. Such a powerful brain rests behind this patch of flesh and bone.

Leo loses himself in the world being created for him. Someone wants to give him all this attention and give it so gently. That finger brushing his hair off his forehead has more caress than most full body hugs. He forgets himself in the moment. The fear it could all be taken away so suddenly hovers just on the edge of his consciousness. He sits up tall, brings his hands to Dave's thighs.

Dave notices that the furrow has returned to his brow. He wants so badly to make it go away for good. There is so much about this man that frustrates him.

What is in there that is so hard to get out?

He takes Leo's head between his hands and leans in to kiss that forehead. "I'm so happy to be here with you."

Leo folds forward and wraps Dave into his arms. He rests his head on a firm shoulder, brushes the warm skin with his lips. "Me too."

They hold on until Dave quietly says, "I think it's dinner time."

Reluctantly they unwind. Leo closes the drapes then they head to the kitchen. Dave pulls the lasagna out of the oven. It is bubbling, almost coming over the top, edges slightly browned. Leo stares at its beauty.

Dave is very pleased. "Want to set the table?"

"Sure. What all do you want?"

"Don't know. Let's see what you got. I'm thinking something a little special but not too formal."

"Which means I'll have to show you what we have and let you decide. Everyday things are in here, but Jay has a lot of nicer things in the dining room." Leo leads them back. "There are all sorts of things in the buffet. I'm familiar with most of it about as much as I was with a pasta maker and food mill earlier today."

Dave opens a door and sees several sets. "Wow, that is a lot to choose from. Any restrictions?"

"Jay says if it's in a shared part of the house, it is meant to be shared."

"He is something else. I like him a lot. Benji too." He starts to pull dishes out to see what he wants.

"I like them too."

Dave holds a simple dish with gold around the rim. "This is beautiful. Too elegant for tonight." He puts it back and pulls out another, also white, but rimmed with a thick blue-black edge. "I like these, simple but very lovely." He pulls out a pair of dinner plates and salad plates. "Now, something for dessert." He finds some smaller oval shaped dishes of a dark green glass. "These. Silverware in these drawers?"

"Yeah."

"You pick a pattern. I'll get what we need from that. In the meantime, glasses?" He sees the china cabinet. "Never mind, I see them." He goes over and pulls out stemmed glasses. "I love the etching on these. We'll have to be careful. What'd you pick?"

"I like these." Leo has picked a very simple design. The handles are rounded and slightly long.

"Unique. Did Jay pick out all of this?"

"I think so. I don't imagine Benji picking out these kinds of things."

"No, Benji seems more the everyday kind of guy. What else? Napkins."

Leo opens another drawer.

"The ones on the far side. And one final touch. I saw some candlesticks in the china cabinet, but no candles."

"Drawers at the bottom."

"Now, we have everything we need." He thought to ask Leo to set the table but didn't want to risk embarrassing him again. It seems so often this sweet, shy man was raised in a vacuum.

"Come on." Dave takes Leo's hand in one hand and carries plates in the other. They return to the kitchen to assemble the salad.

Lettuce is torn into bite-sized pieces. Dave opens a jar, pours off most of the liquid and dumps them in.

"What's that?" asks Leo.

"Artichoke hearts." He picks one out and feeds it to Leo. "Hope you like them. I should have asked."

"Different, but yeah, good."

Dave cuts up and adds radishes and cucumber. "Get the herbs we set aside earlier." While Leo does that, he pours olive oil and wine vinegar onto the vegetables. Leo returns with the herbs.

"Make a cup with one hand." Leo does so. Dave brushes the herbs into it. "Close your other hand over it." Dave guides Leo's hands over the salad bowl. "Now, rub your hands together, moving them all over the salad until all the herbs are gone."

Leo is delighted. He almost starts to go to wash his hand but stops. He brings his herb infused hands to his face to breathe in the sweet aroma. Instead of rubbing them on his face and neck like he had earlier, he rubs them on Dave's chest, very pleased with his innovation. So is Dave.

At the table, candles are lit. They start the meal with a kiss and dig in hungrily. They sit close, Leo at the head of the table, Dave to his right. Stolen touches with a free hand or a bare foot occur while making quick work of the salad. They lean back and look at each other giggling.

"Guess we were starved," Dave observes. "I hope we savor the lasagna a bit more."

"More than likely. It smelled so good when you took it out of the oven."

"You sit. I'll get it for us." Dave takes the used salad plates and forks.

Leo leans back in his chair. He lets his head fall back.

This is more than I ever dreamed.

He runs over events of the day. How gentle and kind Dave has been. Even that horrible episode in the car was taken in stride. Leo tries to avoid thinking about that. Too confusing. He replaces it with sweeter events: Dave speaking that beautiful language; holding him naked on the bed or shirtless on the couch. Much better.

Dave sees Leo in that position when he returns and after quietly putting the plates down leans over to kiss his full, red lips. Tongues perform a brief dance before Dave breaks, "Dinner is served, my sweet."

"Wow, that is pretty." The green beans have been arranged in a fan with the lasagna anchoring the hub. Grated cheese tops the entire plate. He looks at Dave and notes a rather curious look. "What?"

"I have a request. It's something I've always kind of thought about doing someday with someone special."

"And that would be me?"

"Indeed."

"What is it?"

"I want us to be naked the rest of the night."

Leo grins and nods.

"Stand up."

He does so, and Dave reaches to undo his pants and slide them down. Tempted to get lost in Leo's thick pubic thatch, he looks up. "Later for that." He continues to strip the jeans down exposing firm calves. Leo steadies himself, a hand on Dave's shoulder for Dave to get them completely off. Once the jeans are cast aside he runs his hands up those legs, then rises to meet Leo in an embrace.

"Now, me."

Leo squats down to start taking Dave's jeans off. He gazes at Dave's erection, but Dave is right, there is time.

They take their seats. "This is so pretty. I don't want to eat it." He is staring at the plate. Dave reaches over with his fork and messes up the green beans.

"Now, *mangiare, splendido uomo.*"

"You talk funny." He takes a forkful of the lasagna. His fork falls from his hand, clattering on the table. "Oh my god, that is amazing." He looks at Dave, chin dropped nearly to chest.

"Best compliment I've ever gotten for my cooking." He takes a bite himself. "It did turn out."

Leo resumes eating. He has never wanted to eat so slowly. "What did you just say to me?"

"I told you to eat."

"Lot of words for that. What else?"

"Promise you won't deny it?"

"Okay, if you tell me how to say, 'this is the best thing I have ever eaten.'"

"*Questa è la cosa migliore che abbia mai mangiato.*"

"*Questa...* I'll need practice."

They start eating again, but Leo stops, "Hey, you were supposed to tell me what you said."

"Oh yeah."

"I'm going to insult your food if you don't tell me."

He feigns slumping in a death swoon. "A knife to the heart. I said, 'Eat, gorgeous man.'"

He looks at Dave briefly. "Good thing I don't understand Italian."

Dinner passes with savored bites and easy banter. Knee brushes thigh. A hand smooths stray hair.

If he thought about it, Leo would wonder where all these words come from, but for the last several minutes his mind has shut off. They eat an incredible dinner together. The best he has ever had. At the last bite, he puts his fork down, leans back, and stretches his legs out.

Dave stretches his legs out beneath Leo's. Leo relaxes his legs over Dave's to deepen the touch. "How do I say 'thank you?'"

"*Grazie.*"

"A whole lot of *grazie.*"

"That would be *mille grazie.* We still have dessert."

"You are so amazing."

"Just trying to sweep you off your feet."

Leo raises his legs in the air under the table. "Done."

"You are delightfully silly right now." He reaches out to take Leo's hand and pull him out of his seat. "Come here."

Leo lands on Dave's lap, his arm around Dave's neck, the other hand on his chest. Dave holds with both hands locked around Leo's waist. "You are so much fun," Dave tells him.

Leo shakes his head, smiles and chews on his lower lip to control his emotion. Emotions with no name as they've never been felt before.

"Let's plate some pears."

Back in the kitchen. "What do I do?"

"Pick out a pear for each of us, take out the cinnamon stick and then slice the pear in half from top to bottom."

"Wow, those turned out so pretty." The bottom half of the pears has taken on the color of the wine sauce.

"Yeah, that is a nice effect." Dave pours some cream into a small deep bowl. "Put them on the dessert plates, and just play with them until you like the way they look."

Dave grabs a whisk and starts beating the cream.

"Is this okay?"

"If you like it, it's perfect. Spoon a little of the wine sauce, doesn't really matter where." He stops beating to add a little powdered sugar and vanilla to the cream, then resumes whisking.

"That looks like a lot of work."

"It is, but I like it." The cream thickens to a soft peak stage. He adds a couple dollops to each plate. "*Voila! Dessert!*"

They carry their plates back to the dining room. Leo starts to sit where he was, but Dave asks him to move next to him instead, wanting to stay close. The tender pears are cut with spoons and eaten in silence. Sitting close and enjoying the sweetness of the dessert is enough.

Spoons down, they reach to find the other and turn for a kiss. Once again, they become erect. All day long, they have passed in and out of phases of excitement. Very soon there will be no more tasks to distract them from the release they eagerly want.

First, there is a final phase: clean up.

"You need a houseboy."

Leo almost asks what's that but figures it out. "Guess we should get it over with." They move into the kitchen one final time for the day. "Tell me what to do."

"Grab a bunch of containers so we can cut up the lasagna. Some can be frozen, some put in the fridge to eat during the week. Pack the freezer containers tight. I'll grab dishes out of the dining room."

Dave returns to the dining room. Gathering the plates, glasses and silverware, he savors the joy with how the meal went. Happier with how the day went. Even that puzzling episode in the car somehow fit. He realizes he is crossing into something deeper with Leo than he has had the courage to go before. So little is known, yet he knows him better than anyone in the world.

He brings the dishes to the sink and carefully places them down. Leo almost completes moving the lasagna into containers. Dave picks a smaller one fit for only a couple of servings. "Bring this one to Tommy tomorrow. He'll be glad to see you."

Leo stops a moment, "Was it really that scary?"

"At the time, yes. Now, it doesn't seem as bad."

"I'll start getting these all in the dishwasher."

Dave scans the kitchen for any stray bowls or remnants from the day's work. The only thing he sees that has not been brought to the sink is the bowl with the whipped cream on the kitchen table. He goes to get it but changes his mind. Instead he finds a spoon and rests it next to the bowl. He returns to help Leo. "These are all so pretty. Jay has good taste. I don't think I've seen anything garish or ugly. The glasses are so simple and stunning at once."

"Probably should hand wash them."

Everything is put into the dishwasher except the baking pan. Leo starts to wash it, but Dave tells him to let it soak. It'll be easier in the morning.

Leo starts the dishwasher then spots the bowl with whipped cream. "We missed one."

"No, we didn't," Dave counters. He pulls out a chair for Leo to sit with his side to the table. Dave faces him on another chair. "There's not much left. Seemed a shame to waste it."

He picks up the bowl and spoon, scoops up a small amount of the cream, and offers it to Leo, who opens his mouth. Dave intentionally puts more cream on lips than in his mouth. "Oops." Leaning forward, tongue replaces spoon to move the cream into Leo's mouth.

A great surprise, Dave's cream-coated tongue is accepted happily causing renewed arousal.

"I'm horrible at feeding, very sloppy."

This time the proffered cream drizzles down Leo's neck. "Darn." Dave very carefully makes sure to lick away every bit of that spill. Leo doesn't mind that it takes much longer than necessary.

The next 'spill' drizzles down Leo's chest; Dave meticulously laps it up, then coats Leo's nipples.

Leo runs his hand over beautiful dark hair. By the time Dave finishes the left, cream runs down Leo's torso from the right. Dave gets off his chair to squat low enough to catch the end of the trickle with his tongue.

Leo squirms. A new line of cream weaves through his treasure trail. Dave laps this up top to bottom, inching lower and lower.

A small amount of cream waits. Dave takes a little into the spoon and brings it up to Leo's balls. Sharp intakes of breath follow as Dave begins to lick.

Leo, hand over his mouth, mutes the delicious noises he emits. "Oh," comes out as Dave runs the spoon up one side of his shaft and down the other.

Dave's tongue swirls rapidly around to gather all the loose cream. Leo repeatedly stamps one foot involuntarily. "Oh, yeah, yessss!"

Leo tries to kiss him, but Dave playfully shakes his head, not quite done. One tiny bit of cream remains. Dave gathers it into the spoon. Kneeling between Leo's legs he brings it to Leo's tip.

Leo's eyes and mouth fly wide open.

Dave swirls the cream into a thin layer, its whiteness now opalescent. He looks up to wide blue gems as he wraps his lips around what he has wanted all day.

Leo's hands grab Dave's shoulders.

Slowly he takes Leo deeper and deeper into his throat.

Leo's entire body spasms with pleasure. Hands grasp the sides of the chair enabling gentle thrusting into Dave's mouth.

Dave pulls off and traces his fingers along the inside of Leo's thighs. "Shall we move upstairs?"

Leo barely shakes his head yes. Dave leads him by hand.

Leo gazes at the whipped cream bowl and decides to leave it.

They reach the stairs, Leo a bit dizzy. Dave starts up. Leo lags, and Dave's hand slips out of his.

Dave turns his head back to see Leo staring. "You looking at my butt?"

"Yes."

Dave reaches back for Leo's hand, guiding it to his ass.

Leo starts tentatively with the palms of his hands. He leans forward, one knee on a step as desire overtakes inexperience. Soon he massages the firm muscles.

Dave leans his elbows on the landing and widens his stance.

Leo moves closer. As his touch becomes more vibrant, he notices the heavier hair inside Dave's cleft and runs a finger starting at the top down between the cheeks, enjoying how much silkier this feels. Repetition brings him deeper and deeper until his finger grazes Dave's anus, causing an even sigh. Lips brush hirsute flesh, growing into a kiss. Kissing his way to the crack causes Dave to moan sweetly. Encouraged, tongue, instead of fingers, runs full length from top to bottom. Pushing the cheeks open, his tongue probes deeper.

Dave leans his head down. "Yes," he softly urges.

Leo gets deeper and deeper, eventually finding Dave's anus, noticing the difference in skin texture and explores it with his tongue.

"Oh..."

Probing as deeply as possible, it feels unlike anything he has had on his tongue: pliant, warm, silky. It reacts to his touch as if kissing him back. He reaches between Dave's legs and caresses his balls. Leo remembers how Dave had guided his fingers inside before. Now he does it himself, touching the soft pinkness, finger firmly against it, savoring the softness.

A gasp flies from Dave.

He sucks on his finger to facilitate entrance. The first time he did this, it was with wonder that it could cause Dave such pleasure. Tonight, the pleasure is shared.

"Oh, yes, Leo."

Dave pushes back. A second finger moves inside.

Leo eases out.

Dave turns and sits on the landing. Leo comes up to meet him in a new kiss. They break to look at each other. Dave's hand runs down Leo's chest. "I got you all sticky," he says feeling residual from the cream.

"I'll take a quick shower." He kisses Dave. "Very quick."

Before Dave can protest, Leo dashes into the bathroom and begins to adjust the water.

Dave, trailing Leo, leans back against the counter to watch him step in and draw the curtain. Its opaqueness adds a layer of mystery to desire. He pulls himself up to sit on the counter between the two sinks.

Leo turns the water off and reaches for a towel, hanging it back up after a quick dry. He steps out and looks at Dave. "You are so handsome."

Dave motions for him to come over. When he does, he takes him in his arms and says very quietly, "No more than you." He places a finger on Leo's lips to prevent protest. He traces the width of Leo's mouth and starts inserting his finger.

Leo accepts. A slight downward tug understood as a sign to lower himself where he begins by licking from the base to the tip deliberately. Tongue lightly circles the tip. He feels Dave's hand on his head gently holding him, the cock slowly accepted, toying with it more consciously than ever. Each step taken with this man releases hidden dormant feelings. He wants this because it feels good. He has tasted others, but none that matter. It is Dave. Dave's soft moans nourish his starved soul, making him want more. More Dave.

Fingers press into his shoulders a little more intensely, then slip under his arm pits, guiding him upward.

"Leo," Dave raspingly whispers.

Leo allows himself to be pulled to his feet knowing what Dave wants: to meet that soft mouth with his own. Soon, Dave's head draws back. Green eyes dart, focusing first on one eye then the other.

"Leo, I want you inside me again. I want to feel you inside me." He takes Leo's hand and leads him to the bedroom, finding an easy assertiveness with Leo. This willingness to ask, almost demand, rises from his desire for this man. Leo's timidity in voicing his own wants fuels Dave's keenness to step forward and drive their coupling. The first time he saw Leo, he wanted this slender, fair man, fantasizing eagerly, drawing him inside. That changed the moment they met. The raw impersonal urge to have an attractive man became more. Not one body part inside another; Leo inside Dave.

Sitting now on the bed, Leo standing before him, Dave opens that glorious box. Gazing up the body, every little flaw tells him this is Leo.

Climbing onto the bed on all fours, he reaches back, guiding Leo's hardness to his softness. A quiet "Oh" falls from his lips as he feels the initial penetration.

Leo treasures a slow entry. Once fully inside, he pauses and closes his eyes. He is inside Dave.

And Dave wants him there.

Dave raises off his hands wanting to feel Leo's body along his. He guides the hands on his hips up to wrap them around his chest holding them there gently with his own hands. A simple push back signals his readiness for the connection with Leo in the most intimate way either knows.

Leo begins to rock his hips leisurely to and fro. Red lips touch lightly on neck. Pink tongue eases out.

Dave sighs contented desire as he feels Leo's warm hungry mouth on his neck. "I want you so much, Leo," escapes.

Lips find Dave's ear. Only that name, "Dave," voiced at random intervals. The grasp on his arms eases, allowing him to rove the body so tightly pressed to his. Left hand stays on the chest while the right moves down wanting Dave's fullness in his hand.

Needing to see Leo's face, Dave bends and slides forward, momentarily breaking their physical connection. He turns upper torso and continues smiling, open-mouthed, as Leo resumes steady, deliberate rhythm.

Pleasurable grunts and nods assure Leo what feels so good for him feels as good for Dave. He leans forward to again kiss.

Dave sighs out as the kiss breaks. "It feels so good. You are." Eyes close to cope with the intense stimulation. "Oh, yes." Other unintelligible vocalizations continue. A shift brings Dave's legs to Leo's shoulders.

Grasping with both hands, one near the ankle, one on the powerful thigh, Leo kisses Dave's calf muscle. Sweat rivulets run down his sides and back.

Releasing Dave's leg, he falls forward, gathering him into an embrace.

Legs wrap around waist. Somehow with eyes closed, mouths meet. The kiss's urgency matches steady building.

Dave opens his eyes to see Leo's face beautifully contorted and reddened with their heat, aware his hands are on the taut flesh along Leo's sweat-drenched torso. The heels of his feet dig into Leo's ass, urging him. Glorious. Craned-back head draws damp, pungent air.

The room fills with their essence. One hand slips from Leo's body to grab at bedding, pulling it loose before reaching to touch Leo's face. Eyes do not need to see how sharp the nose, how red the lip, and how blue the eyes. He knows the fine arch of the cheekbones, how that brow furrows in worry or concentration, almost knowing the difference between the two. Touching that face or moving his fingers in that thick pale mane feels required in the moment. Struggling with the growing and growing urge for release, desire continues to build as Leo becomes more vital. This energy could last forever.

Leo raises up slightly, arms letting go of Dave's body to brace his own. His back arches as thrusts become more powerful, instinctive. Expelled breath grows in strength. Even the sound as his body rushes into Dave's gathers volume. Eyes open to see Dave's handsome face, wanting one more feature. "Dave," he whispers.

Incredible eyes open, focusing on Leo's urgency. Dave swallows hard, surrendering to passion.

Leo calls out, back arching, legs pushing up onto toes.

As Dave witnesses Leo's orgasm, he grasps himself more firmly. Head arcs back. "Ohhh!" Body shakes, legs wrap tightly around Leo as streams of white effluence spray.

They wrap themselves in a tight ball for several minutes. Ragged individual breathing synchronizes.

Finally, they roll onto their sides. Dave looks at Leo. Leo looks at Dave. Their shared exhaustion evolves to mutual smiles. Gentle touches reassure. For one, two more moments nothing must change.

Exhausted, a sweet shyness comes back to them.

Dave wants to tell Leo how deeply he feels, possibly loves. Tempted down that path, but always pulling back, he knows the difference with Leo.

Leo's feelings for Dave are uncharted territory. No role models showed him a path to explain the incredible happiness of being naked in bed after this day.

Dave's eyelids open slightly less with each blink until finally they close for the night.

Leo watches Dave drift while fighting his own demons, terrorized of having to give up all of this. That damn project, why is it so difficult? Numbers don't stump him! Too bound up in it, he sees no other options. Sleep remains on the fringe, so he goes downstairs. He happily finds the bowl and spoon and cleans them with care before returning. Dave looks so wonderful on his side facing away from Leo. He carefully kisses Dave's cheek, thinks for a second and kisses his ass cheek also.

He turns on his computer and opens e-mail, nothing from school or George, but one from Jean.

Dear Leo,

Someday I hope to really discuss your mother and why you never knew about me or the rest of your family. It is hard to say this about my own sister, but she was very strange. Growing up, I never knew her. I knew the garbage collector better. It was quite a surprise to find out she married your father. She never introduced him to anyone and did not inform us she had been married. At the moment, I don't remember how I found out. I suspect your father was the same.

There are so many reasons I am glad you are making a new life yourself. I am very pleased to hear about Dave. He sounds wonderful.

You'll have to tell me how your day with him went.

Love,
Jean

Life would have been a hell of a lot better with this woman in his life all along. After thinking a moment, he replies.

Dear Jean

Regarding day with Dave:

!!!!!BEST DAY EVER!!!!!

Hugs,
Leo

He sends, turns the computer off, and climbs into bed, takes Dave's hand, who squeezes his, and instantly falls asleep.

18

Jay sips coffee on the deck, holding the mug close against the morning chill, not wanting to go back in for more clothes.

The eastern sky begins to brighten. Colors define themselves across the beautiful landscape. A mild breeze ripples the lake and tousles his hair. He wishes Patrick could come off the road if for no other reason than this marvelous home would be more accessible. Jay knows Patrick loves this home as well as he loves his own. Odd, he ponders, how both received the places they love due to family and how differently. This home was part of a trust when Patrick's family returned to Australia.

The lake takes on the first blue tone it will carry on this sunny day, the morning blue deep and soulful that fades during the late morning and early afternoon before beginning a descent into the purple-blue of evening.

The door slides open behind him. Likely Patrick. Most guests never rise this early, especially Benji. That sweet man has never been a morning person.

Indeed, Patrick slips an arm around his waist and in his rich voice utters, "Morning."

Jay turns and gives him a friendly peck. "Morning. You take care of Sleeping Beauty?"

"Yeah," he yawns out. "This Steve. It's really serious."

"Think so."

After a pause, Patrick continues. "I don't know if I fucked up my chances with Benji or what we've always had was never going to be more. Sorry, bit maudlin this morning."

"Could be the end of an era." He looks at Patrick and puts his arm around him. "I'm sorry. He sleep with you last night?"

Patrick nods. "Still asleep."

"Doesn't work until tomorrow anyway. Funny. You and Benji. Always seemed a part of this place. Not every time, but I think of you guys together, and it's always here."

"Part of the problem. It was only here. Never in the city, not even once." A resigned sigh flows out. "Maybe it would only be good here."

"Maybe." Jay looks out on the view. The sun is almost up. "Gonna be too cold to come here in a few weeks." The breeze dies, and the lake sluggishly settles. More details emerge; trees become distinct. "Guess others will be getting up soon."

"Need to start some breakfast. Want anything?"

"Whatever you're making."

They hear the door and turn to see Diego who wears one of Jay's sweatshirts that comes nearly to his knees. "Morning."

"Good morning," they both say. As Diego approaches, Patrick notices a dry patch on his cheek. He glances at Jay and brushes his cheek.

"Tell you later," Jay whispers.

"Want something to eat?" Patrick addresses Diego.

"Toast?"

"Coming up." Patrick closes the door behind him.

Jay touches the slight man's cheek. "You did let it dry. Everywhere else too?"

"Yeah," he says almost proudly. "You leaving soon?"

"Nothing specific. You need to get back right away?"

"Would be good to get back by 11 or so."

"That'll be fine. Barring unexpected traffic, we have time to eat." He finishes his mug. "I want more coffee. Come on."

Other risen houseguests mill in the kitchen downing coffee. Patrick prepares a large pan of scrambled eggs. A covered plate for toast and a bowl of fresh fruit sit on the table.

Jay pours coffee for Diego and himself. He grabs an apple to munch and sidles up to Patrick. "Need help?"

"No, under control. So what's with?" He indicates Diego's patch.

"Dried cum fetish," Jay says quietly.

Patrick rolls his eyes from the eggs to Jay and back with an accompanying smirk.

"Should I get Benji up?" Jay asks.

Patrick stops turning the eggs and looks at Jay. "I'm going to be selfish. Leave Benji. I'll take him back."

Jay lightly grabs Patrick's arm. "Got it."

Benji woke shortly after Patrick left the room to use the bathroom, but that's all. Talking and making nice offer no appeal. He'd rather wait until everyone leaves except Jay and Patrick. Gazing out, unable to see the lake from this bedroom, he sees a few cars still in the driveway. Back to bed.

Last night upset him. In addition to sleeping through the party, he dislikes how he came on to Patrick and wonders if it truly is over. There's no guarantee with Steve. but Patrick is too decent for a backup. One car pulls away. Determined to stay all morning in bed if needed, he refuses to become sociable.

Finding his phone, it bears a message from Steve.

Hey Boss, have a great weekend.
Don't hold back.
Thinking of you and getting hard.

That endearment. He smiles and replies before slipping back into sleep.

Weekend progressing. You make me hard too.

―――――――

"I want to talk to Patrick a little then we can go," Jay tells Diego who has washed his face.

"Yes, sir."

Patrick stands on the deck gazing across the lake, a few boats dot its surface.

Jay walks up and starts to massage Patrick's shoulders. "We're taking off soon."

Patrick covers one of Jay's hands with his own.

Jay says, "I've been thinking about your suggestion, about planning a few trips together."

Patrick turns. "Popped into my head that day. But I like it."

"I want to do it. It gets too dull on the road. I'm tired of being disconnected and alone."

"That is quite a shift for you."

"Things are changing, it seems."

"I know I'd like it. Sometimes I get so sick of the asses I meet. All those spoiled little shits. Maybe having a friend along would keep me from burning out."

"Be easier to work my schedule around yours."

Patrick sees Diego pacing inside. "I think 'cum monkey' is ready."

Jay laughs, "I better get him home." They head inside. "Take care of yourself. We'll meet later this week. And take care of Benji." He herds Diego into the car, and they take off.

Patrick goes to the kitchen and prepares a carafe of coffee, adds mugs to a tray, and goes to the bedroom.

Benji sprawls naked on his stomach, mocha skin vibrant against the sheets' startling whiteness.

Setting the tray on the nightstand, he sits on the bed and gently touches Benji's shoulder. "Hey."

He stirs, turns, and raises his head. His eyes focus on Patrick. "Hi. Fell asleep again."

"Were you up earlier?"

"For a little. Jay ready?"

"He left. I promised I'd get you home later."

Benji rolls on his back taking that information in. "Good." He sits up. "I'm sorry last night wasn't right. I didn't like what happened."

"What are you talking about?" Patrick stops pouring coffee.

"I was selfish. Greedy."

Patrick is thrown. "How?"

"I was using you."

"I don't feel that way. Look I know you've met someone. It's not good news, but I don't get how you feel you were using me."

"I tried to use sex to soften the blow. Making you think we could still have a chance."

Patrick sits back and looks at him. "You know what? You have never laid such a load of shit. What the hell are you thinking?"

Benji is shocked. "But, I..."

"But nothing. What the hell kind of chance have we ever had?"

"Patrick, what are you saying? We have had some wonderful times here."

"Precisely. Here. Nowhere else. Only here. Have we gotten together for dinner? No. Have I called you because I wanted to hear the sound of your voice? No. Have you? No. It's always been here."

"You've been to the house, Patrick." Benji grabs the sheet and jerks it over his body.

"When you guys had a party, Jay would invite me. Vince would invite me. You didn't. Did I ever stay the night at your home with you?" He puts the carafe down, wanting talk more than coffee now.

Benji pauses. "No."

"Be very honest. Think before you answer. Do you actually ever think about me unless you know you are coming up here?"

At a loss, he reviews all the years they've known each other. "I have thought about you," he says very quietly.

"How? What did you think?"

Unable to look up, embarrassed. "Fantasies," he finally mumbles.

Patrick lets that hover. "I bet you didn't fantasize about cuddling in front of the TV."

"No."

"Not about where to go for dinner or what movie we should see."

"No."

"How about," Patrick tilts his head, "fantasies about my cock in your ass?"

A tear falls down his cheek.

"Look at me," he says quietly.

Benji looks up.

"I'm not being cruel. I am *not* angry. I'm facing the truth. We've had wonderful times together. Great conversations, but only before or after sex. And we never, ever, took it off the lake."

"No."

"Steve."

Puzzled, "What about him?"

"You think about him. You call him. You send him messages. You wonder what life would be with him."

"Yes."

"You've taken him off the lake." Patrick caresses Benji's face. "Benji, we fucked this up a long time ago. I should have called for a date. You should have asked me to stay over after parties. But we didn't. We were content to know that we could find our way back here. Damn it, Benji, we had the best we could ever have between us. It amazes me, now that I think of it, we managed to make it last this long."

"Are you saying we've had nothing but sex between us?" He twists around partially uncovering his quite-awake body. "Because that is bullshit."

"Sex has been a great part of it. But no, it's more. Last night? I was not being used. But I've been facing the truth since Jay told me you met someone. We have this golden, special, but very limited relationship. We gotta face it to move on. You can't pursue Steve or anyone and hang on to me. Let me go."

Benji sits quietly digesting the hurtful truth. "Then, what now? Do I never come here again? Do I tell Jay to not invite you to parties? What happens?"

Patrick relaxes. "No, you're always welcome here. Something tells me I'll be connected to your house forever. I'd be very hurt if I could never see you again. When you come here, you can no longer assume we'll end up in bed. It's not like we always did. We have to start looking at each other as whole men, not my cock and your ass." He watches as Benji busies himself with the bedding. Replacing a pillow, pulling the cover straight. "Tell me about Steve."

Benji reaches for the partially-filled coffee cup and takes a few sips as he regroups. He starts to talk about Steve, how they met, how it developed. Patrick, now sitting on the bed, asks questions. Benji answers.

Finally, they begin to wrap it up. "I hope things can work out for you. Not easy with the distance. Plans to visit?"

"He's too wrapped up in school for me to visit. Might be possible for him to stop for a day or two over holiday break when he comes this way to see his family."

"That would be nice. I hope to meet him someday."

"I've told him about you. Even about coming up here this weekend."

"What'd he say?"

Grinning, "Have fun."

"I'm starting to like him." Patrick takes his shirt off.

"What are you doing?"

"Getting ready for fun." He stands to remove his slippers then takes down his pants.

"What makes you think I want that kind of fun?"

"That," he says pointing to Benji's growing erection. Patrick puts on a condom.

"No preliminaries?"

"This is us."

Benji lies back, his legs apart, knees bent. "True."

Patrick climbs onto the bed and positions himself. He takes hold of Benji's ankles and raises them. "I could suck you or eat you out first."

"Fuck you." He chuckles. "No, fuck me."

This is what we are. This is all we were always meant to be.

He is glad to be here taking Patrick inside, likely for a final time.

They eventually calm, Benji's head on Patrick's chest.

"You better now?" Patrick asks.

"Babe, I'm more than fine." His white teeth flash against the dark tones of his flesh.

Patrick raises Benji's head up and examines him. "We need to clean up and get you home."

Diego falls asleep soon after they get on the road as Jay hoped. Last night was fine, but he wants quiet. Driving relaxes him, at least until he hits city traffic. He looks over at Diego. Fun? Yes. Permanent? No.

Nearing the city, traffic picks up. He wakes Diego for directions then lets him drift back to sleep. It takes about a half hour more before finding the address. Two cars are parked in the driveway. Diego's roommate must be home.

He pulls over and rouses Diego. "One of those Carlos's?" he asks, indicating the cars.

"Yeah, he must be home."

"I want a little more information about your business. I really think Leo might be good for you two."

"Sure, come on in. Might be pissed at having to come home alone."

Inside Diego calls out for Carlos who comes out of his bedroom dressed in grey slacks and a forest green shirt, open at the throat. His dark eyes flash between Jay and his roommate.

"You remember Jay?"

Quietly, with no tone of hostility, he replies, "Yes. How you doing?"

"Not bad, and you?"

"Fine."

"I wanted to touch base about something we discussed last night. I mentioned my roommate Leo and was wondering if you had some interest there. If so, I'd like to get you all together."

"Might be good. Worth meeting him anyway." Carlos glances at the groggy Diego. "*Chico, Duermete. Yo atendere a esto.*"

"*Si, hermano.*" Diego slumps back to his bedroom.

"I take it you kept him up quite late. You don't look any worse for the wear. How's that possible?" They move into the living room to sit.

"Good genes?"

He laughs and straightens the cuffs of his shirt. "He gets carried away."

"You're not upset? Diego thought you might be."

"Frankly, I'm jealous he hooked up and I left alone, but given his tastes...? Not sure."

"His little peccadillos?"

"The submissive dynamic and the cum thing? Not me."

"No secrets between you. Submissive/dominance has its place. The fascination for dried cum is rather unusual, I'll admit. What about you? Any special desires?"

"Thought you wanted me for a business contact for your roommate." Carlos leans back slightly.

"That's for him. I'm always curious about sex habits of cute guys."

"Cute." Carlos shakes his head. "Not sure that's quite how I want to be perceived."

"You moved here to start up a new business. And one that requires a form of intelligence I can't claim to possess. That's why I want you to meet Leo." Jay lets a smile light his face. "Perhaps cute isn't quite right either. Actually, you present a rather striking image." Palm toward Carlos, he circles his hand. "You're dressed as meticulously this morning as you were at the party. That's a compliment, if it didn't sound like it."

"I'll thank you for that one." Carlos tilts his head slightly. "Maybe you see meticulous. I feel comfortable." He pauses and thinks, "Ah hell, why not? Fantasies that I'd like to fulfill maybe. Nothing drastic."

"Such as?"

He shrugs his narrow shoulders. "Being watched. Be kind of cool to figure out a way to do that... Unusual places too."

"I need to get going soon, but if you're up for it, I'd be willing to see what could be done to make that happen."

"You're sick. In the best way, of course." Carlos moves forward again.

"You're not angry with me? Good."

"It gets frustrating around Diego. He's aggressive, so he gets a lot of guys I would like myself. But ultimately, we're good business partners. We also have a long history, and there's pretty much nothing left to get us really upset."

"Good to know that. You know, I never got a chance to find out how you guys ended up here."

Carlos laughs slightly. "Don't imagine that was topic of conversation with Diego."

Jay chuckles in response.

Folding his hands in his lap, Carlos explains, "In college, I worked for a computer repair place near campus. Patrick came in one day needing some work on his laptop, and we kind of connected." He notes Jay suppressing a laugh. "Not like that. Boy, you do think sex all the time."

Tossing his hands up as in surrender, Jay responds, "I said nothing of the sort."

"Not with words." Carlos ventures a smile, acceding his enjoyment of this. "Anyway, we got to talking. I mentioned about wanting to start up a business, and well, we just kept contact. I researched the market and thought we'd have a more realistic shot here than in our hometown, Deming, New Mexico."

"Never heard of it."

"Very southern New Mexico. West of Las Cruces, if that helps. Very poor too. Not a good place for two Latino, gay computer nerds to start up anything."

"I guess Patrick was a lot of help. That would be like him."

"Very true."

"Well, I do need to get going for now, but I mean it about Leo." He looks at Carlos. "I might get in touch with you for my own purposes too."

Carlos reaches into his back pocket for his wallet extracting a business card. "Planning to fulfill my fantasy?"

"Maybe one of my own." Jay accepts the card. Both names are on the card: Carlos Delgado and Diego Corrales in addition to the name of the business. "Interesting, your initials are switched." Jay slips the card into his pants pocket. "I'll make sure Leo gets this."

Outside he ponders what just happened. He has set up yet another encounter.

I need to go home.

19

Dave and Leo wake for good around 10:00, much later than either usually sleeps, but they exhausted one another. They kiss again. Dave checks the time. "Leo? When are you meeting George?"

"Around one, why?"

"We slept in, sweetie, but you should be okay." He tells him the time.

The day before yesterday he would have been very upset, this morning, only mildly annoyed. "I never sleep this late." Moving onto his back, he brushes something and grabs it: a condom from the middle of the night. A slow dawning, "Oh wow, that wasn't a dream."

Dave takes it. "I am shameless. Okay, I guess you've figured it out. I love getting fucked. Especially by you."

"I have no problem with that."

"I'd say let's have another round, but I really have to pee. C'mon." He pulls Leo out of bed.

As their streams flow, Dave asks curiously, "Do you mind that I always want to bottom? It would be fine with me if you ever want to switch it up. You do have an awfully cute butt."

Leo can't yet admit he has never received. He likes the idea Dave could be the first. "I'm okay."

"I'm not sure if it's the idea, but you are liking something. Oops, I must be liking something too."

"Um, could we get away from the toilet?"

Giggling their way into the hallway, they decide to make some coffee first.

"I can handle making coffee. You relax," Leo says as they enter the kitchen.

Dave sits at the table and looks around. He starts to shake his head in amusement. When Leo sits, he gives him a decidedly pissy stare.

"What?"

"Did you actually get up after all that last night and come down to clean?"

Leo covers his face. Slowly he draws his hands down looking between his fingers at Dave. The corners of his eyes have been comically drawn downward. "Yes, I did do that. I did. I really did do that."

"What am I going to do with you?" he says with a delighted smile.

He continues holding that goofy face as his voice takes on a whacky, robotic tone. "I do not know the answer to that."

Dave scoots his chair up to get between Leo's knees. "I could let the tickle monster loose."

Leo widens his eyes, and in his own, anxious voice says, "That would not be welcome. I would not like that. One little, tiny bit." He stiffens his body but does not retreat.

"That *is* one possibility," he traces a finger along Leo's cock. "But there could be a different way to let you know how I feel about this situation."

Leo, keeping his hands in place, protectively covering his sides, looks down at his emerging erection. "What is this alternative you are proposing?"

"Instead of taking you back upstairs after coffee and letting you fuck me, I could suck you to oblivion right now."

"My choices are?"

"Tickle or oblivion." He strokes Leo lightly with one hand, the other inching toward Leo's side.

"Um, I think I'd prefer oblivion?"

Dave crouches between Leo's legs, looks up, "Are you sure?"

Hands drop away from face and grab the sides of the chair seat. "Very."

Dave teases Leo with several tongue flicks, hand securely wrapped around the shaft. He licks and suckles the glans until it gleams, then circles the opening with his forefinger. The crown next receives full attention.

Leo's grip tightens on the chair.

Dave takes Leo an inch or so into his mouth then pulls back, the corona firmly held by lips, as tongue rolls around the tip. More is taken in. Full creative play involving varying depths and brief withdrawals ensue. Dave looks at this cock: Leo's. He takes it in to about half its length, the base circled with thumb and forefinger.

Leo relaxes his grip to slide his hand over the hand on his thigh. Leo exhales.

Was I holding my breath?

Very aware of Leo's hand, he turns his so they can hold each other. With Leo fully inside, he rests. Free hand cups the balls, gently supporting, lifting them. After slowly releasing, he looks to meet blue eyes. A smile flashes before returning attention to sucking, building pace bit by bit. A hand now assists mouth's action. Letting go of Leo's hand, he gently tugs on his balls. One finger slides under to apply pressure to his perineum, causing an involuntary jerk.

Leo doesn't know where to put his hands. Stroke Dave's hair? Dig his fingers into those shoulders? Run them on his own body? Grip the chair so he can thrust his hips into Dave's mouth?

Head bobbing, Dave rakes his fingers up Leo's inner thighs then gently urges him forward on the chair for better access to his balls, every move about giving Leo pleasure.

"Oh, oh, oh." Leo's hips begin to buck.

Dave continues as warm liquid infiltrates his mouth.

Leo's hands clamp Dave's head.

Dave's mouth fills with the slight sweetness and slight saltiness that is Leo.

"Oh my god!"

Leo trembles as Dave lifts his head to see the wonder-filled face of this entirely enthralling man. He rises to his welcoming kiss.

"Thank you."

Dave pulls back.

Leo stops shaking, hands cover his mouth. "Wow, I finally stopped. Is that possible? How did you do that?"

Dave tenderly rubs Leo's arms. "Is what possible?"

"That shaking, like I was still cumming. All over. My whole body. It wouldn't stop. It was incredible...wonderful."

"Wow." He stops and look at Leo with a delighted smile.

They sit with mugs of coffee when Jay enters from the back door.

"Oh my god, naked men."

Leo and Dave laugh.

"I forgot all about clothes," Dave admits.

Leo cannot find a trace of embarrassment.

"Hey, not complaining." He surmises from what he sees the date went exceptionally well.

Leo looks expectantly past Jay. "Where's Benji?"

"He stayed up to work things out with Patrick. They've had an off and on thing for years, and well, now with Steve in the picture, that may have come to an end."

"Benji seems so sweet," says Dave.

"Patrick too. They'll work it out. Oh, and Leo, I met a couple guys at the party who would like to meet you. They have some sort of startup company doing computer design of some sort. You'd understand better than me, but they may have use of your brain power."

"Sure. My, look at the time. I have to get ready to meet George."

"Guess I should get ready too." Dave follows Leo back to his room.

Jay puts his bag down by the stairs leading to the basement. He pours coffee and checks the fridge for something to nosh and is amazed to see many leftover containers. He opens one to get a scent.

Wow, that is going to be heaven.

Pouring a little milk in his coffee, he heads to the living room to check mail. Hearing the couple heading down the stairs, Jay goes to lean on the arch between the stairs and the living room but holds back giving them a chance to say their goodbyes.

"Midterms are this week, so I'll have to grade a ton of papers in addition to writing assignments of my own. Looks like another busy week," Dave says.

Leo responds, "I have to start some preliminary work on a paper. Maybe Wednesday around 3?" It doesn't look good for more than a few stolen moments.

"Guys?" Jay interrupts. "What's wrong with tonight? I looked in the fridge, and there's enough leftovers to get us through a blizzard. I was assuming you'd be back to help us eat it, Dave."

They cast shy glances at each other. It was so good yesterday and this morning, neither wanted to press their luck.

"Um, that would be good if you want," Leo ventures.

Dave barely holds back his smile. "I'd like that, yeah."

"Good. Dave if you have a minute, after you two say your goodbyes."

Dave nods, and Jay leaves them alone.

"That was nice," Dave starts. "I was afraid to push even though it was the most phenomenal day of my life."

"It was that good, wasn't it? I was afraid too."

"Uh, can I hope for even more and bring an overnight bag?"

"Counting on it." He kisses Dave. Desire urges, but he will be late if he doesn't take off now. "See you tonight," Leo says, grinning the width of a soccer stadium.

Leo's light and quick pace buoys by delight. If only it could last. All of this is wanted so desperately. His mood darkens the farther he gets from the house. Too much at stake. Winning the stipend is paramount. Some traces of his mood linger when he reaches George's.

―――――――

Dave watches Leo head out, then shuts the door and joins Jay. "Hey, what's up?"

"Nuffin, wanted to spend some time. I get to see Leo all the time, but the only time I see you, he has your full attention."

Dave grins, "He does have that effect on me."

"You guys are adorable together. How is everything going?"

"With Leo or in general?"

"General won't happen until gushing over Leo subsides."

"The word is smitten." Dave executes a slight dance step crossing the living room.

"He is too, but it doesn't show as clearly until you're around."

"Thank you, that's sweet of you." Dave starts to walk, arms held out, very deliberately one foot in front of the other, sometimes pausing as if catching his balance.

"That is not something I'm usually called."

"You hide it but not as well as Leo hides so many things."

"I'm glad you see that side of me." Jay briefly looks at Dave, pleased there is no evident denial.

His eyes are wide open.

"What are you doing?"

Dave looks at Jay with a silly grin. "Playing circus. Pretending I'm on a high wire."

Jay laughs softly. "Kind of dangerous?"

"Nah, someone's there to catch me."

"Who?"

Dave stops and faces Jay. "Who do you think?"

Shaking his head in amusement, Jay adds, "You really do have it for him."

"Well, I think he'd catch me. If he's not too wrapped up inside his brain to notice." Dave sits in the easy chair.

"Leo is one huge mystery." Jay crosses one leg over the other knee and absently scratches his ankle. "I never really get the sense he intentionally is trying to hide or be deceptive, but there's something he doesn't talk about. Something very off about his family."

"We all have secrets, but yeah, I don't know what it is."

"Dave has secrets? I thought you had the perfect family."

"Perfect families don't prepare you for an imperfect world."

"Dave?"

"For example, I'm horrible at handling conflict. We were always so rational at home."

Jay reaches out and puts his hand on Dave's knee. "I promise you, I am going to sit down with you and tell you about my sordid past. My entire life was dependent upon exposing one fucking hell of a secret that likely makes most seem like a school girl kiss."

"Now, I am curious. How bad could it be?"

"My name was not Jay Freed growing up. I changed it when I basically blackmailed my family."

"What about your brother?"

"When I left, I forced my family into sending Tim to an undisclosed boarding school year-round to remove him from the situation. Yeah, that bad."

Dave sits back. "I can't imagine anything so horrendous." He looks at Jay while cocking his head. "You'd trust me with it, though?"

"I'm not sure even Tim knows it all, but yeah. And Leo's the only other one who knows my original name. I was born James Martin Harris, Jr."

Dave removes his shoes as he lets that sink in. "I share one thing with Leo. I was my hometown's resident genius."

"Kind of figured that."

"Thanks. I doubt it's easy for anyone in that position. Very isolating. Kids think you're weird. Doesn't help teachers love you. Kind of brands a target on your back. Oh, and making it even better, I was small and ungainly."

"Formula for disaster. I've seen that enough." Jay turns and stretches out on the sofa.

"Well, when I started to understand my feelings for men, I kind of already knew I had to hide them. My family's cool. They have gay friends. I have a couple of lesbian cousins too. But when it came to school, I knew I'd be even more of a prey."

"Beat up?"

He lets out a nervous laugh, "No nothing like that. Kind of the opposite." He goes into detail about encounters with several boys from his neighborhood that left him ultimately feeling both used and isolated, survival the best spin to give it. "That is the pathetic start of Dave Azzurri's sexual awakenings.

"You are not pathetic."

"Jay, I know that. The experience was pathetic. I was naïve and let myself be used. Yes, at times I blame myself, but who gets prepared for shit like that?"

"Good point."

He smiles. "Enough of the Dave Azzurri tale. Walk me home? Show me some scenic routes."

Jay returns very pleased, finding Dave the most genuinely kind man he has ever known.

Leo sits in the easy chair focusing on his laptop. Jay gives him a peck on the top of his head, bringing Leo out of his ponderings.

"What's up? Any progress with George?" Leo's scowl is all the answer he needs. Jay sees Leo's screen. "My computer looks like that, I assume it crashed."

"Thought I'd start working on a class assignment since the project sucks major."

"I'd ask what it's about, but pretty sure if you told me it would be like you were speaking a foreign language." This brings a smile, a complete change of mood. "That's a much prettier Leo face. What brought that out?"

Leo tells Jay about the trip to the deli.

"Dave is truly remarkable. Spent the afternoon with him. You guys are both very lucky."

Leo manages a bashful thank you.

"I told him to come by around 7:00 for dinner. Thought that wouldn't be too late for a school night."

"Jay, thanks for inviting him." He hesitates, not sure what he wants to say.

"You and Dave have quickly vaulted into being two of my favorite people in the world. You know he's always, and I mean always, welcome." Leo nods. "And speaking of favorite people, have you see Benji?"

"No. Shouldn't he be back by now?"

"Knowing him, he probably went straight to his room. I'll check."

"I should have thought of that."

"You will when you know us better."

Jay heads upstairs and knocks on Benji's door.

"Enter."

"You're back."

"Yep." He curls, facing away from the door on his bed, hugging a pillow.

"Want to talk?"

"Nope."

"Want to cuddle?"

"Yep." He scoots over.

Jay joins him on the bed and spoons him. "Dave's coming for dinner."

"Good. I like him," he whispers.

"Me too."

"And Leo." He pulls Jay's arm fully around him.

"Most definitely."

"And them together."

Several minutes later, a phone call rouses Jay. He rolls onto his back to answer.

"Jay, this is Carlos. I do have a few projects I'd like to run past your roommate to see what he's got."

"Great! We'll be home all evening, if that's okay. Otherwise, we can find time later in the week."

"Couldn't make it until 10 or so tonight."

"I'll be up. Can't guarantee Leo." He replaces his phone and re-spoons Benji.

Benji selects a good-sized container of the lasagna. Opening it, he relishes the rich aroma and transfers it to a baking dish. Rummaging through the refrigerator reveals the lovely pears. Avoiding the temptation to wolf them down after a taste test, they are chopped up to serve warmed over vanilla ice cream. A book awaits in the living room, but from the dining room window, he spots Dave coming down the block.

Dave arrives early not wanting to appear too anxious, but it is hard to rein it in, especially after Jay's words of encouragement.

Before knocking, Benji opens the door. "Hello. Good to see you."

"You too Benji. I missed you."

"That's sweet." He leans forward and conspiratorially adds, "Somehow I doubt you thought about me at all."

Dave chews on his lower lips, stuffs his hands in his pockets, and says timidly, "There was at least a minute there somewhere...I'm almost sure." He looks at Benji. "Anyway, how'd it go?"

"Thanks, better than I thought it would be. Lasagna's heating up. Smells incredible."

"It was fun making it."

"And I appreciate how nice you left the kitchen," he says teasingly.

Irony raises Dave's eyebrow.

"Speaking of Leo, go. He is dying to see you."

Dave takes the stairs two at a time and knocks lightly on Leo's door. Leo opens it with a look of pleasant surprise.

"I'm early, couldn't wait."

Leo steps aside. "I don't mind."

Benji reads until time to call all to dinner. Leo and Dave straighten their clothes as they come down to the table. Benji and Jay sit on the ends, Leo and Dave close on one side.

The lasagna has been arranged on plates with a side of broccoli. Jay, first to sample, exclaims, "Wow!"

Benji takes his first bite. He puts down his fork. "Dave, I hate you." He picks up his fork for a second bite. "That is the absolute best I have ever tasted."

Dinner passes lightly. Jay tells Leo about the work Carlos will bring by later in the night. "He might be late, so don't worry about staying up. He said you could look at them anytime in the next couple of days."

Dave returns compliments to Benji when the pears are presented in their new incarnation.

The night continues in the living room, but Dave and Leo have trouble concentrating on conversation. Curled into the big chair together, they try their best to comprehend something one of the others says.

Looking at Benji, Jay says, "You two look exhausted. We'll clean up here."

Dave and Leo very civilly leave the living room hand in hand. Jay and Benji listen to the scuffling sound as the two scurry up the stairs. As soon as they hear the door to Leo's room slam, both break into laughter.

"Bet they're already naked," Jay says.

"Too easy. We'd better really clean up here so Leo doesn't spend too much time in the middle of the night." Neither of them fully understands why the clandestine manner, but they accept it. Of course, neither objects not having to clean.

"I like Dave," Benji begins. "Don't know him much yet but like what I see."

"Spent time with him today. I think he may be the nicest, most decent man I've ever met. He genuinely and quite simply wants Leo."

"I know one thing about him." They rise to clear the dining room. "That boy can cook."

"No shit. That was incredible."

"He'll be good for Leo, won't he? Maybe he can draw him out. He's such a mystery."

"They're good for each other. No telling if Leo will ever let anyone know what is going on in that fabulous brain. He may not know himself."

With no major cooking, cleaning takes little time. Once done, Benji grabs his book and heads to his room, hoping for a response from Steve. Passing Leo's room, muffled sounds of pleasure squeak out including something that sounds like Leo giggling.

Dave must be doing something right.

Jay stays downstairs to read. Legs stretched lengthwise across on the large sofa, he receives a text from Carlos.

On my way

Jay smiles and picks up his phone, "Tommy? Question. Do you like to watch?" A pause. "You know damn well watch what... Thought so." Jay outlines his plan. "He'll be here soon."

Carlos arrives about five minutes later wearing a light jacket over a short sleeve, buttoned shirt and loose, crisply pressed pants. In his left hand, he grips a briefcase. Not as small as Diego, he stands considerably smaller than Jay. He knocks a few short raps and waits. "Nice place."

"Thanks, come on in."

Carlos moves in an easy gliding step into the foyer. "Even nicer inside. This is a great house." A hand brushes the hardwood railing of the stairway.

"Again, thanks. Come on into the kitchen. The light's better. You can show me what you've got."

"Leo around?"

"Yeah, but he's busy fucking Dave."

"That was blunt."

"Saves time."

They settle at the table. Carlos hangs his jacket on the back of the chair.

"I'd say let me see what you brought, but I'd have no idea what it is. What do you want Leo to do with it?"

"I brought three projects we've been working on that are giving us trouble." He pulls a folder out of the case placing it on the table. "Something's wrong somewhere, and neither of us can see it. A fresh pair of eyes might. If he does any good and we sell any, he'd get 10%."

"Doesn't sound like much."

"It is for this. If he ever developed an idea or did something more intense, he'd get more. But this is just fix a problem for something that's nearly done."

"Makes sense. I'll make sure he gets them tomorrow."

"What's he like?"

"Quiet, coming out of his shell, in large part due to previously mentioned boyfriend. Super genius-level smart."

"Kind of a nerd?"

"If he wasn't so sexy, yeah."

"Sexy nerd. Sounds good."

"You should know about sexy nerds."

"Oh?"

"That's kind of what you are, isn't it?"

He looks at Jay in puzzlement. "There is a Leo, isn't there?"

Jay pulls out his phone and finds a picture of Leo. "Right here. See what I mean?"

"Cute and nerdy, yeah."

"Like I said, kind of like you."

"I'm not sure I like that."

"The nerd part or the cute part."

"What's going on here?"

"Basically, taking advantage of a situation that presented itself."

"Go on."

Jay reaches to unbutton Carlos's shirt. "May I?" No resistance arises. "I knew Leo and Dave would be busy when you called."

Carlos, bare chested now, says, "You couldn't have known I would call."

"True, but when you let me know you'd be alone, I hoped you wouldn't mind more than dropping off papers." He starts to slip Carlos's shirt off his shoulders and down his arms. "Nice body."

"Thanks, but shouldn't we move this somewhere more private?" He reaches to pull Jay's shirt up.

"Nope, giving you something you want." Carlos's shirt slips off. Jay picks up his phone and scrolls to a picture of Tommy. "See him?"

"Bearishly handsome. So?"

"That's my neighbor, Tommy." Jay points with the phone across the yard. "See that window?"

Carlos strains to see in the dark. "Yeah?"

"He has a very clear view of this table from his kitchen."

A jolt blazes through Carlos. "No shit?!"

"If I call him, you'd see the phone light flash." Jay removes his shirt.

Rasped through a dry throat, "You don't have to."

Jay leans in to kiss Carlos whose arms go around his neck. Jay's hands run over the slight man's carefully groomed chest.

Jay gets a reaction as soon as he brushes one of Carlos's nipples. He rubs it between a finger and his thumb causing a sigh of pleasure. "You like that. Stand up. Let me suck on them."

Carlos can't quite make out the outline of a man watching. The mere possibility heightens every nerve. Jay's mouth ignites his nipple, more erotic than he thought imaginable.

Jay kisses down his body. Looking up, he unfastens Carlos's belt. "Let's get naked."

Tommy has been naked for some time, fascinated how Jay takes charge of this intriguing man. He wasn't sure about this, but this guy keeps getting better as clothes disappear: nice tight little body, surprisingly round ass.

Clothing discarded, the table has been moved aside, giving Tommy a full view. Carlos crouches, his back to the window pleasures Jay, hoping the show looks as good as it feels.

Pulling him to his feet, Jay wants more, giving him a deep lingering kiss. "Ready to put on more show?"

"Yes."

Jay turns him so Carlos presents a clear side view. One hand toys with himself as the other plays with Carlos's smooth firm ass. His finger probes, producing a quick body shudder and sharp intake of breath.

"That's right, show him how much you love it. Don't stroke. Let him see your reaction each time my fingers dig into you. He wants to see how much you want it."

"It feels so good, Jay." He widens his stance to steady himself.

Tommy cannot believe how this guy reacts, bringing him to a rare level of excitement.

Jay keeps Carlos turned and leans to briefly suck but not for long. He stands back up and kisses Carlos's smooth neck. He whispers, "I'm going to spin you now to face Tommy. I'll lick my way down your spine. Avoid stroking. Makes a better show. When I get to your ass, reach back and place your hands on my shoulders. If you can, open your eyes. Focus on Tommy."

"Got it. This is amazing."

Carlos toys with his nipples, sending Tommy the message: I like this. The electricity he feels as Jay's tongue starts to probe reminds him to reach back to find his broad shoulders. He gazes across the yard to where he thinks Tommy stands.

Unknowingly he manages to look right at Tommy, who utters slowly, "Fuck." He especially loves Carlos's modest endowment, fighting a desire to run across the yard and take this guy into his mouth.

Jay stands and begins to enter.

Carlos leans his head back and swallows hard. "Oh, fuck..." He wants to get lost in the moment, but remembers Tommy. His gaze again steadies toward the man shrouded in darkness. Heavy diaphragmatic breaths match Jay's thrusts. He improvises a new pose by placing a foot on the closest chair.

Tommy yearns to join, or better, replace Jay.

Their height difference makes this angle awkward, but Jay has an idea. "Turn around and put your arms around my neck." Carlos obeys.

"I am going to lift you up. Throw your legs around me. I'm going to try and lower you onto me."

Missed attempts for this position appear merely as a teasing prelude. "Fuck me," Tommy says aloud. "Wow!"

"Ready for the finale?" Jay asks Carlos.

"Oh, yeah!"

Jay eases Carlos off and down. They move the table back in place. With Carlos now on the table, Jay gives specific verbal and physical directions.

From across the dark yard, Jay's instructions appear as tender caresses. Jay starts again.

"Jay, this is so fucking tremendous." Instinct would have him roll his head back or watch his strokes. He fights that by directing his gaze across the yard. Once locked where he thinks Tommy stands, he climaxes in rhythmic gratification.

Jay pulls out and soon adds his fluid to Carlos's. Across the yard, Tommy quickly follows suit.

Panting, Carlos gets out, "That was so intense." He stays on the table for a few moments and accepts a dish towel from Jay.

Soon they are dressed, and the kitchen is back in order, leaving no evidence. They talk quietly. Carlos, overwhelmed his fantasy has come so gratifyingly true, needs a moment before he can leave.

"Sometimes playing out a fantasy can be very disappointing. Glad I took the chance," Jay comments.

"How'd you get your neighbor to agree?"

"I asked him if he wanted to see me with a really cute guy who likes being watched."

"Why were you so eager to get involved?"

"Never back down from new experiences or interesting sex. That's both admission and advice."

"Thanks. I wonder if your neighbor was there. Never really saw him. Thought I heard something once but couldn't be sure."

"He'll let me know. You want a review?"

Carlos thinks, "Maybe. It was a performance after all. I mean, I don't need you to tell me what you thought, but he was the audience. Be interesting."

"True."

"Better get going. Get those back to me as soon as Leo has a look. Still want to meet him."

"I'll call you to let you know."

As Carlos reaches for his jacket, they hear voices from the living room.

"Hold on. You may be meeting him in a moment. Leo? Dave? Are you guys out there?"

The pair had taken a brief shower then decided to come down for a snack, wearing only towels.

"Hi," Leo says with some embarrassment. "Didn't know anyone was here."

"Leo, this is Carlos. He's one of the guys I was telling you about. Carlos, this is Leo. And the other handsome guy is Dave."

Leo steps forward and extends his hand. Dave follows. "Hi, sorry about the lack of clothes."

"No problem," says Carlos.

Glad they didn't come in ten minutes earlier. A willing man in the shadows watching is one thing...

"Carlos brought some stuff for you to look at." Jay gets the folder.

Leo takes the folder and starts looking at the documents with no hesitation. After a moment, he requests something to write with and sits. Pen in hand, he starts making notations and asks Carlos brief questions. Carlos alternates his gaze from Leo to a window that seems even darker now.

Dave and Jay have retreated to the other side of the room. "Kind of late for a visitor," Dave teases.

Jay just smiles.

"Story to tell?"

"You're creating your own story these days."

Dave takes his turn to smile. He finds a plate, opens the refrigerator, and selects snacks. Using the plate to point toward Leo, "He jumped right in."

"Don't worry. He'll be done soon enough. Then you can whisk him back upstairs for round two. Or is it three?"

"He's finishing already." He puts the full plate down so he can tighten his towel. "Oops. At least round four."

Leo hands the papers back to Carlos. "That should do." He looks over to Dave. "Good, you got us something." He reaches out his hand for Dave to take. They head out of the kitchen.

Carlos watches in bewilderment. "Uh, what just happened?"

"You met Leo. You said you wanted to."

"Okay, two hairy men walk in wearing only towels. In the time one fixed a simple plate of food, the other read through six months' worth of work making occasional notations saying that should take care of it. Then they leave hand in hand."

"Yup. That's my Leo. And his Dave. Kind of my Dave too, but in a different way."

"I need home and bed." He picks up the folder. "I'll look at this tomorrow."

"He'll be right."

"I'm believing that."

Jay walks him to the door.

Carlos looks up the stairs then back to Jay. He shakes his head. "I'll call," he glances at the folder, "soon."

20

"**G**uys? Can I ask something?" Leo puts his laptop aside. Jay and Benji glance away from vegging with the TV.

Jay mutes it. "Anything."

"At the risk of sounding like the world's most naïve person, what's Halloween all about?"

Leo and Benji exchange looks.

"You want to take this?" Jay offers Benji.

"Halloween is a wonderful excuse to decorate your body with outlandish costumes and makeup. In the right setting, you can win all sorts of prizes. Yay!" He imitates swirling noisemakers in each hand. "Of course, there are those who insist it's related to various religious beliefs, but that's not as much fun. With children, it's connected to Trick or Treat in which they go around their neighborhood, knock on people's doors, yell 'Trick or Treat', and get candy or other treats."

"Is that what makes it a big deal?"

"Maybe. Why?"

"Dave's going to his family's to help with his nephew's costume and wanted me to come along. It sounded kind of important. He seemed really disappointed when I told him no."

Jay turns off the TV and tells Leo to join them on the couch. Once there, he takes Leo's hand. "Dave didn't really care about Halloween. That's not the big deal."

"I'm missing something, aren't I?"

"Yes. Something rather important. Dave wants you to meet his family."

Leo shakes his head uncomprehendingly.

"If I was to ask you to meet my family, except for Tim, it would be a horrible insult. If Benji asked you to meet his family, that would be dementia. Dave likes his family. From all accounts, they're decent. He wants you to meet them. It means he is taking the two of you pretty seriously, Leo."

"Really?"

"And you truly like him, right?"

He looks down slightly, smiles, and nods.

"It's a compliment. It may have hurt him when you turned him down but not irreparably," Benji interjects.

"I am so tired of being so damned stupid about these things." He rubs his forehead with the heels of his hands. "I've committed this weekend now."

"Call him," Jay urges.

"Staff meeting. I guess I'll have to leave a message."

Leo reaches for his phone, but Benji intercedes.

"Are you seeing him tomorrow?"

"We're meeting for coffee."

"Tell him then. More personal. He'll understand."

"See, that's the kind of thing I mean. As soon as you say that, it makes sense."

"Hmm," Jay muses.

"I don't like that sound," Leo admits.

"I do," adds Benji.

"It's time to contribute," Jay says to Leo.

"Do I have to?"

"Yes!" Jay and Benji squeal simultaneously.

"I'm going to run out of stories. I don't have the experience you guys have."

Benji, hand to cheek in mock insult, says, "Are you calling us sluts?"

Leo folds his hands in his lap and looks shyly at them. "Maybe...if I knew what that meant."

More sure that he is kidding than not, Jay states, "I thought of something that is kind of appropriate given the topic of naiveté."

"Gee, thanks."

"There are all sorts of things that were strange or foreign when we first encountered them that now seem tame."

"Intriguing."

"Today's subject is 'seemed kinky at the time.'"

Leo looks skeptical and confused at once.

"Yay!" Benji responds.

"We'll go first. Benji, tell us the first time you encountered a dildo."

"That would have been when I was 18. I was very wild then," he explains to Leo. "I was turned loose on the streets of El Paso with no means of support other than what I could provide with my ass."

The look Leo gets on his face makes Benji pause. "Babe, I had to survive. Finding tricks paid a hell of a lot better than flipping burgers. The wardrobe required was much more fun too." He notices Leo's knitted brow. "Of course, some tricks can also be treats."

Leo, wary of looking terminally innocent, makes note of the word "tricks," having downloaded a dictionary of gay slang to consult in private.

"Anyway, soon after I was on my own, I found my way to Phoenix during summer. We were at a pool party thrown by this guy who hired a bunch of hustlers to pretty-up the party and be used as favors.

"Then he was there. Could not figure him out. Too old to be a party favor, but younger than most of the host's friends. Not the usual guilt-ridden jerk you encounter. And decent looking. Had to know more. A lot of the guys targeted him, so it took some time to get close to him. His name was Ray. The hustlers were all over him, but he kept rebuffing them.

"Leo, let me explain something. Most johns want you dumb. They don't want a kid with a brain. Anyway, all the hustlers were coming on to Ray with that street sass and attitude, acting far stupider than they actually were." He touches Leo's arm. "You can't survive too long without some brain power. I noticed as soon as whichever guy trying to hustle him started in on that shit, he'd send them away for something then move on before they got back. So, he made some comment to one of the host's friends about a book he was reading by Michael Cunningham. I took a chance, 'I don't know that one. I've read *The Hours* and *Specimen Days*. Loved *The Hours*.

"He zeroed in on me, and we started to talk books. He asked me to leave with him later. Turned out he lived a few houses away, which is how he knew the host. I had to ask him if he knew what I was. He replied he fully expected to pay. 'What's a guy like you doing paying? You're like, hot,' I said. He explained he sometimes got an urge for a peculiar thing and found it easier to pay.

"Hearing that made me nervous, but I went anyway, figuring I'd at least get to see him naked. Plus he had agreed to pay even if I wouldn't indulge him. I'd just get more if I did. So, we get to his place. Not as fancy as where we'd left but nice. He started kissing me and stripping me down the second the door closed. Who was I to stop him? He had a decent body. Not over developed. He led me to the bedroom and had me suck him while he stood up and I was seated on the bed."

Leo, unsure if he likes this much detail in these stories, shifts in his chair, realizing at least one part of him is enjoying the embellishments.

"He pushed me back and started going down on me. Totally unexpected. It's usually one or the other. I couldn't remember a paying customer wanting both. He was good too. Then he raised my legs and started tonguing my ass. I was so ready for him to get inside me, then he stopped. 'Here's the deal,' he told me. 'I fuck you now, and you go away with the amount I promised. You can make a lot more if we don't.'

"He headed to this built-in cabinet. It was floor to ceiling, about six or seven feet wide. It wasn't very deep, so I had figured it hid a flat screen TV or something. Wrong. He opened it up displaying the hugest collection of butt plugs, dildos, and other toys I'd ever seen outside an adult store. More complete than a lot of them. They were lined up by size. The top row had butt plugs and other small toys, the dildos started on the second. They varied in length and girth. The largest one being maybe twenty inches long and the size of a very large fist in width."

Leo's eyes dart back and forth between Benji and Jay throughout the story.

"He gave me the scenario. He'd start with a dildo about his size and work his way up. I'd earn fifty bucks for each additional one as he used larger and larger ones. I think I had to last three minutes for each. If I came, that's as much as I'd earn, and the game would be over. He continued, 'If you get all the way through, then we both cum while using a double-headed dildo up both our asses for an extra thousand. You don't make it to the end because you've hit your limit, we still use the double-head, but the bonus is only $500.' I think I had to make it through at least fifteen to earn any bonus.

"'Which is the starting one?' I asked. He pulled it off the second shelf. 'This one.' I ran my eyes along the rows. There had to be at least fifty, probably more. I knew I could make it through at least two rows," Benji says with a flip of his hand, "if I really tried.

"'Do I get a break between each one?' After some negotiations and an enema, I was ready."

Leo sinks lower in his seat, not quite believing this story. Seeing Jay's bemused expression somehow helps him relax.

"I couldn't believe he was so matter of fact, but trust me, Leo," Benji says as he leans forward, and conspiratorially whispers, "I'd seen weirder."

Leo's eyebrows knit enough for a winter sweater.

"He sucked me hard again and started. I thought he was going to shove them in and out of me then move to the next one. But he was skilled. He worked them around, in, out, twisting, tapping the bottom, and all kinds of things. There were several times I got very close and had to concentrate until that short break between. Can you believe he actually set a timer for each one?"

Leo's not sure what to believe.

"At first I was counting to see how much money I was making. I lost track and got into it. I knew I didn't dare touch myself or I'd never last."

Benji grips the sofa cushion he sits on to feign restraint.

"Sometimes I would see where we were because I was watching him. He was gleaming with sweat. His body looked so hot, his hair wildly sticking out everywhere." Benji growls. "So sexy.

"Eventually, it started hurting, but nothing I couldn't handle. It didn't last long. Usually only when a new one would penetrate. Then it started to take five seconds for the pain to become pleasure. With each new and larger one, it took just a little longer and a little longer. I was reaching my limit. I didn't care if I made it to the end. I decided to keep going until the pain was worse than the pleasure. I didn't want to stop, but there was only so much I could do. I finally had to tell him to stop. My voice sounded weird. It was hoarse and raspy. He told me later I had been yelling.

"I thought about asking for a break, but given how keen I was for money, I let him get the double-head ready. He asked if I wanted to do this on my back or on my knees. It didn't matter as long as I could touch him with my free hand. I needed that connection. Once on my back, he inserted a head into each of us then kept scooting forward working it deeper inside both of us until it was in deep enough for our asses to touch.

"He stretched his legs along my body, and I rested mine on his. I could caress his leg with my left hand and was even able to suck on a toe with my mouth if I bent enough. He started to stroke himself and told me to do the same. It didn't take long. Fucking amazing orgasm. Shot clear over my head.

"After crashing, I asked how I far I got. He pointed to the cabinet. There were less than ten left. 'Damn, how many did I do?' He told me I had taken 56. He left the room returning a few minutes later with an envelope full of money. I figured I had earned around $3500 at least once the base pay was added to what I had done. I took some of it out, partly to verify that it was real money, partly because I had never seen that much money in my life. I didn't count it. It looked like there had to be that much.

"It was kind of hard to stand up steady, so he offered to drive me home. I gave him an address close to where I hung out. I didn't really have a home and had to hide all the money. As he dropped me off, I asked if we could get together, meaning not as a trick. He laughed noncommittally. I was a bit upset as I still wanted to feel him inside me. Come to think of it, looking back and knowing what I know now, I think I would opt for him instead of the money.

"Anyway, with all that money in hand, I did what any street kid would do. I took off. Gathering my meager things, I bought a bus ticket and a few books for the ride and immediately found ways to blow through the money. I had just landed here when I took the last of the money out of the envelope. I finally saw he had written a note with his phone number. Can't believe I missed that chance."

Leo and Jay are silent for a bit. Finally, Leo says, "Fifty-six dildos in one night? I've never even touched one."

Benji bolts from the room.

"I should have kept my mouth shut."

"You may be right."

"Okay, Jay. I know I'm pretty naïve and all, but isn't that still a bit kinky? I mean one I could see as being strange at the time, but 56?"

Jay scrunches his face, "I'd heard that story before. When I asked about the first time he'd seen a dildo, I kind of assumed there would have been at least one prior encounter. Guess not."

Leo slowly shakes his head in disbelief. "I hope your story will be tamer. I am not going to have anything to come within a galaxy of that." He can only laugh.

Benji comes bouncing back into the room with a box. "Here. Your very own dildo."

Leo opens it. "What am I supposed to do with this?" He holds one hand to an ear. "Don't answer."

Benji, in a friendly mode, teases, "Well, if you don't want to use it on yourself, I bet Dave wouldn't mind if you used it on him."

Leo looks at him, pointless to deny the image in his mind. The tip of his tongue pops out as he dips his head and blushes. "Maybe we should get back to the game."

"Okay," Benji states. "Jay, tell us the first time you tied someone up."

"This will be gentler," he reassures Leo. "Probably.

"My sophomore year, Paul lived in Tommy's house. I was horny and enjoying my freedom, also very frustrated because I was not having luck meeting guys. Almost every morning, I would see some hot guy leaving Paul's. Rarely, the same one twice. My tastes were limited back then. I only chased pretty boys so didn't see the appeal of a beefy daddy frequently swathed in leather. Paul was always nice, but I wasn't in return. I couldn't get why so many of the guys I wanted would end up with him. I assumed everyone shared my tastes.

"He tried to make friends, but I ignored him. I should have at least treated him as a good neighbor. One day he brought something over, cake or pie, just an excuse to get to know his snotty neighbor. I saw who was at the door and was going to brush him off. Before I could say anything, he barged in and headed to the kitchen. 'Where's plates?' It threw me so much I told him, and he cut a couple pieces. 'Sit.'

"He tore into me. I started to get defensive, but he just looked at me. 'Jay, you're one of the hottest guys I know, and you're pissed because some old fart like me gets all the men you want.' I think someone I had bitched to reported it back. I stared a hole through his head not wanting to admit the truth. He blew right over it. 'You can have all of those guys if you'd change your attitude.'

"I was angry and wanted to yell, but he just went on. 'Tonight you're going with me. Point out the hottest man in the bar, and we'll take him home. I'll guide you through it, and you'll literally have your way with him.' I started listening. Couldn't deny his success.

"He came by around 11:00. He told me I looked like I was ready for a business partner, not a sex partner. He had on a leather vest, tight jeans, and boots. 'I don't have clothes like that,' I said.

"'Not asking you to be my clone, just for you to look more like who you are.' We went up to my room, and he rummaged around in the closet, picking out a more form fitting pair of slacks and a rich blue tapered shirt. I changed in front of him. 'Better. This is how I look when I'm saying I'm available. That is how you look.' I looked in the mirror and could tell the difference. 'Get rid of the crap in your hair. It makes you look like you'd get pissed if someone messed it up.' He was right. I rinsed all the product out, towel dried, and shook it into place.

"Around midnight we arrived. It was busy but not overwhelming. He told me to look around until I found the one. There were several attractive guys, but I wanted the best. Maybe twenty minutes later, I spotted him in the back near the pool tables. He was long and lean. Muscular, but not bulky. He wore his dark wavy hair somewhat long, not quite to his shoulders. Too dark and far away to be completely sure about eye color. He was laughing easily with friends. He looked in his mid-twenties, maybe older. I pointed him out to Paul, who asked, 'What do you want to do with him?'

"'I want to fuck him.' Paul wanted more detail. 'I want to fuck him all night. I want to fuck him until he cums and then fuck him until he is ready to cum again. I want to fuck him, so he'll never want another man to fuck him. Is that enough detail?' He told me he could work with that.

"I watched Paul separate my intended from his friends. Paul pointed me out. The guy nodded at me. I did the same. Paul brought him over.

"'Paul says you want me for something.'

"I glanced briefly at Paul. I almost said I want to fuck you but caught myself. 'I'm going to fuck you. All night. If you cum, I will continue to fuck you, using your cum for lube. I will fuck you until you are ready to cum again. I will spoil your ass for other men.'

"The guy just looked at me. 'To do that, you'll have to tie me down. At least part of the time.'

"'Deal.'

"He went to the bathroom, saying he'd be right back. Paul assured me he'd return. I told Paul I had nothing to tie him with if it came to that. He suggested neckties but not to make the bindings too tight. 'It's more psychological than physical. He needs to know he can break out if it's too weird. You're not going for sadism, just bondage. There's a difference. You could be dominant, never cruel.'

"The guy came back, and we took off. Paul drove, the two of us in back. I unzipped my pants, and he went down on me. I pulled his shirt out of his pants and slid my hand into his waistband until I found his hole. I finger fucked him while he sucked my cock the whole ride home.

"Paul pulled into his driveway and said goodnight. 'You're fine on your own now,' he quietly told me. I pulled the guy inside and stripped him down immediately. God what a body! Even better naked. Smooth, barely a dusting of hair on his chest. Full dark pubic bush. Nice firm cock I had to suck. Then I turned him around and ate him out. I told him to get upstairs.

"In my room, I grabbed a handful of ties out of the closet and threw them on one side of the bed, telling him to get on his back. I put on a condom and got between his legs. His ass had been so primed between my finger on the ride home and my tongue downstairs, I entered him easily. I went at it for a good hour, sometimes leaning in for kisses while his legs wrapped around me, sometimes leaning back or holding his legs out. At some point, he came and was ready to stop, but like I had promised, I just wiped up a huge glob of his cum and rubbed my dick.

"'You really going to keep going?'

"I turned him onto his stomach then grabbed one of the ties. I used it to tie his left hand to the corner of the bed. I continued around until all four limbs were loosely tied down. With a final inspiration, I used one as a blindfold, then started again. 'God, you're doing it,' was all he said. No struggling, he took it. That gorgeous ass took me over and over. All kinds of positions. When he began to moan, I knew he was hard again so I reached around to stroke his erection. 'Don't,' was all he said.

"I untied him. By that time, the sun was up. This whole time he had avoided touching himself, but at some point, he had to.

"As soon as he shot, I started too. It felt like it lasted hours. I collapsed on him, and we slept until afternoon.

"Paul and I got along great after that. I was sorry when he moved. Tommy's been a good replacement."

Leo, who had been leaning forward, listening intently, flops back in his chair. "Wow, that was amazing," he declares. "What about the guy? What happened to him?"

Jay speaks, "Benji?"

Leo, bewildered, shifts his gaze.

"Jay left his name out intentionally. That was Patrick."

Leo tilts his head. "The guy that gave the party?"

"Yeah," Jay answers. "We've been great friends ever since."

"Jay, I never know if you two are teasing me or not."

"One of the rules is to always tell the truth. Truth can change in hindsight. You must always tell it as true in the moment, so made up stories aren't allowed."

"How do I know you're not making something up?" Leo asks.

"Trust."

"I'll say this," Leo starts. "From what I've heard of bondage, I've had kind of gross images of cruelty and forcing people into doing things they don't want. But it wasn't. You weren't the least bit cruel. Patrick agreed. It was his suggestion to start with and didn't object when you brought out the ties or when you slipped them on him."

"Since then I've gotten bindings designed specifically for that purpose. Ties will do in a pinch, but there's too much potential for getting caught up in the moment and making a binding too tight or something."

"Guess what, Leo?" Benji interjects. "Your turn."

Leo feels inadequate. "I have nothing like those stories. The little sex I've had has been pretty basic. Certainly, I haven't done anything anyone would think of as kinky."

"Don't think kinky," Benji says. "Just something that seemed strange or unusual, but when you look back, it wasn't really so weird."

"Everything seems strange at the time." He is not sure if he is joking or not.

Jay queries, "Even Dave?"

Leo smiles. "Most everything."

They wait.

"A few weeks after that nasty roommate incident, I ran into Aaron, one of the jocks that used to come over. He tried to talk, but I walked away. He called my name, but I couldn't respond. It happened again a couple days later, but I ignored him. Later that week, he taped a note to my door. He wanted to sit down and talk. He proposed a time and said he'd be at this coffee shop, kind of like where you work, Benji."

Jay and Benji exchange worried looks. "Are you sure about this?" Benji asks.

Leo looks back and forth at them and then realizes, "Guys, this turns out nice."

Reassured, they both relax somewhat but remain wary.

"I stood him up. I avoided going where I thought I'd run into him. About a month later, there was another note. I almost threw it away without reading it but went ahead. It was more of a letter. He wrote about what had happened. Fucking Asshole got expelled. A lot of things came out about his crap, and Aaron only wanted to know if I was all right. I remembered how Aaron was the tall one who always got between Fucking Asshole and me and deflected things when Fucking Asshole started to get abusive. Anyway, the letter went on to say he was leaving at the end of the semester for an opportunity at a different school and just wanted to make sure I was okay. He proposed another meeting."

Leo places the box with the dildo on the coffee table as he pauses to gather his thoughts.

"This time I went. What was the worst that could happen? It was a public place, and he had been nice to me. He was there already when I showed up. I recognized him from behind. There aren't too many guys that tall. I think he played basketball. I sat down, not sure what to say. He smiled. I remember he covered my hand with his huge hand. I felt like a child. I pulled away.

"He started to talk about all kinds of things that had happened. He gave me a little detail about Fucking Asshole and how he was glad to see him gone. He also told me about his school experiences. He was transferring. He wanted a school that would give him a better education. Then he gave me a surprise, 'Besides, I'm tired of hiding being gay, and that is not mixing well with sports. It will soon, but I can't do it anymore.'

"I had to confirm that, and he said, 'Yeah, haven't told a lot of people. You're one of the first.' I wanted to know why me. 'I thought you might be gay too.' I didn't say anything, then he added, 'plus I think you're cute.'

"That threw me. It was the first time I'd heard that. It was strange enough he had told me he was gay, but that he found me attractive seemed absurd."

Jay breaks in quietly with, "Leo, he found you attractive. We've been telling you that all along."

"It was my truth," he says looking at Jay. "I hadn't expected anything he had said. No one had told me they were gay until then. I hadn't told anyone about myself yet. I was only 18.

"I took it all in as best as possible. He was leaving soon and wanted to make things right between us. I was thinking how could there be anything wrong between us when I never thought there was an 'us.' Then I remembered how he had been nice to me, how he had tried to protect me. It started to make a little sense. I still wasn't sure what to do with all the rest of the information. We talked more. He asked me about my school, and eventually we got silent. I didn't know what was happening. He finally asked if we could go for a walk. It was kind of nice but awkward. He was at least 6'8". Then he stopped in front of this building. 'This is where I live. I want you to come up. I'll understand if you don't.'

"Not sure why, but I agreed." Before Jay or Benji can react, he quickly adds, "And yes, now I do know. We got inside. It was small. The only place to sit was his bed. No way to do that without touching. Everything was so small around him.

"He said he wanted to kiss me. I tried to be casual, but as he started, it felt so good. We took our clothes off. He had close-cropped red hair, handsome too. Amazing body. Like I said he was an athlete, so he was very muscular." He pauses, unsure.

Benji perks up and asks, "What about the rest of him? Was his cock pretty?"

Leo stares at Benji. "I have no idea what that means." After a moment's contemplation, he continues. "Very pale, so his nipples really stood out. Oh, yeah. He had this massive tattoo down one arm."

Benji looks at Leo through one eye. "Better."

Leo resumes. "When he pulled his pants down, I tried to suck him as well as he did, but I'm sure it was a poor imitation.

"His legs were massive too. I swear his thigh was as big as my waist. Now is the part that was strange. After we took everything off, he put his shoes back on. After he gave me a condom, he got on his back holding his legs up. I wasn't very experienced, but he seemed pleased enough. I kept getting distracted by the shoes, though. Once, when he wrapped his legs around me, they dug into my back. It didn't last very long but was the best ever..." He shyly glances at his roommates and softly adds, "...until recently.

"We talked a couple times after that day, but then he transferred."

The three sit in silence for a moment.

"I warned you that it wasn't going to be too kinky."

"It was to you, and that was the point." Jay adds, "I would imagine if you ran across that today, you'd think it was peculiar at most."

"That seems right." He shifts in his seat and grins. "Probably use a different position that avoided the shoes digging in."

Benji and Jay laugh along with him.

Benji gets up and announces that he is done for the night, leaving Jay and Leo.

"Jay, do you think I'll ever stop being so innocent? It is very frustrating."

"You've changed more that you realize. Someday you'll figure out what happened in your past to get you to be like this."

Leo gives a short shrug and picks up the box with the dildo. "Nothing happened."

Leo arrives early for his rendezvous with Dave and selects the table where they met.

Dave approaches from behind and brushes a hand on Leo's shoulder.

Leo turns and smiles, watching as Dave takes the seat next to him. He reaches out to take the hand Dave lays on the table.

"It bothered you when I told you I wasn't going with you this weekend, didn't it?"

"It did." Dave looks to the side then meets Leo's gaze. "I really want you to be there."

"The subject came up with the guys last night, and now I understand." He looks at Dave, his eyes eager for comprehension. "I didn't understand you wanted to take me home. Halloween was a convenient reason. That it was important. I'm sorry if I hurt you. I never want to do that."

Dave takes Leo's hand in both of his. Leaning forward, he brings them all up to rest his chin. He takes a breath, then kisses one of Leo's fingers. "It's fine. I understand now. Next time I can be clearer. I still wish you'd join me."

"Me too, but I promised to lead a study group. I'm really sorry." He bends forward and kisses one of Dave's fingers.

21

As Thanksgiving approaches, the coffee shop slows, normally making the night easier, but two employees called in sick. Benji works the line more than usual, leaving less time for paying attention to the public areas. Because of that, a backpack lingers unnoticed at a back table. Near closing, a customer points it out. "Never saw anyone near it," the woman informs him. Most customers carry backpacks. This one could belong to anyone.

No one on staff remembers anyone near that table either. All he can do is put the pack behind the counter out of sight. Hopefully whoever forgot it will retrieve it tomorrow. Reluctant to rummage through it, he sees no identification on the outside.

Benji completes checkout, making sure to stock everything for the morning crew. Eventually no coworkers or customers remain and all task delaying his departure resolve. Grabbing his jacket and pack, he sets the alarm before shutting the front door. It locks automatically when the door shuts.

Starting for home, he hears, "Wait!" from a young man running toward him. Benji figures the guy's 19, maybe 20. Lanky dark hair flops over his left side and cropped very close on the other. Several piercings adorn each ear, one in his left eyebrow, another in his nose, and a stud beneath his lower lip. Tattoos show on his arms and legs, probably more under clothing. "I'm so fucking glad I caught you."

Benji interrupts, "You forgot your backpack."

"Oh, shit yes." Wearing only shorts and a t-shirt, he shivers. "I thought I'd be too late. Didn't know I left it."

"Sorry, but you are too late."

The guy moves around a lot, trying to stay warm as the night has become chilly.

"Once it's locked, I can't get back in. I don't need keys to close so they're not with me. Your pack is safe, though. I put it behind the counter."

"Crap! Double fucking crap!" The guy hops from one foot to the other over and over. "Damn, I can't believe I did that. Such a fuck up."

"Easy. You can get it in the morning. Not really a big deal."

"Damn it. Damn it." He looks at Benji. "Fuck, I'm sorry I'm not making sense. I need that pack. My keys are in it. I can't get back in my room. And fuck! I have a jacket in there too!"

"Okay, calm down." Benji sets his own pack down and opens it up. He finds a sweatshirt and offers it. "Put this on."

He slips it on. "Thanks."

Benji guides him to a bench in front of the coffee shop. "I'm Benji Martinez." He extends his hand, fleetingly shook by a very cold one. "Now, suppose you tell me what's going on?"

"Mitch." He gives a half smile, but doesn't look directly at Benji. "I'm maybe starting school next term. Crazy all day." He fidgets, picking at threads on the bottom of his shorts but slows slightly now that he is not quite so cold. "I met with a couple people in the bio department, that's what I want to study, then came over here to kind of go over things in my head. I have to sort things out like that." He laughs nervously. "Anyway, I ordered coffee, sat down, and tried to call my brother but couldn't find my phone." He draws his arms around himself shivering. "Damn, it got cold."

"Cold, or is more going on?"

"Fuck, I'm sorry. Yeah, more. I get hyper when things go wrong. That happens more than I want, so I start to get down on myself which makes me more hyper, and I lose track like I did with my phone even though I remember telling myself when I put it down not to leave it. I don't even know why I took it out of my pocket. Wait, no! I got a text signal so I took it out to see who it was from. It was my brother. Damn it, that must be when I put it down." He slaps the top of his thighs with open hands a few times. "Oh, shit, now he's going to be all worried because I didn't answer. That was hours ago. Fuck. So fucking stupid. I got here, and before I even sat down I remembered the text, and then I couldn't find the fucking phone. Must have been when I remembered putting it down 'cause I took off running. But then the backpack got left even though I swear I had just put it down a sec. I don't even fucking remember. Shit, then I got lost and all turned around."

Benji clamps his hand lightly over Mitch's mouth. "I get it."

Mitch looks at Benji with his soft brown eyes. "You think I'm crazy."

Benji cocks his head and strokes his chin with his right hand. "Cold more than anything." He then turns fully facing Mitch.

It seems to have calmed him. "Anyway, I finally got back to the biology building, and it was locked, got lost on the way there. Had to back track three or four times so that made me late. I guess they closed the whole building. Decided I'd go back to the dorm I'm in. Had trouble finding it, and when I did, I realized I left my backpack here. The keys to the dorm are in the pack, so I had to get back here. Of course, I got lost trying to find this place again, like the little fuck up..." he looks at Benji, and turns to face him. "I'm starting to work up again, aren't I?"

"Yep. But good you caught it."

"Shit, I fucking hate this. How am I ever going to be ready for school if I can't get though one fucked-up day. I'm sorry. I cuss too much."

"You can say any goddamn fucking thing in the shitass crazy world for all I give a flying fuck." He meets Mitch's stare. "Clear enough?"

Mitch laughs. "Oh man, that was the best thing anyone's ever said to me about it. Thanks, guy."

"As for crazy, I'm kind of thinking, and you better not take offense, you are late taking medication. Hopefully in your dorm room, not the backpack?"

Mitch looks at Benji for quite some time before turning away. Very quietly he says, "Atavan, dorm room."

"Good. Definitely the better place. Now, which dorm?"

He closes his eyes to think. It feels good having someone take this all so calmly. "Damn it, I don't remember the name." A shallow swaying signals a potential new rant.

"Only two used for guests, so it'll be easy to figure out. Older brick or newer high rise?"

"Older."

"McNeil, okay that's not far."

"I don't have my key." Slight swaying resumes.

"Stop," Benji steadies him using a forefinger on each shoulder. "You're registered. Have your ID?"

He pulls his wallet out.

"Put it back. Don't want to lose that too." He waits a second then playfully nudges a miserable looking Mitch. "That was called a joke. Far from my best, but not bad under the circumstances."

Mitch manages a bit of a smile.

"Do you want me to walk you there?"

Mitch nods dejectedly.

Benji stands and offers his hand to help Mitch up.

As he takes it, "How come you haven't run away yet? Most guys find a way to get rid of me by now."

Benji exaggeratedly looks under the bench, "I think you dropped your self-esteem."

"You're very strange."

"Glad you noticed. Now as we find your dorm, tell me why biology."

Mitch talks about his love of plants and making things grow. "I fell into it playing around in the backyard, noticing things about different plants, how some only grew in one area and others in different areas." Focusing on this so intently, he doesn't notice when they arrive.

Benji holds the door open for Mitch. At the reception desk, nerves ramp up trying to explain the situation to the woman staffing the desk. "I lost my keys, no, I mean my phone, but when I went to find it, I lost my keys. Wait, no, I know where they are, but I can't get to them because they're locked up, so I can't get in. Fuck, oh god, I'm sorry." He falls silent.

The woman simply responds. "You're locked out?"

"Yeah," he says quietly, his head down.

"ID." He hands it to her. "Room 326." She returns his ID with a key.

He turns to Benji. "Thanks, you really helped."

"You going to be okay?"

Mitch shrugs.

Benji addresses the desk clerk, "Okay for me to go up?"

"Sure." She pays no more attention.

"Thanks."

They get on the elevator, not speaking during the ride up.

Inside the room, Mitch kicks his shoes off, flips on the overhead light, and flops on the bed. "I am so fucking glad this day is over. What a bitch. Thanks."

"It's okay. How're you doing?" Benji shuts the door and leans against it.

"I've been better."

"I've seen worse. Should I remind you about meds or let it go?"

"Fuck, how the hell am I going to do this?" He goes to the desk for his suitcase. Pulling out a medicine bottle, he downs a two pills and grabs a couple of power bars, downing them in the few steps it takes Mitch to return to the bed.

"Benji, can I ask you something?"

"Sure. Of course, it would be my choice to answer."

"You're teasing me, right?"

"That's what you wanted to ask?" Benji's hands, fingers spread, go to his chin in faux surprise. "Babe, that was teasing. My first answer was serious. What do you want to ask?"

"Can you stay here tonight? I'd let you fuck me."

"Mitch." His shoulders sink with sadness. "I've been kind. You don't have to jump to sex."

"Too much again, Mitch." He slaps his head, not hard, but not play-fully. "I'm sorry. You can go. I'll be gone tomorrow."

"Please, I was just starting to like you. You have some completely inap-propriate bullshit, but you're nice beneath it. I mean, are you even gay?"

Mitch, disgusted with himself, slowly nods his head.

"Damn is that how you relate to people?"

"Yes."

Benji looks at the young man who now holds his head down. "There were two questions, which one did you answer?"

Mitch, back on the bed, studies the sweatshirt, "The first. Maybe both."

"That's good. The first anyway."

"Really?"

"If you truly want company, I'd love to stay awhile. As for sex, maybe yes, maybe no. Gotta tell you though, I'm involved with some-one. Unfortunately, he doesn't live here and, if anything does happen," he pauses dramatically, "I will be the one getting fucked, not you."

Mitch's eyebrows knit, and his mouth is slightly open until he can finally say, "I don't know what to say."

"You could say if you want me to stay or not, but to talk."

"No sex?"

"Not off the table, not guaranteed. Now, stay or go?"

"What would we do?"

"Talk. I liked what you said about plants. Sounds like the right choice for you."

Benji, still leaning against the door, looks around the miserable room. The overhead florescent light glows unnaturally. Four pockmarked beige walls, one narrow window, the bed almost as narrow. A grouchy chair faces a despondent desk adorned by a crooked lamp. "Before you get started," he turns on the lamp and turns off the overhead. "Much better." The resulting dimness helps the room's inherent ugliness.

Mitch starts to talk about plants again, but only gets a few sentences out. "Benji, why are you being so nice?"

Benji pats the feet of Mitch's outstretched legs to make room at the foot of the bed.

"How old are you?"

"22."

"Little older than I thought." He points a thumb at himself. "Clinically depressed with a large helping of compulsive behavior. I've been on…" He holds his left hand up and touches his thumb with his right index finger. "…Prozac, with little effect…" He continues to move down his hand as he recites his list. "…Zoloft, again not much help for me. Remeron, little better. Wellbutrin, you name it. I will not even begin to list some of the not very delightful experiences some of them provided." Benji lets out a sigh and sticks out his tongue. "I've been stable on Effexor for quite some time, even managed to avoid the side effects. Offering sex in trade for kindness makes sense. I have traded sex for money, food, shelter, and various commodities."

"No shit?"

"Yeah, no shit. Now, let me see if I can guess your delightful life." He studies Mitch.

"Don't get the feeling you've been diagnosed and are kind of playing with meds and dosage. Hopefully you didn't try to self-medicate with whatever was handy, but if you do…" Benji places a gentle hand on Mitch's leg. "…you're playing with fire. Too easy to get hooked. Probably school was the shits. Wouldn't doubt you were thought a behavior problem by teachers who could never get more creative than giving you detention. Didn't make a ton of friends either. Maybe dropped out? Being gay didn't help either. How'm I doing?"

Mitch stares at Benji bug-eyed. "Holy fuck." He backs up against the wall at the head of the bed.

"Must have gotten pretty close." He absentmindedly kicks off his shoes.

"Not officially diagnosed, but yeah, all the rest. You too! Really? You look so normal."

"I am deeply wounded." He laughs. "Before things got better for me, I did all sorts of things to telegraph what was happening and how strange I felt and how strange I thought I was. You've done it with piercing and ink. I used to dress in some of the most outlandish clothes. Acted out a lot sexually too." He's drawn his feet up and now sits cross-legged.

"Do you think I look weird?"

"Maybe you're trying to tell people how weird you feel."

"Thanks?"

"You seem much calmer now. That would have sent you down a spiral earlier."

"Yeah, I feel better."

They fall silent for a few moments.

"Benji? How'd you get to this," he indicates with a sweep of his hand, "from all that?"

"Lots of help from two very special people I met, getting the right treatment, and refocusing my obsessions in better ways was most of it. But it's been a lot of work that never fully ends."

"You just look so...I don't know. I mean, look at you. No way I guessed any of that."

"No one does. But it used to be very clear."

"Are you telling me to ditch the metal? My brother pushes that constantly."

"It serves you for now, I think. Besides if you come here, you'll see people a lot more over the top than you."

"How can any of that happen to me? I can't just find two guys who will take me in." He starts moving away from the wall a little.

"That was luck, but you can do the other things. The student clinic has a great program for guys like us. It helped me. You'd meet others. And as for refocusing your obsessions, you may have taken that step with botany."

"What do you obsess about?"

Benji pushes his shirt sleeve up and flexes.

Mitch laughs, the first comfortable one of the night. "You're huge. I don't think I could ever have a body like yours."

"Not exactly, you're taller with finer bone structure, so you wouldn't get the bulk. I used to be skinnier than you."

Mitch leans forward, one leg up, an arm resting on it. "Can I ask you something?"

Benji has an urge to tease him about asking permission again, but holds off. "Sure."

"Do you think I can do this?"

Again, he fights the urge to tease, but senses direct answers would be better now, "I have no idea. I've known you, what? Maybe an hour? Hour and a half? Have you asked yourself?"

He looks up to meet Benji's eyes briefly. A look of confusion takes hold. "I don't know." Shifting around, he sits next to Benji.

"I would love to tell you I think it's the best thing for you. What would you do if you stay in…? I don't know where you're from."

"Bum-fuck middle of nowhere northeastern Colorado. No place you've heard of, nor should."

"Bum-fuck would tip the odds in favor of school."

Mitch starts to laugh in earnest and reaches for Benji's hand. "I have to think more about it all. If I did come here, could I get in touch with you? It would help to know a friendly face."

Squeezing his hand, he says, "I think that would be fine."

"I would also like to ask you if you'd stay tonight. We don't have to do anything, just sleep."

"Get serious." He feels Mitch start to pull his hand away, so he holds it tighter. "Look at this room. The floor is disgusting. That chair will collapse if I look at it too hard, and the desk's wholly unsuitable. That leaves this narrow bed for both of us to sleep in. There is no way I could sleep that closely to someone as cute as you and not have something happen."

Mitch feels better than he has in months, if not years. Maybe it is possible. "Can I ask you something else?"

"Okay, but you don't have to keep asking. I give you full permission to ask anything the rest of the night." He shifts closer.

"What you said about meeting other guys like me. I wouldn't be alone here? Back home I was the only one who looked and acted like this. I was the only gay kid too."

"You were the only one who admitted to being gay, not the only one. Yeah, there are others like us. Both in terms of dealing with mental health crap and being gay."

Mitch leans into Benji who puts his arm around the younger man's shoulders. They sit that way some time as Mitch processes a lot of new information. Up and down all day. At times, flying, at times, very close to crashing. Now with this man's arm around him, a sense of seldom felt calmness kindles. Wanting desperately more out of life, his head lazes on Benji's solid chest. His arm goes around the firm waist as Benji strokes his head.

Curling into a comfortable fetal position, "Benji, can I kiss you?" comes out faintly.

"Promise me one thing, I know how it works with guys like us."

"What?" He turns his head to face Benji.

"Promise not to fall in love. It never goes well. We'd be better as friends."

"That happens to you too?"

"More often than I'd like."

"I can try." Stretching up to meet Benji's soft lips, a tentative tongue flick finds welcome into a warm mouth. He accepts the tongue offered in return and twists around until his body presses into Benji's.

They pull apart to look at each other. "You have such soft, dark eyes," Benji states. "You're going to become a very handsome man."

Mitch presses back for more kissing. Talk like that makes it difficult not to fall for this diminutive muscleman.

They maneuver until both face each other on their sides. He feels Benji caressing his bare arms. Mitch's hands explore. He tugs at the tautly worn shirt covering a body he must see. They become naked on the tight bed, Mitch's piercings and tattoos now on full display for Benji to wonder at in the dim light.

Both nipples have posts. A ring garnishes his navel. Small metal rivets form a short line on the left side of his torso.

A poplar tree rooted in ground at his left elbow grows to reach the shoulder. His right arm has his name in script, starting at the shoulder going to elbow. From what Benji can tell at this angle, graceful fern fronds unfurl on each calf. A garland of red roses mixed with leaves drapes from one shoulder to the other in a graceful downward arch. Oranges and reds form a sunset surrounding his navel. A vine seemingly grows out of his crotch and winds down to end very near the left knee.

Benji starts kissing the poplar, works up that arm, over his face and down the other arm to his name. Roses are savored as if they produce scent. Both nipple posts receive gentle nibbles. Tongue flicks at the navel ring, moving it luxuriously from side to side. Saliva cools the burning sunburst. A metal stud, visible now between erection and lovely balls, accepts kisses, a ring embedded in his perineum is gently tugged first with finger and thumb then between teeth. Mitch's leg is raised so a tongue can trace the length of vine from root to tip. Benji coaxes Mitch onto his belly.

Now Benji sees the rest of Mitch's work. Both calves indeed have fern fronds. The trunk of an oak tree starting at the crack of his boyish ass develops into full foliage across the top of his back. The only animal, an orange tabby, sits on one of the branches. Pale flesh offsets the ink colors. The ferns are properly misted. Finally, the tree is massaged under strong fingers. The cat receives extra attention, its purring resonating in Mitch's mind.

Done in stubborn defiance to a drab life, all piercings and tattoos, no detail ignored, gain acceptance through dozens of kisses and nibbles, as beautiful as he wants to believe. These marvels created on his body find acceptance and love for the first time.

The body itself receives attention. Still on his stomach, Mitch feels powerful fingers dig stalwartly into his flesh. That tongue that told the beauty of vine's tendrils and fern fronds laps at his crack before finding its way into the only hairy region. The forest parted, his sensitive anus receives the same ministrations given his body art.

A minor confusion intrudes as he remembers what Benji said about who will be doing what. Then Benji turns him over.

His testes next welcome exquisite treatment from warm mouth and gentle, capable hands. Finally, his erection receives attention, the shaft soon glistening. Lips and tongue tenderly tease the head.

"Incredible," quietly slips between his lips. "This is fucking incredible."

Embers smoldering through the careful stoking of body burst into flaming passion. Animal passion wakes. Hips thrust. Hands reach to knead flesh.

Mitch feels strong.

He takes charge with new confidence and unfamiliar proficiency. Dormant skills burst forward to pleasure this man who gives so much.

Legs parted and raised, Mitch begins pleasuring Benji's ass, a previously repugnant concept. Eagerness replaces hesitancy. Tongue probes followed by finger.

This man wants me inside. Me inside him.

As it sinks in, a sad realization dawns: no protection.

He was ready to let himself bottom, damn the consequences, but he cannot do that to this man. "Benji," he starts apologetically, "I didn't bring condoms. I didn't think I'd need them."

Benji grins at him. "Front pocket of my pack. Lube too. Ya never know."

He finds Benji's pack and soon rolls the condom down.

He finds no distraction nor hope to complete hurriedly, only a desire to be inside this man. Beginning slowly, Benji's legs around his waist, he focuses on the powerful body below him. Pleasure written on the dark, roundish face gives permission to become more forceful.

They kiss as Mitch adjusts to this less familiar role, loving it, feeling as strong in spirit as Benji's body. Too skinny legs now possess potency to power his thrusts.

Mitch finds new delights in each position discovered, finally settling on his back with Benji straddling him. Unable to hold off any longer, his fingers dig into powerful thighs. Panting builds volume until one thrust carries him over the top.

Benji's own orgasm follows, depositing satiny globs onto Mitch's verdant torso.

They gaze at each other. Mitch rubs Benji's cum into his skin.

Benji eases Mitch's waning hardness out of his body.

Both awake and eager to talk, Benji starts while holding one of Mitch's hands. "You surprised me."

Mitch smiles. "I was doing things I never thought about as if they were completely natural."

"Babe, they are natural."

"Yeah, that isn't quite what I mean, but you understand." He looks at Benji with a new curiosity. "No one's ever done that to me. With the ink and metal. It felt incredible."

He mulls it over then laughs. "Compulsion comes in handy sometimes. Did you design them?"

"Most."

"I don't imagine Bum-fuck has a slew of talented tattoo artists. Where'd you get them done?"

"The sunburst was first. I ran away to Denver when I was 15 and hooked up with a bunch of kids that all had tattoos. It's the only one I didn't design. Found ways to get back to have the rest done over the years. Not sure if I'll get more or not."

"You really have a passion for plants. Makes sense the sunburst wasn't yours. The rest are all living things. Anything special about the kitty?"

"Memorial to Linus, my cat when I was growing up. Loved that little guy. He was in trees a lot."

After a few moments of silence, Mitch asks, "Benji? You know how I promised not to fall for you? After this, how?"

Benji starts to laugh in a kind, unteasing way. "Mitch, I suspect you don't know many who revel in being gay."

"Uh, none."

"When you start, you're going to meet guys who'll look into your liquid brown eyes or see your lithe sweet body and readily give it up for you." He casts a glance at Mitch, "And I suspect you'll meet a few who'd like to get inside that pretty ass of yours too."

Belief he can do this germinates. "You really don't like to fuck?"

"I'll do it once in a blue moon. I have the feeling you'd want to switch it up a bit more. Besides I'm not your type."

Mitch starts to protest.

"Close your eyes," Benji suggests.

He obeys.

"Think about all the times you've jacked off in the last month. Take your time and let me know when you're done."

A few moments later, "Okay, done."

"Did you remember all the guys you fantasized about?"

"Yeah, so?"

"Any of them remotely look like me?"

Mitch looks at Benji for a few seconds before his face slowly dissolves into an easy smile. "Shut up."

"What did you see?"

"Well, not exclusive, but yeah. Skinny, nerdy guys."

"Oh lord, I better not introduce you to Leo."

"Who's that?"

"Roommate. Very definition of gorgeous nerd. Slender, super-super smart, and more handsome than he'll ever realize. He's taken though. Enamored with Dave."

"They the two you mentioned?"

"No, Leo came into the house this semester. He met Dave a few weeks later. Jay, my other roommate is one of the two. The second used to live there, but now lives in Germany."

"What kind of a house do you live in? All these perfect guys are gay?"

"We're not without flaws and not all gay men you meet are good. You'll meet all sorts as you go along, probably not in Bum-fuck, though."

Mitch yawns, it is very late. "Are you staying?"

"If you want."

"I want."

"How long are you going to be here?"

"Leaving tomorrow evening. Have an appointment at financial aid in the early afternoon then go home and figure out how to make it work."

"You going to be fine tomorrow?"

"Yeah, this helped more than you know. If nothing panics me, I'll be fine. I don't always dissolve into the mess you met earlier.'"

"If you like, I'll walk you back to the biology building in the morning and give you a tour. And we'll have to get your pack. I'd love it if once you're done with financial aid you stop by the coffee shop to say farewell."

"That'd be good."

Mitch falls asleep in Benji's arms.

Rising too early for the biology building to be open, they retrieve Mitch's backpack and find breakfast. As Benji guides a much calmer Mitch around the campus, the sense of disorientation dissipates. He identifies landmarks. Benji's presence calms him too.

Once they retrieve his phone, he immediately calls his brother to explain, not an easy scene for him to play out in front of someone new.

"Al, stop. I'm okay. It got crazy. I nearly lost it, but I met someone who helped." There is a pause while Mitch listens.

Benji tries keeping his attention on everything else, but it's difficult.

"Look, I'm going to say this once more. Listen, okay?" Another brief pause. "It was stupid leaving my phone, and it set off a series of panics, but I met this guy who seems to be like me in many ways who took me under his wing." There is another pause, but he cuts in with a little anger, "No, not like that. Damn it, listen! It was good, really good. I feel great today." He looks at Benji and shrugs. "Al, listen to my voice. How does it sound?" He sticks his tongue out at the phone as he listens. "Right, not hyper, not crazy. I'm very glad you offered to come with me but very glad you didn't. You can't come up here all the time. I got through one day, I can get through more. I already know I'm not alone here. There are other people just as crazy. There are other guys who are gay."

He puts the phone against his chest to shield so he can look at Benji, "Oh my god, I've never said it out loud like that. Fuck, that's incredible."

He returns to the call. "Yes, I did say that, and you have known it for a long time. I can't be who I am back there. We both know it." He wanders away so Benji hears no more.

When he returns, he grabs Benji's arm. "Oh my god, I came out to my brother. I can't believe it. Feels fantastic."

Benji gives him a hug. "No going back now."

Mitch, not used to being so public with affection, tenses when he hears laughter. He glances to its source: a woman on her cellphone paying them no attention. "You know, even if school doesn't work out, I have to get out of Bum-fuck. I wish I was staying now I'd take you to dinner to celebrate, course it would be cheap."

"It would have been an honor. You okay on your own? I have to get home."

He takes note of himself. "Yeah, I really am. I'll stop by the coffee shop after financial aid. It should be around 2. Will you be there that early?"

"Sure. I'm on afternoon shift." They exchange numbers and share a hug.

Mitch looks around the coffee shop until he sees Benji step out of the office. Their eyes meet and both break into smiles.

Benji asks the woman he is speaking with to take the counter and goes up to Mitch. The grinning greeting says all went well.

"I'm registered. It's all set." The young man jumps up and down, the scariness of last night's excitement, now infectious and good.

"Grab a seat. I'll fix something special."

While Benji makes a cappuccino, Mitch orders some pastries and finds a seat.

When done, Benji joins Mitch to go over the events of the day. Mitch, while nervous, remains lucid.

"So, it's all set?"

"Mostly. I gotta go home and get everything ready there. Frankly that scares me. Bum-fuck is not a very accepting place."

"Your brother?"

"He's the only one that never gave up on me. It didn't surprise him when I told him I'm gay. It was more that I finally actually said it. No, it's all the rest. They may try to sabotage it."

"Can you survive it?"

"Yeah, but I may be a mess when I show up here. Hope I get an understanding roommate."

"Took care of housing too. Good."

Seth's approach distracts them. "Benji, I came in for my paycheck. Madison said you'd have to get it out of the safe. Sorry to interrupt." He exchanges glances with Mitch.

"Pull up a seat. Seth, this is Mitch. He just enrolled and will be starting in January. Mitch, this is Seth Ng, also a student, and he works here evenings." They shake hands.

As Benji rises to get Seth's check, he hears them engaging in the initial chat of students everywhere involving majors and classes. Upon returning, he sees they easily engage in conversation. Current subject seems to be tattoos. Mitch has drawn up the bottom part of his shorts to show off the vine as conversation transitions to flirtation.

Benji holds back. Seth responds to Mitch by raising his shirt and turning to show off something not visible from Benji's view, something he had not known about Seth. He gives them a few more moments before returning to give Seth his check.

"Thanks, Benji. I'll see you Saturday." And then to Mitch, "It was really good to meet you. I hope I'll see you in January." He starts to head off, but Benji tells him to wait at the counter.

"I'll be with you in a moment." He turns to Mitch, "So that didn't take long."

"What?"

"I told you you'd meet lots of guys who would fall for those eyes. Looks like one just tripped."

"He's cute. Did you see his ink? Called it ying-yang?"

After a little contemplation, Benji gets it. "Oh, yin-yang. Couldn't see from my angle. Did you even exchange numbers or anything?"

"Shit."

"You are green. Mind if I play matchmaker?"

"Um, I don't know."

Benji rolls his head back, lets out an extravagant sigh, and lets his arms fall to the side feigning exhaustion. "Pathetic. Seth, come back here."

"What's up?"

"Are you free this afternoon?"

He glances at Mitch hoping this somehow involves this new man. "Yeah. No more classes."

"Mitch has to catch a bus this evening but needs someone to keep him entertained until then. You up for it?"

He looks at Mitch expectantly, encouraged by a small nod. "Sure, if you'd like."

A floored Mitch manages to agree. "Let me say goodbye to Benji."

"Thanks for everything," Seth says to Benji as he heads out, pausing at the door.

When Mitch joins him, Seth asks, "You already got a college sweatshirt? Cool."

Mitch looks down and pulls it off.

Seth nonchalantly gazes at the hint of flesh and ink this action exposes.

"Be right back." He charges back to Benji to thank him for the shirt.

"Mitch. You're going to be all right here," Benji says delightedly. "There'll be lots of ups and downs. You've had an amazing day. Call me when you can. Now, a prince awaits."

I'm already in the rearview mirror.

Mitch, though grateful, gives in to a hormone-driven quick goodbye and rushes to meet Seth. Benji watches as they head down the block, crashing into each other every few steps.

Never noticed what a skinny nerd Seth is.

22

"I was hoping you could meet Mom during a quieter time."

Leo and Dave sit on Dave's roof at sunset wrapped in a blanket against the cold. Dave holds both of Leo's hands in his lap as Leo leans on his shoulder. "There's going to be cousins and aunts and uncles and all sorts of people dropping by. Barbara, my sister, will be there with Kevin and Caleb, my nephew. He's a delight but can get rambunctious and whiney when tired." He looks at Leo. "Please tell me you never want to have children. Love Caleb to death but no way."

"Never met one who could hold an intelligent conversation."

"Knew you were a keeper." Dave smiles and gives him a peck. "Of course, my mom will be cooking her fingers off."

"Is she as good as you?"

"Better, but it's Thanksgiving so it'll be turkey. Something spectacular may show for dessert."

"How many people will be there?"

"No telling during the day, but for the meal itself, only immediate family, just Mom and Barbara's family. The rest live close by and have other relatives, so they all take off."

Leo ponders this. There was never more than three, holiday or not. Holidays meant no school. Now he knows that was not normal. "Was it always that way?"

The question warms Dave. "No, it changed when Dad died. He was the one to gather the whole tribe. It was too much for all the aunts and uncles to do without his organizational skills, so it quickly evolved into what it is now."

Leo ventures, "How did he die?"

Dave usually tenses up when people ask this, but oddly he feels happy.

"Cancer. Started in the stomach. Or at least where it was first detected. It took a little time, not much more than a year. Got rough at the end. That was a little over three years ago now." Dave looks to the side and quickly shakes his head. "That seems weird."

"Do you miss him?"

"At times. Most at holidays. Like I said, he was the organizer. We stopped doing a lot of things, like driving around to see Christmas lights or shopping for a tree. Mom bought an artificial tree." He holds Leo's hand tighter as he contemplates asking. Finally, he dares, "Do you miss your parents?"

He expects Leo to withdraw or tense, but after a momentary silence, he simply answers, "No."

Unsure what that fully means, Dave understands the depth of this admission. "Getting colder. We should go in."

"I like being up here with you. What's happens when it snows? You'll miss your sunsets."

"There's a couple buildings on campus with decent views, but you can't always find a seat."

They sit silently enjoying simple touch as the sky slowly and fully darkens. Cooling temperature gives them a logical, if unnecessary, reason to huddle closer. Reluctantly they head downstairs, blanket now draped around their shoulders. At Dave's door, they pause. "I wish you'd stay tonight."

"I don't have my laptop and have to get up too early to get home and all," he says unhappily.

"It's cold out there too. I don't like your walking across campus all the way home in this."

"Kinda sucks."

A gleam grows in Dave's eyes, "You know there is an alternative."

Leo, eager to know Dave's plan, adds, "Go on."

"I could give you a ride."

Leo cocks his head to the left. "That would be appreciated."

"And," Dave sways seductively, his hands on Leo's hips. The blanket slips off, "since I'd be all the way over there and it's getting late..."

Leo discovers his hands now on Dave's hips. "Sounding better..."

"I could throw a change of clothes in my gym bag and instead of you staying with me, I stay with you."

"Ooh, let me think... Yes! I like that."

Dave opens his door, grabs the blanket off the floor, and tosses it on his bed, then seizes his gym bag, pulls a fresh shirt and pair of jeans out of drawers, finally adding adds a sweater and socks. Packed and ready in less than a minute. It takes the elevator agonizingly long seconds to bring them to the parking level where they jump into Bart and head home.

Jay rinses out dinner dishes as they arrive. "Welcome home, guys."

They stop long enough for a polite hello before rushing up the stairs.

Jay follows shortly thereafter. As he passes Leo's room, he faintly hears muffled preliminaries of the two in lovemaking.

Need to insulate these rooms better.

Jay continues to his room and turns on his computer.

Leo stands naked before Dave who sits on the bed. Dave's hands run up and down Leo's torso. Dave loves these light-hearted preludes. Leo's sounds let him know how much he relishes the attention. One of Leo's slender hands combs soothingly through his dark locks as he continues giving attention.

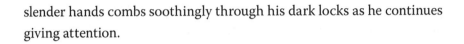

Jay logs onto a favorite hookup site, thinking someone nearby, a little older, late thirties to early fifties.

Nice to have someone taller than me for a change.

He scans through profiles matching his parameters.

Leo crouches between Dave's legs taking him fully, his turn to give pleasure. He'd tried with others but they were either too big or he couldn't relax. Discomfort with this man never arises. Dave's sighs of erotic contentment encourage him.

Well, this is no fun.

The men's interchangeable profiles produce little interest. Loosening his age parameters from thirty to sixty, brings up another few profiles. He opens a new message.

Fuck me 2nite.

No profile pics. He sends back a thanks-but-no-thanks message.

Lying on the bed, Dave holds both cocks, stroking languidly in no rush to learn Leo's body. What matters is they kiss. Leo's left hand skims his chest, his right hand in Dave's hair. Dave's left arm forms a pillow for Leo's head. Importance lies in pressing closer.

Jay find a couple of men in his new search interesting. The first calls himself Jon, but the guy signs off before he sends a message. He pulls up the second, only the screen name BTM4U. Not the best, but the picture shows a fairly handsome man claiming to be 32. He scans through the profile until he sees the guy only plays bareback. A new message pops up, a ballistic response to the rejection he sent. He deletes the message and blocks the profile.

Maybe I'll have better luck with an app on my phone.

They enjoy mutual oral pleasure crosswise on the bed. Leo's legs are stretched out long, Dave's bent at the knees.

Dave's hand steadies Leo's as he alternates from cock to balls. Dave loves the all-natural furriness of Leo's testes, easily disregarding the need to occasionally spit out a stray pubic hair.

Leo, both hands on Dave's hips, uses his mouth to offer and receive gratification.

A shift in bodies finds Leo kneeling over Dave, whose knees bend, legs slightly spread.

Jay checks a site catering to a more discriminating clientele: men who want domination or bondage. He sees Justin, the guy he met several months ago.

That was a depressing place.

But again, the profiles seem copied from one to another. An attractive man who writes decent sentences intrigues him initially. A visitor, he wants to meet in his motel in a risky part of town.

Leo still kneels above, tongue ravenously gorges on Dave's sensitive bud.

Dave's head falls back, luxuriating in pleasure. His hands are on Leo's ass, fingers grazing the fine hairs. He raises his head and looks at Leo's crack. Spreading the cheeks, he moves forward to find Leo with his tongue.

Leo gasps from the unexpected pleasure.

Soon Dave pulls back slightly to stare in amazement, realizing he has never done this with Leo before.

This also marks the first time anyone has tasted that part of Leo. Joy accompanies knowing Dave broke this barrier. He shakily reaches back to gently hold Dave's head in place.

No wonder he loves this.

Jay has uncontestable requirements, though sometimes difficult to identify all his standards, tonight, no one meets them. If the next few profiles provide no satisfaction, he'll switch again.

They are on their knees. Leo wraps his arms around, holding him near. Dave guides Leo inside. Leo easily complies in wonder and contentment. Dave crosses his arms over Leo's while gently pushing back.

Jay tries one more rarely-used site, hoping at least for new pictures. Most here seek dates. Nice, but not what he wants now. The more detailed profiles provide interesting reading that might be fine if he ever looks for more than one night.

Prone with Leo inside him, Dave reaches back over his shoulder with his right hand to feel that thick blondness. His left hand snatches a fist-ful of sheet. With Leo, his world melts into a space comfortably large enough for two.

Leo still holds Dave close, hips swaying into him. During this aston-ishing sensation, the feeling of Dave's tongue on his ass lingers.

Jay closes this site. Back on his computer, he surfs gay porn, not really craving that either. Finally, he shuts the machine down and crawls on top of his bed.

Too early for sleep.

His mind drifts over men he has encountered the past year. All let Jay take charge and call the shots. He initiated, made the next move, and decided when he would fuck and how.

Then, a small realization: an angel abandoned by a trail did not.

As they first coupled, Dave on his back, Leo driving into him with steadily increasing tempo, Dave again cums. Inside Dave, Leo cums.

Jay heads downstairs. Sooner or later Leo will descend or Benji will come home. Maybe even Dave will come down.

Dave asks if Leo is going to get up.

"Probably later."

"That's normal for you." He runs a finger down Leo's breastbone.

"I rarely sleep more than a few hours. Even as a kid I'd get up. Nice to live where there's things to do."

"Like clean?"

Leo accepts the mild tease. "Yes, like clean. But other things too. I'll do some studying, maybe send an e-mail. Sometimes go in the backyard and look at the sky." No one knew about that one.

Dave reaches to pull him in for a kiss. He learned one tidbit of his childhood. It is not a totally closed book.

During the night, Leo wakes. He writes an e-mail to Jean, in part telling her about his Thanksgiving plans.

> Dave has invited me to spend Thanksgiving with his family. In ways, I don't fully understand, I know this is a big step. I can't imagine what it would have been like having a dinner guest, holiday or not.
>
> I'm excited and nervous. What is the right thing to do? What should I do or say? What if they only speak Italian and I can't understand a word the whole time? LOL.

He adds a few other things before sending and heads restlessly downstairs. Leo sits on the end of the sofa and starts to rub a sleeping Jay's bare foot, another new gesture but so natural in this home.

Jay stirs and smiles when he sees Leo. "Hi gorgeous. What time is it?" He doesn't pull away. Leo keeps massaging.

"Late, not sure." He waits as Jay comes to a little more. "I have news."

"Good or bad?"

"I'm going with Dave for Thanksgiving to be with his family."

Jay bolts up, fully awake, "Holy shit! That's incredibly good news. When did this happen? Are you nervous?" Dozens of questions form.

"This afternoon and yeah, I'm very nervous. I don't know how I should act or what I should say or not say."

"Well, what was it like when people came to a holiday for you?"

Leo shrugs, "I don't remember anyone coming over."

Easier to believe Leo has memory gaps, Jay takes Leo's slender hand. "Be yourself. They'll love you like we all do."

Leo allows a smile. "Thanks." He giggles. "Doesn't really tell me what to do or say, but it helps."

Jay begins gently tickling his friend who tries to counter. Both howl with laughter bringing Dave downstairs, fully enjoying the scene from the edge of the room.

Benji, also drawn by the sounds, stops with Dave. "Hey, babe." He winds an arm around Dave's waist and plants a kiss on his t-shirt clad shoulder. "What's going on?"

"They're tickling each other. Leo's loving it."

Benji contemplates this information. "You ticklish?"

"Nope."

"Me neither." He takes Dave's hand. "Jay's as bad as Leo. You get him. I'll take Leo." They race into the living room and before either Jay or Leo have a chance to react all four playfully wrestle. Their laughter fills the house and can be heard out to the street.

23

"**R**eady for your trip, babe?" Benji greets Leo when he comes into
the kitchen.

He shrugs. "I don't know what I'm getting into."

"First time meeting a boyfriend's family?"

"Benji, I am so tired of everything being the first. I feel like I'm two
years old." He fixes coffee and joins Benji at the table. "Yes, it's the first
time." An overriding warmth counterbalances his frustration.

"I actually know the feeling. When I first moved in here, oh my god."
He leans forward and spreads his hands on the table. "Hustling didn't
prepare me for the stability of Jay and Vince."

"Wish I could meet Vince. I hear so much about him."

Benji thinks, trying to figure how to give Leo a good sense of Vince.
"He is kind of a mix between Jay and Dave. Very sweet and decent like
Dave, self-assured as Jay. Closer to your looks. Handsome, slender, and
very blond. There's pictures of him all over."

"Sorta figured out which one he is."

"When's Dave coming?"

"Anytime now. Kind of wish we were staying here."

Benji smiles. "Kind of wish you were too." He glances over and sees Leo lost in thought.

He is so completely there one moment, then the next? Another planet.

Unable to fathom the depths of thought this man must have, that clear intelligence tempered by vast naiveté fascinates him. Benji grasps more clearly than anyone Leo's lack of guidance growing up. When Leo says nothing happened, Benji considers the frightening truth of it.

As they sit, Leo starts, "The other night? When we were all wrestling?"

"Yeah, that was fun."

"It was. It was really fun." A slight smile lightens his face. Stumbling how to continue, he finally adds, "I liked it."

The doorbell sounds. Benji moves to get the door but turns on his way and shouts back, "I liked it too."

"Good morning, Gorgeous Number 2. Gorgeous Number 1 is in the kitchen."

Dave laughs. "Would you be number 3? Or is Jay 3 and you 4?"

Benji fans his fingers out. He places a hand on each side of his face and pulls the skin back taut. "I'll take 4 since I'm *vastly* younger. Come on. He's on pins and needles."

Leo brightens as soon as he spies Dave. They move into each other's arms, exchanging hellos and kisses.

Dave's effect on Leo touches something very deep in Benji.

Dave is Leo's "on" switch.

"You ready, sweetie?" Dave asks, his arms around Leo's waist.

"I'm packed. Don't know if I'm ready."

Dave rewards that comment with a peck on the cheek. "Neither am I, sweetie."

Benji asks, "When are you guys taking off?"

"We're going to stop at the deli to pick up some things for my mom. Be good to see Salvatore again. Called ahead to let him know what I wanted. Probably hit the freeway around noon."

"I can't wait to hear you speak Italian again. It's so lovely," Leo says.

"That would be fun," Benji adds.

"Benji, you'd love it," Dave considers and offers, "We should cook a meal together. We can go there to get what we'd need."

There are few cars at the deli, last minute Thanksgiving food not usually sought here.

Salvatore spots them as they enter, "Dave, Leo, *ciao ragazzi. Bello rivederti.*"

"*Ciao, Salvatore. Siete pronti per il* Thanksgiving?"

"*Sì. Tutta la famiglia sta venendo su. Festa enorme.*"

"*Suoni celeste. Mia mamma è già cucinando. Non vedo l'ora di sfoggiare per Leo. Portandolo a casa per la prima volta. Tipo di emozionante e snervante. Augurarci fortuna.*"

"*Grande passo. Infatti buona fortuna.* Hey Leo, good to hear you're visiting his family."

Leo grins. "Yeah."

He wags his finger at Dave, "*Se a loro non piace Leo, è ancora possibile incontrare il mio Roberto.*"

They both laugh.

He heads to the back and returns with a good size package. "Leo," he beckons him over. "You take good care of my Dave."

"I'll do my best, Salvatore." They shake hands.

"*Ci vediamo quando torno. Avete una grande,* Thanksgiving," he says to Dave. They also shake hands warmly.

Outside Leo asks, "Did he try to push his son on you again?"

"Um, yes… Please don't tell me you're picking up Italian after hearing it one time." Dave looks quizzically at Leo over the top of the car.

"I heard the name Roberto. Have you ever seen Roberto?"

"Not yet. I keep telling Sal I only have eyes for you, sweetie."

Dave's mother lives in a small mountain town a few miles on the other side of the continental divide. They soon leave the interstate for two-lane back roads with lots of twists, turns, and hills that gradually transition into mountains. Leo gets lost in the landscape. He passed though similar places on his trip from Tucson but was in no condition to pay attention. Now, the crisp sky above the rugged magnificence of the mountains fascinate him. Valley vistas open from time to time on one side of the road or the other with no hint when this will occur next.

Trees, save evergreens, stand naked after losing this year's foliage. Scant traces of early snow, a rare occurrence for Leo, peep out in odd corners. The low desert heat chased away the sporadic flurries that would make their way. Fascinated now, these little patches are more than he has seen in his entire life. "There's so much snow."

Dave finds Leo's excitement charming. Any endearment for snow withered dozens of storms ago. But as Leo's exhilaration builds, he finds himself embracing a new appreciation, putting words to each patch now, noting how each hugs a tree or rock, none found where sunshine falls thus giving light to the normally darkest shadows. He reaches for Leo's hand when driving does not require both.

"This is all so beautiful," Leo states. "Very different from the desert."

"Desert sunsets are incredible. The colors are so intense."

"Until you taught me about sunset, I never paid attention, but now thinking back, you're right. There were times I couldn't help but notice. Didn't need a roof. They were just there."

'Yes! Amazing. A few summers ago, I participated in a writer's workshop in Las Cruces. Not the best time to visit, but the sunsets were abundantly exquisite. And there's these stone mountains on the east side, the Organs, that reflect back intense oranges and reds. Something like 90% of all the stories from the class either were about sunsets or included them as a plot device."

"Bet you wrote the other 10%."

"I saved the sunset stories for other classes."

The flow back and forth from periods of silence to bursts of conversations, usually fueled by some new aspect of landscape, continues as daylight fades.

"Dave? I've been thinking, can I see some of your writing sometime?"

"I've never seen you read other than your studies. What do you like?"

"I'm not really sure. I rarely have had time to read for fun. I read books for English classes, but that's been years. I'd like to read something you wrote."

"Admission time." Dave lets out a sigh. "It's hard to show people my writing. It never feels ready. Even the pieces I've published don't feel done."

"How much have you published?"

"I've had a few pieces in small literary magazines."

Leo lets that simmer as he gazes onto a new broad panorama to his right. "That's pretty impressive."

"It is a great view. One of my favorites along this road."

Leo chuckles. "I meant you being published."

Dave exhales warily. "It's good, not great." He reaches over to touch Leo's hand, needing physical reassurance before continuing. "I struggle a lot with this. I chose a field that depends so much on people's opinions. Can it sell? Will anyone read it? Will critics trash it?"

"So, letting me read your work is kind of like me meeting your family. It's a risk. You think I'm worth taking the risk. Your work is worth the risk too."

Dave feels a shroud lifting. "Thank you. How'd you get so smart?"

"Haven't a clue."

Taking a tight curve, the beginning of a series of switchbacks, Dave cannot see the gleeful look on Leo's face.

"Okay, there's a lot of things stored in my bedroom. I guess you can dig through it. Give you something to do when you wake up during the night."

"Kind of figured it wouldn't be too good to roam around at night. I didn't want to bring homework, plus I couldn't take another look at that project without screaming." He gazes out and sees several snow-capped peaks across a new valley. "Wow."

Dave slows to give Leo more time to take in the scenery while the light lasts.

Silence envelops. Dave needs to focus on the road. Leo rests his hand on Dave's thigh. They've said enough. Sharing presence suits them the rest of the trip.

Arriving later than planned, the cold slaps them unexpectedly when they step out of the car. Grabbing as much of their bags, including Dave's package from the deli, they rush inside.

Dave calls out, "Mom?"

As they move into the living room, Mrs. Azzurri emerges from the back. "Dave." She opens her arms for an embrace. Slight and rather quiet, Leo sees parts of Dave in her face: the same mouth, definitely her nose, and the texture and lack of curl in her greying hair.

"Mom, this is Leo Graham," he says as he steps aside. "Leo, this is my mom, Mrs. Azzurri."

Unsure, Leo steps forward and reaches out a hand. She takes it warmly in both of hers.

"Welcome, Leo. Did you have a good trip?"

"It was very pretty."

"Leo was excited to see all the little snow patches. He's from Tucson, so he hasn't had much experience with it."

She keeps hold of Leo's hand with one and takes one of Dave's with the other. "You boys must be hungry. I'll fix something."

"Thanks, Mom. Anyone here?"

"Barbara, Kevin, and Caleb." She leads them to a counter where they sit on stools. "They went to bed already. Drove directly from his family in Albuquerque. Caleb was disappointed you weren't here."

Dave rushes back into the living room. "I almost forgot." As he quickly returns with his cooler, he says, "I brought you some cheeses and sausages from that deli."

"Grazie, Dave. You put them away while I fix you two a plate. I made gnocchi yesterday. Do you like that Leo?"

"I don't know what it is."

She laughs. "Gnocchi, it is."

Dave intervenes. "It's a pasta made with potatoes instead of just flour. I love it. I'll make it sometime for all of us. Mom, I made Noni Azzurri's lasagna for Leo and his roommates."

"That was the best thing I've ever tasted," Leo adds.

As she warms up gnocchi, she says over her shoulder, "Dave always watched his grandmothers and me when we were in the kitchen. Barbara did too. Dave, *volete qualcosa da bere, tu e Leo? C'è anche latte se ne preferite prendere.*"

"What do you want to drink, Leo? Wine, juice, milk?"

"Whatever you want is fine."

"Leo," Mrs. Azzurri says, "Dave is the only one who learned to speak Italian. Excuse me if I start in with him. I don't get to speak it much anymore."

"It's fine, Mrs. Azzurri. I love hearing it. Surprised me the first time."

Dave sets two glasses of wine down. "Mom, do you want anything?"

"No, I'm fine." She piles two plates and sets before them. Dave also brings a grater and some Romano cheese, putting some on his then some on Leo's. "Dig in."

"It looks like little pillows." Leo raises a forkful to his mouth. "Oh my." He stares at the plate. "Dave, your lasagna just got bumped to second place. This is incredible. What is it?"

She repeats the dishes name, and he tries to say it but can't quite get it, causing gentle mirth.

"Whatever it's called, I love it." He digs in with relish.

Mrs. Azzurri takes Dave's hand. "You got here late. I was getting worried. No trouble?"

"No, took my time so Leo could take in more scenery."

They chat while Leo finishes his plate.

"If I knew you'd like it so much, I would have made more."

"That was plenty. It was wonderful. Thank you very much."

Leo looks around. This house, very different from the place he thinks of as home, bears its own message of welcome. Touches of Mrs. Azzurri assert themselves everywhere. Pictures of family members hang on the walls. One must be Dave's high school graduation, too young for college. As he continues scanning, a barefoot little boy, dressed in pajamas, steps into the light rubbing his eyes. Leo pokes Dave. "We have a visitor."

Dave turns. "Cabers!"

The little boy looks up and immediately brightens. "Uncle Dave!"

He charges over, suddenly all words and laughter as Dave scoops him up. The verbal barrage covers his trip, how he has something to show his uncle, and how he missed him when they arrived. The nonstop chronicle continues until he turns a bit and notices Leo for the first time. He stops talking and turns full face to Leo, staring in wonderment with nearly the same impossibly green eyes of his uncle. Hiding his words with one hand while pointing to Leo with the other, he whispers something to Dave.

"Cabers, this is my very good, extra special best most delightful friend in the world. His name is Leo. He's kind of quiet, but very nice. And Leo, this is my favorite, though only, nephew in the entire world, Caleb."

Leo reaches out his hand. "I'm very pleased to meet you."

Caleb cautiously takes Leo's hand while eying him up and down. "You like my Uncle Dave."

"Oh, very much. Yes, I do."

To Dave, "And you like him?"

"Yes, very much."

"Okay." That settled, he launches right back into a vocal torrent on Dave. Leo meets Mrs. Azzurri's eyes.

She shrugs, "He likes you. You must be fine. I'm going to bed, boys. Don't keep him up too late. Dave, you boys are in your room, Caleb in the guest room. The big boy wanted it to himself." She comes around to give Dave and Caleb a kiss each. She considers for a moment then gives Leo one on the cheek also.

"Goodnight," he says very softly.

Dave smiles at Leo over Caleb's rambunctiousness. "Cabers, would you like to help us take our things to my room?"

"Yes!"

The second feet hit the floor, he runs to the living room to inspect the bags, suspecting something waits for him somewhere. "Can I help with this one?" is his best way of guessing which one holds his surprise.

"That's Leo's," Dave says while crossing toward his nephew. "I have one more out in the car you can help with."

He catches Caleb. "It's cold out there. You can carry it in from the porch, okay?"

"Yes, Uncle Dave." He squirms with delighted anticipation.

Leo, watching this exchange, owns no reference for this completely enchanting scene.

"Leo, take our bags to our room. Down that hall, first on the left. Hey, just like at home."

Leo carries the bags to Dave's room, still filled with mementos from an earlier life. He wants to explore, but finds the story unfolding in the living room far more tempting.

Caleb quivers by the front door waiting for his uncle's return. Dave reenters, shivering from the cold, carrying a bag Leo never noticed. "This bag is so heavy, Cabers. I think there's too much inside."

"Really?"

"I think we need to take something out. I don't think I can carry the whole thing all the way down the hall unless we remove something."

Caleb jumps up and down, struggling to keep his voice down.

"Don't you think this bag is too stuffed? Maybe there's something we can take out to make it lighter."

Caleb, giggling too hard to talk, shakes his head.

Dave unzips the bag and pulls out a package wrapped in comics from last Sunday's paper. "Now, what is this? What do you think it is?"

"Open it."

"I don't know how." He holds it out to the boy. "Do you?"

"Yes!"

"Here."

Caleb rips the paper, revealing a Dr. Seuss book. His face brightens in excited delight. "Read it to me. Read it to me!"

"Are you sure? You can read yourself, you know."

"I want you to read it. Make it funny!"

"If you're sure. We could wait until tomorrow when your mom's awake. She might want to hear it too."

"Now." He is tugging on Dave, trying to get him into the living room.

Leo watches in sheer delight noting yet another first. No delightfully excited child could be found in any of his classes. Such unbridled enthusiasm makes it hard for him to not burst out laughing, but he reins it in, not wanting to interrupt the sweet interaction.

"Okay, then." Dave lets himself be dragged to the sofa and turns on a lamp. Caleb crowds next to him. Dave looks up at Leo, glowing. "You know, Cabers, Leo doesn't know Dr. Seuss."

The little boy looks at Leo with wonder. "Really?"

"It's true," Leo admits.

Caleb looks back to his uncle, the solution so obvious to him. "Read it to him too."

"Where can he sit?"

Caleb looks at Leo, excited having a new book and a new friend. "Right here." He points to the sofa on his other side and says quietly to Dave, telling a secret, "Then no one else can hear. Just you and me and Leo."

Leo sits. Dave opens the book and begins reading using an unfamiliar voice. He changes pitches and tones as different characters speak, enthralling Leo almost as much as Caleb.

So, this is Dr. Seuss.

From time to time, Dave pretends to stumble on a word. Caleb readily offers tittering assistance.

Shortly, Caleb begins to drift off and falls asleep before the story is half finished. "I think we need to get this little guy back to bed." He gently lifts his sleeping nephew and carries him to the guest room. "Pull down the bedding, sweetie." Once they tuck him in, they return to the living room. Leo plops down on the sofa. Dave starts to get the bag, but notices Leo. "What?"

Leo pats the spot on the sofa where Dave had been reading. "Finish the story." Dave grins and returns. Leo cuddles into his side with Dave's arm around his shoulder.

"You won't fall asleep on me too, will you?"

"Not a chance. You better use those voices too."

After a nearly three-hour workout, Benji hears Jay rummaging around in the kitchen as he climbs the stairs. "Hey, babe." He goes to kiss his best friend.

"Everything ready for tomorrow?"

"Think so. Pies and cranberry sauce are done. Everything else can wait. Less here than I'd hoped there'd be."

"Yeah, just four. Well four and a half since Tommy will be stopping over briefly."

"It'll be nice. Wish Leo and Dave were here."

"Me too."

Benji leans against the counter, simply gazing downward.

Jay goes up to him and drapes a comforting arm around his shoulders. "You want Steve here."

"I didn't think it would be so hard."

He squeezes a powerful shoulder. "You hanging on?"

"Yeah, I'm coping better than I used to. I met someone the other day that made me think of those early days." He tells Jay about Mitch.

"Sounds high maintenance, but worthwhile."

"He touched me. My mind has been kind of twisting around since. Haven't figured it out yet."

In his old bedroom, Dave becomes intimidated. He wants to rip Leo's clothes off and go crazy, but this is his mother's home. While neither he nor Leo are particularly loud during sex, an occasional outburst can't be helped. Barbara and Kevin are right on the other side of this wall, his mother and nephew not much farther.

"Dave, is something going on?" Leo sits on the bed.

Dave settles nervously next to him and explains the situation.

"You mean I've done something sexually you haven't?"

"You had sex in the bedroom of the house you grew up in?"

"Yeah, when I was in graduate school."

"I have to think about it." He starts unpacking as a distraction.

"Dave, remember telling me I could read some of your work if I couldn't sleep?"

"Yeah." Dave rummages in the closet and pulls out a box. "It's all in here. Most on flash drives. The computer on the desk is slow but works. Now, I'm really nervous." A yip of laughter escapes.

Leo picks his way into the box. "Any way to tell what's on each?"

"Not really. Sorry."

"Anything you don't want me to see?"

Although difficult, he trusts no one more than Leo. Eyes closed, he sighs. "No, anything you find is okay." He sits on the edge of the bed.

Leo sets the box by the computer to investigate during the night, returns and leans his head on Dave's shoulder. "It's not as scary as I thought it would be. Your mom is great. Caleb is hilarious. I had no idea a child could be so funny."

Dave lets his hand run up and down Leo's thigh. He turns his head and kisses the top of Leo's.

Leo turns to look up at Dave who takes his face between his hands.

"Crap, I can't resist you."

He starts to kiss Leo.

Pulling back with an impish grin, Leo suggests, "You know, if you start to moan too much, I think I have a solution."

Dave cocks his head to one side. "What's th—?"

Leo immediately clamps his mouth on Dave's and resumes kissing for a few seconds before pulling back again. "Think that will work?"

"Very innovative, sweetie." Both resume kissing.

Hesitations fall as easily as discarded shirts. Dave's hands range over Leo's slender body. He loves finding the edge of Leo's beard and running his tongue between the soft hair of the beard and the rougher stubble.

Leo leans his head back. His fingers lightly scruff Dave's hirsute chest, snatching small furry bits between his fingers. Oh, and how that tongue works into his ear. He gives in to the pleasure Dave willingly confers. The sensation of tongue on his ear and the gentle raspy sound it produces brings him to a wondrous state. He caresses Dave under the soft denim. And that tongue now explores his neck, easing its way downward. He feels his arm being raised.

Dave's inviting mouth explores the pit, breathing musk and tasting dampness.

The slight tickling is more than compensated by the electric pulsations for Leo. Subtle whimperings encourage Dave's explorations. Gracefully, they slide themselves fully onto the bed, Dave's mouth maintaining contact with Leo's increasingly receptive skin.

Sweet, gentle lovemaking, interspersed with frequent kisses to ensure they create little noise, continues for the couple.

On this night, in this bed very familiar to one, novel to the other, Leo crosses a new boundary. Tonight, if only with one slim finger and for too brief a time, his first anal penetration occurs.

They end quietly, Dave unaware of the sweet significance of his actions. Dave holds Leo's face with one hand. "You are so beautiful, Leo."

A grin develops, starting with his eyes. Leo, at last, believes him.

Some moments later while sitting up against the headboard, Dave's leg draped over Leo's, he suggests, "We should hit the bathroom, so you'll know where it is if you have to get up during the night."

Leo opens the door, but Dave grabs his wrist. "Leo," he says as he gazes down their bodies, "we're not leaving your bedroom." Quickly shutting the door, they throw sweatshirts and sweatpants on before heading down the hall.

Next, Leo flicks on the computer while Dave settles into bed. Leo cuddles as Dave drifts off. It feels weird holding him with layers of cotton between them. After a short doze, Leo wakes, gets up, and takes the computer out of sleep mode. Then, as it warms up, he selects and inserts a random flash drive. It appears to hold a collection of stories, mildly surprising him, as Dave talks more about poetry. This is better. Leo spent little time reading anything non-technical. Poetry will initially require Dave's guidance.

The first, a very short work, simply describes a man walking down a street, exquisite detail given to what the man sees, even things not registering on a conscious level. Its brevity makes Leo wonder if this may have been a class assignment. That assumption deepens as he continues. No true stories occupy this drive, only similarly detailed descriptions.

On the second, he finds "Trying to be Seen," the first full, though brief, story about a boy named Dallas trying desperately to meet a new guy in school. Both sweet and sad, Dallas makes several attempts, more unnoticed than rejected. It ends with a hopeful Dallas feeling the future holds one who can see him. Rough, even to Leo's undisciplined ear, it has a touching, sweet truth. Leo looks at Dave's sleeping form, gets up, and kisses his smooth forehead gently. Dave stirs slightly and rolls over. Leo enfolds Dave in his arms and drifts off.

24

Sensing a presence, Leo slowly opens his eyes. A pair of green eyes and a tiny waving hand await. He reaches back to poke whatever part of Dave he finds.

"Leo, are you awake?"

"You definitely are, Caleb." Leo hears Dave's very soft snicker behind his back.

"Where's Uncle Dave?"

Dave raises up and peers over Leo's shoulder. "Right here, Cabers."

"Yay, come on. You forgot to finish the story."

Both men laugh.

"Okay, let me wake up. I'll meet you on the sofa."

Caleb darts raucously out of the room.

"Sorry about that."

"Guess I should get a shower." He looks at Dave. "Don't suppose you can join me."

Dave pouts out his lower lip. "No, darn it."

They meet in the kitchen where Dave has coffee ready.

"Where's Caleb? I thought you had to finish his story." Leo wants to hear the story again.

"No telling. Got distracted between bedroom and living room."

A smaller female version of Dave enters, sees Dave, and brightens. "Hey Dave." She crosses to give him a hug.

"Barbara, I'd like you to meet Leo. Leo, this is my sister Barbara."

"I've heard good things about you," she says softly as they shake hands. *She's so quiet. More like Dave than Caleb.*

"I'm sorry," she continues, "we couldn't wait up for you guys, but I guess you met Caleb."

Leo grins. "He's quite a character. Where is he?"

"Back in his room. He brought something for you, Dave, and he's looking for it." She pours herself coffee then addresses Leo. "He was saying quite a bit about you, Leo, but I need some of this before I can process all he had to say." She sips her coffee. "Basically, he likes you." She notes how Leo, blushing, turns slightly away.

Caleb returns proudly, presenting Dave with a simulated turquoise ring from Albuquerque. Disappointment follows when clearly it is too small. Dave reassures him he will find a very special place to display it when he gets back to school, promising to send a picture. Caleb then pulls both Dave and Leo to the couch to resume the story.

Kevin, Caleb's father, appears next, easily the largest person present, towering over the others. He wears his longish dark brown hair tied back. He greets Barbara with affection and is introduced to Leo. Mussing Caleb's hair, he goes to grab his own coffee.

Dave finishes the delightful story, but Caleb asks for a repeat.

"Your grandmother is about to serve breakfast. How about after?" Indeed, the room fills with a heavenly cinnamon aroma from a freshly baked coffee cake.

"Caleb," his father calls, "time to get ready. C'mon, let's clean up."

"I'm already clean, Daddy."

"Good, then you can help me."

Caleb scurries off.

"He has two speeds, slug and cheetah," comments Dave. The scent lifts him off the sofa. Reaching back, he offers Leo his hand.

The aroma alone would have been enough for Leo to rise, but he sees nothing wrong in accepting Dave's assist.

Despite the cold, Jay's shirt has sweat patches from his morning run. He leaves his clothes by the washer with other laundry accumulating for Leo, a now accepted practice once understood he enjoys performing household chores, similar to Benji cooking or Jay taking care of household repairs like that drip that is trying to form in the downstairs bathroom.

He finds Benji in the kitchen. "Surprised to see you up," he starts. "Lot of preparation to do?"

Benji looks at Jay, a smile dashing across his roundish face. "That too, but have some great news. Got a text last night from Steve. He's going to see his family over break but is stopping off a day here first." He starts to clap. "I couldn't wait to tell you."

"Fantastic news! That will be so good for you." He hugs Benji.

"Hope so." He lets the hug linger until breaking with, "Guess I better get started with dinner stuff." A slight dance motion modifies his step. With the refrigerator door open, he says over his shoulder, "Heard from Mitch too. Almost forgot after seeing Steve's text."

People start arriving late morning. Leo gets introduced to so many aunts, uncles, cousins, spouses, significant and not so significant others he loses track. The hoard prevents him from staying as close to Dave as he'd like, causing him to shy away from the general din, more content watching from a short distance. Better not put his social inadequacies on display. He makes visual contact frequently with Dave who can only smile and shrug. From time to time, they find each other for a brief, reassuring touch.

He works his way to a door on the opposite side of the kitchen opening onto a previously unnoticed den, a welcome escape. Furnished with the same sense of comfort as the rest of the house, he slips into it, hoping to reenergize. Expressed in a very different style, it reminds him of home, how Jay filled it with pieces providing comfort above style.

As he studies the room bit by bit, he hears his name softly called. Turning to find a forlorn Caleb sitting dwarfed at a large table on the far side of the room, book and paper in front of him, he asks, "Hi, what are you doing in here?"

"Stupid arithmetic" is the reply.

He moves towards the boy. "Homework?"

Clearly not pleased, he states in a crushed tone that melts Leo's heart, "I'm stupid."

"No, that's not at all true. I saw how you helped your uncle read. Only a very smart boy could do that."

Caleb brightens a little but admits, "I don't get this."

"Would you like help?"

Caleb eyes him suspiciously. "How?"

"Show me what you're doing." He pulls a chair over and sits at the side of the table.

Caleb turns his work to Leo. Only one calculation dejectedly crams into a top corner of the page. He doesn't understand the problem:

$$\begin{array}{r} 25 \\ + \ 25 \\ \hline 410 \end{array}$$

Leo asks a few questions to understand the method Caleb's teacher uses. "I get why you think this is right, Caleb. You know how your Uncle Dave is so good about writing stories and having you show him words and all that?"

Barbara, coming in to check on her son's progress, watches unawares.

"Yes," Caleb answers hesitantly.

"Well, I get numbers the way he gets words. I know what your teacher is saying, but she doesn't know how to tell you in a way you understand."

"So, she's stupid?"

Chuckling, he continues. "No one is. I have an idea that may help. Give me a sheet of paper and we'll see if this works."

Barbara backs out quietly, satisfied.

Leo draws lines down the page. "The thing about numbers is that they are very stubborn. They want to do things the same way over and over and over." He has written down:

$$
\begin{array}{cc}
|2|5| & |5| \\
+|2|5| & +|5| \\
\hline
|\ |\ | & |\ |
\end{array}
$$

"Add the 5 plus 5."

Caleb correctly writes 10, but it is very hard to get it into the narrow column that Leo has drawn. Leo redraws it.

$$
\begin{array}{c}
|5| \\
+|5| \\
\hline
|1|0|
\end{array}
$$

"See what I did? Only one number at a time can fit. One of them must move over. Numbers are very stubborn about how they move. It is always the one on this side that moves over. It never works the other way. Does that make sense?"

"Yeah."

"We'll practice with a few more."

He writes similar problems. Soon, Caleb gets that part of the problem.

"What you've been doing with that one each time you moved it over is called 'carrying over.'"

Caleb grins ear-to-ear. He nods enthusiastically when Leo asks if he is ready for the next step. It takes a few minutes and several columns being drawn, but soon Caleb masters this step. Leo writes out a new problem without the columns.

$$68$$
$$+\ 57$$

Intentionally one step higher, Leo wants to see if Caleb truly understands. The boy writes 125.

"That is absolutely and completely correct. See? You are very smart. Now, why don't you do the rest of your homework? I'll check it when you're done, then you can show your parents. I bet they'll be very proud of you."

The boy sets to work with newfound happiness, completing the ten problems quickly.

Leo checks them and proclaims, "You're a genius."

Caleb gives him a big hug and, paper in hand, runs screaming out of the room. Leo follows at a more casual pace. When he reenters the main part of the house, he locates Caleb by his volume. "Look what Leo showed me. He says I'm a genie."

Barbara looks at the paper and passes it to Kevin. "You did this all by yourself?"

"Leo showed me how." He squirms with pride.

Barbara looks around, spots Leo, and walks over to him. "He's had so much trouble with this."

Leo watches her take his hand.

Why do so many people touch me? Is it normal?

"I get numbers. He needed it explained a different way."

"Math has always been such an issue for him. Thank you very much."

"Um, I tutored a lot of math in college. It always goes back to the place they first don't get it, usually fractions. Little earlier for him. He'll be fine now. Well, until those pesky fractions appear." He feels an opening in his chest, his eyes slightly tear up. The smile loses a bit of shyness.

Barbara has not released his hand. "All these people are over-whelming you."

He nods the truth of that.

"I'm kind of glad. Otherwise you may not have stumbled onto Caleb." She gently pulls him into the room. "Come, we'll find Dave. I suspect you'd like to be near him."

Friends and relatives stream in and out during the day, but this begins to slow midafternoon. Caleb, put down for an unwanted nap, is appeased by another story from Dave. Once Caleb sleeps, Dave asks Leo if he'd like to escape. He suggests they grab Barbara and Kevin for a walk. Leo gratefully agrees but admits, "I don't have a coat."

Dave finds one in his old room and adds a spare pair of gloves, scarf, and knit hat. Properly bundled, the four head out.

Barbara and Dave hang back while Kevin and Leo forge ahead. Once Kevin expressed his thanks to Leo for what he did for Caleb, the two simply walk along, a refreshing change for Leo to be around someone not making demands. Everyone always seems to want him to talk so much.

Brother and sister lock in conversation. Family gossip is glanced over before the true subject intervenes: Leo.

"I like him," Barbara avers. "He's quiet, but I'm used to that with Kevin. What he did with Caleb was flat out amazing." She updates him.

"He's sometimes too quiet. His parents were killed last spring, but he rarely refers to them. Almost like they didn't exist."

"Families can be very strange. Maybe he's still in grief. It was hard enough losing Dad. Both at once with no warning must be devastating." She gazes ahead at Leo. "He doesn't show any signs of abuse, does he?"

"No. Mostly a huge naiveté. Odd for someone as intelligent as him." Dave fixes his eyes on Leo. "It stuns me how sharp his mind is."

She laughs. "That must be quite a shift. You've always been the smart-est one in the room. But, yeah, it's very clear with him. The way he got Caleb to understand, I don't know. He's a different league. What do your friends think?"

"What friends? If I'm not doing things for my degree, I'm with him. The people there I think of as friends are his roommates, Jay and Benji. They've only known Leo a few weeks longer. But yeah, they are definitely friends."

"What are they like?"

"Benji's all heart. Hard to imagine a more giving, gentle man. I get the sense underneath there's a steel core. Jay is something else. He comes off as the most self-assured guy you'd ever want to meet. He's someone who came from an extremely abusive background. He's let me in on a little of it, but wow, what he's done with his life is amazing. The house they all live in is his, officially, but in a sense, all three of them share it. I have been welcomed into it like 'hey, come on in, you belong too.' He's very protective of both guys. I would not want to cross him regarding them."

"Sounds kind of harsh."

Dave shakes his head. "I know this would never happen, but imagine if Kevin hit you. What would Mom do? Kind of like that."

"She'd eat his brains for breakfast before he knew what was happening. Yeah, I get that. How do you fit?"

He stops walking and takes a big breath, turns away overtaken with the realization. "I think I'm already part of the family. Jay and Benji constantly let me know they like me, and they like me with Leo."

She slips an arm around him. Up ahead Leo and Kevin pause, clearly discussing the landscape as they point out different things. Barbara squeezes Dave a little tighter. "We're both very lucky."

———

The turkey tucked in the oven, Jay and Benji go for a walk around campus eerily devoid of students. The shops near campus are also closed, including most restaurants. The open ones have few people. Later that will pick up, but this early in the afternoon only pitiful workers stand about forlornly. The coffee shop seems unnatural with no lingerers guarding their tables. Both have urges to call Dave or Leo but resist. It doesn't stop them from admitting their desire. They want Leo and Dave home.

Later, Tommy stops by before heading to the south side of town. Jay opens a bottle of wine and all three have a glass. "To friends," Jay toasts.

"Where's Leo?"

"Making his first visit to Dave's family," Jay states.

Tommy raises his eyebrows. "Big step."

"Inevitable. Dave's apparently pretty close to his family."

Benji adds, "We were just talking about how we both wish they were here instead."

"Who will be here?"

"A couple of guys Jay met at a party. They have some sort of business designing computer stuff. They had Leo look at some things for them. I haven't met them."

"Diego and Carlos." He looks at Tommy with an ironic glint. "You've seen Carlos."

"I have?" It dawns on him. "You mean...? Okay, yes, indeed I have." His eyes grow quite large.

"I'm not sure I want to know what's going on," Benji says looking back and forth between the two, "but I have a feeling you're going to tell me anyway."

"We helped Carlos fulfill a fantasy. That's all."

"Oh, bullshit, Jay. That is not the whole story."

"Thought you didn't want to know."

He stares Jay down. "I lied."

Looking at Tommy, "Okay with you?"

"Sure."

"Carlos had a fantasy about being watched during sex. I seduced him in the kitchen so Tommy could watch from next door."

"You fuckers. That was very rude..." He crosses his arms and taps his foot petulantly, "...to not invite me."

Tommy adds through laughter, "Now, I really wish I was coming here. I really liked what I saw."

"Really?" Jay asks as he arches an eyebrow.

Benji recognizes Jay's look. "What are you planning now?"

"Satisfying a friend."

"Last time we did something with someone else it got very intense. Kid's doing great now, by the way." Tommy states.

"You've kept in touch. Good."

"What now?" an exasperated Benji asks.

This time Tommy tells the story. "Remember back at the party you guys had when Leo moved in? Jay and I had a three-way with a younger guy, Carl, who had shown up with a friend. Got very intense. Kid shot his load without touching himself, he was so turned on. Kind of freaked him out, but now he's moved to Denver and chasing every boy he can."

"Carl?"

"Yeah, you remember him?" Tommy wonders.

Benji turns to Jay, "Steve's cousin?"

Jay nods.

"Damn, I don't remember that. Steve's never mentioned it either."

"You and Steve had absented yourselves."

"Oh. I was distracted."

"And ever since," teases Jay, "but in the best of ways. Tell Tommy the good news."

"He's coming for a visit over break," Benji quavers gleefully.

"Fantastic! You're unmistakably excited."

"And nervous. It's been all e-mail, texting, and phone calls for months. Scary to know it will be face to face."

"Well, I always wish you the best." He turns back to Jay. "Tell me about Carlos."

"Lord," Benji breaks in, "I think it's time to baste a turkey and start some side dishes. You guys make your plans. I expect to take at least five and no more than ten minutes." Benji begins a retreat to the kitchen, but he turns with hands on hips and adds, "Maybe I'd better take twenty."

"He and his business partner, Diego, are coming over for dinner. I wish I'd known you were interested."

"I can't promise when I can tear away, but if I see the lights on when I return, I'll stop by. Didn't get a clear image of his face, but what I did see? He could fulfill many of my fantasies."

"You did help fulfill one of his quite nicely."

"In a way, I guess he kind of owes me." Tommy laughs heartily. "Seriously, I'll try and stop by."

Leo and Dave set the table. Caleb offers help, but Kevin shrewdly takes him to clean up instead.

As the turkey rests, Mrs. Azzurri puts final touches on side dishes. Barbara fills serving dishes with mashed potatoes, broccoli, salad, cranberry sauce, olives, dressing, and manicotti. Family tradition requires at least one pasta dish every holiday.

Caleb wanted to sit between Dave and Leo, but Barbara vetoes, explaining, "Honey, we're not pulling the table out. There's not enough room for three on a side." She places him next to her on one side with Dave on the end. Leo sits across from Caleb keeping him next to Dave. Mrs. Azzurri sits at the head of the table with Kevin on her right side, Barbara on her left.

Mrs. Azzurri considered asking Leo to carve, but noticing his awkwardness during the day, she bestows the honor on Kevin who handles it with aplomb. Plates passed, Leo asks for a little of each since others said that. Seeing no one starts right away, he waits. Mrs. Azzurri calls for a moment of silence and asks all to join hands. He closes his eyes as soon as he notices he is the only one who hasn't.

Silence ends when Dave's mother simply says, "Thank you." The table erupts into conversation and eating.

Leo feels out of place until Dave's foot finds his under the table, calming him enough to pay more attention.

Kevin asks him if this was anything like Thanksgiving growing up. When he answers with such sincerity that they never celebrated Thanksgiving, it stuns the family.

"What about other holidays like Christmas?"

"None of them, really."

"Was that some kind of religious thing?"

"No, they just didn't."

This oddity briefly halts conversation until Dave steps in. "If we could, I'd like to take a moment to remember Dad." He raises his wine glass. "I miss his presence. He made holidays more special. I want to honor how he helped make me who I am today."

Leo looks at Dave.

For that I am grateful.

Except for pasta, the same feast adorns the table, beautifully laid out by Benji, at home. Carlos and Diego experience the first big holiday away from their birth families.

Jay carves for this more informal dinner. No silence, no rituals. They simply eat. Carlos and Diego talk about their struggles with the business despite some encouraging inquiries.

"I'm very hopeful for the projects Leo reviewed," Carlos elaborates. "We've had a bit of interest on those."

At one point, Benji returns to the kitchen the same time Diego takes a bathroom break. "Carlos, I have a question. Would you like to meet Tommy from next door?"

"If he's half the handsome bear you showed me on your phone that night, sure. Why?"

"He wants to meet you and may stop by. He liked what he saw, and I don't mean just the scene."

Carlos sits for a moment letting this digest, until now uncertain anyone had watched that night. "I'll meet him, sure," he continues with a nervous laugh, quickly composing himself, and adds, "After all, I never did get a review."

Returning from the kitchen, Benji hears that and decides discretion may be a rare, but good, choice for him.

Dinner recommences, Carlos a bit quieter, but otherwise it picks right back up.

The feast lasts a couple of hours, culminating in a grand Italian Cream Cake. The family splits up after dinner. Kevin goes into the den and turns on the television. Dave takes Caleb into the living room to read more where the boy will likely fall asleep again. Barbara decides to join them. She has not heard her brother read a story in quite a while.

Mrs. Azzurri, wanting to know this young man who has apparently taken her son's heart, gratefully accepts his offer to help clean up. She asks about his school work and living situation. Leo's brief admission at dinner steers her from his past. That Leo has some trouble making eye contact and constantly blushes causes no concern. She asks about Dave.

Tension flows out of his face. His forehead unfurrows, and he smiles as words flow. She needs no more information.

Once done, he goes to the living room where Caleb holds his seat.

Barbara finds her mother. "I was beginning to wonder if Dave would ever bring someone home. What do you think?"

"That boy?" Mrs. Azzurri starts, "He's too thin and quiet. His past is a mystery. But he's good."

The four men sit back slightly past gorged. Benji wrangles Diego into helping him clean up. Jay and Carlos move to the living room. As they sit, Jay receives a text from Tommy.

On my way home. Hope you're still up.

"Our neighbor is going to stop over," he notes casually.

Carlos looks at Jay, nods once, and straightens the seam of his pants.

"Think you might want to stick around a bit longer?"

Carlos resists an urge to throw a pillow at Jay. "Possibly."

The evening draws on pleasantly.

Diego puzzles why Carlos ignores hints about time to leave.

About 9:30, Tommy arrives. "Damn, snowing out. Really coming down." After introductions, the handshake between Carlos and Tommy lingers. "I've seen you before, I believe."

Carlos finds Tommy more appealing in person. "Very possible. Not my first visit."

"Very nice to meet you. I didn't get a good look at your handsome face last time," Tommy says as he grins broadly.

"You saw more of me than I did of you."

"Very true."

They find seats next to each other on the small sofa.

The family starts to disappear. Caleb is put to bed. Mrs. Azzurri gives kisses all around and heads off, followed shortly by Kevin. Barbara hangs back. As Dave gathers dishes that snuck into the living room with 'one more bite' snacks, Barbara sits with Leo. "I'm so glad you came."

"It has been wonderful."

She hugs him. "Thank you for Caleb. He's as crazy about you as Dave, you know."

He turns the brightest red he has been for days. "Thank you," he says very softly.

Dave and Leo head for bed. Once inside, Leo says, "Guess we'd better put the sweats on again."

"Not yet," Dave leans against the door. Reaching behind him, he locks it. "Look at me."

Leo stands facing Dave. "That's a nice shirt. You look so handsome, Leo." He walks over and takes him into his arms. He begins to kiss him, hands work their way down the shirt, undoing button after button. He runs his fingers down Leo's partially exposed chest. "That is so sexy," he says as he steps back to see. Eyes a twinkle, he adds, "Leave it on, like that."

Leo steps up to him and covers his mouth in a kiss. He considers following Dave's lead but wants to see all. His hands glide up the skin of Dave's arms. The shirt, soon a forgotten heap, solaces in company of soon discarded shoes and socks.

Dave reaches to undo Leo's belt then top button.

Each movement brings Leo deeper into himself, mind swirls with sensations as the connection with Dave deepens. Further and further, he willingly enters this cosmos of sensation: cock, mouth, hands, ass. The fabric still on his back. By the time he enters Dave, the rest of the world, including financial concerns, dissipate.

Dave reaches up and in the dark calls softly, "Leo."

He calls my name. My name. Leo.

Dave's fingers slip behind Leo's head, pulling him in somehow for more intimacy. "It feels so good, Leo. You."

Leo's eyes focus on Dave's, one after the other.

I do that. I make him feel good.

They kiss. Dave utters something unintelligible into Leo's mouth. A brief break gives him enough time to draw a damp breath before the kiss resumes. In the next break, Dave moans out, "Leo, you feel so good."

Leo raises up by straightening his arms. His eyes feast on Dave's torso, slowly savoring the furry chest, the belly expanding and contracting.

I never looked before. I didn't care until Dave. Dave.

"Dave."

It feels so good to say his name.

Dave's hands explore Leo's body, always something new to discover.

Leo grasps Dave's fullness gently, needing to hold it.

This will be inside me. I don't know how, but he will be my first one. Dave's. It can only be Dave.

He begins stroking this wonderful man.

Legs wrap tightly around Leo's body as Dave's orgasm forms. His muted groans pull Leo forward for one more kiss.

Leo collapses down onto Dave who holds him tight, spent.

Sometime in the night they put on sweats.

Carlos and Tommy sit very close on the small sofa. Benji, Jay, and Diego distribute themselves loosely on the rest of the furniture. They lose track of time until Benji begins to feel the length of the day. He yawns and checks his phone. "Oh my, it's almost midnight."

A round of amazement at the lateness of the hour meets this statement. Making his goodbyes, Benji heads upstairs. Diego and Carlos start making noises about leaving.

Jay carries a few stray dishes to the kitchen and looks across the yard. Snow falls so hard it is difficult to see across to Tommy's. He walks to the alcove and opens the front drapes.

"Guys, it's coming down like crazy."

They all join him. Early for a snow this hard, but not unheard of. A keen wind makes it worse. Jay's mind goes to Leo and Dave.

With virtually no snow experience growing up in southern New Mexico, Diego and Carlos discuss how to get home.

Closing the drapes, Jay announces, "You guys are going nowhere. Tommy, the drifting looks crazy bad. You stay too."

That averted, they return to their seats. Tommy and Carlos snuggle now on the small sofa. Carlos turns into the crook of Tommy's arm and slowly reaches between two buttons on his shirt to feel flesh. Undoing one button gives better access.

Tommy looks at that hand with a slight scowl, but finds Carlos hard to resist, especially with the attention his nipple receives. He glances over to Jay and Diego wondering if Carlos wants to put on another show. For Jay, that would be fine, but Diego? He catches Jay's eye and gives a brief shake of his head.

Jay addresses the group, "It's time for bed." Both Diego and Tommy clearly register relief. "Tommy? Carlos? You guys can take the guest room. Diego this sofa folds out. It's made up and very comfortable."

Jay shuts the door behind him in his room. Going to a window to survey the progress, his concern for Leo and Dave increases. Storms like this back up to the mountains. They may not be aware. Setting his phone alarm in case he doesn't rise early, he plans on calling them first thing tomorrow.

25

Before the sun rises and the alarm goes off, Jay wakes. Muted street light allows judgment of the storm's severity. Drifts rise over three feet with flurries still coming down. There will be lots of digging. Throwing on a pair of sweats and a t-shirt, he decides to start coffee. Guests need to be dealt with. Grabbing his phone, he heads downstairs. The doors to the spare bedroom and Benji's room are closed. He passes Leo's room and wishes he and Dave had stayed here.

Coffee started, he makes the call.

Leo, at the computer reading some of Dave's stories, sees Jay's name on his phone. "Good morning, what a nice surprise! Did you guys have a good Thanksgiving?"

"It was good." Jay says. "And I want to hear all about yours, but I need to check in first. Is it snowing there?"

"Let me see." He stands and moves to a window.

As he stirs awake, Dave says, "Good morning, sweetie. What's going on?"

Covering the phone, "Jay's calling. Wants to know if it's snowing." He gazes out the window. "No nothing. Why?"

"Leo, we had a huge storm here yesterday. Easily over two feet, maybe as much as three. Driving's going to be horrible."

"Wow, there's not a hint of anything here." He looks at Dave who gives him a curious look. "Jay says there's been a ton of snow back in the city. There's none here."

"Let me talk to him." He takes the phone from Leo. "Jay? What's going on?"

"Snow started coming down hard around 8:30 or so and went on well into the night. Lot of wind too, so drifting is way crazy. I've only looked out and haven't turned on the news yet. We kept our guests here it was so bad."

"Shit. There was a slight warning before we left, but it wasn't really expected. This is really fucked."

Jay laughs, "That is more cussing than I've heard out of you ever. Yeah, not good here. Can you guys stay over another day? I want you here, but I want you safe more."

"Thanks, and yeah. Leo, what's your schedule like?"

"Getting to crunch time."

Dave touches one of Leo's legs with his free hand. "Tell someone to get the news on. We need to see what travel's going to be like." Leo heads out. "Jay, Leo's going to get the news on. I'm not sure we can wait, nasty time of the year. I have tons of papers to grade, two stories to finish by Monday and polishing up a few poems. Crap I could have done all but the grading from here if I'd brought my laptop."

"You guys both have your phones. Do you have your charger?"

"Yeah for both, and it'll charge in the car if we need. If we do leave today, I'll make sure to have a full tank too. Wait, Leo's back."

Leo takes the phone and puts it on speaker. "The news isn't great. Storm dumped up to 40 inches in parts. They've got road crews out everywhere, but that's about it. Sorry, I'm not familiar with all this."

Dave adds, "We're going to have to think about it. I wasn't planning to take off real early. Maybe we'll see as the day goes. I'll call you back once we know."

"I'll be here digging out. Can't go anywhere. Good thing there's plenty of food."

"Same here." Dave heads out of the room.

Leo takes the phone off speaker. "Is this really bad?"

"Possibly. Partly depends on what the roads will be like for you guys. Shitty timing."

Caleb comes charging into the room, yelling Dave and Leo's names in his normal morning excitement.

Jay pulls the phone away briefly. "What the hell is that?"

"Dave's nephew, Caleb." Leo holds the phone to his chest and greets the boy. "Good morning. Dave's in the living room." The little boy grabs Leo's leg in a raucous hug then runs to find his uncle. Leo resumes his conversation with Jay. "He's very active."

"Sounds like you hit it off with him."

"Jay, it's all kinds of strange but wonderful."

"I'm very happy for you. I miss you though."

"I know. I wish I could be both places. I want to come home."

"I want you here too. Dave too. But I want you safe, so if you can wait a day, it would be better."

"I have so much to do down there. Should have brought my laptop."

Jay laughs, "Dave said the same thing. I should let you go. Guests will be getting up soon. Even made Tommy stay."

"Wow, it was that bad?"

"Oh yeah, so please be very careful."

"Okay, we will."

Jay clicks off.

Damn, I love those guys. They better get home safe.

Jay pours a mug of coffee. The house should begin stirring soon, so he pulls out sugar and milk, setting them on the kitchen table. He's going to have to start shoveling soon too.

Surprisingly, Carlos appears. "Morning."

"Morning. Want coffee?"

"God, yes."

Jay pours some.

"Sleep well?"

"Eventually," he says with a bit of a smile. "Not what I expected, but yes, very well."

"What'd you expect? I got the feeling you wanted to put on another show last night. That what you mean?"

"That was probably the wine. Not sure I want to go into it, but, well… there were pleasant surprises. I'll leave it at that."

"You have gotten my interest up, but fine. Others'll be getting up and about soon. You up for shoveling?"

"The least I can do. Let me get dressed."

"There's extra coats and overshoes in the closet under the front stairs, a couple of snow shovels in there too." He goes to the window. "It's finally stopped. Good time to get started. See you outside."

Jay finishes the front steps as Carlos joins him. They work down the entry walk to the sidewalk. "You take right, I'll take left." They continue to work for half an hour before Tommy and Benji emerge.

"Need help?" offers Tommy.

"Only have the two shovels, but if you guys want to take over, no argument from me," says Jay.

Benji grabs the shovel from Jay as Tommy goes to Carlos.

Jay tells Benji, "I called Leo this morning to warn them. They haven't had any snow up there."

"They staying over?"

"Not sure yet. Waiting to hear from them."

"I hope they can get home soon."

"Me too. But safely." He heads inside noting Tommy and Carlos pay little attention to shoveling.

Diego is sitting up as Jay passes through the living room. Jay offers coffee.

When he returns, Diego thanks him and asks, "Did you know about Carlos and your neighbor? I kind of thought there was a bit more going on."

"I thought you two didn't keep secrets."

Diego shrugs his shoulders. "Just because he hasn't told me doesn't mean he won't." He walks to the front of the house and looks out the window to see Carlos and Tommy huddling together. "Guess I better help out too if we expect to get out of here anytime today."

Looks like it will be a few hours before all can leave, but Jay's mind drifts to his friends on the mountain. He absently nods agreement to Diego.

Barbara's family leaves around 9:00. They do not live far and on this side of the divide. Boisterous declarations about Christmas from Caleb accompany their departure.

Mrs. Azzurri puts a tray with coffee, cups, cream and sugar, and the remaining coffee cake down, and then sits with Dave and Leo at the dining table. "I wish you boys would stay over. This isn't good."

"If either of us had brought a laptop, I'd agree," Dave starts. "There's so much to do at this time of year. None of it can be done from my old computer or yours." He looks between his mom and Leo. "I'll think more while I get a tank of gas." Dave rises and returns to the bedroom.

Mrs. Azzurri touches a hand to Leo's arm. "Stay with me. I'd like to spend some time with you."

He pours himself coffee. "Thank you. This has been very nice."

"Very different for you, I think."

"Yes."

Dave comes out dressed for the cold weather.

Mrs. Azzurri gets up from the table to walk him to the door. "Leo's staying with me." She gives him a kiss as he leaves.

Passing Leo on her way to the kitchen, she tells him, "Cut some cake while I get plates and forks."

Leo does as he's told, transferring a generous slice to each plate she places in front of him.

"Dave likes you. He doesn't bring friends home."

Leo naturally brightens to red. "I like him too."

"You are perhaps more than friends?"

Leo looks her in the eye but has no idea what to say. "I would like that. He's amazing."

"He says that about you too." She pats his hand. "I think maybe he's right. What you did for Caleb was very nice. You are as smart as Dave says."

"Thank you." He pauses. "But you know? People always see how smart I am because it's math and science. I think Dave is highly intelligent too. Not the same way and in different fields. He's made me see things I never noticed before, I mean really see them. He can describe things in ways I'd never dream." Leo has no difficulty talking about Dave.

"Growing up he was always writing. Making up stories. It's his gift."

They continue until the subject of their discussion returns. They both smile at him.

"What?"

Mrs. Azzurri goes up to her son and gives him a hug, "Any decision?"

He turns to Leo. "What do you think, sweetie?"

"No idea. The snow coming up here is the most I've seen in my life. Maybe we should call Jay and see how it is down there." He pulls out his phone and hits Jay's name. "Hey, we're trying to figure out what to do. What's it like down there?"

"Digging out all morning, barely starting the driveway. No more falling and the sky's starting to clear. What about you guys?"

"Nothing here. Wouldn't have known if you hadn't called. I'm going to put Dave on. He's the driver."

"I wish you boys would stay an extra day," Mrs. Azzurri tells Leo.

"We should have brought our laptops," Leo tells her. "Then we could work from here. Never anticipated this."

Dave paces the living room while talking to Jay. "I'll have to see if I can find more information online. The news doesn't carry anything about the roads. Thanks, Jay."

Dave ends the call when he returns to the table and hands Leo his phone. "I don't want to, but I think we have to get going. The snow's stopped, and sun is starting to come out. There's around an hour before we hit the divide." He shakes his head. "We have so much to do back there."

The decision made, they load Bart. Dave loans Leo a coat in case they stop on the way.

Mrs. Azzurri, after handing Dave his cooler packed with leftovers, pulls Leo aside to say her farewell. "You take care of each other. Come back soon when there's not all the extra people."

She turns to Dave, "I love you, son. *Egli un bravo ragazzo. Abbiate cura bene di lui. Mi piace lui.*"

"*Anche a me place lui. Molto. So che lui è tranquillo. Ma lui è molto buono in tutto che importa a me.* I love you, Mom."

Following them to the door, she stands in the frame, pulling her sweater close and watches them get in the car.

Dave waves, causing Leo to turn to her. He raises his hand, tentatively at first, to wave to her also. She rewards that with a more enthusiastic wave and smile while watching them turn out of the driveway and pull away.

She doesn't want us to go. She cares about us.

Leo looks at Dave. "I like your family."

Dave looks at Leo, "Thanks. Think they kind of like you too. A whole bunch."

Jay and Benji rest on the front porch, leaning on the shovels for a few moments to regather energy.

"I'm glad they're gone," Benji says as he looks over to Tommy's house.

"Me too," replies Jay. "Didn't expect overnight guests but nice to have help digging out. They didn't go very far."

"Carlos and Tommy hit it off." He playfully shoves Jay. "Hope Diego can keep himself entertained." The humor melts. "Dave and Leo coming home?"

He nods bruskly. "You're going to worry until they're sitting on the sofa holding hands."

The image makes him smile. "They're so damned cute together." He pokes Jay with one foot. "You can admit you're worried too, babe. When can we expect them?"

"Normally five to six hours. Could be more like eight to nine. Fuck."

Once inside they start to pick up the living room. Soon they merely pick things up only to put them down in another spot, not enough cleaning to keep their hands or minds occupied.

"Jay, this is going to drive us nuts. The Powell's went to Anne's for the holiday. Let's clear their sidewalk. Keep us busy."

"Excellent idea."

Outside, other neighbors emerge to dig themselves out. Shared looks of disbelief and exaggerated shoulder shrugs pass along the street.

Dave mentally gears up as they climb higher. Clear roads may disappear. Puffy white clouds dot the sky, unlike the dull grey ones currently exiting the city. He starts to withdraw from the enjoyable discussion with Leo so he can concentrate. "We're getting near the top. We'll get a pretty good idea soon of what the rest of the trip will be like."

Leo hears the tension in Dave's voice but doesn't know what to expect. Excitement for a new adventure mixes with fear. Dave's hands visibly grip the wheel more firmly, his eyes focus more keenly on the still clear road.

"Sweetie, there's a place to charge our phones right under the dashboard on your side. You might want to plug yours in now." He pulls his out of his pocket and places it in the tray between the seats. "When yours is full, switch to mine."

Leo hears the note of alarm in his own voice. "Going to be that bad?"

Dave shrugs, "Maybe, maybe not. Better to be ready. There'll be a lot of dead spots anyway." He glances over at Leo, sees the worry, and bestows a reassuring touch. "I've driven in a lot of snow. It may be tense, and I may have to ignore you to focus, but if it gets too bad, we pull over. Mom packed plenty of leftovers in the cooler. We have lots of extra clothes to keep us warm." He takes Leo's hand to his lips. "I'll be extra careful."

"Okay." There seems nothing other than to sit uselessly in the passenger seat. "Wish I could do more."

Dave pulls over, turns to Leo, and pulls him in for a kiss. "I may not be able to do that for a bit. You being here in the same car is plenty, okay? See the top of the hill there?"

Leo nods.

"That's the divide. Let's hope for the best. We can take it as a good sign the road is open. Look to the side of the road up ahead. See the gates on either side? If it was too bad, they'd be closed and we'd have to turn back. That doesn't mean it will be easy, but the road is passable. Best case, the road crews have cleared it all the way, and the sun will melt what's left."

"What's worst case?"

"The road would be closed."

"Any way to get more information? Maybe the radio?"

"You can try, but the only stations I've ever picked up here are from further west, usually Grand Junction or Craig. If they're talking about the storm at all, it'll be jokes about how they dodged this one." He squeezes Leo's hand. "I suppose you could see if you can find anything online with your phone. I checked right before leaving, and there wasn't much about the roads where we'll be for the next few hours. They said the storm moved north and is disintegrating."

Leo kisses Dave. "Let's do it then."

Dave pulls back onto the road, very thankful for no traffic, an extra hazard best not encountered.

The change is not immediately evident as they cross. Dave sees smatterings of snow ahead, meaning only the storm blew north before coming this high. He can stop at a small town twenty miles ahead for more information.

As they start to descend, they see glimpses along the way of what to expect. Every time a view of the lower lands breaks out, white dominates, if not completely overtakes, the vista. The brief scenes give no real concept of depth or road conditions.

Leo, studies in wonderment at these glimpses, offering a baffling beauty: soft, inviting, yet perilous.

While the road remains clear, Dave pushes Bart, figuring to make up time at the beginning of the drive. By the time they hit the first little town, snow transitions from random patches to shallow ground cover. The road sports an occasional wet patch from melted snow. These will be treacherous later. A local service station provides little helpful information. Crews have been seen heading down the mountains, but traffic reports continue saying slow going with major delays. Fortunately, traffic has been nonexistent, at least so far. Before getting back on the road, he tops off his windshield washer reservoir, a task he forgot before the drive began.

Wet patches start showing with uncomfortable frequency, causing Dave to slow a few miles per hour. No ice yet but that seems inevitable. They come upon a stretch of road displaying an extended white-blanketed vista covering the entire valley. Snow remains on tree branches blending them with the ground cover and making it difficult to judge snow depth. The road thankfully shows in black swaths.

The first car heading the opposite direction passes, going slow enough to see the passengers' expressions, but hard to figure out if their bored or stressed.

Uncomfortable for some time now, Leo finally asks for information.

"I'm sorry, Leo. I forget this is very different for you. So far, we're all right. The valley we're about to enter looks worse than where we were but not by much. Seeing more cars would be a comfort, but that may not happen. It's Friday after Thanksgiving, so there won't be much traffic anyway. I'm afraid it will be worse after the next rise."

"Hate that I can't help with driving."

"Actually, there may be something you can do, if it gets rough up ahead. I'll start getting tense which is not good. You can keep my mind relaxed. I may ask you to sing me a song or tell me a story. Radio reception is spotty and poor up here. There are some CD's in the glove box I might want to hear at some point too."

"Not much of a singer or storyteller."

"Doesn't have to be a storybook story. Everyday stuff would be good. What do you do with Jay and Benji or your course work? Things we've done that you liked. You're good with that. Oh, one more thing you can always do."

"What?"

"I hate that I have to keep both hands ready. I'd rather be able to hold yours or rest my hand on your thigh. But there's nothing that says you can't put your hand on my thigh."

Leo does so.

"Better already."

Leo smiles.

Despite his fears, Leo admits to the beauty. Before meeting Dave, he would have looked at this snow as ice crystals stacked logically due to weather conditions. Now, he sees subtle variations, spots of grey, blue, even purple. Patches where a log or rock pokes up assert more under this blanket.

"I've never seen anything like this. The desert never was anything different." He glances at Dave, amazed at how his focus remains solid on the road, scanning ahead constantly. It dawns on him, people tell him the same thing about himself, how he focuses on a task. It pleases him this wonderful man does that too. "I remember walking so much around the city. I wish now I'd paid more attention to the landscape. Something about the monochrome of this snow reminds me of Tucson."

They make it across the valley floor with little incident. As the car starts up this slope, the drive's difficulty rises a notch. No sun warmed much of this section of road. Ice laces through wet patches. Multiple switchbacks add to the danger.

Breaking over the ridge, snow depth clearly deepens across the next valley.

"Start thinking of stories, sweetie. I may need one going into that curve. How about the best meal Benji ever made?"

Once they hit the curve, driving difficulty for some time becomes evident. Bart slips once, causing a slight jolt for Leo. He quickly looks to Dave and sees him taking it in stride, back to driving after a quick adjustment. A smile blossoms.

He's keeping us safe. Us. He deserves a good story.

Leo thinks back on so many delicious meals since arriving and decides on his first meal in his new home. Benji has made better since then, but none has surpassed its importance. He winds around the meal, including how he helped with measurements, his first experience with fresh asparagus, and how everything tasted better and better.

Amazed with the detail Leo gives, Dave drives out of this difficult section and cruises along a decent stretch on the basin's floor, dry from hours of caressing sunshine.

"Thank you. That was lovely."

"I wish I could kiss you right now."

"Put your hand to my lips."

Leo obeys and is happily rewarded with a very loud smack of a kiss.

The snow level deepens. Wet patches from melt cause some splash back. Snow, blown back onto the road, taunts in other places.

Dave again slows. "I may need a song soon."

"I don't know many."

They start up another rise that is the most difficult yet. Dave drops his speed to ten miles per hour on some curves. "Sing. Please."

Leo works his way through the only thing that comes to mind, "Three Blind Mice."

"Sorry that wasn't very long. I never learned a lot of songs. I'll try a story instead." He tells about Jay walking him around the backyard, explaining the different plants. The story takes them over the rise and well into the next smaller valley.

Snow becomes still more abundant. Larger drifts linger threateningly close to the road; several encroach nearly a foot onto the pavement. Grit tells Dave a road crew passed through here.

Traffic picks up. Cars confront them every few minutes. Dave had to pass a couple of cars driving scarily slow. Another passed him going frighteningly fast. "Put some music on. Please. Whatever you find."

Leo pulls out a CD of a men's acapella group and slides it in.

Dave visibly relaxes. He hums along unconsciously with a noticeably good voice, the familiar distraction enough to get him over the next two small rises and valleys. The snow level inches up the longer they are on the road and the lower down the mountains they get. The next town offers a chance for a bathroom break and much needed movement. Pulling into a fast food joint, they also order a bite to eat. Dave calls his mother while Leo calls Jay with a progress report.

"They're about halfway," Jay reports to Benji.

"That's good. Been about three hours."

"Yeah, but the second half will be worse. They haven't hit the worst snow and traffic's light. What's the news saying?"

Benji scans until he finds a station covering the storm's aftermath. "Road crews out all over the city. Interstates are clear, but dense traffic for the most part." He watches for a bit. "Nothing about mountain roads."

Jay thinks. "I don't remember if the news usually covers them. Never cared before."

"I'll make soup from some of the leftovers. That'll be good when they get home."

The road steadily degrades. A light wind twirls snow around. Patches of ice pop up with disturbing regularity. Bart moves with the care of a cat on aluminum foil. Leo continues thinking of stories to tell and has put in a third CD, fascination for snow quite deceased. Each valley opens to another rise on the other side. Each crest discloses a new basin. It seems they will never find that final valley or crest.

Leo looks out at the latest vista. It is difficult to place it in relation to the trip to Dave's mother's, the landscape completely different, but somehow familiar, under the white blanket. It hits him why. "This makes me think of returning from some conference or symposium when I was back in Tucson. Coming in on the plane, the landscape had this same lack of variation. The desert sand was kind of like the snow. The few cacti or rock formations that stood out are like the trees and things that aren't covered."

Leo glances at Dave, noting the tension. Stories and music no longer ease his clenched jaw as he focuses on the road. Leo settles into a quiet sulkiness. His hand drifts over to rest on Dave's thigh again.

Unable to think of something new to say, Leo decides to pull out a new CD. Listening to Dave's soft singing, he enters a funk regarding his financial situation.

I have to find a way to make this work. I cannot lose all this. I cannot!

His focus drifts absently along the scenery, settling on a granite outcropping dominating a section of the road ahead. Its jagged crags fascinate him.

A sudden shift in the car's direction causes the scenery to blur at his sides as he hurtles out the windshield toward the stone wall. Unable to turn his head away as his trajectory impels his body toward the crag, granite transforms into a solid concrete wall. Two bodies hurl past him at unbelievable speed. Knowing they will slam into the wall before he can look away, he forces his eyes to close—

"Lord! That was scary," Dave says as the car jerks to a stop. "That came out of nowhere."

Leo turns quickly. "What?"

"You didn't see it? A deer darted right in front of us. Barely had time to stop and almost went into a skid." He shakes his head and reaches over for Leo's hand. "You okay?"

Leo looks at Dave then the now normal outcropping. He stammers, "I must have nodded off..."

That was a dream? Must have been.

Dave laughs lightly. "Well, I'm definitely awake now." He leans over for a kiss before resuming the drive.

Dave has driven under worse conditions and heavier snowfalls. The storm has, after all, ended. Leo sits right there next to him, but not being able to touch makes him feel like he may as well be on the moon. The stories help as does the music, but ultimately it comes down to him and the road. Beginning at 10:00, they now hit the two-thirds mark at 3:00.

Traffic steadily picks up. They face one or two cars every minute. At one point, with few safe places to pass, they lolled behind a car creeping at 20 mph until it finally turned off. The snow level seems to have stabilized, but the steady breeze causes drifting. Dave wants to get off the mountain before dark. Once on the interstate, at least that won't be a problem. Increased traffic could take its place.

Leo sleeps.

Dave glances at him. Leo's hand slips off Dave's thigh. He gently puts it back, causing Leo to stir.

Looking around at the surrounding mountains, Leo sighs in frustration. "How much longer?" comes out harsher than meant. "Sorry."

"It's okay." Dave feels tired too. "We should be able to get to the interstate in less than an hour. After that? Depends on traffic." The car clock reads nearly 4:00. "I'm hoping we get home by six."

"But could be later, right?"

He lets out a long breath. "Yeah. We'll have to make a stop for gas too. All this slow, fits-and-starts driving really drinks it up. We can dig into the cooler then. I'm hungry."

"Me too, come to think of it. I could dig into it now."

"No. Too dangerous to take off your seat belt and crawl around. Sorry." He risks a moment to caress Leo's hand.

"I can wait. I better think of another story, or food's all we'll both be able to think of." He tries to think of something and then begins to giggle.

"One day, I came home from a department lunch. I had to get slightly dressed up, so I wore a pair of pants Jay had given me. Benji was sitting in the living room. He had been promising for weeks he'd hem them up. Suddenly, it was the exact time for him to do it." Soon Leo is lost in the tale that lasts nearly twenty minutes. "I thought it would be a truly tedious project, but he kept telling all those stories and jokes during the whole process, keeping me in stitches the entire time he re-hemmed both pair."

Dave begins to laugh. "Did you just really say that?"

Leo isn't sure what Dave means for a moment until he gets what he said.

"Sweetie," Dave says with delight, "I may steal that line for a story sometime."

He has been talking for hours trying to keep me alert. I know tons of things about Jay and Benji. He's talked about George, Tommy, and even about some of his teachers and other people in his program. He has told me about the desert. He has told me about our trip. He has spoken on and on yet still so little of his personal past. Not one word about his parents or what it was like growing up.

Dave recognizes the final hill. After it will be mainly downhill to the interstate. With the temperature starting to cool, soon the patches of water will become ice. As they start the climb, he says, "This is the final rise."

"Good," comes the grateful response.

Over the top, they get the first view of the interstate. With the sun getting quite low in the sky, it heartens Dave. As they get nearer, his heart sinks again. He sees the faint glow of red: brake lights. Lots of brake lights.

―――――

Jay and Benji pause longer and longer every time they pass a window with a view of the street, hoping to catch the first sight of Bart. Nothing keeps them distracted any longer. They know what they're doing doesn't help. Logic is water to worry's oil.

―――――

Dense interstate traffic stretches the two-mile drive to the next exit into a thirty-minute trek.

Darkness sneaks in as they pull into a service station. The price screams of gouging, but Bart is parched from all the driving in lower gears. They wait several minutes for a free pump. Leo hurries inside to use the bathroom. Dave fills up, pulls up to the front of the station to free the pump, finds his phone, and calls Jay who answers immediately.

"We're at a gas station off the interstate."

"That's the best news of the day. You guys must be beat. Benji's got some soup on the stove for you."

"God that sounds heavenly. Traffic is crappy, so it'll still be some time."

"How's our flaxen-haired boy?"

"Tired. Hitting the bathroom. Which I need to do myself. Wait, he's coming out now." He gets Leo's attention and hands him the phone. "I called Jay. My turn for the bathroom."

"Hi. I'm tired of being in the car," Leo says, barely keeping the whine out of his voice.

"Won't be too much longer now. Wish traffic was better."

Hearing Jay's voice, he wants to be home.

When Dave returns, he suggests, "How about we crack open the cooler before getting back on the road. Benji has soup brewing, but I need something now."

"Sounds wonderful."

Dave opens Bart's hatchback and grabs the cooler. A chilling breeze makes Leo very glad Dave loaned him this coat. They pull out turkey and eat it with their fingers. They lean against each other as they gorge, feeling so good to touch. "Our fingers are greasy," Leo says.

Instead of giving in to the temptation of licking the grease off Leo's fingers, Dave reaches for his pack and pulls out a t-shirt. "Has to be washed anyway."

Dave notes how filthy Bart has become on this drive, his even blue now transitioning to a lower level of wet, tawny road goo. They return to the line of cars on the interstate. "This is going to take forever. But driving will be easier, so..." He takes Leo's hand.

The closer to home they get, the longer it seems to take. Inch by inch they crawl along.

"Dave? When we do get back...stay over."

Dave laughs. "I would like nothing better."

———

Their vigil continues as day fully becomes night. Benji placed the pot of soup on low and splits his time checking to make sure there is enough liquid and watching the street for oncoming cars.

Rare cars come up the street, none the desired one. Both receive periodic progress texts from Leo. The last one, thirty minutes ago, let them know they were in the city limits, but traffic is obnoxious, and most side streets are ice-packed.

Jay sends other calls straight to voicemail, leaving his phone open. Nearing 8:00, nothing keeps him away from the window. After a lull, a car finally appears, moving slowly down their frozen street. "Benji." It approaches.

Benji joins him at the window.

"Fuck! Finally!"

Bart pulls into the driveway. Jay and Benji throw on coats and run to meet them at the garage. Jay, flustered, must enter the code twice. As the car pulls in, they flank Bart, Jay on the driver's side, Benji on the passenger's. Dave barely turns the car off before doors open and the two are pulled into relieving arms. Visibly drained, the couple welcomes the warmth given by these two anxious friends. They meet in the back of the car so each can trade.

Leo shakes in Jay's arms from an overwhelming combination of exhaustion, relief, and gratitude. "Welcome home," he hears whispered tenderly, giving strength to deepen his hold.

Each man grabs one bag leaving an arm available to hold another man. The cooler, in no danger of becoming warm in the unheated garage, remains for a later trip. They clumsily make their ways around the house to the kitchen. Coats are discarded. Dave and Leo's shoes come off. After making a bathroom stop, Jay guides them to the living room, seated side by side and told to relax. Benji returns to the kitchen as Jay scurries upstairs. Both return to find Dave and Leo leaning into each other, hand in hand. Dave talks to his mother to let her know they arrived.

Jay brings each man a soft set of sweatshirts, sweatpants, and a fresh pair of socks. Gladly Leo and Dave strip out of the clothes they've had on way too long.

Leo's mind drifts back to when Jay and Benji bathed and clothed him. Dave at his side, Benji and Jay close, happiness envelopes him.

Comforted by the lush softness of these clothes, Dave murmurs his gratitude and snuggles up closer to Leo. His magnificent eyes focus on Jay, then Benji.

Benji serves bowls of soup. Jay and Benji listen as the pair on the sofa share the grueling story. But their exhaustion from the trek catches up. First Dave, then Leo, dozes off. Benji removes their empty bowls.

They look down at their sleeping friends. "We can't leave them there. They need to be in bed," Jay says.

Benji agrees. "They're too cute to wake."

"I can carry them one at a time." Jay considers. "You take their bags."

Dave is positioned in a way that makes lifting him easier. Jay gently slips an arm under Dave's knees, takes an arm and wraps it around his neck before slipping his other arm under the sleeping man. Steadying himself, making sure he has hold, he eases Dave more fully into his arms. Pushing off with his legs, he stands, finding Dave more solid than anticipated, but Jay is strong enough. When Benji comes down for a second load, Jay, without a clear sight line, quietly asks for guidance to maneuver out of the room and up the stairs.

"I pulled the covers down," Benji tells Jay.

Once in the room, he eases Dave onto the bed.

Dave curls up without waking.

Jay returns for Leo. As Benji comes back down from taking all the bags up, he again guides Jay. Leo, lighter than Dave and easier to carry, does stir, but only to snuggle more into the arms bearing him.

Jay lowers Leo to the bed and pulls the covers over the couple.

Briefly, Leo opens his eyes enough to find Dave and moves over to spoon him and returns to sleep.

Dave shifts to find Leo's arm and wrap it around him, uttering simply, "Leo," before dropping back to sleep himself as the roommates steal out of the room.

The sun blazes brightly. Dave awakes alone. He feels the soft fabric against his skin and remembers pulling on this pale green sweatshirt and pants.

How did I get upstairs?

Standing, he gazes around the room, Leo's room. Little to tell him that. The glorious box, Leo's computer. No pictures of his parents or a younger Leo. No art. No books other than texts. Such a puzzle. His present life? An open book, all chapters available. His past life? In a treasure chest on a sunken ship deep in the ocean. But Leo lives here. He has shared this room several nights now. His heart resides here far more than his own tiny apartment.

After a bathroom stop, he goes downstairs and passes the front window offering a view of the snow, still piled high.

We made it through that, sweetie. You and me.

Muffled voices coming from the kitchen lead to Jay and Benji.

"Good morning, guys." They greet him in return, Benji offering coffee as he sits. "Where's Leo?"

"Downstairs doing laundry," answers Jay.

He accepts coffee thankfully, vaguely noting it is prepared to his liking. "He didn't have to do that."

"He's Leo," Jay offers mirthfully. "Yes, he did."

Leo enters, "What's so funny?" He goes to Dave to share a morning kiss and is drawn onto his lap.

"You are, my gorgeous cleanaholic genius."

Leo makes no argument, settling into Dave's embrace.

26

Leo notices how little snow remains merely a week after Thanksgiving, the streets and sidewalks virtually clear. Mounds of now discoloring remnants of the storm blemish lawns. Piles, shoved by city crews, sit in extreme corners of parking lots like punished children. He would spend time contemplating how the bright sun helps take care of all this except for one thing. Yet another first: Christmas presents. He ponders that on a detoured walk to class, taking extra time to pass stores along the streets lining the campus. Nothing satisfies, too pricey or trivial, another expense.

There always seems to be a new way for Leo to spend what little he has. Only yesterday he checked with the department to find still no positions for tutors or T.A.s, even with a new semester starting next month. Recently, he found out Jay and Benji plan to exchange presents. Dave will likely give him something too.

He heads back to campus and passes several itinerant vendors set up on the campus mall. One, selling homemade jewelry, catches his eye. Nothing fancy, mostly necklaces or bracelets of simple stones woven into leather or hemp straps. The vendor perks up when he stops. The work, less flashy or polished than others, draws only occasional interest. "Did you make all these?"

"Yes, except the earrings. My friend does those, but never has enough for a booth. See anything you like?"

"Maybe. I like your work."

"Thanks. Something for yourself or someone else?"

"Someone else."

The young man studies Leo and starts to smile. "Boyfriend?"

Leo meets his eye and grins. "Yeah, and my roommates. Your work is very affordable." He knows he'll get something now. Nothing more than $10, many pieces sell for considerably less.

"Materials are pretty cheap. Frankly, it's not great stuff. I'm learning."

Leo is eyeing some of the bracelets, simple strands with one or two stones. He picks one up. "Lapis?"

"You like it?"

"Very much. I'll take it." He studies the other bracelets as the vendor sets the first one to the side. "What are these?" He points out one that has a red stone and one that has purple.

"Garnet and amethyst."

Even at $5 each, it's a healthy bite out of his budget. He likes the work and the artist. "I'll take all three."

"Wow, great. You need a box?"

He hands the man the twenty previously placed in his wallet deciding that was his maximum. "No." He slips them in a pocket of his pack.

This brings me down below the $200 per month until September.

"Can I give you my card? Never hurts to advertise."

The question snaps Leo out of his concerns. "Sure." He accepts the card and reads it. "Thanks, Ty. I'm Leo." They shake hands, then he saunters away, happily poorer.

Heading up Jewel Street, Dave sees Leo's blond head as he waits on the porch. They will spend their first full day and night together since the Thanksgiving holiday two weeks ago. He picks up his pace, almost skipping.

Leo looks up and jumps to his feet to meet Dave. "I didn't think you'd ever get here," he says as they collide into each other's arms and share a tottering kiss.

"That is exactly what I've needed." Dave says, spinning Leo around. "You look extra scrumptious this morning."

"Benji fixed breakfast. Come on."

They giggle their way across the living and dining rooms to the kitchen.

"Good morning, Benji," Dave sweeps him into a dance. "Isn't this a wonderful day?"

"Lord, you two are impossible today." Benji laughs. "Leo's been silly all morning, now you."

"Where's Jay?" Dave wants to include him in this festive mood.

"Visiting his brother," Benji replies. "Mostly fun, but I think there were some more family issues going on. Not sure. Jay just hinted that Tim wanted him for more than just a visit."

Dave gives a pouty face then twirls Benji around again. "Then you get his dance."

A laughing Benji manages to ask what their plans are for the day.

"The art museum offers a free day for students today," Dave starts. "Then we may find a tour of the historic district."

Giddiness continues through breakfast and down the street to the campus where they catch a bus taking them downtown. Except for the deli, neither Dave nor Leo has been more than a few blocks away from the neighborhood.

They step onto a crowded bus and struggle finding space for them to stay together. No adjoining seats available, they stand close. Each grabs onto the same pole. In no time, Dave's hand covers Leo's, enhancing their desire after not being together for two weeks. The swaying and general bumpiness of the ride adds to the sensation as they crash into each other constantly, somehow managing to avoid other riders. Every stop adds a few more people until, by the time they arrive downtown, being jammed together needs no pretense.

After a short walk, they find the museum, also surprisingly busy. Sharing a pair of headphones to follow the recorded tour keeps them in close contact.

For lunch, they squeeze around a tiny table in a crowded, inexpensive café. Hands sneak under the table between bites of food until activity under the table flows as busily as customers in the aisles.

A crammed shuttle brings the couple down the main street of downtown where they join a walking tour of one of the city's historic districts. The guide keeps the larger than normal group closely packed to complete on time.

The cramped nature of the day continues on the return shuttle. Dave backs up close to Leo, deciding to take advantage of the situation rather than fight it. Leo feels Dave's ass bump into his crotch continually during the ride and braces to receive the full benefit of Dave's friskiness.

Exiting quickly, they dash the short trip to the bus stop and find seats together for the trip home. Their hands rove more adventurously as darkness steals in. By their stop, all they want is to gratify what has been building all day.

Benji sees them come in and starts to greet them, but they don't notice him in their rush to get upstairs. Instead he waves to the eddying current left in their wake. "Welcome home. Sounds like you had a wonderful time."

The door slams behind them. Leo leans against it as Dave kisses him passionately.

The constant teasing quality of the day adds to the frustration built from being apart. Dave wants Leo.

Holding Leo's hands, he backs up to the bed and sits.

Leo expects Dave to start gently.

Instead Dave spots the wooden box and pulls out a condom. "I want you inside me so much, Leo."

A puzzled look requests further information.

"Sweetie, this whole day has been one long foreplay." He turns to bend over the bed.

Leo enjoys the difference of Dave's sexual drive. Assertive, aggressive, at times demanding. Leo eagerly complies to the current demand, caught up in the heat of Dave's passion. Neither holds back any longer.

Eventually, Leo puts Dave's still partially-clothed legs over one shoulder, causing Dave's torso to turn fully onto his back. Gazing into each other's eyes brings them closer. Leo leads, erupting inside Dave, moaning out his orgasm. As his subsides, Dave's begins. The dark hair on belly and chest looks drizzled with icing. They wrap into each other after finally getting rid of their clothes and fall into a nap until Benji calls them for dinner.

As they emerge from the room and head down, Benji waits for them at the bottom of the stairs, hands on his hips and petulance on his lips.

Dave and Leo exchange glances. Dave asks, "What's going on?"

Benji breaks into a smile. "Just wanted to make sure I was visible again." Then he pirouettes and heads for the dining room.

They can only shrug their shoulders, completely unaware of their earlier snub.

A Mexican feast awaits: guacamole to start, followed by flat enchiladas and rice. A dessert of sopaipillas with honey follows the wonderfully spicy dinner. Afterwards, Benji suggests a walk around the neighborhood.

Given the holiday, several houses boast decorative statements. Dave walks between the others, one hand holding Leo's. Knowing not to ask about Leo's past for such events, he asks Benji if he ever decorated for Christmas.

"Depends on where I was placed. Some years I was in a home that did, some years not. What about you?"

"Yeah, we did. Nothing elaborate like these homes. A simple strand of lights around the front window framing the tree would be about it. Mostly it was about the tree. When we were small, my sister and I would try to see who could hang the most ornaments. Then, of course, we'd see who got the most presents. My parents always made sure it was a tie, I recognize now, but it was fun." He feels Leo listening and senses the desire to know. "Mom always trundled us off to midnight Mass. After, we'd get to pick one present to open. The rest had to wait until morning. We'd try to argue every year that technically it was the next day already, but she was always firm."

"What's midnight Mass?" ventures Leo.

Questions like this from Leo no longer surprise him. "I was raised Catholic. Not a part of my life now, but we went to Mass every Sunday. I was even an altar boy." Sensing that may need some explanation, he adds, "I kind of liked helping the priest with the services. The rituals were comforting back then. Anyway, twice a year, Christmas and Easter, there's a special Mass celebrated at midnight. It was a rite of passage when you were old enough to stay up."

"I had weird all over the place religion thrown at me," Benji injects. "Sometimes I'd be in a home that had religion, other times little. The worst was the super fundamentalist family I was placed with one year. Horrid experience for a little gay boy who never could hide his fascination for other boys. That was a tricky one to escape." He laughs about it.

Feeling strange having nothing to share, Leo can only add, "We didn't do anything for holidays." Increasingly believing life did not start until he talked to Jay on the phone and decided to move into this magical house, it makes him begin to realize how truly bizarre his rearing was.

Dave squeezes his hand and brings it to his lips. He turns his head toward Benji. The two of them exchange smiles acknowledging the depth of this tiny admission.

"Dave," Benji says, "I believe you are the only person I know who had anywhere near a normal Christmas."

Dave chuckles in reply.

"Even Steve," Benji continues, "His family's relatively average, but they were one of only two Jewish families in his small town. That caused all sorts of holiday issues."

After about an hour of touring the neighborhood, they return home. Benji brings out three mugs of eggnog laced with a splash of rum. Soon after, they retire for the night.

Dave and Leo make love again, a slower, more languid event since the afternoon's intensity largely slaked desire. Gentle sharing of bodies and ample kisses replace the afternoon's frazzled desperation.

They fall asleep, Dave wrapped in Leo's arms.

27

Dave and Leo greet each other with a series of kisses and get up to head for the bathroom. Coffee aroma draws them downstairs where they find Benji, up early considering he works the late shift today. The three men chat at the kitchen table genially over breakfast. With tests completed and final assignments turned in, both Leo and Dave can afford to linger over an extra cup. A short stack of papers for Dave to grade sit leisurely on his desk at his apartment in no rush for completion.

Leo plans time to meet with George to go over the project.

Leo tenses at the thought of that but cannot see other opportunities that allow him to continue this life he delightfully discovered. A couple of minor consults for Carlos and Diego offer little payoff yet, and the continued dearth in T.A. or tutor positions continues to frustrate him.

Dave and Leo return upstairs as Benji stays in the kitchen to clean up and have another cup of coffee. Getting dressed, Dave, hoping to find a little time they could meet later, asks what time he is getting together with George.

"I'll need to contact him."

He picks up his phone and pulls up a text from George.

Bad news. Bill and Karla turned in
their work on the project. Contest over.
Sorry. Guess we won't need to meet.

Dave puts on the last of his clothes and turns to observe a very stricken looking Leo. "Sweetie?" He tarries in the partially opened doorway, sensing a drastic change.

Dread and fear grow rapidly in Leo's mind. Quietly he utters, "No," repeated louder, "No." Repetitions continue, "No. No. No!" Each louder, more drawn out. "Noooo!"

The protest evolve into screams, causing Dave to freeze.

Leo builds, finally emitting a long terror filled, "NOOOO!" that reverberates throughout the house.

Benji, hearing it in the kitchen, drops his mug and runs stopping at the landing of the stairs, seeing the door to Leo's room slightly ajar.

Leo's eyes raise slightly.

I've felt this before, where? Dave's car. The world disappearing. No, different, not all encompassing white.

Color fades from the extreme reaches of his visual field. He gets up from the bed and backs into the chest of drawers unaware of what stops him. Spinning around, a drawer is opened to find clothes still solid, but the sides of the drawer fade to grey tones. Dave, his adorable Dave calls, "Leo, what is it? Leo."

As Dave reaches out, an encroaching circle of grey surrounds him.

It will swallow him. That cannot happen. I must protect him. Dave cannot be swallowed.

"Go," he commands. "Go!"

Fearfully, Dave takes a step forward, hand extended. "Leo, what the hell is going on? Please, sweetie, talk to me."

Leo sees Dave getting closer to the hideous greyness.

I cannot allow that. It cannot take him. Dave cannot fade.

He holds a protective hand up to stop him. "Go! Now!"

He spins, reaching back into the drawer and pulls out a t-shirt, noting its still vibrant green, like Dave's precious eyes. He cannot bear seeing them swallowed into that grey.

Unable to turn back, he waves his hands towards Dave's pleading voice, screaming out, "GO! Please!"

He shuts his eyes to the circle of grey swallowing his dear world and, most horribly, Dave.

Sobbing out now, "Please, please, go away. You can't be here. It's not safe."

Voice getting more frighteningly softer, he continues ordering Dave to leave. The final statements barely audible from across the room. "You're not safe. Go."

Dave backs out of the room, partly in obedience to Leo's command, partly in fear, partly not knowing what else to do.

Benji watches. When Dave obliviously gets too near the top of the stairs, he rushes up to stop him before he falls, catching hold of him as Leo slams the door. "What the fuck?"

A trembling Dave turns, shakes his head in shock.

"Dave, come on. What the hell?"

Benji guides him safely down the stairs, both arms fiercely protecting him, seating them both near the bottom. Dave, face covered in tears, gasps from crying.

"Breathe, babe, breathe. I'm here. Breathe."

Benji's quiet voice encourages him to speak. "I don't know what happened! I turned, and he was looking at his phone. Then he started saying 'no' over and over and over, and it kept getting louder." He turns into Benji to let out a deep, gut wrenching sob.

"Let it out, baby, let it out. I heard him too. Scary."

Dave settles enough to continue. "Then he kept telling me to go. I don't understand." He folds into Benji's embrace and lets the raw emotions flow.

Leo sits with his back against the door. Color, except for the green t-shirt, drains from his world. He tries to focus on it, hoping color will grow out from it and return to the rest of his world.

Is this what their world was like?

He rises, letting the green shirt drop, and goes to the bureau, pulling out everything he owns piece by piece. All his old things have color. The lovely, cherished blue sweatshirt from Jay… colorless.

Am I as mad as they?

Again, the question suddenly materializes. Going around the room in near panic, he surveys shirt after shirt, all pants are pulled off hangers in his closet. The same. Only new things have faded. The precious box on the nightstand: slate with lighter and darker bands of grey.

Grey as they were.

Wincing, a whispered rage emerges. "Who, damn it, who?"

Returning to the chest, he sits, finally opens the bottom drawer, pulls out the eerily vibrant folder and sets it on the floor. "That can't be," he wonders out loud, "it's beige."

Them. That's who. Mr. and Mrs. Fucking Graham.

It gets shoved to the foot of the bed. Overwhelmed, Leo picks up the sweatshirt lying next to the folder and turns away. A now slate grey flash drive with Dave's stories sits on his computer desk. He takes it, wraps it into the sweatshirt, then crawls onto the bed. Holding them tight, he curls into a fetal position and falls into a sleep-like state.

Benji moves Dave, clearly stricken to the core, onto the large couch where his crying subsides. Able to speak again, he looks at Benji, "I have to go."

"Dave, no. We'll talk to him together and find out what's going on."

Dave shakes his head, not quite understanding why, but knows he cannot be around Leo. "It's no good, not right now. I can't be here. He can't have me here."

He starts to rise, but Benji holds on.

"He needs you, Dave. You can't just let him go."

"Not now. I don't know why, and it hurts like hell, but I can't be here now."

He gets up and starts to head out the door, but hesitates, wanting badly to run upstairs and force Leo to... Then it hits him hard. Leo's whispering becomes clear.

Quietly he says, "He doesn't think I'm safe."

Benji reaches for Dave's arm. "What? That makes no sense."

Facing Benji he states, "Benji, take care of him."

"You can't just leave him, Dave. You guys love each other. I know that and so do you."

Dave, vision clouded from tears, tries to focus. "I can't explain, but for right now, I cannot be here. I do love him. I know he loves me. I know that more than ever. I'll only cause harm right now." He looks down, trying to understand. "He can't have me here."

"What am I supposed to do?"

Dave takes Benji by the shoulders. "I will be back. I don't know when. Right now, Benji, you can be there for him. Take care of my Leo."

He hates leaving, but breaks free and races out the door.

Benji stands alone at the open door, wrapping his arms around his body as he watches Dave disappear down the sidewalk.

I love you too Dave. I hope you know what you're doing.

He shuts the door, turns, and leans against it. His eyes laboriously crawl up the stairs. He moves to the landing and focuses on Leo's closed door. He wants Dave back. He wants Jay to come home and take care of this, but it's up to him. Step by step he ascends, trying to figure out what to do.

At the door, Benji listens, but hears no commotion. Fearing what he will find, moving his hand forward requires immense concentration. The knob gratefully turns, and the door silently swings open, revealing Leo curled up on the bed, apparently asleep. The mess shocks him: clothes everywhere, drawers open.

This is not Leo.

Approaching gingerly while stepping over strewn clothing, he notices the tightly held sweatshirt. He sits on the bed and reaches to touch Leo. "Babe? It's Benji."

Rousing from his state, Leo blurts out as if far away, "I sent Dave away to keep him safe." He doesn't face Benji and soon escapes back into slumber.

It makes no sense to Benji, but he rubs Leo's back, "I know, babe, I know. We'll get him back when the time's right. I promise. I'm here until then." He continues to rub his back until he knows nothing more can be done.

Later, Benji brings Leo a sandwich. "I brought you something to eat." He barely rouses him to eat, but not talk.

Leo lets go of the sweatshirt. He reaches out, eyes closed tight. Benji places the food in Leo's hand and watches in complete confusion as Leo mechanically eats.

The only response Benji gets is when he asks if he can call Dave and have him join them. Leo answers simply, "No."

Benji stays with him until the sandwich is gone.

Leo gropes for and grabs the still- grey sweatshirt. The flash drive slips out and falls to the floor. He blindly retrieves it and wraps it carefully in the sweatshirt before curling back up to sleep, both precious items pressed tightly.

Benji, heart rending, covers his mouth with both hands, watching these movements in stunned silence. Tears well up and spill from his eyes. How can he help this dear man without understanding any of this? Grasping the empty plate, he backs out of the bedroom, closing the door softly.

In the kitchen, he debates calling Jay. Instead he calls Dave. "Hey, babe, how are you doing?"

"I can't make sense of any of it."

"It makes none. He hasn't left his room. I got him to eat a little, but it was like he was in a dream. He didn't even open his eyes." Benji wants to be there for Dave but quickly realizes his limitations. Dealing with whatever is happening to Leo surpasses anything in his experience. "Dave,

I haven't called Jay. You call. Tell him what you can. He'll be there for you like I can be here for Leo."

God, I hope I can be there.

Dave hesitates, "I can't right now. I will. Tomorrow."

28

Leo wakes in silent darkness, his body not needing the sleep his mind does. Fear of the grey elevates the task of turning on a light gargantuan. A shaking hand reaches for the lamp, closing his eyes the moment before the light comes on. Slowly he forces them open. He buries his face gratefully into the again-blue sweatshirt. Rising he sees the mess.

I did this?

He drops the sweatshirt on the bed causing the flash drive to slide out. Picking it up gingerly, too keenly aware of what he has done, he kisses it before putting it back on the computer stand, believing in this moment it is all he will ever have of Dave. He knows he hurt Dave badly, possibly irreparably. Tightly squeezed eyes force tears away.

Near trance, he goes to the bathroom. The mirror reflects back a visage as wild and ugly as he feels. "Leo, you really fucked up."

Robotically he restores his room. Shirts and pants are picked up and placed back on hangers in their previous order. Carefully folded T-shirts, socks, and underwear return to the chest. The only thing left out is the folder. It sits there; only cardboard filled with paper. No more fear. It is time.

He opens it and begins reading, vaguely remembering requesting all these documents: the accident report, the emergency room records, and the autopsies. Jean helped obtaining some even as she doubted what good they could provide.

Page by page, he reads the entire contents, finishing well after sunrise, horrified by his discovery.

"Fucking assholes!" he screams out. "This is how you leave me? Goddamn you two!"

Benji, wakened by the outburst, rushes to Leo's room and opens the door without warning, fearing Leo may be experiencing another episode like yesterday's.

"What's going on?"

The return to order reassures him.

Leo looks up, his face a study in anger. Embarrassment ties his tongue.

"Are you okay?" Benji inquires.

Leo can only shrug.

"What's all that?"

"Reports from the wreck."

"Your parents? How they...?"

"Yeah." He sees Benji wants to know more. "I've been avoiding it."

"Is that what you were just yelling about?"

Leo nods and rubs his face with his hands. "I need to do something."

He turns on his computer and signs onto his e-mail, needing to contact Jean. Writing won't do. Scrolling to the first e-mail, he finds her phone number, writes it down, and looks for his phone, forgotten during the blow up. "Damn it, where's my phone?"

"Hold on. I'll be right back." Soon Benji reenters, his phone in hand, and punches Leo's speed-dial number, causing a dull ring.

Leo follows the sound and finds it on the floor barely under the side of the bed by the computer. He looks at Benji. "I have to talk to my aunt."

"Do you want me to bring you something? Coffee, something to eat?"

"Both. Please." Finally looking directly at Benji, aware of his crazy state, he states flatly, "Benji, I fucked up."

"Okay." He hesitates, then adds, "Can I call Dave and get him over here?"

He so much wants to say yes, but it isn't safe. "No. He can't be here now." He turns away.

Benji's heart sinks as he moves toward the door. "I'll be back."

Leo waits. This dreaded call must be made. Where to start? A second study of the reports achieves only stalling.

Benji returns with coffee and a bowl of cereal. "If you want more, I can make some eggs or something."

"Thanks. This is more than enough."

Benji sits. "Babe, please let me know what's going on." He touches Leo's shoulder getting no initial reaction, but at least the hand isn't brushed off.

Leo slowly looks at his friend who he may soon lose also. "I don't know myself."

"You're hurting Dave. He loves you. You know that."

A sole tear escapes Leo's eye. "I'm trying not to."

How can this grey world make sense? How can I doom that sweet man to a relationship with my bleak future? Dave must be safe.

"That makes no sense, Leo." No more forthcoming, Benji finally gives up, hoping for better after Leo talks to his aunt. "I'll be downstairs for a while. I'm cancelling work this evening. You are scaring me to death. I can't leave you alone."

Leo sees the fear in Benji's face and reassures, "I won't do anything."

Benji reluctantly closes the door behind him.

Leo punches in Jean's number.

"Hello?"

"Jean? It's Leo."

"Oh, what a wonderful surprise! How nice to hear your voice."

His aunt, breaking the tense silence, interjects haltingly, "Leo? What's going on?"

"I'm sorry. Don't really know where to begin."

"Has something happened?"

"Yes." He takes in a big breath and lets it out. "I screwed things up. I'm not sure I should have come here."

"Leo, everything you've told me has been wonderful. Have you had a fight with Dave or something?"

Leo slumps onto the bed, sitting cross-legged, his back against the headboard. "God, Dave. No. No fight, but I... Jean, I need to find out about Mom and Dad."

The shift confuses her. "What about them?"

"The wreck, all that happened. Something's very wrong. They were crazy, weren't they?"

"Oh, boy, Leo. That's a very dangerous word. They were indeed very strange, yes, very likely something wrong with both of them. What's bringing this out?"

"It wasn't an accident. It was deliberate." His free hand absently brushes through his hair then falls limply into his lap.

"What? Why on earth are you saying that?"

"It's the only way it makes sense. Remember all those reports from the accident and all the medical reports, all that I made them give me?"

"Yes, I never understood why. Leo, I'm still not sure it will do you any good."

"Too late for that now. I finally read them. The only way it makes sense is if it wasn't an accident."

"Leo, why are you doing this?"

"I know they pushed you and everyone else out years ago before I was aware, but you're the only person I can ask." He squeezes his eyes shut, forcing tears back. "I don't even know if Dad had family."

"Frankly, I don't either." She takes a couple audible breaths. "Leo, what can I say? Your mom was always very strange."

"She always did everything the same way, time and time again, right?"

"Yes, wouldn't vary an inch, if possible. That's true."

"Mom had her role, Dad had his. No change, one day to the next."

She wonders how her nephew survived such starkness.

Leo continues, "I cannot for the life of me remember anything both would do. Each had assigned roles. That was what made me realize this was all wrong."

"Leo..."

"Jean, Mom was driving. Not Dad. She only drove when he was gone somewhere."

"Maybe something was happening to him. She was driving to get help."

"No. The autopsy notes no contributing factors. He is described as a healthy 48-year-old man, no physical issues. Died from trauma due to injuries from the wreck."

"Leo, why are you doing this to yourself? Please don't."

"The car was too fast. It was always a mile or two below the speed limit. She was going a good twenty over. There were very short skid marks. Jean, there were no mitigating weather factors. No rain, nothing noted on the road. The sun was to the side. Nothing to cause an accident. Witness reports mention no interference."

"Leo, stop!"

Tears flow now. "They shut everyone out, even me."

"Leo, sweetheart, slow down. What's causing all this?"

"It's true, isn't it? Why were you listed as contact, not me? When was the last time you talked to Mom?" His tone, clearly not accusing, possesses an aching need.

"All right." She takes a gulp of air. "I'll tell you what I can."

She pauses briefly to collect herself.

Leo holds his breath, waiting for her to continue.

"I was on the insurance probably because she put me there when she first got the policy and never bothered to change it. I doubt it occurred to her. I don't remember exactly the last time I talked to her, no more than a couple of years after you were born. Your grandmother, uncle, and I were very apprehensive when we found out she was pregnant. We tried to intervene, take you away, but there were no grounds. No signs of abuse. You were fed, probably not well, but enough. Nothing we could use. Any reasoning made her withdraw even more. Talking to your Dad was as bad, if not worse."

"Wait... I have an uncle?"

"You did. He died years ago. The two of you would have loved each other. Dean was smart like you, but he was never healthy. Your grandmother used to tell me she had only one whole child. Dean wasn't given a body and your mom didn't have a head. Her words, not mine."

"She was right about Mom." He slumps off the bed to the floor next to the desk.

"I remember the last time I saw you. You were maybe old enough to walk. I dropped by. I rang the bell, I knocked, but no answer. I knew she was home... You're right, every day the same. It was not time for her to be out. I went to the living room window and I could see you on the floor with some paper or books open. You looked up and waved. I rapped on the window."

A vague awareness tugs at Leo.

She tries to compose herself, her voice heavy. "Then I saw her. She must have been sitting in a chair next to you. She picked you up and carried you to the back of the house. Leo, I wanted to kill her right then. I hate to say that, but it was so mean of her."

A flash of memory vibrates through Leo.

The episode in Dave's car. Jean was the angel at the window.

"Oh my god, I remember. I was reading. I looked up and saw you. I thought you were an angel. You were so pretty. Then she took me away. I don't remember if she said anything or not."

"You were only two or three and already reading? I missed too much. She never contacted us. Shortly after that, you all moved. The next time I knew anything about you was when you made the news for your beautiful intelligence. I don't know if I told you, but I saved every article and picture. Wish there were more."

Leo sits in a cocoon of silence.

"Leo, are you with me still?"

His voice nears nonexistence. "Yeah."

"Leo, are you crying?"

"Yes."

Slowly and with quite a bit of urging, he tells her what happened. The whole ugliness comes out.

"Leo, I don't know what to say. You must be terrified."

"I'm so sorry, Jean. I must sound as crazy as them."

"No. Not at all. Are you going to call Dave?"

"I can't. I'm afraid."

"Afraid of what?"

"Me."

"I don't understand."

"Look at them. How can I be their son and not be crazy? I'm so afraid I'll be them."

"Oh, honey, no. Don't do that. You're not your mother or your father."

"How can I know? I don't want to turn into them."

"Leo, you are not like them."

"I'm their son. I must have gotten something from them. I look like my father, but there has to be more," he stammers.

Jean stays silent for a moment. Only her breathing slips out. "Leo, I don't know what to say. I can't speak for your father. I barely learned his name."

Leo focuses on a crumpled piece of paper apparently lost under his desk. He picks it up and casually moves it on top of the desk. "You know something about my mother..."

"All right, there is something you may not know. It didn't surprise me when you made the news for your intellect. You do get that from her."

"I don't understand."

"Your mother. When she started school, as my mother tells it, no one was sure she would ever learn to simply read. Although she never participated in any activities or showed interest in the least social approaches, she excelled in coursework. It was like she had to write things out in order to express herself. Especially math."

Leo sits up, confused. "What?"

"She'd pick up a pencil and work it out, whatever it was. Soon as she was done, pencil down, no comment. She was never wrong."

"I never saw her do anything like that."

"Did you ever put a piece of paper down in front of her with some math on it? Didn't matter what, basic math, algebra, geometry, whatever."

"Of course not. Why would I?"

"You'd have no reason to. I don't remember her seeking it out, but she couldn't resist if it was placed in her hands."

After an almost uncomfortable length of pondering he finally states, very flatly, "So I am like her."

"No, Leo," she nearly shouts. "You are not her. Your mother never did what you are doing right now. You are not them."

"What am I doing? I just called you."

"Exactly. I have known you less than a year. I knew your mother all her life. She never reached out like this. Damn it, Leo, you have called me more than she ever did."

"I've never called you before."

"That puts you ahead of her by one." Her voice takes on a strident tone. "You are not them. You absolutely must believe that."

"I don't want to be them, but I think I may turn into them. I can't be with someone as wonderful as Dave and turn into them. I can't do that to him. I can't do that to anyone."

Jean sighs and says softly, "You have to believe in yourself. Give Dave more credit too."

"I have to be sure."

"Stop, please stop. You are not them. You are not!"

"I'm scared."

"What about your roommates? Can you talk to them?"

"I don't even know right now if I can afford to stay here much longer."

"That's not an answer. Can you talk to them?"

"Maybe, I don't know." He becomes yet quieter, this call both helped and scared him. "Jean, I think I have to go now. Thank you, though. I needed to know. I have a lot of thinking to do."

"I'm not comfortable ending right now. I wish I was there."

"Me too. Will you feel better if I promise to talk to Jay or Benji? Maybe not today or tomorrow, but I can try."

"Please do. I want to hear from you too. Sooner than later."

"I will. Thanks." He ends the call.

Surer than before that his parents' deaths were not accidental, he knows they left him alone all his life, a state continued with their deaths. Anger for them exhausts him.

Leo crawls up on the bed and gazes out the side window at the cloudy, grey day. Winter-bare branches show no movement. Groggily, he gets up and moves to a front window. No people wander the neighborhood.

Returning to the bed, he curls up and escapes back to sleep until late afternoon. Upon waking, Leo notes the wan light filtering in from the side windows stirring the memory of Jay selecting light as the reason for this room over the back bedroom. Feet firmly planted on the solid wood floor, he rises and moves to his door.

Silence envelops the house outside his room, although his head rings with memories anywhere blue eyes focus. Leo reaches out.

Touching now familiar things, he moves through his home, the first he has known looking for Benji.

Money won't last.

Thinking maybe Benji could be working out, he tries the basement. Nothing. Stopping at the refrigerator to get a bite to eat, he finally sees the note Benji left.

> Leo, went out for a minute to get more food.
> Fridge is kind of bare. Back soon.
> I know we need to talk but when you're ready.
> Love, Benji

Leo opens the refrigerator and pours an anonymous liquid into a glass. It disappears in one long gulp. Setting the dirty glass on the counter, Leo heads back upstairs, sleep the only reasonable activity.

Benji knocks lightly on Leo's door the next morning. It is not right he hasn't been up. Leo opens his door, bringing some relief, but the utter dishevelment of this beautiful man shocks him. Leo wears the same clothes, the t-shirt rumpled and stained. Even the socks show grime.

Benji looks him up and down. "You look like shit. Get in the shower and meet me in the kitchen in fifteen minutes."

Leo looks down his body, noticing a stain for the first time. He rubs it with a thumb.

When Leo shows no inclination to leave his room, Benji shakes a finger, adding vehemently, "Oh, no, no." He stands firmly, feet shoulder width apart and crosses his arms. "Not a request. I will drag your ass in there and strip you down if I have to. Whatever else is going on, you will take care of yourself." He steps aside and thrusts an arm out, finger demandingly pointed toward the bathroom. "Now!"

Leo, partly in shock over this unknown side of Benji, obeys.

Benji heads to the kitchen and prepares coffee. He picks up the abandoned glass with a bit of a jolt, realizing the grim depth of the situation.

Soon a slightly better version of Leo shows up, sits, and accepts a cup.

Benji lets Leo take a few sips of coffee before reaching to gently hold his hand. "Now, suppose you tell me what's going on?"

"Benji, I don't know where to start."

"Same as always, where it's easy."

He sits and thinks. "I called my aunt. We talked about my parents."

"What's that got to do with what happened with Dave? He left here absolutely stricken."

"Everything and nothing. Fuck, there's so much. Wait."

Leo starts to get up, but Benji grabs his wrist. "Where are you going?"

Confused, Leo answers, "To get my checkbook."

"Babe, I don't need visual aids. Just talk."

Leo settles back into his seat.

Benji watches his friend struggle. "What happened right before you started screaming?"

"George left a message. That project I've been working on? Another team completed it. I was depending on it for income. There's no openings for T.A.s or tutoring. I was sure I would win. Now, I have no source of income. I have very little money left in the world. I should have never come here. I wasn't ready. I don't even have enough to cover rent for the next semester."

"There's more than money. Leo, you're not going to be kicked out. You're family. You know that, don't you?"

"I don't know if I can do that."

"You can if you have to. I still don't understand what this has to do with Dave. Or your parents."

"My parents..." He starts to cry. "God-fucking-damn them!" He buries his head in his hands, barely feeling Benji's touch. "The wreck."

"You mean the accident that killed them?"

He lowers his hands surer than ever. "No accident. Intentional."

Benji jerks back as if he has been slapped, "How? I mean, what? Fuck, what do I mean? Leo?"

"They did it... Telling no one... Giving no clue, just... Fucking did it...," he accuses. "Leaving nothing. Nothing. Always nothing from them."

"Nothing. You've said that over and over. That's what it always was, right? Nothing. No anger, no abuse, no ridicule." Benji closes his eyes against welling tears. "No caring either. No joy. No love."

Leo only nods.

Slowly shaking his head, Benji continues. "But why Dave? Do you think he won't understand?"

"Maybe. Part of it."

"You need to talk to him."

Before Leo can protest, he raises his hand to stop him.

"I get it, not right now. I can barely fucking process what you just told me. I doubt it's clear to you either. Fuck."

Neither moves for several minutes.

"We can't do this all day, babe." He shoves away from the table. "Get on your computer, find us a movie, and grab a jacket."

Leo is puzzled at the request. "Benji, I just told you I can't afford anything like that."

"Fuck you. I can. We are going to find the most innocuous fluffy mindless comedy possible. There's three theaters within walking distance. Others we can get to by bus. You need a break."

Walking back, Leo remains lost. The film, whatever it was, never penetrated his memory. Meaningless conversation snippets bring them home.

Benji attempts to talk about the film, commenting on its content or surprising length but gets little better than grunting acknowledgements in return. His nervousness of the situation drives his desire for some reaction. He finally looks up at the sky and comments, "That is the orangest sunset I've seen in ages."

Leo stops dead and finally looks up, staring at the horizon.

Benji studies his roommate with measured discomfort. "Leo, what's going on?"

No immediate response surfaces.

"Leo," he continues, reaching out for an elbow. "Is it happening again? Are you slipping away?" Panic edges into his voice.

The touch causes Leo to glance where Benji's hand has landed. He looks back to the sky and utters, "Carrot."

"Uh, I beg your pardon?"

"The sky. Not just orange. Carrot."

Dave would know. I want him to see this...with me.

Benji shifts his focus from Leo to the sunset and back. "Carrot it is." He shrugs his shoulders before adding, "Come on. Let's get home."

"Leo, can I ask you something?" Benji sits on the large sofa and pats the seat next to him. "I'm trying not to pressure you, but I care about Dave too. You really think he won't understand?"

Unable to voice his fear of becoming his parents, he sags onto the seat. "I don't know."

"He will. He cares too much not to." Benji studies his confused friend trying to make sense. "This is all about what happened growing up, isn't it? Dave, us, this house, your program. We're all secondary."

Leo flops his head on the back of the sofa. "It was so bizarre. I don't understand how I got here."

"What does it matter how we got here? We're all here now." Benji pauses as he considers. An image builds in his head. "Think of it like we've been invited to this wonderful party."

He turns on the sofa to face Leo.

"We all got here and can now join the gathering. Each of us travelled this long way to get here. Everyone's path different from the others. Jay had to conquer a huge mountain. It was hard and he had to struggle like hell, but when he got over the top, it was smooth sailing.

"I had to wind my way around the worst urban streets. There were constant detours, potholes, assholes, and distractions on the side.

"It's not Dave's fault for most of his journey he was on newly-paved interstates with little bad weather. What matters is, we are all here. The past is stories, nothing more than conversation starters. Right now, you are fully wrapped up in your story. You can't get stuck there."

"What's my story?"

Benji thinks a moment, "Babe, you were on a long, unwinding road crossing stark, gloomy flatlands, under a grey overcast sky, stuck in low gear, with no radio reception and a broken CD player."

Leo looks at Benji, eye to eye for the first time since his blow-up.

Am I back on that road?

He looks down.

I need to know before I can move on. Or out.

ACKNOWLEDGEMENTS

The Men of Jewel Street began life as a one very long book. Having never written anything other than a few short stories, I had no idea what I was getting myself into. After the initial outline, I wrote pretty much from the beginning onward. It took quite some time to complete, but I was quite pleased that I stuck with it.

I received much support from my partner, Mark Clinard. It had to be frustrating for him as I would not allow him to read any of it during the entire process. I may have shared an occasional sentence I thought he'd enjoy but nothing more. His constant encouragement and support were invaluable.

When I was ready to get the book into shape, I began working with Wayne Smith. He took one look at it and let me know either major edits were in order, or I had written a series, not a single book. After a critical look at what I had done, I decided that it was to become a series. Work on what was to become *Touching Now Familiar Things* or at that point, Book 1, began. With much help from Wayne, a novel began to emerge that could stand on its own yet still make sense as the first part of a series. His guidance was given with humor and grace, taking me through an unfamiliar journey. Throughout, he listened to me, gave incredibly constructive feedback, and eased my fears as they arose.

David Wayne Fox, a very long-term friend, created a wonderful image and designed the cover. It was a joy finding a way for us to combine our talents on this project.

Lorikay Stone took wonderful photos for my author headshot. I rarely like pictures of myself, but I love the ones she did for this book.

My brother, Richard, was instrumental in helping with the Italian dialogue. We grew up around this lovely language, but he paid attention and actually learned to speak it. For this and all the moral support, I thank him.

Charles Wildes assisted tremendously in setting up social media accounts, guiding me through uncomfortable territory with great humor.

At one point it became necessary to share this work with others for feedback and suggestions. I would like to thank my readers: Franklin Abbott, Frank Wilms, Anne J. Temkin, and David Salyer. Your insights were very helpful.

Other friends offered encouragement along the way. Specifically, I want to mention Dan Heidel and Glenn Faulk who listened often to my tales of the—at times, seemingly endless—process of bringing this book out.

ABOUT THE AUTHOR

Roger V. Freeby grew up in a small town in western New Mexico, part of a predominantly Italian neighborhood. English, Italian, Spanish, and Navajo could be heard daily. A lifelong hobby took a firm grip with the writing of what was to become *Touching Now Familiar Things*. He currently lives in Atlanta with his partner Mark.